same beach, next year

same beach, next year

a novel

Dorothea Benton Frank

WM

WILLIAM MORROW
An Imprint of HarperCollins*Publishers*

This is a work of fiction. Names, characters, places, and incidents are products of the author's imagination or are used fictitiously and are not to be construed as real. Any resemblance to actual events, locales, organizations, or persons, living or dead, is entirely coincidental.

SAME BEACH, NEXT YEAR. Copyright © 2017 by Dorothea Benton Frank. All rights reserved. Printed in the United States of America. No part of this book may be used or reproduced in any manner whatsoever without written permission except in the case of brief quotations embodied in critical articles and reviews. For information, address HarperCollins Publishers, 195 Broadway, New York, NY 10007.

HarperCollins books may be purchased for educational, business, or sales promotional use. For information, please email the Special Markets Department at SPsales@harpercollins.com.

FIRST EDITION

Designed by Bonni Leon-Berman

Library of Congress Cataloging-in-Publication Data has been applied for.

ISBN 978-0-06-239078-3 (hardcover)
ISBN 978-0-06-274048-9 (BAM signed ed.)
ISBN 978-0-06-274050-2 (B&N signed ed.)
ISBN 978-0-06-274049-6 (Target signed ed.)

17 18 19 20 21   LSC   10 9 8 7 6 5 4 3 2 1

contents

prologue 1

1   meet adam 3
2   meet eliza 17
3   eliza's new friends 31
4. eliza's merry christmas 46
5   adam's merry christmas 54
6   eliza and the unexpected guest 60
7   eliza 77
8   bonded 99
9   eliza's catching up 121
10 adam 137
11 eliza's fury 150
12 adam 173
13 corfu 190
14 adam 212
15 eliza 226
16 adam's snake in the garden 247
17 eliza 262
18 back in corfu 282
19 eliza 304
20 eliza 323
21 eliza 340

epilogue 364
acknowledgments 371

For
Victoria and Carmine
And all the joy to come!

"It is important to our friends to believe that we are unreservedly frank with them, and important to friendship that we are not."

Mignon McLaughlin

"One measure of friendship consists not in the number of things friends can discuss, but in the number of things they need no longer mention."

Clifton Fadiman

prologue

isle of palms, south carolina, 2016

The conversation that launched my need to tell you this whole crazy story actually came from our son Luke, who, like his twin, is practically an adult. Okay, they *are* adults. But only because of their age, which is still completely astonishing to me. How dare they grow up and make us, God help us, almost sixty? Some nerve.

They asked us to come along with the Landers family, to spend New Year's Eve 2016 on the Isle of Palms. Adam and I and our boys have vacationed with Eve and Carl Landers, their daughter, Daphne, and Eve's mother, Cookie, for decades. We all love Wild Dunes and being together so much that we bought condos near each other and watched our children grow up to the music of the Atlantic Ocean's changing tides and the squawking of thousands of generations of seagulls. In the early days, we drank enough white wine and various trending cocktails to float a container ship. Mai Tais. Stormy Weathers. Salty Dogs. Moscow Mules. And we cooked dinner together more times than I could count. We were better than best friends, which may have complicated things. Okay, it made things complicated in the extreme. But why wouldn't you love who you love loves? It's sort of like you are what you eat eats.

Adam and I rarely, if ever, go to the beach in the winter. Well, maybe my husband takes a drive there occasionally to do repairs or to assess the havoc a renter has caused on the plumbing or to fix a leak. But generally, we stay away because the weather is freezing cold and I can feel the dampness in every one of my bones. I hate winter. But New Year's was such an unusual request that we all agreed to go. And needless to say, Eve, Carl, Adam, and I were as thrilled as we always were to see each other. Honestly, any excuse to see each other would work, and maybe we are finally all old enough to admit it. Before I go any further I want you to know this wasn't like that old movie *Bob and Carol and Ted and Alice,* the one where two perfectly nice married couples swap spouses. But boy, there was a moment when it could've been. And I'll get to that steamy business later on.

But for now, we have to begin at the beginning. Even though it's New Year's Eve and I'm on my way to a freezing beach. Save your fireworks for a little while and relax while I tell you how the saga of our epic friendships all began. And how we learned what matters. It might matter to you.

CHAPTER 1

meet adam

isle of palms, south carolina, 1994

My fabulous wife, Eliza, has an opinion on everything, but she's not from here, and it's always been hard for her to get a grasp on what it means to be from the Lowcountry. So how can she explain the Lowcountry to you? She can't. The pluff mud is in *my* veins, not hers. This whole business of Lowcountry versus the rest of the state of South Carolina goes back several hundred years. All you have to do is visualize Charleston, South Carolina, as the center of the universe. To know the Holy City is to love her, but to understand her might take several lifetimes.

In the best of seasons, Charleston is a dowager queen, but still plenty sexy and sultry despite the centuries of her age. She charms the hearts and souls of legions of visitors, year after year. Tourists arrive in droves from all over the world, the same way they do to any other world-class destination.

They come with cameras and guidebooks and restaurant reservations to witness Charleston's illustrious history, her legendary beauty, and her unique way of life. These visitors confide to shopkeepers and guides that they are here just because they wanted to see what it felt like to be southern. Authentically southern. A Lowcountry daughter or son. They seldom leave disappointed.

However, in the height of summer Charleston finds her ferocious core, breathing fire, bringing on swoons and foul moods. And, perhaps most interestingly—because Charleston is a port city—once home to more brothels than churches, her sweltering season invites and coerces every flavor of dangerous seduction. She plays with your soul and doesn't care if you go to hell. You would return home to wherever you came from in a stupor. You've been kissed by the devil herself and someday you'd be back for more. Charleston is as intoxicating as she is addictive.

Here is how our friendship with the Landers family began.

It was July 1, 1994. Every detail of that day is as vivid as though it happened just yesterday. The temperature must have been close to one hundred degrees and the sun was unrelenting. There was not a wisp of a cloud in the sky. I was poolside reading a novel, with one ear cocked toward the background laughter and taunts of my young twin sons, and enjoying a well-deserved vacation. Having lived almost every day of my life in the Lowcountry, I was only too aware of the dangers of extreme heat, but I stupidly believed I was immune to heat stroke, melanoma, or seductive temptations. Despite pretty humble origins, I liked to think of myself as a gentleman. And, okay, maybe sometimes I was a little smug. Still, I was usually smart enough to know that peril is sometimes shrouded in complacency. For all I knew, or for all anyone knew, at any moment Lady Lowcountry might laugh and mock and challenge us by raising the temperature a few more degrees. With a smirk, she might stoke the humidity to such levels that we wouldn't be able to hold a coherent thought. We could find ourselves walking down a sidewalk in the city, literally unable to go on. It has happened. As it was, my upper lip tasted of salt and the hair on the back of my neck was wet. I was on guard and ready for anything.

Or so I thought.

I glanced at my watch. It was only eleven in the morning. Every hound dog in Charleston County had surely claimed a piece of shade, including our old black Lab, Rufus, who was nestled under my lounger. Except for the occasional jumping fish in the surrounding waters, there was not a sound from nature to be heard. Even the bugs were taking a siesta.

So, with an ear perked for my boys and an eye on the heat of the day, I was slathered in sunscreen and stretched out on a lounger, wearing blue swimming shorts covered in miniature smiling orange goldfish, just like the snack. I was relaxed and thoroughly engrossed in a legal thriller, and in a weird way, I liked feeling the heat bake my skin as though it was good for me.

I'm getting some massive vitamin D, I thought and smiled.

I was a mere twenty or maybe thirty feet away from the condominium we rented in the Wild Dunes Resort. But I didn't hear Eliza's approach.

"Sweetheart? You know our lovely neighbor Mrs. Shannon from Aiken, who's staying in the condo next door?"

Faithful Rufus raised his big squarish head and gave Eliza and then me a questioning look. Seeing it was Eliza, whom he loved, and that this had nothing to do with him, Rufus put his head back down and resumed his nap. I looked up from my novel. There stood my wonderful wife behind her retro cat-eye sunglasses and under her enormous sun hat. Of course, I knew who Mrs. Shannon was. I had never seen a woman with more elective plastic surgery in my entire life. She was the one with a thirty-year-old head perched atop a sixty-something-year-old body. The stuff of nightmares. Eliza's hands gripped her elbows across her gauzy striped caftan. The set of her jaw resembled one of those guys on Mount Rushmore. Bad body language. She was very annoyed.

"Is something wrong, sweetness?" I said, hoping to lighten my wife's mood.

"Nice job watching the boys, Adam. Our little darlings tried to assassinate Mrs. Shannon's miniature Yorkies with their fun new semiautomatic Super Soakers. She just had them groomed. She wants to sue us unless we pay for them to be regroomed. In cash. This minute. I didn't go to the bank."

I considered the situation for a moment. I had definitely flunked her mandate to watch the kids.

"Take what you need from my wallet and tell Heckle and Jeckle I want to talk to them."

She nodded her head and called out with exasperation, "Boys!" She caught their eye and hooked a thumb in my direction.

They looked like a couple of textbook imps. I thought, Well, at least with my boys, what you see is what you get.

Inside of a minute, my five-and-a-half-year-old twins were standing at the foot of my lounge chair with their water guns resting against their shoulders, like soldiers at attention. I could tell by their disingenuous expressions that there wasn't even a smidgen of regret between them. Max had a deadly serious face and Luke was fighting back giggles. I removed my sunglasses and stared down my nose at them with the most authoritative look I could muster. I struggled to sound provoked.

"I'll bet you boys think you're funny, don't you?"

"We thought they were rats, Daddy. We really did!" Max said.

Max was the older twin, having burst into the world five minutes before his brother, Luke. Max was the wise guy of the family. Luke was the sweet one, always in cahoots with Max.

"Uh-huh," Luke said, bobbing his head in agreement.

I looked over to old tight-as-a-drum-faced Mrs. Shannon and her little dogs, which were perched on her flabby lap as she dried them with a beach towel, fluffing their fur and cooing apologies. One of the little varmints wore a fake diamond collar and the other wore fake pearls. Are you kidding me? Both had their facial hair restrained with tiny rubber bands and wet ribbons, sad little bows that had come untied in the fray and hung down like overcooked strands of fettuccine. The dogs actually appeared to be frowning. They were ridiculous dogs, I thought, if you could even call them dogs at all. I've never been a fan of little yippers.

I looked back to my boys. They were right. Sort of. When drenched, her tiny terriers absolutely resembled rats in black tie.

"Did y'all apologize?"

"Yes, sir," Max said. "We sure did. They ain't *real* dogs, are they?"

"Of *course* they are, and you know it. And don't say *ain't*. It's not nice to shoot animals or people with water guns. You boys know better. You should be shooting each other." I realized how crazy that might have sounded to a passerby.

"It was by accident, Daddy," Max said, practicing his Academy Award acceptance speech for Best Actor.

"I doubt it," I said. "I was a boy once, you know!"

"You were?" Max said.

"I know. Hard to believe," I said.

"We thought that mean old lady was gonna hit us, Daddy!" Luke said.

"No one's going to hit anyone. Do you hear me? Now, behave yourselves or no Nintendo! Is that clear?"

"We don't have Nintendo. Momma says we aren't old enough," Max said.

"I'm gonna be six soon," Luke said. "That's old enough."

"Not if your mother doesn't think so," I said. "But you boys cross the line again, no TV!"

The threat of no television instantly sobered them. I was pleased with myself then, feeling I had successfully laid down the parental law.

Max saluted and then Luke did the same.

"Yes, sir!" they said.

"All right, now get out of here and let me read my book! You leave those water guns right here. They're in time-out."

"But it's so hot!" Luke said.

"We're dying!" Max said, performing a dramatic, drunken, weaving and staggering walk.

"Go jump in the pool."

They dropped their weapons on the ground and ran back to the pool. I watched them and thought that they were really good kids, just given to mischief. I sighed and took a long drink from my can of lukewarm Coke.

I'd kill for a glass of ice, I thought.

I reminded myself that if I had been paying attention, Mrs. Shannon's dogs would be dry. But hell! Wasn't I entitled to some downtime too? I'd been working my construction crews almost around the clock to get the new strip mall on James Island open by the Fourth of July. The stores had all opened by June thirtieth. Four days early! I was mentally and physically exhausted and very glad my father could watch the site office for me. I'd taken over the family construction business ten years ago and quickly quintupled its size. My father was extremely proud of that, and his approval meant a lot to me.

I could hear the boys' shrieks of laughter as they cannonballed and belly-flopped into the pool over and over again. Then the music became *Marco!* and *Polo!* as they bobbed underwater and jumped up as high as they could. They were having a wonderful time driving everyone else in the complex crazy.

I was just starting to think about lunch. I looked up to see Eliza crossing the terraced area and coming toward me again.

"Did your tummy start to growl yet?" she said.

"Kill me. I'm predictable," I said.

"I love you being predictable. How do you feel about BLTs on toast with basil mayonnaise? The bacon is smoked with applewood."

"If I had a diamond necklace in my pocket, I'd give it to you."

"Really? You sweet thing!" Eliza giggled. "How many carats?"

"A thousand."

"Then I'll make homemade cottage fries too." Eliza smiled and her dimples showed. "Lucky for you I packed my mandoline. And my fryer."

Eliza was a very serious cook who brought her own knives and other accoutrements with her on vacation. Including, apparently, her mandoline, which I had recently learned was not a stringed instrument but a gizmo with a blade used to slice vegetables so thin that you could see through them.

I lifted my sunglasses and looked up at her.

"You are the finest woman who ever lived."

"Ha ha! I love you, Adam Stanley."

"I love you too," I said.

And it was true. Eliza was an amazing wife.

"I'll bring a tray out in about thirty minutes or so. Pull our monkeys out of the pool in about fifteen. Good grief, would you look at them?" Eliza shook her head and laughed.

"Should we feed the little snipers? Or should we make them suffer for their crimes?"

We watched as the boys threw plastic rings to the bottom of the pool and dove in to retrieve them with the same frantic energy crazed dogs burn while chasing tennis balls. They were long skinny string beans, tanned to the hue of peanut butter, who could swim like fish. Their olive complexions, black curly hair, and blazing blue eyes were a result of Eliza's Mediterranean origins. But they would grow tall like me. Their height belied their age, and people frequently assumed they were older than their five and a half years, expecting more from them than what they were mature enough to deliver. In other words, they caught a lot of hell.

"We have to feed them. It's the law. They're just little rascals, that's all. But they're too tall to be tormenting dogs," I said, delivering the family joke for the hundredth time. "Did you give our nice neighbor the money?"

"Yeah. She's a . . ." Eliza mouthed the word *bitch.* "Now we have to go to the bank. Okay, I'm gonna go fix our lunch."

"Hurry back. I'm going for a quick dip to cool off."

I'd always thought that renting a condo made much better economic sense than buying. I wasn't a reckless man, with money or anything else. And I never invested in anything without tons of due diligence and consideration. But I also recognized that if this year's vacation lived up to last year's I might change that position and entertain the idea of buying something, sometime down the road. If I rented it out when we weren't there, over time it would pay for itself. Maybe.

I stood up, walked to the edge of the deep end of the adult

pool, and considered my next move. Rufus remained behind, sleeping like the old dog he was. Dive in? Slip in? A gradual immersion in the shallow end? There were not many people around the pool, because most of them were either on the beach where it was considerably cooler and beyond the shouts of *Marco! Polo!* or they had already gone inside to escape the merciless heat.

Perspiration was pouring out of me and the sun was blinding. I took off my sunglasses and put them on the edge of the pool. I dove in the deep end and for the first moments my body was shocked by the cool water. I wondered if that kind of cold shock could cause a heart attack. Yes, I was a worrier, but not excessively so. I surfaced, backstroked over to where my boys were standing in waist deep, and hoisted myself up onto the side of the pool.

"Nice dive, Dad!"

"Thanks! Whew! That felt great! Mom wants y'all to dry off soon. She's bringing lunch down here for us."

"Great," Luke said. "I'm starving!"

"What else is new?" Max said and pushed water toward his brother's face with the heel of his hand.

"Hey!" Luke said. "Stop!" He pushed a wave of water back toward his twin in retaliation.

"All right, you two. Out of the pool. Adult swim time. I'm going to do a few laps and then I'll dry off too. Why don't you boys gather up all your stuff and get a table for us? One with an umbrella."

"Does that mean we can have our guns back?" Max said.

"Do you think y'all can use them responsibly?"

"Yes! Yes, sir!"

"Okay, then. But no shooting little dogs. Got it?"

They scampered away toward my lounger and I slipped back into the water.

God, this feels so good, I thought.

I turned on my back and began doing backstrokes. When I reached the end of the pool, I turned over and began doing breaststrokes toward the shallow end.

Swimming gives me time to ponder my life—you know, assess things. Lucky for me, I'm about as satisfied with my lot in life as any man I know. And not too terribly arrogant. I hate arrogance. And I don't take anything for granted. But I think my male bravado and swagger is in the acceptable zone, and if I'm hiding some great mountain of hubris, no one has ever accused me of it. I'd say my friends and colleagues view me as a reliable, good-natured, well-mannered fellow. A man's man. But most important, I've got the steadfast support and admiration of my father, Ted.

If I ever get a little free time I like to hunt birds and fish the rivers. I can swing a golf club and a tennis racket well enough to play nine holes or doubles. But I sure as hell will never be a club champion, because sustaining any level of success would be impossible if I spent my time chasing balls. Besides, I'm not all that competitive. And I'd say I'm a respectable golfer and tennis player nonetheless.

I swam a few more laps and continued thinking about life. I knew I wasn't exactly curing a terrible disease when I built another shopping center or apartment complex, but you know what? I took a certain pride in the fact that the work I did had provided enough money at thirty-seven years of age to buy a large tract of land outside of Charleston and build a home there for my family that resembled Tara, but on a much smaller scale. And I loved my little family and our menagerie, which seemed to be growing all the time.

The problem with buying a property that came with a barn was that it called for animals. Before I knew it, we had horses, goats, and a brace of German Shorthaired Pointers that loved to flush out coveys of quail. Next came the peacocks and chickens, followed by a cat who we named Crank. And naturally all those mouths to feed needed supervision, so we hired a property manager, Mr. Proctor, who saw to the animals and did all the landscaping and house repairs as well. Mr. Proctor was the same age as my father—too old to really work full-time but too young to retire at sixty-eight. Crank and Rufus were house pets. Everyone else lived in the barn. Oh, Mr. Proctor.

He's a good guy, I thought.

I swam to the deep end of the pool once more and stopped. Suddenly I had a sense of being watched. There were two feet in front of me at eye level, female feet with a pedicure that I seem to remember Eliza called *French* for some baffling reason. They were very pretty feet and they did not belong to my wife.

"Adam? Is that you?"

I looked up. The feet in question were connected to perfectly tanned, very long, beautiful legs. Above the legs was a turquoise tank suit and a super flat stomach below perky, if smallish, breasts. The sun was so bright that I could not make out the details of her face. But I knew that voice. It had haunted me for more than half my life.

"Eve?"

"Oh, my gosh! It *is* you. I remember you swimming laps like this when we were teenagers. I'd know those shoulders anywhere."

You knew my shoulders, all right, I thought, and every other part of me too.

I climbed the ladder in the deep end and sucked in my stomach when I emerged from the water. Regrettably, my six-pack had morphed into a little paunch. I lifted myself out with a little swinging movement, hoping it would make me seem more fit and virile.

"Nice swimsuit," she said and covered her mouth with her hand to hide her laughter.

"Father's Day gift. What are you doing here?" I said. Jesus, I thought, she's still devastatingly beautiful. My heart was racing. Be cool, I told myself. I picked up my sunglasses and put them on. Joe Cool.

"Why, I'm on vacation with my family. You?"

"Yeah, me too. You have a family?" What a stupid thing to say, I thought.

"I sure do." She turned and pointed to the little girl in the kiddie pool. "That little angel is mine."

I looked and there she was. She was around the twins' age, with blond, blond hair and no doubt blue eyes like her mother's. I sighed. Of course she had a child! Why wouldn't she? The daughter that, in a different life, could've been ours.

"She's beautiful," I said. "Like you."

"Oh, Adam. Go on now. You don't look so bad yourself."

All I could manage was "Thanks." But then I finally found my voice and said, "Why don't y'all come over for a glass of wine around six? That's our condo right there."

"Sure. I'd like that. It'll be fun to catch up!" She kissed my cheek and turned to go back to her daughter. "Can I bring my husband?"

"What kind of a question is that? Of course! I have to meet the guy that stole my girl!"

Yeah, I thought, *that* son of a bitch. Let's see what he's got.

"I thought I'd never see you again. What a coincidence," she said.

There are no coincidences, I thought.

"See ya later!" I said cheerily.

I felt like a young man of eighteen then. Adrenaline rushed through me and I was energized and excited. I could run a marathon! By God, I could!

What *were* the odds on this serendipitous meeting? But if I didn't believe in coincidence, what was the meaning of seeing her again?

Across the terraced area, I spotted Eliza setting the table with our lunch. She was hairy-eyeballing me with grave suspicion.

Eliza's probably not going to like this, I thought.

meet eliza

You did what?" I said.

"I invited her over for a glass of wine. With her husband, of course," Adam said as he surveyed his lunch. "Wow, this looks great, sweetheart. Thanks!"

I detached the straws and pushed them through the tiny openings on pouches of Capri Sun for the boys. Then I poured iced tea from a covered plastic pitcher for Adam and myself. The boys scraped the heavy metal chairs across the cement closer to their food and then climbed over the arms to sit. The enormous patio umbrella was situated to keep us all in the shade. If need be, we could reposition it as the sun traveled across the sky.

"Well, that's fine, but who are they?" I asked.

"She's a girl I knew in high school. No big deal. You'll like her."

I smelled a rat. I had been standing right there watching Adam preen and hold in his stomach.

"What makes you think I'll like her? She's nine feet tall,

skinny as a stick, and blond. She's going to wonder what in the world you ever saw in the likes of me!"

"No, she won't! She's going to know in less than a minute that I married the most glamorous, fabulous woman in the world! Isn't that right, boys?"

Luke and Max, who were almost completely self-absorbed, were totally oblivious to the fact that I was feeling a little insecure. They didn't understand the word or the concept. Thus far, their young lives had been a succession of brass rings. As far as we knew they had yet to experience even a playground bully.

"Uh-huh," Luke said. "Pass the ketchup, please."

"Yep," Max said. "More potato chips?"

"Say the magic word," I said.

"Please?" Max said. "Hey, Mom? You know what? I like eating lunch in my bathing suit!"

Anything new and different was okay with Max.

"Good, sweetheart." I passed the platter to him and said, "Save some for your father."

"Thank you," Adam said, "but I think I should start watching my weight."

"Really? Thirty minutes ago, it was okay for me to hang over a pot of boiling oil to make them for you."

"Oh, okaaaaay. I'll have a few." He took a handful and dropped them on his plate.

I scrutinized Adam as he sucked in his stomach muscles again and could see that his mood had changed. He was considerably more lighthearted than he had been in the morning when he was offering me diamonds in exchange for cottage fries. He hadn't stopped smirking since we sat down for lunch. I hated smirkers. Who was this woman, anyway? And what had she meant to him? Did he sleep with her? Was I really supposed to be nice to a woman who'd slept with my husband? Was Adam losing his mind to invite her over? Did he think he could *will* away his gut by the cocktail hour?

Men are so stupid, I thought. And vain.

"What's her name?" I said.

"Eve. She was Eve Church . . . I don't know her last name now. She's got a husband. It will be very interesting to see who she married."

The fact that Adam thought meeting Eve's husband would be *very* interesting, not merely *interesting*, told me that Eve had been more than a fling.

"Her name is Eve? Really? Like Adam and Eve? You're kidding, right?"

There sat my husband, giddy with excitement, mouth full of sandwich, looking pretty silly in his giddiness and excitement. He was smiling even as he chewed. "Yeah. Eve. Isn't that funny? Anyway, that August we went off to different colleges and I never saw her again," Adam said as a nearly tangible air of gloom descended around him.

I knew there was no way he would be this animated if that woman meant nothing to him. Plus, he had never mentioned her name before today. And I knew the name of every single girl he had ever dated. Why? Because boys like to kiss and tell.

If I were in his shoes, I'd never let on that I was that excited to see an old flame. Not in a million years. Why didn't he even have the good sense to mask this tsunami of rapturous glee?

Because he had been in love with her, that's why. Men!

I waited for a moment and watched his face as he stared off into space, wistful and remembering. "So, she broke your heart, did she?"

"What? No, no, no. That's ridiculous," he said. "Anyway, it was high school, for heaven's sake! Ancient history! They're just coming for a glass of wine. No big deal."

I could tell by his sudden change in expression that Eve had, in fact, broken his heart. Suddenly, instead of feeling insecure, I was annoyed. Who was this Eve person who had hurt the man I loved? I'd show her what she had walked away from! Who did this Eve think she was? Why, she was a fool! A damn fool!

"What time are they coming?"

"I think I told her six."

"I'll be ready," I said and thought, six o'clock can't get here fast enough.

As we ate our lunch, a warm breeze began to swirl, enveloping us in thick, salty air. Adam and I sighed deeply and fell under a mischievous Lowcountry spell. Our shoulders relaxed and we smiled for no reason. Gulls squawked all around. The rhythm and the incessant movement of the rolling tide was like a beautiful Strauss waltz. We looked at each other, beaming really, with an inexplicable happiness.

It was a satisfying moment for me. My boys were sitting politely and using nice table manners. And Adam seemed to be thoroughly enjoying his sandwich and gulping down copious amounts of iced tea. An old girlfriend? Who cares?

I was so happy we were all together and I ticked off a list of all the things I felt grateful for. I had beautiful children and a wonderful husband. I was just thirty-seven and I felt very much like an adult. Technically I knew I was a wife and mother, of course, but the realization that I wasn't ever going to be that hot young babe again had taken a while to adjust to. But if the trade-off was to be Adam's wife and the mother of our two scallywags, it wasn't so bad. Who cared about stupid Eve Church?

All I had to do was look at Adam to see that he was having similar thoughts. He was very proud that he was able to give us a nice vacation. Everyone knew he adored his boys, and yes, it always seemed as though he was crazy about me. But at that particular moment, it seemed like he was feeling much younger than his years, macho in fact, anticipating the evening to come. If we hadn't come to Wild Dunes for this vacation he might never have run into Eve again for the rest of his life. I knew my husband, and right about now he was feeling a twitch in his personal Lowcountry and was trying to redirect his thoughts to something benign, like throwing a Frisbee with his boys.

"This was delicious, Mom," Max said.

"It was great, Eliza. Just hit the spot. Thanks! You boys want to build sand castles this afternoon? Maybe throw the Frisbee around"

What did I just say?

"Yeah!" Max said, and Luke bobbed his head.

"Y'all are welcome! Okay, boys. Give me a hand cleaning up lunch and I'll take you to Baskin-Robbins," I said. "I want to see what looks good at the Pig for dinner."

The Piggly Wiggly was my favorite grocery store.

"Baskin-Robbins! Yay!"

Ice cream? On a blazing hot day? The boys were understandably jubilant. They quickly gathered up the paper plates and the collapsed juice pouches and rushed toward the public garbage cans.

"We'll play with you when we get back, Dad," Max said.

"Okay," Adam said.

"Let's go, Mom! Let's go!"

They were literally jumping up and down in place.

"Go put on a T-shirt and put something on your feet!" I turned to Adam and said, "I wish they still took naps."

"Don't worry. I'll wear them out this afternoon when you get back."

"Well, behave yourself until I do, okay, Mr. Romeo?"

"Eliza? You know I only love you."

I pointed my finger at him and shot him some stink eye. We both laughed. I laughed to let him know I was onto him. And Adam laughed to try to make me believe there was nothing to this unexpected meeting with an old friend. We both knew better.

I withstood the bombardment of the highly elevated level of testosterone emanating from Adam, and I was reasonably certain that a trip to the grocery store would not wreck my marriage. He wasn't going to run over to Eve's condo and throw her in the sack. The worst that could happen was that he might spend an hour doing sit-ups and flossing. I could leave home with some level of confidence.

I loved shopping at the Piggly Wiggly. They always had a wide variety of Lowcountry specialty foods and condiments, including especially Mrs. Sassard's artichoke relish and okra pickles. As I gleaned the aisles, I thought we might stop at the vegetable stand on Highway 17 to pick up tomatoes and cucumbers. And maybe we'd pop into Simmons Seafood to check out their daily catch.

By four o'clock that afternoon the boys were back on the beach with Adam, having eaten double scoops of rocky road and pralines and cream ice cream. I watched from the window as they sat on an old palmetto log, working on a large slice of watermelon. In accordance with the Lowcountry traditions of Adam's childhood, he drew a line in the sand and they had a contest to see who could spit the seeds the farthest. To Max's chagrin, it looked as though Luke won every single time. Of course, it didn't hurt that he was missing a front tooth. Finally, Adam whispered something in Luke's ear, and when the very next round of seeds went flying, Luke's came up short. Max was so relieved to have won at least one round. And Luke had learned the first of many lessons he would learn about sportsmanship: sometimes it was better to be gracious than to pound your opponent into humiliation. I loved Adam then.

When the seeds ran out they had races to see who was the fastest. Next came practice for a running broad jump. Now that the boys were sticky and salty, Adam threw them into the pool and made them race the length of it over and over. Adam was true to his word. The boys would sleep very well that night. He was a great father.

Meanwhile I was in the kitchen, making hors d'oeuvres I hoped would impress my husband's old lover and whoever her stupid husband was, who probably didn't realize he had married a slut. (Yes, my imagination was in overdrive.) Miniature crab cakes would be topped with frizzled leeks and red pepper jelly. Fresh-caught shrimp, deveined and made into ceviche, marinated in scallions, cilantro, lemon zest, and a citrus vinaigrette, would be offered with toothpicks. Sweet sausage baked golden brown in puffed pastry rings would be served with a piquant honey mustard laced with traces of horseradish. And of course, I was making a tray of tiny pigs in blankets, which the boys loved. I seldom worked so hard in the kitchen while on vacation, but the prospect of an old flame dropping by for a glass of vino demanded extra effort. When our guests left I'd just put some burgers on the grill for the boys' supper if they were still hungry. Depending on his behavior, I might or might not feed my husband, especially since I knew he was feeding me some massive bull.

Don't screw with my intuition, Mr. Stanley, I thought. And then I laughed out loud.

Once I had the kitchen under control and a bar set up, I went to our bedroom closet to see what to wear. I try to be stylish in my wardrobe choices and in every area of my life. I chose my clothes carefully, looking for flattering silhouettes, generally in solid colors, and then accessorized accordingly. The truth was that my body had betrayed me by failing to return to its normal size after I delivered the twins. It didn't matter how much jogging I did or how many hours I spent in exercise classes. I'd never have a tiny waist again. Other assets seemed to be traveling south as well. But there was nothing to be gained by fretting over things that I could not change. So I continued doing aerobics and hoped for the best. I placed several sundresses out on the bed and stood back. One was a long white tank dress with a deep V-neck. It showcased the girls. The other two were black. Black was too serious. The white dress would look better on me with my tan. So I showered, moisturized from one end to the other, and piled my crazy hair into a knot at the nape of my neck.

I owned a lot of turquoise and silver Native American jewelry—mostly Zuni. And I loved coral too. I had been collecting pearls for years and owned yards of them in every size and hue—white, pink, champagne, and gray. I had my eye on a pair of South Sea deep-charcoal-colored pearl earrings with little diamonds around them. Adam knew it.

"Maybe for a significant birthday," he had said.

I had brought some great outfits with me to the Isle of Palms, but none of them were clothes to leave my husband's old girlfriend in a state of wonder.

While applying my makeup, I could hear Adam and the boys rummaging around downstairs. They'd want a cold drink. I heard the refrigerator door open and close several times. I was right. I hurried to the stairwell and called to them.

"Did you kids shower off outside?"

"Yes, ma'am!" they called back.

"I made sure they did, and they're sort of dry," Adam called to me.

"Boys! Don't sit on the sofa in a wet swimsuit!" They'd ruin the night before it got started. "Get up here! We have company coming!"

I went back to my bathroom, but when the twins failed to appear, I quickly went to the stairwell and called to them once more. I intended to get them moving before they picked through the cocktail food and got sand everywhere, wreaking mayhem on my carefully orchestrated party scene, such as it could be staged in a bare-bones rental house.

"Max? Luke? Y'all come when I call you, you hear me?"

"Coming!"

The boys ran up the stairs, taking them two at a time. I had to back up against the wall so they wouldn't plow into me. I looked at them and my heart melted a little. They were shirtless again, and the freckles that were scattered across their noses and cheeks were becoming more pronounced with each passing day. And they had peanut butter and grape jelly around their mouths. I thought then that the good Lord didn't make little boys any more adorable than mine.

"You know, you *are* going to have supper," I said.

"We were starving," Luke said.

I just shook my head. Boys are simply eating machines.

"Okay, I want y'all to get out of your swimsuits right now, put on your pajamas, and brush your teeth. We have company coming in less than an hour. I'll let you skip your baths tonight."

"We swam off all the salt in the pool anyway," Max said.

"That's not the same thing as a warm bath with soap," I said.

"Yay! No bath!" Luke said.

"Can we stay up late? Please? Please?" Max said.

"If you behave yourselves. Got it? Okay, I'll fix your tooth-brushes for you. Let's get going!"

I put a squirt of toothpaste on their toothbrushes, hurried down the stairs to preheat the oven, and rushed back up the stairs, checking on the boys' progress. For once, they were doing as I asked them to do.

"Good boys!" I said. "Brush every single tooth and rinse good, you hear me?"

I went back to the bathroom once again and finished ap-plying my makeup as well as I could without a magnifying mirror. I stood back and looked at myself.

Not bad, I thought.

I was about to meet my husband's former paramour. I wished then that I was entertaining this awful woman in my own home, surrounded by our belongings, instead of in this rental condo that came fully furnished with utilitarian, clunky things we wouldn't have even considered owning. I felt if Eve could see all the photographs of me with Adam and our sons she'd back off—that is, if she had any intentions that were not honorable.

"I must be out of my mind to let this woman in here," I said to the thin air.

Ten minutes later, promptly at six, the doorbell rang. Adam and the boys answered it as I looked across the long dining room–living room. There came Eve in the palest blue linen shirt and white pants with white sandals, gliding into our lives like a swan. Her blond hair was blown out straight and hung below her shoulders. She looked angelic. I hated her on sight. But behind her was the most handsome man I had ever seen in my entire life, if you liked his type. He was tanned and fit. Obviously athletic.

A Norse god! I thought.

I liked his type.

I was paralyzed, totally unable to put down the sheet tray of pigs in blankets to leave the kitchen and greet my guests. Maybe I wouldn't hate the evening as much as I thought.

Move! I told myself. Close your mouth! Your jaw is hanging open!

Finally, I cleared my throat, tightened my abdominals, and moved out into the living room to say hello. And I managed to put the tray down on the coffee table.

We were all struggling with our abs today, weren't we? Except these two, I thought.

"These are our boys, Luke and Max," Adam said.

"She doesn't look like a stick," Max said.

Adam covered Max's mouth with his own hand and said, "Max is the family comedian."

"That's okay," Eve said. "I'm *still* too skinny. *Still* can't gain weight!"

Oh please, I thought, go kill yourself.

"Make yourself scarce," Adam said to Max and Luke.

"Okay!" they said and took off for upstairs with Rufus. "Come on, boy!"

"And this is my wife, Eliza," Adam said, smiling as widely as a largemouth bass.

"Hey! How're y'all doing?" I said, trying to relax.

"Let's get you a glass of something?" Adam said and moved toward the bar I had set up on the dining table. Eve was right at Adam's side. "What'll it be? White wine? Scotch? Vodka? A beer?"

I looked at Eve's husband, who finally made eye contact with me, and when he did I was sure I was naked. Or at least half dressed.

"Hi, I'm Carl," he said. He took my hand into his and held it as he appraised me with his sparkling green eyes.

He had the thickest eyelashes I had ever seen on a man, blond fringe awnings, actually. And he was still holding my hand.

"I'm Eliza," I said and was suddenly overcome with hot flashes and giggles.

He grinned at me and said, "Eve said she saw you this afternoon, but she didn't tell me you were gorgeous."

"Okay. *That's* it! I'm gonna die right now!" I said, feeling like I had just fallen into one of those dreams where the impossible was happening, like flying. And I thought my laughing would never stop. I didn't even care if he thought I was completely crazy.

"Are you all right?" he said.

"Um, yeah, really, I'm sorry. I should've known. That's all."

"What? You should've known what?" He was smiling and politely waiting to be let in on the joke, whatever it was.

I was not about to say what I was thinking.

"Listen, Carl. I'm sorry, but no one has ever called me gorgeous."

"Really?"

"Yep. Really. It's okay. I was just surprised."

"Well, you are."

"Well, thanks. You're not exactly Uncle Fester yourself."

He shook his head in agreement. After all, he knew what he looked like. "Uncle Fester. Remember that guy?"

"Yes. Um, okay, how about an adult beverage? A California agricultural product?"

"And you're funny too. Well, I'm sure glad we met. It's going to make this vacation so much easier to take!"

CHAPTER 3

eliza's new friends

The notion that Carl and Eve were just stopping by for a glass of wine and that then they would be on their way was not what Fate had in mind. Once we all started talking, it was clear they were there for the duration of the evening.

We sent the boys off to their rooms again and again, telling them they could watch television for an hour. Between pigs in blankets, PB&J sandwiches, and snitching the adults' hors d'oeuvres, their seemingly bottomless stomachs were finally full. There was no need to fire up the grill for burgers.

"At eight thirty I'm coming up to turn out the lights!" I said. "Give your dad a kiss."

"Yes, ma'am!"

They gave us a peck on our cheeks and ran up the stairs, thrilled at the idea of watching an hour of unsupervised television.

"Are your boys always so well behaved?" Eve said.

I said, "No. They most certainly are not. But overall, when they're not sassy, they're really great."

"My Daphne is a sneaky little hellion," Eve said.

"That's because you give her everything she wants," Carl said.

"Oh, you! I do not!" Eve said and gave him a little pinch on the arm.

"She spoils her rotten," Carl said.

"Where *is* your daughter?" I asked. "I was looking forward to meeting her."

"She's at our condo with our au pair. My sweet mother, who usually travels with us to watch her, sprained her ankle on a cobblestone street. She's at home on crutches," Eve said. "Hey! Here's an idea. We can throw the kids in the pool together tomorrow, if you'd like."

"Wonderful!" I said, finally but only slightly warming up to Eve. "I'm sure the boys would love a new friend. And I hope your mom's okay."

"My mother-in-law's a good egg," Carl said. "She always babysits for us when we need her."

"Where do you live?" Adam said.

"Raleigh," Eve said. "Anyway, Carl's right. My mother is a bona fide saint."

Adam lifted an eyebrow, and I knew he disagreed for some reason. He said, "Well, we always say it's too bad kids don't come with a manual on how to raise them."

"Listen, earlier today our little devils nearly drowned a couple of dogs with their water guns. Nice, right?" I said.

"I feel better," Eve said.

As the evening rolled along a camaraderie was forming. Before we finished the first bottle of wine, which after all is only five glasses, everyone was feeling more comfortable with each other, except me. Something about Eve irked me. But I remained congenial. A second bottle of wine was opened.

"So, y'all live out on 17?" Eve said.

"Yes. We do," I said with an unintentional bit of emphasis on the *we*.

"What do you *do* out there? I mean, it's like—"

"A wasteland? Yeah, it's half an hour to anywhere. But Adam always wanted a river house, and he found this property that was an old farm on the Stono River. Then he built our home and a dock, which is really terrific for him and the boys." I didn't say it was my dream home, nor did I brag about how Adam had insisted on my having my dream kitchen. Or that we hand-selected each stone for the fireplace together or that the mantelpiece was hand-hewed and carved by my father's father. Our house was the perfect expression of our love for each other in so many ways.

"But what about for *you*? Do you even *like* living in the country? I'd lose my mind!"

Then it's a good thing Adam didn't marry you, I thought.

"It's not the worst thing. I handle all the accounting for his business, so I get to work from home. And then I can see about the boys too. Would you like one of these?"

Eve had unearthed a secret I harbored and worked hard to hide. But I wasn't quite ready to abandon caution and bare my soul to her. It was true. Sometimes when I was there alone at night with just the boys, I'd hear a noise and it would frighten me to death. I definitely had moments of feeling vulnerable. In fact, I really didn't like being alone. It was so dark at night that if I went outside I couldn't see my hand in front of my face. Adam proposed having a gun in the house, but I was terrified of them. To my mind too many terrible accidents had happened with guns.

I offered Eve one of the sausage-in-puff-pastry nibbles and her eyes grew large as she took a bite.

"This is delicious!" Eve held her cupped hand under her chin to ensure that flakes of puff pastry wouldn't fall to the floor. "Honey? Try one of these!"

I turned and offered the platter to Adam and Carl. Each man promptly took one, dipped it in the mustard, and popped it into his mouth. Then they moaned in unison.

"Ma'am?" Carl said. "Please stand right here until that platter is empty." Then he picked up another one and ate it, grinning like a teenage boy. "Outstanding."

Not to be outdone, Adam had two. And then I broke out the marinated shrimp, which brought about more wide eyes and moans of simple pleasure.

"Eliza? Please tell me how to make this! The shrimp are so fresh and light. I love them!" Eve said.

"I'd be happy to give you the recipe, although it's just something I made up," I said. "I think it's the cilantro and lime zest that make it sing."

"Eliza is the best cook in the world," Adam said and gave me a kiss on the cheek.

"Wow," Eve said. "I can hardly boil water. Now, tell me more about living outside of the city. Isn't it lonely?"

Eve had done it again. Of course, it was lonely. And it was damned inconvenient. It took thirty minutes to get to the worst grocery store and almost an hour to get to the better ones. And with traffic? It was a huge pain to get anywhere. But I wasn't going to let the conversation go there.

So, ever the trouper, I began telling them about the good things about living in the country.

"It has some drawbacks, but it has lots of benefits too. The very first thing you notice is the clean air," I said. "And I love watching the water. But I think what I enjoy most is the quality of life it gives our boys and my garden."

"Really?" Carl said. "Somehow I can't see you getting dirty."

"You should *see* her garden," Adam said. "Vegetables on steroids. No lie."

"It's because of the compost," I said, thinking, these birds have no idea how to make compost or why anyone would.

"Ew! Compost? Nasty. What do you grow?" Eve asked.

Maybe this sounds a tad superior, but now I really didn't like Eve so much.

"Oh, you know, the usual stuff. A row of beefsteaks and other kinds of tomatoes, a row of Silver Queen and bicolor corn, collards and romaine have a row. Then sometimes I put in asparagus and cantaloupe, cucumbers, bell peppers, and then jalapeños and herbs. And I grow zinnias too. There's just something about them I love, with their sticky stems and weird medicinal smell. This year the boys planted sunflowers. They'll probably be taller than them by the time they go back to school!"

Eve was rapt but obviously having trouble envisioning the joy of gardening.

"How big is it?" Eve asked. "It sounds like a small farm and an awful lot of work!"

"Not that large, really. And it's especially fun for the boys. They help me pull weeds. In the fall, we grow pumpkins."

"What do you *wear* when you tend your garden?" Carl said.

I looked at Carl to see if he was serious. I almost said, black lace panties. Propriety aside, I could be outrageous with the best of them. But I didn't know them well enough to be bawdy.

"Well, sunscreen, for sure, and a big hat."

I laughed over my naughty thought and Carl seemed to have heard it in the ether. I caught his eye and he wiggled his eyebrows at me. Eve saw him wiggling his eyebrows at me, got the joke, and gave him another pinch.

Sometimes even poker players could have their lewd thoughts discovered, I thought. The poor man's inner arms must be black and blue all the time.

Adam, unaware of any sort of flirtation going on in the room, kept going on about the things I grew and the animals we kept. "You should see the chickens and the goats!"

"Good heavens!" Eve said, honestly shocked over the idea of voluntary ownership of goats and chickens. "Why on earth would anyone—"

"*Want* goats and chickens? Eggs and weed killers. We have peacocks too," I said. "A peahen and a peacock just appeared one day and took up residence. Now we have six!"

"Good grief!" Eve said and laughed. She looked at me like

I had teleported straight from the set of *Little House on the Prairie.*

"Watch where you're walking!" Carl said.

"Exactly!" Adam said.

It should be noted that, while Adam was as gregarious and hospitable as I had ever seen him be, he was stealing a multitude of glances at Eve, thinking he was unnoticed.

I said, "Well, when I was a little girl my grandparents had a farm in upstate New York. Columbia County. I spent my summers there and loved it. And I guess in some perverse way I still think it's fun. The kids sure do."

"Yes. It was *really* fun the time the boys let the goats in the house and they ate the sofa cushions," Adam said. "You can't believe how much stuffing is in a sofa."

"I turned my back for *one* minute," I said.

Everyone laughed.

"Where did you grow up?" Carl asked.

"Winchester, Massachusetts. A suburb of Boston."

"I went to school in Boston," Carl said. "How did you two meet?"

Adam looked at the ceiling. I could read his mind. Were they about to get a lecture on the history of Harvard and how Carl was the smartest guy who ever went there?

"Business school. Adam and I went to Carolina. He borrowed my statistics notes and the rest is history."

"I still hate statistics," Adam said.

"Love it," Eve said.

Eve was smiling and complimentary and seemed to be no threat at all, I thought. I mean, now that they had seen each other again, would Eve do something insane like leave Carl for Adam? Probably not. There was something a bit snooty about her, as there was about Carl. No. Adam and Eve would not have been a great match.

"So! We've got a couple of MBAs, down by the riverside, living the organic dream," Carl said. "Not too bad. Not too bad at all."

"How about y'all?" Adam said. "How did you find each other in this cold cruel world?"

Eve drained her glass of wine and refilled it herself.

"Friends set us up," Eve said. "I was visiting an old roommate in Raleigh and we went to a party. There was Carl standing by the bar. We were introduced and the first thing he said to me was *Don't you think we'd make beautiful children?*"

Carl chimed in, "I did say that. Shameless."

Adam cleared his throat and I knew he was thinking, Well, aren't you the stud?

"I know, very presumptuous of me. But she said, *maybe*. I took that as a good sign."

"And making that baby brought us to the altar," Eve said, taking a big gulp of wine.

What? I thought. They got married because Eve was pregnant?

Eventually, it came out that Carl was a pediatrician. Not only was he a pediatrician with a huge practice, but he taught at Duke and did research and was always out on speaking engagements. But he didn't want to brag.

I looked at Adam and he pretended to gag. I didn't blame him, but I was still impressed.

And somewhere along the line and that third bottle of wine it was revealed that Carl wanted more children and Eve did not. Her pregnancy had been difficult and she didn't feel like she had the wherewithal to endure another one.

I thought about that for a while. What woman on this earth wouldn't want to have babies with Carl? Then I thought, what woman wouldn't want to at least *try*?

The evening finally came to an end around eleven.

"Max and Luke will be up by seven, raising hell," Adam said.

"Well, if you're up at seven," Carl said, "why don't we go play nine holes?"

"Actually, I brought my clubs," Adam said. "But you have to know I'm not much at the game."

"Oh, hell, don't worry about that! We can play best ball? I don't really care," Carl said. "I just like to get some exercise before it gets to be too hot."

"Okay. It's a deal," Adam said.

Later, when we were in bed and had just turned out the lights, Adam said, "So what did you think about tonight?"

"I don't know."

"Oh, come on. You know you have an opinion."

"They're both too good looking. Being that good looking is a curse."

Adam was quiet for a minute. Then he said, "Please tell me why?"

"Because you're never satisfied."

"Really?"

"Yeah, really. And you know what else?"

"Tell me," Adam said.

"It's harder to know what's true and what isn't."

"You mean like did you get the job because of your looks or your résumé?"

"Yes. Or does someone like you for your looks or because of what kind of person you are. And you want to know what else?"

"Sure." Adam yawned and rolled over onto his side and threw his arm around me. "God, I love lying down next to you."

"Me too, baby." I smiled then, thinking Adam could be so sweet.

"So? What else?"

"I think he screws around on her."

"Why would he do that?" Adam said, trying to sound blasé.

He knew I was always right about these things.

"I don't know. But I'd bet the ranch on it. One other thing."

"What's that?"

"If you think I'm going to spend this vacation watching you drool over her like a puppy, we may as well go home tomorrow."

Among the pillows, the sheets, and the comforter there was silence followed by more silence while I bunched them and twisted the covers, sending a clear signal of my annoyance. Adam was as still as a corpse, probably hoping I would think he had already drifted off to sleep.

The last thing he heard me say was, "I mean it, Adam."

Morning came earlier than expected for Adam and later for me.

"Tell Mom I love her, okay?" Adam said on his way out the door.

"Where're you going?" Max asked.

"To make a fool out of myself," Adam said.

"I love you too!" I called out from upstairs.

"Have fun!" Luke said.

"See you later," I said.

I came padding down the stairs in a tie-dyed caftan and bare feet.

"Morning, boys! Don't sit too close to the television," I said. "You'll ruin your eyesight. Did you eat?"

"Yep," Luke said. "Dad made us breakfast."

"What are you watching?"

"*Rugrats*," Max said.

"*Ren & Stimpy* is on next," Luke said.

"Okay, well, what do you say to brushing your teeth and then let's hit the pool?"

Max stood up. It looked like he wanted to go put on his bathing suit but he couldn't tear himself away from the television. He was hopping from one foot to the other.

"Go use the bathroom, Max."

"When a commercial comes on!"

"Now!" I said.

Max ran down the hall.

I looked at the kitchen counter in dismay. The knife that had spread peanut butter on the toasted waffles was stuck to the counter, the open box of waffles was thawed, and the cap for the container of milk was MIA. I sighed, counted the remaining waffles, and knew that my boys had eaten two apiece. I poured myself a mug of coffee and began putting everything away. I hated buying that kind of food for my children, but when we were on vacation I let a lot of rules go by the wayside. Otherwise it wouldn't have seemed like a vacation.

It wasn't too long before everyone was ready for another day in the sun.

"Rufus? You want to go sit in the sun?"

Rufus knew better. Sit in the sun? Rufus looked at me as though I had asked him to sit in the oven. He turned, directed his body to the tiled area in front of the refrigerator, lumbered over to it, walked in a circle, and curled up on the floor. He raised his eyes to me, big, watery, red-rimmed, chocolate bonbons that they were, and he sighed the most world-weary sigh that a dog or a man had ever emitted. My heart melted.

God, I love this dog, I thought.

I leaned down and scratched behind his ears.

"You rest, old man," I said, "and I'll see you around lunchtime."

At last, I was able to get my sons organized with all their toys and gear and off we went to the pool. Eve was there reading a book while her daughter splashed around in the shallow end of the adult pool.

"Come sit with us!" Eve called out, waving me over.

"Thanks!" I said and dropped our towels and so forth on a

lounge chair next to her. "You'd think we're going on safari with all this stuff!"

"It's the truth!" Eve said and called out to her daughter. "Daphne? Come say hello to Max and . . ."

"Luke," I said.

"Max and Luke!"

Max and Luke were very busy putting on their goggles, and before Eve's little girl had time to get out of the pool Max and Luke cannonballed into the deep end, sending up a huge plume of water. Fortunately, Eve and I were the only adults there.

"They're river rats," I said. "What can I tell you? They started swimming the day they were born."

"They're boys! What do we expect?" Eve said, not bothered by their antics in the least.

We watched as my boys swam underwater to the shallow end and pulled Eve's little girl underwater. Screaming ensued and a morning of endless competition was born. Eve couldn't stop laughing as she watched them get to know each other.

"They're like puppies," she said, "sort of sniffing around each other before they get into the games."

I shook my head in agreement. "This is the best thing that could happen to them! A diversion."

We watched them for a bit, then I said, "Where's your au pair?"

"Oh, it's her morning off," Eve said.

"Say, how's your mom feeling?"

"Cookie? Oh, she'll be fine."

"You call her Cookie? That's so cute!" I said.

"Well, Daphne started it when she was just starting to talk. She would see her and ask for a cookie. Naturally, she gave her one. So she became *Cookie*. Anyway, she never sits in the sun. She's trying to avoid aging."

"How's that working?" I smiled.

"Well, she *looks* great, but I think she's getting a little batty."

"What do you mean? Is she forgetful? I mean, that's pretty normal."

"No! That's the whole problem. I wish she would be forgetful! She's . . . well, sometimes she can be very inappropriate."

"Oh," I said, wondering what that could mean. "Well, we have to love our parents, warts and all, right?"

"Yes, I suppose so. Hey, Daphne! Give Max his noodle back!"

The pool was a bowl of Chinese soup and the kids were the wontons, floating, bouncing, and bobbing. Unfortunately, they began to play Marco Polo at the top of their lungs.

I looked at Eve and said, "I despise Marco Polo."

Eve soon came to understand why. The Marco-ing and the Polo-ing was an incessant barrage of highly irritating noise pollution.

Eve went to the edge of the pool and said, "Kids? It's time to play something else."

Luke and Max looked to me as if to say, She's not our mom!

"Don't even start," I said. "Noise pollution. Got it?"

Their faces were dramatically sorrowful, so much so that when Eve's eyes met mine we had to put our hands over our mouths so the children wouldn't see us laughing. At last we had found common ground. By the time Adam and Carl returned from golf, sweaty and laughing, we were all practically old friends.

Later, when Adam and I were alone, I asked about the golf game.

"How'd it go?" I asked.

"He just had to play eighteen holes. I lost eighteen dollars and had to buy him a beer."

"A dollar a hole?"

Adam nodded his head. "Pissed me off." He was accustomed to winning. Well, not really, but for reasons obvious to me, he didn't like losing to Carl.

"So it's safe to assume you'll be taking golf lessons starting tomorrow?"

"I'm meeting the pro late this afternoon on the putting green."

"That's so great! Why not take the boys?"

"Eliza, this is serious. I can't have them driving me crazy when I'm trying to concentrate."

"Oh, okay." I looked into his eyes. "I never knew you to be so competitive."

"Between us? This is war."

CHAPTER 4

eliza's merry christmas

home on the stono, 1994

L uke and Max were out of school for their winter break. None of the schools called it Christmas Holidays anymore because not everyone celebrated Christmas. Everyone in America, or so it seemed, was suddenly twisting themselves inside out trying to be politically correct. Call the season what you like, but it was the end of another year and most people were feeling celebratory. And it had been a darned productive year for our little family.

I had a bumper crop of vegetables pickled in jars and in the freezer, and I was working on that cookbook I'd always wanted to write. Adam had the most profitable year in his business's history and bought us matching red SUVs. The boys had started kindergarten that prior August and their first semester had been one of many challenges and small victories. They made lots of new friends and took up hand-bell ringing and Bitty Basketball, the sport redesigned for kids under four feet. Because they were like asparagus in a field of sprouts, my twins were the stars of the team. But they were not exactly the descendants of Mozart, so when they performed in what was billed as a winter concert, they didn't distinguish themselves for the right reason. They somehow stayed a little behind the class, ringing with dramatic enthusiasm a few seconds after it was their turn to chime in, causing lots of tittering among the audience members. Of course, Adam and I nearly burst with pride watching them onstage. I blotted my eyes with a tissue, surprised at my tidal wave of emotion, while Adam held his movie camera over our heads, hoping to capture the boys on film. After the concert the little rascals were officially on vacation, free from the extraordinary stresses of elementary school until the first week of January. They were practically convulsing with excitement over what Santa might bring and on the best behavior of their young lives thus far.

The afternoon of December 16 found them on barstools in our kitchen at home under my watchful eyes. Dozens of cookies doused with liberal shakes of green and red sprinkles were cooling on wire racks strewn across the counters. They were the same type the boys had proudly given their teachers as a holiday gift, and this batch was destined for Mr. Proctor and for our few neighbors. But for the moment, Max and Luke were stringing popcorn for our enormous Christmas tree, which they had cut down with their father in the deep woods on our property. I was a little nervous about them handling needles, but so far there was no blood.

"You boys are doing a fine job, but be careful, okay?" I said.

"We handle fish hooks and they're much worse," Max said.

"Dad does that. Not you," Luke said in a whisper.

Max knitted his eyebrows together, disappointed that his twin had exposed his exaggeration of the facts. Luke usually agreed with whatever he said. Had something changed?

"Tell Luke to quit eating all the popcorn! There won't be enough for the tree!" Max said in revenge.

"But I like popcorn!" Luke said with a frown. "And besides, I'm—"

"Starving?" I laughed. "Oh, Luke." I tousled his hair and said, "Precious child. I can always make more."

Adam had taken the week off too. He was in the next room, all snug in his favorite recliner reading *Field & Stream* while the fireplace hissed and crackled from the flaming logs our caretaker had chopped for us. The enormous family room was where we congregated because it was the most comfortable. There was a game table, three deep sofas, and several club chairs. There was always a jigsaw puzzle in progress and stacks of magazines, as we subscribed to many. Hundreds of books lined the shelves, with framed photographs interspersed between inexpensive but nice replicas of antique Chinese blue and white ceramics. And of course, the biggest television in captivity stood opposite the fireplace. Adam loved his new television. The New York Philharmonic's rendition of holiday favorites filled the air with music streaming from the discreetly placed speakers of our mini stereo system. The disposition of the Stanley household was just right.

I was humming along with the music and going through the mail, opening holiday cards and stacking catalogs to recycle.

"Oh! Adam? Look here. We got a card from Eve and Carl. It has one of those annual newsletters in it."

"Really? Read it to me," Adam said, trying to sound blasé. He was fooling no one.

"It's three pages long," I said.

"Well then, just give me the highlights," Adam said.

Who has three pages of news about themselves? I said to myself as I began to read. The largest section was a chronicle of all their daughter's activities. She had started school too. Daphne was artistic and becoming quite the little ballerina and only wanted tutus from Santa. My eyes traveled to the *what we did on summer vacation* part of the letter. I was astonished to read Eve's feelings about us.

> . . . as unpredictable winds seem to blow throughout our lives like the breath of Mischief itself, we had the occasion to connect with an old, dear, and precious friend of mine and to become friends with his beautiful family. We have never enjoyed a family vacation as much as we did during the brief period we were their neighbors at Wild Dunes on the Isle of Palms.

I wondered if Carl felt the same way, because he had flirted with me relentlessly throughout our stay on the island. Naturally, I'd been flattered, but I quickly recognized I wasn't getting special treatment, as he spouted the same nonsense to every waitress, checkout girl, and any other female we encountered. When I realized he considered himself to be an intergalactically ranked Don Juan, I began to think of his ridiculous flattery as actually very funny. Still, I wondered what part he had in choosing the wording of Eve's holiday letter. He probably didn't even know she'd written one.

"Well, butter my butt and call me a biscuit," I said to the room in my best southern accent.

"Mom! You said 'butt'!" Luke said.

Max began to singsong my words and Luke joined in. *Butter my butt and call me a biscuit* rang through the air like a doorbell that wouldn't stop ringing until Adam called them down.

"That's enough!" he said.

Given the proximity of Santa's sleigh, they fell silent.

I went over to the counter, where the boys were nearly collapsing in stifled laughter.

"Okay," I said, "here's the deal. Singing a song about butts *is* truly funny, but Santa can hear you."

Max and then Luke pulled their thumbs across their closed lips like zippers and broke out in giggles all over again.

In a matter of just a few days it was finally Christmas Eve, and by then our whole house smelled and looked like the season in all its glory. The air was laced with the rich smells of glazed ham, apple bread, and minced meat pie, and of bayberry, cranberry, and citrus from the fat candles that burned in oversized hurricanes all over the house. In the bay window of the breakfast area, aromatic clove-studded oranges filled a hand-hewed antique wooden bread maker's bowl lined with tiny branches of pine and colorful holly. One afternoon I sat for hours with my boys pushing the spikes of tiny cloves through the tough skin of oranges in decorative swirls and geometric designs. When we were finished, I rewarded them with steaming hot chocolate and marshmallows before moving on to their next project, which was to set up the old train set with Adam. Crank the cat had draped herself over the back of the sofa, curious about the train and its whistles and whirrs but not so curious that she would get involved.

"She's gonna pounce," Max predicted.

"No, she ain't," Luke said.

"Don't say 'ain't,'" I said.

Miles of strung popcorn garland were carefully draped around the Christmas tree in dramatic loops. Our monogrammed stockings were hung across the thick oak mantel, which was covered with a parade of red candles in shining brass candleholders tied with red and green plaid ribbon bows. The crèche set of Adam's childhood was carefully positioned across the sideboard in our dining room on a bed of pine needles interspersed with tiny pinecones. More red candles that smelled of cranberries were placed in glass hurricanes with gleaming silver bottoms. There were wreaths on all the doors and tiny white lights nestled into all the foundation shrubs around the front of our house. At five o'clock in the afternoon the yard came to life, and at ten o'clock it fell into darkness. Adam had installed the timer for all the holiday lighting, and he was pretty proud of that.

Even Rufus was wearing a special needlepointed holiday

collar with a design of red Santa hats with tiny white pom-poms on a background of deep green. Most days he lumbered around the house between dog beds, one of which was in almost every room.

"All right!" I said, draining a pound of pasta through a colander. I had prepared an early supper of spaghetti with tomato sauce and lots of grated Asiago cheese instead of Parmesan. I pulled two crusty loaves of garlic bread from the oven. "The candlelight service starts at six o'clock. I expect to see you boys for baths by four. I laid your clothes out. Do y'all hear me?"

"Yes, ma'am!"

There would be no resistance about baths. No. Not on Christmas Eve. I could have asked them to scrub the kitchen floor grout with a Q-Tip and they would have done it with a smile on their faces.

"Okay, good. Now go get your daddy and let's eat."

Later, in church, I caught Adam's eye and smiled at him. We weren't ardent churchgoers and not especially devout, but we gathered there that night and were touched by the spirit of the holiday. I found God in nature, and when I asked Adam, he said he felt the same way. The many cycles of life were always there right before your eyes. And it was just a fact of life that came from living in the Lowcountry of South Carolina. But we had started to go to church again for the first time since our college days because I really wanted our boys to have a religious foundation. And the boys were finally old enough to behave themselves throughout the service.

I felt deeply blessed to have the precious love of my husband, who worked so hard to give us such a wonderful life. Even after all these years, I still got excited when I heard his car come into the garage after work. Maybe that sounds silly, but the best part of my day was always when we were all together.

I looked down at the boys in their navy blazers and khaki pants, with their hair wet-combed into place. So innocent! Oh, I thought, this is the sweetest moment, this one, right now. It was so sweet that I had a thought of perhaps another baby. Maybe a girl would come to us?

adam's merry christmas

I was on another planet, having unfortunate and inappropriate thoughts. In church, on Christmas Eve, of all places and times! I had not stopped thinking about Eve since Eliza read me excerpts of her newsletter. Thoughts of her had tormented me from the moment we said good-bye on the Isle of Palms last July all the way through Thanksgiving. Just when I was finally able to get through a day without obsessing over her, here came the Christmas card.

Earlier that afternoon, when Eliza put the boys in the bathtub, I'd hurried to the stack of holiday cards that were tumbled together in a sweetgrass basket. I found Eve's card and brought it up to my face, inhaling deeply, hoping for a trace of her. It had no smell at all, and that was disappointing. I read the letter carefully, looking for clues about her state of mind. Was she really happy with Carl? How could she be? He could be such a competitive, arrogant asshole. But there wasn't a hint of dissatisfaction or sarcasm in her writing that indicated anything less than a great year for them all. Was that really true?

I had always wondered, what if things had worked out differently? Could I have been happy with Eve today? Was it worth the risk of undermining and jeopardizing the stability of my family to find out? No! I told myself. Eliza was a one-in-a-million girl. She lived to make me happy in every single way. Beautifully kept home, gourmet cook, wild in the sheets! What else could I want?

I shouldn't even be *thinking* about Eve! What's the *matter* with me? Here I am in *church*! On Christmas Eve! And my wonderful little family is all around me, but what am I doing? I'm thinking about what it was like to make love to Eve to the music of Frankie Valli singing "My Eyes Adored You" in 1975. Yes, I thought, that's what I'm doing and I don't care. The thought police couldn't hear me. I could think about whatever I wanted and I was still safe. I was a man possessed.

So I indulged my memories, remembering how wonderful, almost surreal it had been. When I was with Eve time was suspended. We were drawn to each other like metal filings to a magnet, one filament at a time and then all in a rush. I had been hopelessly and completely in love with her, lost in her beautiful eyes, her breathing and her heartbeat pounding against mine. I remembered it. I remembered it all. I reminded myself that a man is very lucky to ever have had a love like that, even once in his life. And her mother had ruined it. Cookie. I would never forgive her. That judgmental, small-minded bitch who found us together, called me a common laborer from a family with no distinction, and said her daughter was destined for a far grander life than I could ever offer her.

As we did whenever possible, we went to her house when Cookie wasn't home. One day, Cookie wasn't supposed to be home until six. We were in Eve's bedroom, in her bed, screwing our brains out with every ounce of energy our eighteen-year-old selves could muster. Suddenly, the door opened and the screaming started. "You! Stop this at once! Leave my daughter alone! Get out of her bed! Get out of my house now or I'll call the police! And don't you dare ever come back here!" I fumbled around trying to gather my clothes, which were flung all over the room. I barely got my pants and shoes on as I left the house. I was still buttoning my shirt as I started my car. I could hear Eve shrieking. I wanted to go back in and rescue her, but I knew better. Cookie was a wildcard. She would have done something drastic, like claim rape. Did Cookie really think Eve was not a willing partner?

Cookie was always trading on her ancestors—someone had signed the Declaration of Independence a million years ago. She was such a prude. Such a snob. I despised Cookie and loved Eve in equal amounts. But we had been too young to fight and too afraid of Cookie.

I wondered if Cookie had even an inkling of how successful I had become. As she lived in Charleston, there was a chance she could've known. But would that change her opinion of me? Oh, sure, Carl was a doctor and he saved lives here and there, but he had no soul. No true passion. At least not one that I had been able to detect.

I glanced at Eliza sitting in the pew next to me and was immediately awash in guilt. She was beautiful, in her exotic way, and I loved her. I did. I loved everything about her. She had no hidden agenda, no guile. No. Eliza only wanted to be my wife, my partner, the mother of our children. And she was an absolute delight to live with. She was a reasonable woman, fair and insightful, not given to moody or bitchy behavior. Her marvelous sense of humor had carried us through so many awkward situations. Her meals had not only warmed and nourished us all but her culinary efforts had won me contracts. When a bid was in question, I brought the client home and Eliza whipped up something mind boggling that brought the client to his knees, singing her praises, begging to sign on the dotted line. There was no doubt that she was my greatest asset. Oh, God, the things she could do with a chicken. My mouth watered for her coq au vin.

I wondered then if Eliza had ever had someone in her deep past who meant to her what Eve meant to me. A first love? A regret? Things we never shared? Was there a man she thought about in a weak moment? Someone she had loved with youthful abandon? Someone who had broken her heart? Did certain music trigger memories? If there was someone like that in her past, she had never said one word about it. Not one word.

But then again, I thought, I never told her about Eve.

The pine-scented air was crisp as we left the church. It felt like a Christmas Eve should feel, a little damp and raw with the promise of something new and wonderful about to happen. It sent a rush of happiness through each one of us and we smiled for no reason other than that we were together.

By the time we arrived home the boys were fast asleep in the backseat of the car. We pulled into the garage and I lowered the door with the remote. Luckily, the boys didn't stir. Ever so quietly, Eliza carried Luke and I carried Max to their bedroom, where we undressed them, pulling on their pajamas as their listless bodies flailed. We kissed the boys on their foreheads, turned down the light to very low, and left the room, leaving the door ajar.

"They ran out of steam," I said quietly.

"They'll be up at five, if we're lucky," Eliza said.

"I'm going to take Rufus outside," I said.

"Do you want to have a glass of wine while we fix Santa?"

"Sure, but why don't we step outside together for a moment? It's so beautiful."

I roused Rufus from his bed in the family room and Eliza followed me through the kitchen doors onto the patio.

"Let's go down by the river," I said.

"Okay, but just for a minute. What if the boys wake up? I need to be able to hear them."

"Don't worry. This is probably the one night of the year they won't leave their room."

I knew Eliza could see me smiling, even in the dark, hoping I was right. She took my outstretched hand and walked with me toward the water.

The full moon was up, high in the sky, surrounded by billions of twinkling stars. Rufus wandered off toward an ancient live oak tree, draped with long sheets of Spanish moss that moved slowly in the evening breeze like a ghost. We could smell the brackish water of the Stono River, brimming with life and death as it flowed in a southwesterly direction. Its ripples shimmered with light reflected from the night sky. We stood there, on our dock, leaning against the railing. I had my arm around her shoulder and hers was looped around my waist.

"Merry Christmas, Mr. Stanley. I sure do love you."

"Merry Christmas to you, sweetheart. I love you too. So much. Man, we sure are lucky."

"Sometimes I can hardly believe it."

We stood there for a few more minutes until Rufus meandered over to us and nudged us with his snout.

"I think our old man is ready for bed," I said.

"Yep, and I think our tree is ready for Santa."

Soon all the toys were arranged under the tree and, weary from the day, we crawled under our own bedcovers, too tired to think of anything but sleep.

After a few minutes, I rolled over on my side and threw my arm over Eliza.

"We sure have it good, babe, don't we?"

I thought I heard her say, "Yep. Don't fuck it up." I sat up and looked at her, but she was already asleep.

CHAPTER 6

eliza and the unexpected guest

There was hardly a sliver of daylight when Luke and Max appeared at the side of our bed.

"Is she awake?" Max whispered.

"No. What time is it?" Luke whispered.

"You know I can't tell time yet," Max hissed.

I groaned and the boys jumped.

"It's too early!" I said. "Go back to bed!"

They scampered from our room.

I took one leg out from underneath the comforter, opened my eyes, and stared at the ceiling. I was wide awake then and resigned to beginning my day. And I really wanted to see the boys when they saw their loot.

How many more Christmases will there be that involve Santa? I thought.

"Adam? Honey?"

There was a moan from his side of the bed.

"The boys are awake."

"Okay, okay," he said. "I'm up."

We got out of bed and pulled on our robes. The floor was ice cold because the furnace didn't cycle on until 6 A.M. Crank the cat wandered in and mewed.

"Merry Christmas, Crank," I said. I reached down and patted her fur. "I'll get your breakfast in a minute."

"I'll push up the thermostat," Adam said. "It's not supposed to reach fifty today."

"Dang, it's early." The bedside alarm clock read 5:15. "Get the movie camera! I'll turn on the coffeepot." Fifty degrees, I thought. It was probably ten below in Massachusetts, where my father and brother lived.

Naturally, the coffee machine was on a timer, but that timer didn't swing into action until six thirty. In any case, this was our division of labor.

"Right! Good idea," Adam said. "And I'll light a fire."

On the way to the family room, we looked in on the boys, whose hearing was as acute as that of any prized hunting dog in the land. Sure enough, they had just hopped back into their beds and were pretending to be asleep. But their rapid breathing, flushed faces, and devilish grins betrayed them. They had probably been having a pillow fight or simply jumping on their beds, trying to hit the ceiling, which was pockmarked with traces of chocolate and only heaven knew what else.

"All right, you two little scamps, let's go see if Santa left you anything besides a lump of coal," Adam said, shaking his head.

Max and Luke leapt from their beds and tore around us, racing to the living room screaming with excitement. More screaming ensued. We looked at each other, shook our heads, and smiled the parental smile of resignation.

"Kids," Adam said and turned on the movie camera.

"Ya gotta love 'em," I said.

I clicked on the coffeepot, made hot chocolate, fed the cat, then opened the back door, giving Rufus the opportunity to sniff around the backyard. The next chance I would have to sit down would be for breakfast and then dinner, so for the moment, I curled up in the corner of the sofa and watched my boys tear open gifts.

The following hour was spent documenting our lives on film, opening box after box, drinking hot cocoa and mug after mug of coffee and trying out various presents. Christmas carols sung by the Mormon Tabernacle Choir played in the background. And a lovely fire crackled again in the fireplace, warming the room. Norman Rockwell himself could not have done a better job of staging a diorama of the Great American Family.

Santa, in his extraordinary generosity, had left remote-control cars for the boys, in addition to boxes of Legos and a bonanza of other amusements. Adam and I exchanged engraved key rings for our new cars. There were many new sweaters, bottles of inexpensive perfume and aftershave the boys bought us from the drugstore with their tiny allowance, new camera equipment for Adam that excited him, and the latest model of a food processor, which thrilled me. My father, John, had sent us a check for four hundred dollars inside of a nice card that said to buy something special for ourselves. And my brother, JJ, and his wife had done the same. I wished my father and JJ were joining us for Christmas. I loved Ted dearly and he was included in every holiday and event in our lives, as it should be. But it's not like that with my family. They are just too far away. If I was lucky, I saw them once a year.

"That's awfully generous," Adam said. "I probably won't buy a sweater."

"Me either," I said.

"What did we send them?"

"Steak-of-the-Month Club. Wine-of-the-Month Club. I guess the divorce courts must be having a good year," I said, rereading the card from my brother. "Still, it sure would be nice to see them once in a while."

"Really?" Adam said in a high voice. "Do you *really* think so?"

"Adam Stanley!" I laughed, knowing that my sister-in-law drove him insane. "You're gonna make Santa turn his sleigh around and come back here and take away all your sweaters."

"Oh, no!" Adam recoiled in mock horror. "Then I'll definitely behave myself."

"Momma?" Max said. "Don't you know Aunt Tasha works Daddy's last nerve?"

Works Daddy's last nerve? Where had he heard that expression?

"You hush! Who told you that? Your daddy loves Aunt Tasha!"

"Little pitchers have big ears," Luke said solemnly. He sounded like an old man.

Adam arched an eyebrow.

"Boys? Here's your Christmas morning piece of wisdom. Families are your given tribe, and you have a duty to your given tribe to take care of them when they need help, to be respectful of them, and so on. But they are not your chosen tribe. Those are your dear friends who you love and treasure because they make your life rich with all the things that matter."

"What tribe are we?" Max said. "Is there a tribe for your kids?"

"Well? Let's see . . ." Adam said, and I could see he had dug himself a rather nice hole.

"You are our precious hearts," I said. "That's the most special tribe of all!"

"Yay!" said Max.

"Aunt Tasha drinks like a fish," Luke said, sucking in his cheeks over and over and making Max crack up.

"Poor Aunt Tasha. I'm sure she has her reasons," Adam said.

"I've only ever seen Tasha like that once when she drank wine on an empty stomach!" I said. "Aunt Tasha does not have a problem with alcohol." She has other issues, I thought, but not booze.

Reluctantly, I left my cozy spot, went to the kitchen, and dug around under the sink. I knew Adam thought that being married to my brother was reason enough to drink your head off. He had said so on many occasions. When it came to JJ, Adam could be the most judgmental and unforgiving person in the world. Maybe Tasha just liked to whoop it up once in a while?

And Adam believes himself to be a Christian. He believes himself to be the picture of benevolence. I thought, true Christians don't judge.

While Adam busied himself putting batteries into the remote-control cars for the boys, I scooped up wrapping paper and ribbon.

"What time is your dad coming, sweetheart?"

"I told him three o'clock. Is that still okay?"

"Yep. It's perfect. How's he doing? I haven't seen him in a while."

"You know Dad. Gloomy Gus."

"This will be good for him. Christmas with kids all around—harder to be unhappy. He needs to get out more." I looked around the room. It was tidy enough. "Okay, everyone! Who wants sticky buns and scrambled eggs?" I asked over my shoulder, heading to the kitchen.

It was a rhetorical question. Sticky buns and scrambled eggs were a tradition for Christmas morning, just like chocolate chip pancakes and sausage for the boys on their birthday. But the boys responded anyway.

"I do! I do!"

The preparation of our Christmas breakfast was under way, and once again the air swirled with the fragrance of butter, sugar, and cinnamon. I also fried a pound of bacon, thinking the salty meat would be a good counterpoint to the sugary pastry. As usual, the smell of bacon sizzling in the skillet inspired Rufus to sit close to me on his hopeful haunches and whimper. I slipped him a strip.

"Merry Christmas, my sweet baby," I said.

It disappeared in a flash, so I gave him another one.

He's seventeen, I said to myself. So he'll only live to be twenty instead of twenty-one.

In truth, Rufus had already far exceeded the expected life span of his breed, and we believed it was because he had it so good. He never imposed himself in an obnoxious way, but he let his feelings be known with a nudge and a glance at the cookie jar or by pointing his nose toward the back door, indicating his need to commune with nature. And he showed his affection for the family in a number of ways. He would amble over to where I was sitting and quietly place his head on my lap, looking at me with those loving eyes of his. Adam was the one who'd brought him home as a puppy, but I was the one who held his heart. And the bacon.

After breakfast the boys wanted to take their remote-control cars out for a spin, so Adam and the boys put on jackets and went out into the yard. Our property had a very long but narrow tarmac road that began at the street and wound its way to our driveway, continued to the barn and then ended at the boat dock. It was a good long run for remote-control cars, which would probably be the favorite toy of the year.

"I'll check on our animals, then I'll show them how the cars work," Adam said and planted a noisy kiss on my cheek.

"I'll be right here for the foreseeable future," I said, thinking that maybe Santa should've brought three cars.

That was how Christmas morning always was. I would be on my feet in the kitchen for hours. This is what women do all over the world when they celebrate holidays. I had heard rumors about men who could cook, but I had never known one. At least not outside the realm of professionals. Adam didn't even like to use the grill. I had been made to believe that southern men liked to invent their own dry rubs, smear them all over meat, then stand around the hot coals with a buddy, watching, talking football, basting whatever they were cooking over and over, and drinking beer. Not Adam. He could mix cocktails and pour coffee, but that was about it.

I sighed hard. By the end of the day my lower back would be killing me and my feet would be throbbing, but making wonderful holiday meals was one of the ways I expressed my love for my family. I checked the pork roast that had been resting in a special brine in the cooler overnight. It was time to remove it, rinse it, and pat it dry. I did, then laid it on a bed of paper towels in the roasting pan so it could come to room temperature.

I set the table for five with our holiday china, red water glasses, our best flatware, and a centerpiece of red poinsettias. It looked really beautiful, I thought. Simple but beautiful. My father-in-law, Ted, would love it. Who didn't love Christmas?

Dinner that day would be served buffet style from the kitchen breakfast bar, as our dining room sideboard was occupied by the Holy Family, angels, and the Magi. Never mind the camels, cows, and sheep. It was too crowded to be of any other use. For me, Christmas Eve seemed to be the more serious occasion anyway, maybe because it involved church and all the anticipation of what surprises were in store for us all. Christmas Day, on the other hand, unfolded as a bighearted family day, a time to have a great meal and enjoy one another's company, to be with our children, and maybe to stop in on neighbors to deliver cookies or some holiday kitchen gift. While I stood scraping carrots, our isolation crossed my mind. There were so few neighbors with whom I could have a cup of coffee or share a bit of gossip. But there was no point in dwelling on something I could not change. Still, I was lonely most days. Adam would have been disappointed if he knew. Now that the boys were in school all day, I had time for my cookbook, but even that wasn't exactly an intellectual challenge. But if I hadn't had that project and Adam's bookkeeping, I would have completely lost my marbles. It was true that JJ's wife, Tasha, could get on your nerves, but a short visit with them might be nice. I missed my brother. And I had harbored other dreams, but they seemed impossible to me now. I'd always wanted to return to Greece and study Greek cuisine, including cheeses and oils. But that would never happen. I shelved that idea and concentrated on smaller goals.

I watched Adam and the boys playing with the cars through the window over the sink. The goats were running the field from behind their fence and one peacock was rattling his train like mad. The boys were racing the cars, laughing and chasing each other.

I remembered my own Christmases in Massachusetts then, especially the last one when my mother was still alive. I was just eleven and my mother was dying quickly from some terrible disease no one would discuss. There was snow all over the ground and everyone was profoundly sad but putting on a brave face to hide their feelings from my mother. JJ and I somehow knew that this was the last Christmas we would have together with her.

I thought, kids know things. No one has to tell them. They just know.

It was true. Despite my young age then and the fact that I wasn't the least bit interested in things that were otherworldly, I could sense death in every corner of the house, most especially in my mother's bedroom.

My grandmother, my mother's mother, had come all the way from the island of Corfu in Greece to visit in early December, flying on a plane for the first time in her life, suitcases filled with gifts from every relative and neighbor. We called her Yiayia. Yiayia's arrival was as spectacular as it was unusual. She was going to stay for as long as she was needed, which in my mind would be forever. My brother and I whispered to each other that the reason for the long visit was because our mother's end was near. And our grandmother wanted to make the holiday as pleasant as possible for us, given the dire situation. It never occurred to us that Yiayia had come to stay because her own daughter was dying.

Her heart must have been absolutely broken, I thought then.

I leaned on the side of the sink and thought if anything ever happened to my children I wouldn't be able to go on.

But Yiayia was able to shoulder on because she was strong and determined, a whirlwind who took over the kitchen and made karidopita, baklava, and Christopsomo (traditional Christmas bread) decorated with a cross. She showed me how to make other Greek dishes like moussaka, and she sang Greek songs, which made us love her all the more. Especially that Christmas. We had never needed tenderness as badly as we did then, and our grandmother had delivered it so sweetly.

I began to feel melancholy then. I missed my mother and my Yiayia. I had Yiayia's hands. When I was very young I visited Greece every summer with my mother and JJ, and Yiayia was always beside herself with happiness to have us with her. It seemed that her whole village came by to say hello, bringing us little treats, Greek coloring books and candies. In quiet moments, my grandmother would take my tiny hand and trace it with the tip of her finger, showing the similarities in the curvature of our fingernails. And she did the same with JJ's nose as he stood sideways looking in a mirror. She thought her grandchildren were a marvel, as if she had never known another little boy and girl besides us.

I wondered what my mother and grandmother would think if they could see me now, with my handsome husband and my beautiful boys. What would they think of my home and how I had just set my Christmas table? Well, they wouldn't be too happy about our not attending a Greek Orthodox church, but I had overdosed on organized religion somewhere along the line and opted out of the rules and regulations of my mother's faith.

And I still couldn't speak a word of Greek. When I was young I knew many Greek children's songs, but I could not remember a phrase from any of them. If I had been the kind of woman who went into therapy, I might have realized that the distance I had taken with my brother and father and all things Greek had everything to do with my losing my mother so young and my grandmother soon after, both of whom I adored. We never went to Greece again after we buried my mother and then Yiayia. It hurt too much to be reminded of them. And when I finally left Boston and went to business school, there was no Greek presence on campus besides sororities and fraternities, which was anything but the Greek life I knew. It was easy to leave my origins behind because I had wanted to assimilate completely. I wanted to belong to something new that didn't hurt.

Life's messy, I thought, and sprinkled olive oil and celery seeds on the carrots.

Soon, the standing crown roast of pork was done and the pies were ready to bake. Mashed potatoes were whipped into thick ribbons of creamy silk. The casserole of sausage dressing was steaming, the cranberry mold jiggled, peas and carrots were mixed together and scooped into a covered bowl. I stuffed the roast with dressing and took pictures.

Promptly at three we heard a car door open and close. Adam's father had arrived. The boys were building a Lego castle and pirate ship in the middle of the family room floor. They jumped up as though yanked upright by some unseen hand and raced each other to the door, skating across the waxed floors in their socks, trying to trip each other.

I turned from the roast, which was resting under a tent of foil on the counter, and looked out into the foyer. Ted, my father-in-law, whose arms were filled with wrapped presents, was not alone. He was with a woman, a very large woman, who had to be at least ten years older than him, if not twenty. She was towering over a grinning Ted, wearing a black mink coat to the ground, high heels that could produce altitude sickness, and enough makeup to scare the hell out of Estée Lauder. Somehow, weirdly, it all worked on her just fine. But the boys had never seen the likes of such a glamazon, so they looked at each other and dropped their jaws dramatically.

"Holy crap!" Max said.

"Double crap!" Luke said.

Adam quickly covered Max's mouth with his hand while extending his other one to his father to take the packages.

"Dad! Merry Christmas!" Adam said. "Hi!" he said to the aged-out exotic dancer from a gentleman's club somewhere in the sticks. "I'm Adam."

"Hey! Merry Christmas, y'all!" she said in a smoky voice that suggested a lifetime of dedication to tobacco products.

I quickly added another setting to the table.

"Are you a movie star?" Luke asked with eyes as large as dinner plates.

"No, darling," said the guest politely. "But I seem like one, don't I?"

"Yes, ma'am," Luke said, completely entranced.

Things were suddenly confusing due to the dizzying effect of the guest's red dress trimmed in red sequins. Adam, who appeared to be temporarily catatonic, could no doubt see himself reflected in the heavy gloss of her ginormous red lips.

I knew I had to swing into action and transform this very startling moment into just another day at the Stanley house, or else old Hot Lips was going to feel very bad about crashing with Pop. But all I could think, in 100 percent agreement with my boys, was holy whopping shit! For what it was worth, it was obvious to me that Pop was in high spirits and that Pop's guest had not grown the hair she was wearing.

What the hell, Ted? I thought. What the hell are you up to?

"Y'all? Say hello to Miss Clarabeth!" Ted said, grinning from ear to ear like a schoolboy.

Hellooooo, Miss Clarabeth! Adam and I thought simultaneously, looking at each other, hardly able to maintain a straight face.

"Hello!" I said, adding, "Merry Christmas!"

Clarabeth said, "Thank you! Merry Christmas to y'all too! I love your wreath! It's fabulous! Gump's?"

Gump's? In San Francisco? Was she kidding?

"No, just me and my hot glue gun," I said. Do I look like a millionaire to you? I thought.

"Somebody's gifted!" she said and winked at me. "And thank you so much for having me!"

"We're *delighted* to have you," I said and meant it. "You boys move and let Pop and Miss Clarabeth get in the door!" Just act normally, I told myself.

"Pop? Do you have a present for me?" Max asked.

"Of course we do! Here you go!" Ted handed a large shopping bag to Max and said, "There's one in there for Luke."

We? What does *that* mean? Are Ted and this woman a *we?* Ted and Clarabeth stepped across the threshold and I noticed the new white convertible Jaguar parked in the driveway. Nice, I thought, and closed the door. I caught Ted's eye.

"Christmas gift," he whispered.

"From you?" I whispered back, having a hard time imagining Ted buying someone a car. He was notoriously cheap.

"No," he said. "*To* me."

Great God in heaven, I thought. Was my father-in-law this large woman's boy toy?

Adam was nervously pouring everyone a glass of champagne to sip while we exchanged gifts. Ted gave Adam a beautiful cashmere cardigan from Ben Silver. "A sweater!" Adam said and held up the sweater for everyone to see. Adam's sweaters now totaled eight.

"I helped him pick it out," Clarabeth said.

"Oh! Well! I don't think I own anything this nice," Adam said. "Thank you!"

"Oh, my!" I said as I pulled off the wrapping paper to find a Vitamix from Williams Sonoma. "I've always wanted one of these! Thank you, Ted!"

"Well, good! I had Adam search through all your appliances and whatnot to see if you had one."

"She has a lot of kitchen equipment," Adam said, as though Clarabeth would be fascinated to learn that.

"Wonderful!" Clarabeth said.

Well, at least she's polite, I thought. "I am delighted to have it! I'm so sorry I don't have a package for you, Clarabeth, but to be honest . . ."

"Teddy didn't tell you I was coming?" Clarabeth said, pleasantly. "Well, it's a gift enough just to be here with you all! I didn't want to intrude, but he *insisted* that I come with him. And you know, Adam, your father can be very persuasive when he wants something."

"You don't have to tell me that!" Adam said with a nervous laugh.

"Yep. I reckon so!" Ted said.

"Wow," said Luke.

Ted announced that he had been keeping company with Clarabeth for quite a while. In fact, he had been living on her plantation on the Ashley River for the past five months.

Shock was all over Adam's face. "How did I not know this, Dad? You've been holding out on me! All the time we spend at work together and you never told me a thing!"

Dad still came to work a few days a week for a few hours.

"Well, you know it now," Ted said. "I think I'm gonna have seconds!"

"I'll get it for you," I said, already on my feet.

"Thanks," Ted said and handed me his plate.

"This roast was absolutely delicious, Eliza!" Clarabeth said. "In fact, everything was delicious."

"Yes. It's wonderful, Eliza. Thank you for another fabulous meal!" Adam said, trying to recover. He raised his glass of red wine. "To Eliza!"

"To Mom!" the boys said.

"To Eliza!" the others said.

"Thank you," I said with a slight curtsy. "Thank you!"

I put Ted's plate before him and resumed my seat. Clarabeth, who swore she never drank any alcohol, was on her third glass of wine and had become very chatty.

"So, after Arthur died—poor Arthur was my third husband—and left me the plantation, I have to admit, things started falling apart. It's a big old house to run and I just needed a man's help. There was just no way around it. I mean, I can't be climbing up ladders to fix gutters. Not at my age."

I had a vision of Clarabeth, dressed up like Rosie the Riveter, climbing up an extension ladder wearing a tool belt and a schmatte tied around her wig.

"Not at *any* age," Ted said, smiling at Clarabeth.

"Are you on the Ashley? How many acres do you have?" I asked.

"Yes. Well, in its day there were probably two thousand or more. Now there's just around twenty-five. But that's still a lot of grass to cut."

"I'll say," Adam said. "Dad? Are you cutting grass?"

"No, I manage the guy who cuts the grass. Do we have coffee?"

"I'll get you a cup."

"Thanks."

"Oh. Of course you do. Somehow, I couldn't see you pushing a mower. So, how did you two meet?"

"Well, Clarabeth advertised in the *Post and Courier* for a caretaker. And you know how I like to be handy, fixing things that need fixing and whatnot."

"What are you telling me, Dad?"

"I'm giving you my two weeks' notice, unless you need me, of course."

"Are you kidding?" Adam was incredulous.

"No, son. I got a better job. Do you blame me?"

Oh, my God, I thought.

CHAPTER 7

eliza

wild dunes, 1995

It was at least a hundred degrees in the shade when we turned into the parking lot of our condo at Wild Dunes. I had Luke in my SUV riding shotgun and Max was riding with Adam. Together we formed a small convoy, the boys making faces at each other as we occasionally passed each other on the highway, glazing the passenger window with their spit. We were returning for another vacation because the boys had begged and because Adam's father and benefactress had petitioned us with surprising fervency to join us. They wanted time with the twins. Family time. This was something new for us—to have Ted more involved with the boys and Clarabeth taking the role of an ad hoc grandmother. But the boys loved the attention and no one seemed to be the worse for it. In fact, over time we had all come to love Clarabeth. I had no objection to her affection or to the idea of them joining us at Wild Dunes, but there were unspoken boundaries that had to be honored. This new togetherness business still had the earmarks of potential trouble. And sure enough, Adam bore the brunt of a badly conceived idea.

"Or, here's a great thought! We could rent a larger condo and all stay together!" Ted had said to him.

Poor Adam had to think fast about that because he knew I wouldn't be receptive to company for the entire vacation—two more mouths to feed at every meal I cooked for two weeks? How could it be a vacation for me if I was entertaining, shopping, cooking, and cleaning up all the time? Never mind listening to Clarabeth the magpie natter on until we all thought we might like to jump off a bridge. Yes, Clarabeth may have been bighearted and generous to a fault, but as we got to know her we realized she could, as my father used to say, talk a dog off a meat truck.

But Ted and Clarabeth under the same roof with us for two solid weeks would have been a prescription for a familial cataclysmic disaster. Fortunately, Adam was on his toes.

He said, "You know what, Dad? Why don't I see about the arrangements? Let's see what's available. But between us? Our boys like to get up with the sun and start raising hell."

"That's what little boys do," his father said and had a little chuckle.

Adam went even further to ensure a separate residence for them.

"Listen, between us? We're having a hard time getting

them to flush the toilets, much less put the seats down. And if Clarabeth likes to sleep in the mornings, she'd need earplugs. For sure."

Adam said Ted looked at him and ever so slowly a smile of understanding crept across his face. He'd had a wife. He knew the deal.

"My dad's no dummy," Adam said. "He said, 'Tell you what, son. Why don't you try to find us something *near* you? A one-bedroom would be fine. We can visit each other. And we're only staying for one week.' Thank God!"

While the limited term of their visit was a relief, Ted's words confirmed what Adam suspected, that Ted was sharing a bed with Clarabeth. We thought, Wow.

"I told him, 'Whatever you want to do is fine with me.'"

"This will work out just fine," I said.

"We dodged another bullet," Adam said nonchalantly, but I could tell he was very happy about the compromise.

So, when July rolled around, we packed our cars to the roof with half of our worldly belongings, including Rufus and this time Crank as well. Mr. Proctor was taking care of the outside animals, but he had developed an aversion to Crank because he claimed she bit him.

"I'm so sorry that happened, Mr. Proctor. Are you sure that you're all right?" He got too close to her mouth, I thought. Definitely.

He stood facing me in the driveway, awash in disgruntlement, with his bulbous thumb wrapped in what seemed to be a truly excessive amount of gauze bandage secured with surgical adhesive. With the bandages his thumb was twice its normal size, a dramatic statement of his pain and suffering.

"I guess I'll live. But I'm telling you, Mizz Stanley, I ain't getting in the ring with that cat ever again. I like all God's creatures 'cept that one," he said. "That's a terrible cat."

Thus, the Stanley family's cat, having lived up to its reputation, was headed to the beach to shed with impunity all over the dwelling of an unseen landlord.

Adam got out of his car first and Max jumped out to direct me into my parking spot as though he were a ground crew member working for an airline, guiding a plane to safely park at its jetway.

I laughed and rolled my car into the spot next to Adam.

"Your brother," I said to Luke, shaking my head. I wondered, did my sons lie around cooking up ways to amuse each other? Or was their silliness just spontaneous?

"He's a nut!" Luke said and laughed.

We began unloading, carrying suitcases, tennis rackets, endless bags of groceries and tote bags inside. It would take many trips back and forth and hours to set up our residence. Luke took Crank's crate into the house, struggling against its shifting weight as Crank mewed in loud protest at being zigged and zagged up the steps.

"Don't let the cat out! Luke? Did you hear me?" I called out. "Not until we are finished unloading the cars!"

"Yes, ma'am!" Luke called back.

"That cat will take off to kingdom come like a bullet," I said to Adam.

"I'll keep my thoughts on that to myself," Adam said.

I could tell by his expression, he was obviously thinking it would be nice if Crank went to that great catnip bar in the sky.

"Come on. You know you love Crank," I said.

"Right," Adam said. "That cat's the spawn of Satan."

Adam had just slung his golf club bag over his shoulder when a door slammed. There stood Carl and Eve on the steps of their condo.

"Hey, there! Y'all need a hand?" Eve called out.

"Well, look who's here!" I said. "What a surprise! I've been meaning to call you since I got your Christmas card! Where does the time go?"

Eve shot a look to Adam that spoke loudly—Adam and Eve *knew* that they were going to be there. I knew in that moment that Adam had been keeping secrets.

I'll deal with you later, I thought.

"Hey! How are you?" Adam said, blushing to a deep red behind his sunglasses. He shook hands with Carl. "How are you, buddy?"

"Good. Good. Uh-oh," Carl said, filled with devilish humor. "Somebody got very serious about his golf game this year. Look at those clubs. I see some Big Berthas in that bag!"

"Well, yes, I bought new clubs, if that's an indication of how serious. I guess we'll see," Adam said, not exactly challenging Carl but challenging him all the same.

"I hope you brought your wallet," Carl said and laughed. "Here, give me that." He scooped up a heavy duffel bag from the driveway behind my car and, to further demonstrate his superior manliness, took the remaining three as well and carried them all inside. "How are you, beauty queen?" He gave me an air kiss.

"Oh, you . . . ," I said and thought, Okay, it's not *so* terrible to see them again, even if he is a bit of a blowhard.

Adam, Eve, and I watched as Carl's biceps rippled and flexed, and I was a little breathless. Eve was not.

"Did you see that?" Eve said. "He's a regular Rocky Balboa. I'm married to a real he-man."

"I feel strangely inadequate," Adam said. "Short between the trousers."

I rolled my eyes at him and said, "Oh, honey. He's just trying to be helpful."

"Right," Eve said.

There was a trace of sarcasm in Eve's voice that was not lost on any of us, and I wondered what had gone on between Eve and Carl in the year we had been apart. She's probably just tired, I thought, and it *is* as hot as the bottom floor of hell. Or maybe something had changed. And *why* didn't Adam tell me that they would be here again?

"Oh, come on. He's a darling!" I said. "So, how's your momma and how is Daphne?"

"Oh, they're fine," Eve said. "Cookie took Daphne to the movies. Why don't y'all get settled in and come on over for an early supper?"

"Oh! That's so nice! Thank you. But we also have Adam's father and his, um, girlfriend with us this year."

Eve's eyes opened wide over the mention of Adam's father having a meaningful other.

"No kidding? Wow! How fun! Bring them too. It will give Cookie someone new to talk to. She'll be thrilled! It's no problem. I'll call Pizza Hut!"

I stood there, suspended in time for a moment, and a thought flashed through my mind. Did I really want to pick up where we left off the prior year? How much of this vacation did I really want to spend with Eve and Carl? Then, just as quickly, I realized I'd sound ungrateful if I declined on the spot without a ready excuse. And I would be sending a message that conveyed a chilly wish for distance or privacy that I wasn't sure I felt. It was Adam's deception that was bothering me. So, even though I wasn't sure about anything, I accepted. One supper together? It was a small thing in the larger scheme of a two-week vacation. And it would give Clarabeth some fresh ears to deafen.

"How's six o'clock?" I said and smiled.

"Great! We can get all caught up."

Eve gave me a tiny princess wave and glided into her condo. I thought to myself, How is it possible that she looks younger than last year? And she's still too pretty for her own good. I wondered what Eve did to herself. Did she have a face-lift? Botox? Fillers? Or one of those other noninvasive treatments? Dang, I thought, whatever she's doing, she looks amazing.

I wasn't too happy with my own looks. Childbirth, sun, and probably my family's DNA were causing slight irregularities in the coloration of my complexion and there were tiny wrinkles in the corners of my eyes when I squinted. My fortieth birthday was approaching and I wasn't too thrilled about that either. But I wondered if I went back to Greece and measured myself against other Greek women my age, how would I fare?

What am I supposed to do about it? I thought and sighed.

I turned to go inside as Carl was coming out.

"Wow! It's so nice to see y'all again!" he said. "Isn't this a happy coincidence?"

So, Carl was unaware as well?

"Yeah, it's great to see you too! Carl? Could you do me a favor, please?"

"Sure! Just ask."

"Take Adam out on the golf course and kick his butt."

"My pleasure!" he said as he crossed the parking lot. His seersucker Bermuda shorts hung from his hips just so and his muscular arms were tanned to a tawny shade of maple. Like syrup.

That sure is one well-made man, I thought. I wonder if he tastes like Log Cabin?

Then I giggled at my naughtiness. I was rarely given to lewd thoughts, but at that moment I wanted to (a) know I was still viable and (b) pinch the ever-loving shit out of the inside of Adam Stanley's upper arm.

For the remainder of the afternoon while I unpacked, the boys swam in the pool under the watchful eyes of Adam, Ted, and Clarabeth. Crank draped herself like an afghan across the back of the sofa in the streaming sunshine, watching me as I came and went. Rufus slept peacefully, curled up in his dog bed by the refrigerator in the kitchen. He was snoring for all the dogs in Charleston County. I thought, Oh, my old sweet friend, you're not long for this world. I thought about all the times I'd told Rufus my troubles and how he would put his paw in my lap while I wept. And when I had shared good news with him he got up on his hind legs and danced with me. When I sang, Rufus howled. He had lived on my heels since Adam brought him home. He was a rescue, but in truth, he rescued us, bringing so much balance and happiness to us all.

As I put away the balance of the groceries, I wondered for a moment how I would handle Rufus's eventual demise and especially how would I handle it with the boys. And then, just as quickly as the horrible thought came to me, I pushed it from my mind. I didn't want to think about it. I couldn't bear the idea of life without Rufus.

I could never replace you, I thought, fully realizing the depth of my affection for my dog.

The clock struck five thirty just as I got the boys into clean shorts and T-shirts. They stood at attention while I combed their wet hair into place. I had barely had time for a quick shower to wash away the grime of the sweaty day, but I managed to steal ten minutes while thinking of ways to kill my husband. As the afternoon passed I became more furious, but I kept it inside. Why had Adam lied to me?

"Now go sit quietly and watch television for a few minutes," I said to the boys.

I went back to my bedroom to finish dressing. Adam was singing like a fool at the top of his lungs in the shower while

I threw on a sundress and coiled my hair into a bun at the nape of my neck. He was too damn gregarious for the mood I was in. I was giving him the silent treatment and he had yet to notice. It seemed pointless to be mad at him if he didn't even know I was mad, so I decided to *completely* ignore him, as though he wasn't even alive. If I knew anything about men, it was that they hated to be ignored.

I put on a little makeup and sprayed myself liberally with cologne, a gift from my boys on Mother's Day. It was just a drugstore fragrance, but I wanted the boys to smell it and know that I appreciated the thoughtful gift.

I looked at Adam's soapy bare backside through the clear shower door and thought, What if I poison him? Then I felt a little bad about indulging in the very idea of doing physical harm to my husband, who'd been, until a couple of hours ago, a pretty great guy. But what was he hiding? How could I trust him? What other lies had he told me? And what wife doesn't think about murdering her husband from time to time? As much as I didn't like confrontation, there was going to have to be one. But I would wait for the perfect moment, I thought, and nail him to the wall like a rat.

Clarabeth and Ted arrived at a quarter to six, ringing the doorbell with an overabundance of enthusiasm. I looked at my watch and became more annoyed. I really hated it when people arrived early, but Ted was my father-in-law, so it wouldn't be nice to complain.

"I'll get it! I'll get it!" the twins said, screaming as though Santa himself was standing on our steps in a Hawaiian shirt and shorts holding a big sack of midyear rewards.

"Calm down, boys! Hey, Dad! Clarabeth! Come on in!"

"I brought you boys a sursy!" Clarabeth said. She reached in her purse and produced two Hershey bars. "I never come visiting without a little something for my sweet boys!"

"Yay!" they said. "Thanks, Miss Clarabeth!"

"After supper," Adam said to them, meaning they couldn't eat them at that moment. "We're going next door for pizza. We're all invited."

"Really?" Ted said. "That's awfully nice."

"But we've already eaten our supper," Clarabeth said. "I just can't be eating all the time! You know, it's not good for your health to overeat—"

"Yes, we had a rotisserie chicken and some salad. We can have coffee, Clarabeth. Who's the neighbor?" Ted said gently as he put his hand on her arm.

Adam could sense a trace of annoyance in his father's voice. After all, he and Clarabeth had come to have some quality family time.

"Remember that girl I dated in high school? Eve Church?"

"Vaguely . . ."

For the next few minutes I had the pleasure of standing at the top of the stairs, out of sight, and listening to my husband underplay the importance of his relationship with Eve.

Soon we were on the doorstep of Eve and Carl's place.

"You okay?" Adam whispered to me.

After a pregnant pause, I said, "Of course. What could possibly be the matter?"

"Am I in the naughty chair?" Adam asked.

But he didn't seem to realize I had picked up on the uncomfortable fact that he and Eve had apparently arranged the reunion without telling anyone else. He looked right into my eyes, which had always looked at him so adoringly, and saw that they were blank. I was saving it for later.

"Why in the world would you be, darling?"

"Oh, God, I'm a dead man, right?"

"Why are you perspiring, dear?" I smiled.

Carl answered the door and we all moved inside. I looked at Adam and I knew at once he was in an adrenaline-induced fog, his mind racing. Everyone was talking at once. Eve was introducing herself to Clarabeth and giving Ted a hug. I realized then that Eve was Cookie's clone, except taller. Cookie, who was all of five feet and maybe a hundred pounds, had her eye on Adam, which for some reason unknown to me exacerbated his discomfort. And boy, was she decked out in Chanel from head to toe with enough gold bangle bracelets to choke a horse! I'm no fashion expert, but she seemed overdressed for the beach.

Our twins and Daphne shrieked to see each other again and ran to the kitchen to get pizza and a juice box.

"Isn't this lovely, y'all," Clarabeth said looking around, taking inventory. "This is so much nicer than our condo! Don't you think so, Ted?"

"Oh, I don't know," Ted said. "We have a nice view and whatnot."

"Everything's on the table!" Eve announced. "Just help yourself."

"So, Mr. Stanley," Cookie said to Adam. "Long time, no see."

"How are you, Mrs. Church? You haven't changed one bit. Still as beautiful as ever."

Now this was false flattery if I ever heard it.

"Have you met my lovely wife?" Adam continued.

"No, I don't believe I have had the pleasure," Cookie said and shook my hand as though it was something dubious. "And I see you all have twin boys! Well, isn't that something? Now, is your daddy married to that woman with him? I know that's not your mother. I remember your mother."

"No, ma'am. He's not."

"Well, that's fine. He looks like he could use a good roll in the hay."

"Mother!" Eve said.

"She's no fun," Cookie said. She rolled her eyes at Eve, then threw back her head and laughed.

I shot Adam a look. We were both horrified and speechless. Cookie was a fashion plate but served up with a side dish of crazy.

"Remember I told you she was inappropriate?" Eve whispered to us. "I think she's losing it."

"It's okay," I said and thought, Well, by golly, this could turn out to be an interesting night after all. "Really."

Carl was standing back assessing me and smiling like he was mentally undressing me. He held a bottle of white wine in one hand and a bottle of red in his other. I felt slightly uncomfortable, but not insulted.

"What are you looking at?" I said evenly with narrowed eyes and a suspicious stare.

"Nothing. White or red?" Carl said to Clarabeth and Ted.

He didn't even have the decency to blush. At least Adam blushed, I thought. Was Carl serious?

"Oh, maybe just a spritzer for me," Clarabeth said. "You know, I try not to imbibe lately. It's not good for my blood sugar or a long list of other things. That's what my internist tells me. He's so darling. Do you know how many pills I take every morning? And then there are more at night!"

Carl looked at her like she was a little cracked, which she was not. She was, well, just long-winded.

"A glass of red would be nice," Ted said. He put his arm around Clarabeth and gave her a squeeze to quiet her.

The usual niceties were exchanged and pretty soon everyone had a slice of pizza on a dinner plate with some tossed salad.

"You know, one of the best things about having children is that you can justify double cheese with pepperoni and mushrooms. This is so delicious," Adam said, finally joining the conversation.

"Isn't that the truth?" Eve asked, and laughed. "I love this stuff!"

It was unclear to me why Eve thought Adam's remark was funny. Maybe she's nervous, I thought. If Cookie were my mother I'd be a wreck.

But soon the wine began to work its magic and I wasn't nearly as annoyed as I had been. In fact, the mood softened all around and Carl had my attention. We were both being duped by our spouses, I thought.

Carl refilled my goblet and then everyone else's—except Clarabeth's. She was already on her second spritzer.

"Gosh, Daphne has grown up so much since last summer," I said. "She must be five inches taller!"

"And your boys too!" Eve said.

"True," I said. "Sometimes I think I can hear them grow-ing in their sleep."

"Daphne already has little boys calling the house," Eve said with pride.

I was horrified. I looked over to where the children sat at the breakfast bar to see little Daphne removing each round of pepperoni with her fingers, blotting away the grease, and then eating them one tiny nibble at a time.

"She's only six and she's already worrying about her clothes and is she getting too fat! Isn't that ridiculous?"

"You know? I just have boys. It's kind of a rough-and-tumble existence."

I said this with a smile because I wasn't a child psychologist.

God, people are screwed up, I thought.

Was Eve pushing her little girl toward serious self-image problems? Eve had obvious food issues. Was she passing that on to Daphne? Why would she? I thought it was completely asinine, even unhealthy, for a child of six years old to be thinking about her weight. I looked back over at Daphne. Max and Luke were entranced with her, arguing over who was the smartest twin, trying to impress her. And Carl was sucking in his abs and leering at me. Maybe alcohol brought out the Casanova in him.

Oh, hold me close, Lord, I thought, there go my babies. Right down the rabbit hole.

Then I had an idea.

"Hey, kids?" I called across the room. "Why don't y'all go down to the playground?"

I turned to the others and said, "We have at least three more hours of daylight, right? Let them all go get good and tired!"

"Excellent!" Eve said. "But you kids come home as soon as the streetlights go on, okay?"

"Shouldn't they have some adult supervision?" Clarabeth said.

"I think so," Ted said. "Why don't you and I watch them? Cookie? Would you like to join us?"

"I can't think of anything I'd like better in all the world!" Cookie said, her voice dripping with pretension.

With that, Clarabeth and Ted stood, and, joined by Cookie and the children, they left the condo single file, promising to be back when the day began to fade.

"Hey, I brought the latest Madonna CD with me," Eve said. "Y'all want to hear some music?"

Carl ignored her and turned to Adam. "So, tomorrow morning? You and me? Eighteen holes?"

"Sure," Adam said.

"I'm always happy to hear Madonna," I said to Eve, thinking to myself that I wished I had a dollar for every time Adam talked over me. "I love her."

The music began to play, more wine was poured, and stories were told. I was feeling pretty mellow and better disposed toward Eve. Adam excused himself to use the bathroom and I was suddenly inspired to use a bathroom as well.

Eve noticed my frown and said, "Just go upstairs and use mine! You know where it is! We have the same floor plan."

"Thanks."

I watched as Eve refilled her glass and drank deeply, as though it was water. I wondered then if Eve had an alcohol problem.

"I'll be right back!" I hurried upstairs and found relief. I flushed the toilet and opened the medicine cabinet to see what products Eve used on her skin. There was nothing there that I couldn't buy at a Rite Aid. Just then the door opened and there stood Carl.

"Oh, sorry! Wait, can I help you find something?"

I was caught in a very awkward position.

"Dental floss. I was just . . . pepperoni stuck in between my teeth."

"Ah, that's the worst."

He stepped past me. The bathroom was so small it was nearly impossible for him to get around me without us having some physical contact. I inhaled and held my breath. Carl reached into the drawer on the far side of the vanity and produced a pack of dental floss. He handed it to me.

"Thanks!" I said with a slightly guilty smile.

"You know, if you didn't have pepperoni stuck in your teeth and if I didn't want to be friends with you and Adam, I'd lay one on you right here and now."

"Really? I don't think so."

"Oh, yes, and you'd love it. And you'd beg for more!"

I flossed, giggling inside. I rinsed my mouth, turned around, and there he was. The next thing I knew he was kissing me. I did not respond, but I also didn't completely resist.

Finally, he stepped back and said, "What's wrong?"

"Are you serious?" I said. "I'm married and I don't want to cheat on Adam."

"Oh," he said. "It's just a kiss."

Just then we heard *"Carl! Come quickly! One of the kids is hurt! Carl!"*

Panic set in and I nearly fought Carl to get out of the bathroom first. We both ran down the stairs. Adam was already running to the playground. Carl was on his heels.

Ted was there in the living room, out of breath.

"It happened so fast!" Ted said to Eve.

"Who's hurt?" I almost screamed.

"It's Max. He fell and hit his head."

I turned on my heels and began running toward the swings and jungle gym, which were only a few buildings away. Eve followed me, jogging quickly, leaving Ted, who was still struggling to catch his breath, to return to the scene behind everyone else.

There was a small crowd gathered, both adults and children. There was a strange quiet to the group which frightened me even more. As I got there I saw Max's limp body in Carl's arms. He was unconscious. Max's head was covered in blood and his arm dangled at an odd angle. I nearly fainted at the sight of him.

"Oh, my God! Max!" I screamed.

"Is he gonna die?" Luke said. He began to wail, and for the first time since he was a toddler, he reached up to me to be picked up.

Daphne began to cry, throwing her arms around Eve.

Adam put his arm around my waist and said, "It's going to be all right."

Of course, Adam knew no such thing, but I knew he wanted to believe it so badly he just kept repeating it over and over.

Eve said, "Shouldn't we call an ambulance?"

Carl said, "There's no time! Let's go! Adam, come with me. Eve, you and Eliza stay here with the children."

"Adam, take my purse! The children's insurance cards are in my wallet!"

"We've got to get him to the hospital. Right *now*," Carl said, looking into Max's eye with his free hand, pulling Max's lids apart. "Probable concussion. Fracture of the arm."

Within a minute, Max's bleeding head was wrapped in a towel and he was in the backseat of Adam's car with Carl.

"Call me!" I yelled out to him.

Adam nodded to me solemnly and I knew that Adam was praying, begging God to make things right.

We all went back to Eve's condo because that was where the evening had begun. Ted, Clarabeth, Cookie, and I sat at the dining room table.

Collapsing into a chair, Clarabeth shook her head back and forth as she wept into her handkerchief. "I feel terrible, just terrible. I wouldn't let anything hurt that precious baby for all the money in this *world*! I feel so *terrible*! This is *all* my fault! I should've told him to come down."

"I didn't see a thing," Cookie said.

"We *did* tell him to come down. He wouldn't listen," Ted said.

"He never listens," Luke said and climbed onto my lap.

I put my arms around him and stroked his hair back from his face.

"Hush now," I said. "What's done is done."

"All my fault," Clarabeth repeated. "Oh, I wish it had been me, and not poor Max."

"It's *no one's* fault, Clarabeth!" Ted said. "It was an accident."

Cookie said, "Ted's right. It was an accident."

"What exactly happened?" I asked.

"He was climbing on the jungle gym," Daphne said. "He got on top of it and I told him, you'd better come down or you're going to fall!"

"We both told him to come down, but you know Max!" Luke said.

"It's not so smart to be a daredevil, now, is it?" I said to Luke and Daphne.

"No, ma'am," they said solemnly.

"I'll make a pot of coffee," Eve said.

She got up and went to the kitchen.

"He was pretending to be a tightrope walker," Daphne said.

"Dear God," I said.

"Dumb idea," Luke said.

Naturally, Cookie, Clarabeth, and Ted were horrified that something like this had happened on their watch. Luke and Daphne were deeply frightened.

"I haven't been so upset since Adam was a little boy and his appendix almost burst. What a nightmare! He had to get blood and oh Lord, I thought his mother would never calm down!"

Clarabeth said, "There's nothing more terrifying than an injured child."

I was in a total state of jangled nerves and struggling to

quell my worst fears. What if? What if? My hands and feet were ice cold. I felt a little nauseated and disoriented and I couldn't get the image of Max's bloody head out of my mind. Concussion? What did that mean? And he was unconscious, which scared me to death. I knew they would set his arm and stitch up his head, but would he be okay? And where was I when this all happened? Snooping around in Eve's bathroom and kissing her husband.

I would've gone back to my place to lie down, but I was afraid I would fall asleep and miss the phone call from Adam or Carl. So I sat there with the others. Eventually Daphne and Luke peeled away from the adults and went to the bedroom to play quietly. Luke was building a Lego fort and Daphne had dolls.

Eve said, "Listen to me, Eliza. Here is the reason I love Carl. He can move the world to make the right thing happen. There's no one I've ever known like him. No one. When the chips are down? Carl takes over and everything works out fine. You'll see."

"God, I hope you're right," I said.

We drank cup after cup of coffee and pushed some second-rate apple pie from the grocery store around on dessert plates. I noticed that Eve opted to continue drinking wine. Ted moved to the sofa and drifted off, seated next to Clarabeth, who had become very quiet. Hours passed and there was still no word from Adam or Carl. Finally, at ten thirty, my cell phone rang. I answered it with shaking hands. It was Adam.

"Hey, sweetheart. It's me."

"How's Max?"

"He's going to be fine. He got about fifty stitches in his head and they set his arm, which was broken in two places."

"Oh God! My poor baby!"

"They're gonna let him come home in the morning because they just want to watch him overnight. He hit his head pretty darn hard."

"Should I come and sit? I'll come and sit!"

"If you want. I'll tell you one thing, though."

"What?"

"God forbid there's an accident, you want Carl by your side. You should've seen him in action. There was no pediatric orthopedist or pediatric neurologist on call tonight. He made two very emphatic phone calls from the car and boom! There was a team waiting for us at the entrance of the ER. And a plastic surgeon. We really owe him. He even wanted to stay here all night. Just to watch over Max."

"Really? Gosh, that's *awfully* nice. Listen, if you think everything's okay, tell him to drive your car home and I'll bring it back. Are you hungry? Can I bring you anything?"

"No, I'm fine. But thanks."

"You sound exhausted. I know I am," I said.

"I haven't even thought about that yet. I'm just relieved. God, Eliza, if he had hit his temple like just one more inch, we could've lost him."

"Don't even think it."

CHAPTER 8

bonded

1995–2008

On the terrible night of Max's accident, I waited for Carl in the parking lot of our condo in Wild Dunes. I stood under a floodlight mounted on the side of the building, pacing, looking and listening for Adam's car to appear. Finally, I heard the familiar approach of his engine as Carl pulled into our parking spot. He got out and even in the dark I could see that his shirt was caked with Max's blood. The sight of it made me weak in the knees.

"How's Max?"

"Fine. Don't worry. He's gonna be fine. Look, here's the thing. With head injuries, you just have to keep watching for complications of concussion. But I saw the MRI. There's nothing to be concerned about."

As he handed me the car keys he took my hand in his and

began to apologize for what he said to me before the accident, when we'd met unexpectedly in the bathroom.

"Look, I don't know what I was thinking," Carl said. "I am so sorry."

I looked at him, almost having truly forgotten about the illicit kiss. Given the events of the day, I could not have cared less.

"It's okay," I said.

"No, really. If there's anything I hate, it's crass behavior."

I smiled then but I was anxious to get to the hospital. I climbed into the car, started the engine, and rolled down the window.

"Maybe wine does something to you—you know, makes you overly frisky or something."

"Maybe. Anyway, I apologize. I can't help it if I am attracted to you." He extended a hand for me to shake and I took it, shaking it quickly. "Friends?"

I thought about it for a minute. Carl was attractive to me as well, but hell would freeze before I let it get the better of me.

"Friends. You're sure Max is okay?"

"He'll be as good as new in no time," Carl said. "Kids heal a lot faster than adults."

"Right. Okay. And Carl? Thanks. I heard you were wonderful with Max tonight. See you in the morning."

He gave me a nod and turned toward his condo. I put the car in reverse and backed out of the parking spot. I didn't look down into the backseat to see what I was sure was a bloody mess. I couldn't. I just wanted to be at Max's side. Being upset about some ridiculous bit of grape-fueled flirtation was stupid. However notable the actual kiss may have been, what mattered was that Carl may well have saved my son's life. He got my little boy to the hospital as fast as possible and, according to Adam, saw that he got the right care. I drove as quickly as I could without getting in an accident myself. And I all but ran through the parking lot and the corridors to Max's room. I burst through the door and there was my son, sitting up in bed, head bandaged, arm in a soft cast and a sling, talking to Adam as though it was the middle of the afternoon, any day of the week.

"Well, here's Mom!" Adam said.

"Mom! Hey! Am I in trouble?"

I went to his side, took him in my arms, and kissed him tenderly on his cheek.

"No, sweet boy. You are not in trouble." Tears began to slide down my cheeks and I began to laugh, truly incredulous, relieved in every fiber of my being, and exhausted all at once. "You're not in trouble. You *are* trouble!"

I had thought that we would go home to the country when Max was released, but as Eve pointed out the next morning, if we stayed rather than cutting our vacation short, Max would have his own personal pediatrician looking over him for the balance of their time there. And he did. Carl absolutely doted on him, taking him back to the pediatric orthopedist to have his hard cast set and showing him how to slide a bamboo chopstick up or down the inside of his cast to quell an itch. Of course, he showed him how to cover it to take a shower. The cast, which stretched from his upper arm down and over his hand, was a cumbersome thing that caused him no end of bother. No one blamed him when he complained.

Clarabeth and Ted couldn't do enough for Max. Even little Daphne, the once and future heartbreaker, spent time just sitting next to him on the sofa. Cookie, however, didn't get involved except to seem to think (almost out loud) that Max's situation was his own stupid fault and he was lucky to be alive.

As a result of all of the attention, Max's spirits remained high. He began to heal quite nicely and quite quickly. But he still had occasional headaches and was more reticent than before. Even though I offered to affix a combo of plastic wrap and a plastic bag over the cast so he could cannonball, he wouldn't go in the pool. The most we could get him to do was to sit in the kiddie pool when the temperature rose to a fires-of-hell level.

Over the remainder of our vacation, Luke was slowly transformed into an alpha male. He began to blossom, taking small but obvious leadership roles in which game they would play or what they would watch on television. And he was especially nice to Max, even protective.

"I'm getting a juice box," Luke said to Max and Daphne. "Y'all want one?"

They were glued to an animated movie on television and they nodded like bobbleheads.

"Good idea, Luke!" I said. "You kids know when it's hot like this it's important to drink a lot of fluids, right? I'll get them for you."

"Luke calling the shots is a good thing," Adam said to me, popping the top from a bottle of beer. "I never liked Luke being a follower all the time."

"I agree," I said. "No reason why they both can't be leaders." I looked at my watch. "A beer before noon?"

"Just hydrating," Adam said. He blew me a kiss on his way out of the kitchen. "Besides, I suffered another humiliating defeat this morning on the golf course."

"Comfort drinking cannot be a good thing, sweetie." Well, he's on vacation, I thought. Just then I had another thought. We excused each other's weaknesses, and that forgiveness is probably, no, definitely, an important key to the success of any long-term relationship. So is an occasional blind eye.

You can't make a second career out of pointing out some-one's flaws and expect them to love you, I said to myself. That seemed to be Cookie's job.

On another note, it was not lost on us or anyone else that Cookie was flirting with Ted every chance she had. Clara-beth pretended not to notice. She was confident that Ted loved living on her plantation and that he would never be as happy living downtown in some stuffy old house museum, which was how I envisioned Cookie's house. And Clarabeth was secure enough about Ted's affection for her, even if it may have been somewhat powered by the lifestyle she provided for him. But still, Cookie gave Clarabeth, Eve, and me plenty of cause to titter. One night when we were all together, Clarabeth left the dinner table to get a glass of water. Cookie made her move.

"Ted, I sure am going to be awfully lonely without you and Clarabeth this winter."

"Well, then we'll have to get together!" Ted said.

"Let me know if she goes out of town," Cookie said.

"Mother!" Eve said.

"Oh, please! You're such a priss!" Cookie said and smiled at Ted.

Adam and I just shook our heads.

And finally, as our time at Wild Dunes came to a close for that year, I took one last walk on the beach with Adam. We walked along the water's edge and the cool salt water washed over our bare feet. We held hands, something we had always done.

"So, there's something we need to talk about," I said.

Adam, who I knew could detect when there was a growing storm within me, tried to steer the conversation into something we had to be happy about.

"What's that? I think Max is almost himself again. What do you think?"

"Maybe. Look, we've always been honest with each other, haven't we?"

"What do you mean? Of course!"

"You've never told me a lie?"

"Not unless I *had* to," he said.

It was the worst possible response. I had planned to discuss the matter calmly, but now, suddenly, I wanted to go for his jugular.

"Oh, really? You mean like when you acted all surprised to see Eve and Carl here the first day?"

I dropped his hand and turned to face him.

"Calm down, sweetheart," he said, which was also an ill-chosen remark.

I felt my blood pressure spike.

"Calm down? Really? 'What a coincidence!' That's what you said! You're a *liar*! You *knew* they were coming! Would you like to tell me what is going on?"

We stood there growing roots into the edge of the Atlantic

Ocean. Adam was staring at the sand dunes and I was staring at him. He was quiet.

"Adam? Talk to me!"

"Well, honestly, I meant to tell you, and I was going to tell you, but the right moment never presented itself and . . ."

"The right moment? There has to be a *right moment* to tell me the truth? I'm your wife, Adam. I expect the truth from you even when it's inconvenient."

"Okay. Here it is. Eve thinks that Carl is having an affair with someone. She called me a month ago. She was all upset."

"Oh? Now she *calls* you? For consolation? Why? To let you know she might be coming back on the market? To do what? Test the waters?"

"Oh, come on, Eliza. She knows I only love you! She just wanted me to keep an eye on Carl and see if I could detect anything funny or different about his behavior. That's all. We were gonna come back here this year anyway. So were they. So we chose the same two weeks. Big deal. Anyway, she asked me to be discreet."

"Are you kidding me? Discreet? Doesn't she know it's not nice to ask you to keep secrets from your spouse?"

"Eliza, you're right, of course," Adam said. "But what would we have done if they *hadn't* been here? Think about what might have happened to Max."

He had me with that remark. It was true. Carl was the hero of the year. I began to calm down.

"I know. It is further proof that there's no such thing as coincidence. But if I catch you lying to me again, I'm gonna skin you alive."

"I love it when you get mad. Your eyes flash lightning. And when you scrunch up your mouth like that? Your dimples show. Have I ever told you how much I love your dimples?"

"I mean it, Adam."

Adam pulled me into his chest and held me close. Then he kissed me on the top of my head.

"I love you, my fiery Greek beauty! I wish I had God's money so I could shower you in diamonds."

"Oh, you."

"You know," Adam said in a cagey voice, "remember last summer when we were here with them?"

"Yep."

"Well, you're the one, missy, who told me you thought Carl screwed around."

"So what?" I said remembering that awkward moment in the bathroom with Carl. I could feel my neck getting hot.

"So do you think he does? I mean, did you see anything weird or out of line with him?"

I considered what I knew in light of what Adam would do if he knew. If I relayed the bathroom episode to him, it would only provoke further phone calls to and from Eve and maybe all kinds of other nonsense. Carl had apologized. There was no real reason to throw him under a bus. Besides all that, I really liked Carl. I greatly admired a lot of things about him.

"No. I didn't. I think he just made an odd first impression. Look, I think he's a little conceited some of the time. And he likes to flirt. But the way he flirts is so overt that it's almost silly. I don't think it means anything."

Now I had a secret too. I could've told Adam everything,

but I knew it would have a negative impact on his friendship with Carl. And in retrospect I felt certain that Carl's move on me had just been some cheap grapes talking. Nonetheless, I kept the facts to myself.

Hmmm, I thought. I've just committed the same sin!

Somehow, it didn't bother my conscience one iota.

We all rationalize our behaviors, I thought.

"So, do you want to see them next summer?" Adam asked.

We began to walk again. He took my hand and held it tightly. I paused for a moment, taking in the spectacular colors of the western sky. I was so profoundly grateful to Carl. The children got along beautifully. Eve was becoming better company, even though she clearly drank too much. And I was amused by Cookie's lewd-lite pronouncements. There was no reason not to see them again because, despite Max's accident, it was the most fun I'd had all year.

"After what he did for Max? I'd go on vacation with them anywhere they want to go. I mean, Adam, even though I know Eve is still sweet on you, I like her. And Carl too. Plus, he's good for your golf game."

"Please. He killed me again this year. Well, that's what I was thinking too. I mean, we owe them. Especially him. Forever. But next year I'm gonna get him out on the tennis court and destroy him."

After that summer, time began to feel as though it was truly flying. As we knew it would come to pass, that fall Old Rufus went to dog heaven. He was just shy of his nineteenth birthday, riddled with arthritis and every ailment dogs can suffer in their old age. One day we let him outside and he didn't come when we called him. Luke and Max were yelling his name for so long that, having a premonition and a sick feeling in the pit of my stomach, I finally went outside in the yard to see what was going on. My worst fears were confirmed. When we found Rufus at the edge of the woods, the boys were very sad and so was Adam, but I cried like a baby. He had probably been trying to chase something, like a squirrel or a skunk, and his heart just gave out. Mr. Proctor dug a grave and we buried him overlooking the river with prayers and flowers.

"He was my best friend," I said to Adam through my tears.

"He was an awfully good dog," Adam said, giving me a hug.

"We can get another dog," Max said.

"We'll see," I said.

Now, a few months later when Crank the cat gave up the ghost, there was no crying and no ceremony. In fact, Crank was merely assumed dead because she disappeared from our property and our lives.

"You think she was catnapped?" Max said.

"Catnapped! That ain't even a word!" Luke said and laughed.

"Don't say 'ain't,'" I said.

"Nobody in their right mind would steal that cat," Adam said.

Despite my most fervent wishes that time would slow down, it did not. My boys were growing up too fast, I began to find white hairs on my head, and my hands and feet ached at the end of a long day in the kitchen. Even Adam was getting gray around the temples. And, as he thought he might, he bought us a three-bedroom condominium at Wild Dunes, blocking out two weeks for ourselves each year. Not to be outdone, Carl and Eve bought an almost identical one two doors away from ours.

I marked the passing of each year by vacations and holidays and photographs. Christmases, Easters, Thanksgivings, pictures taken around the Christmas tree, the table spread with food, or all of us gathered in my garden, holding tomatoes or corn. Pictures of the boys holding pumpkins they had grown, grinning widely, front teeth gone missing. Then there were my boys of summer, shirtless and freckled, tanned to a beautiful shade of café au lait, holding up watermelons so big they could take a prize at a county fair.

There were pictures of Luke and Max on their first bicycles and then later sitting up tall in the saddle on their horses. There were dozens of fish they caught spread out on the dock. Panoramic pictures of Luke and Max casting nets across the Carolina sky, standing in their johnboat out in the middle of the Stono. When they were about twelve, against my wishes, Adam bought shotguns and taught the boys how to hunt birds. There were pictures of ducks and pheasants they shot spread across the tailgate of Adam's pickup, which kicked up great clouds of dust on dirt roads when they went hunting with their dad and their Pointers.

Adam had taken most of the pictures, but I was the one who edited them, carefully cropping and color-correcting each one. After deliberation over the worthiness of each photo, I printed and framed the ones that represented those moments in the most appealing and memorable way. Indeed, the walls of our den and the halls of our house were a chronicle of our lives. And interspersed between them all were favorite memories from all our summers at Wild Dunes with Eve, Carl, Daphne, and Cookie. Of course, Ted and Clarabeth continued to join us each year.

Whenever Eve paid a solo visit to her mother in Charleston, Ted and Clarabeth met them for dinner. They had become quite good friends. Clarabeth would confide to me that yes, she had seen Cookie and Eve, and naturally she would make a remark about Cookie's very high opinion of herself and that perhaps she understood why Eve held such an affection for alcohol.

"I can't imagine having Cookie for a mother," Clarabeth said after the night she and Ted met them for dinner at Grill 225 to celebrate their recent marriage. They finally tied the knot! Clarabeth wanted no fuss about a wedding, so they went off to New Orleans, said nothing to anyone, and came back married. "I'm sure she never did a thing to boost that poor child's self-esteem."

"Cookie can be a bit of a stinker," I agreed.

"Well, she has other redeeming qualities."

"Such as?"

"She can be very entertaining. You know, most people think white wine is harmless, but it isn't," Clarabeth said.

"Do you think Eve has a problem?"

I had noticed the last time we were together at Wild Dunes that Eve seemed to be guzzling a whole lot more wine than usual, even for someone on vacation.

"Well, she drank an entire bottle herself."

"Good grief!"

I didn't like to think of Eve as an alcoholic, and I wasn't proud that I was sort of secretly glad to have someone remark that Eve wasn't perfect.

But all around, life was a whole lot better than merely satis-factory. Adam's construction business continued to grow and I finally amassed enough photographs and tested enough recipes to piece together a draft of my cookbook. Sadly, all of it re-mained in a big box in the bottom of the guest room's closet, be-cause my growing boys and their very busy schedules devoured nearly every waking hour of my time. And I asked myself over and over, did the world really need another cookbook?

Once a year, while on a road trip to Florida, my brother, JJ, and his wife, Tasha, stopped by to spend the night. It always proved to be the predicted painful endurance contest for Adam, and by the time they left in the morning Adam was wrung out. After dinner the night before, when I'd grilled gorgeous rib-eye prime steaks, they said they really didn't like to eat so much red meat. And, well, they were right, of course. I knew red meat was bad for you, but in my mind, it was a special treat. The next morning, I made them all breakfast—eggs, grits, and sausage with scratch biscuits so light they nearly floated across the room from the oven to the plates. JJ and Tasha pushed their food around their plates and ate like birds.

"Eliza, your biscuits are the best I've ever eaten, but I've never understood why people eat grits and say they actually like them," JJ said.

"They're gritty," Tasha said.

"That's why they call 'em grits!" Max said.

"Hmmm," Adam said for the maybe hundredth time in the last twelve hours, checking his watch.

"It's hard to find common ground," I said, waving good-bye to them as they pulled away in their car with bottles of my homemade jams bubble-wrapped and tucked into a canvas tote. "I'll bet they're saying the same thing."

"One can only hope," Adam said.

"I did my best," I said wistfully. "He's my only brother, you know? I love him."

"Pearls before swine," Luke whispered to Max, who nodded his head.

"What did you say?" I asked.

"I said, why does Aunt Tasha laugh like that?" Luke asked. Luke had become a gifted liar.

"Because her mother was a hyena," Max said. "It's inherited."

Luke and Max went on to imitate Tasha's unfortunate shrill and gulping laugh, which sounded like some godforsaken animal screeching from deep in the bush of the Serengeti.

Both boys doubled over with laughter. Adam and I looked at each other and grinned. What could we say? It was true. My brother was married to a hyena.

The months and years continued to fly. By the time 2007 rolled around, the boys were teenage jocks with driver's licenses and testosterone oozing from every pore of their perfectly toned bodies. They were going to college in the fall, thinking about girls and probably about getting laid.

That last prospect was pretty slim for the moment, as our whole tribe was on its way to Wild Dunes once again.

Of course, on the day we arrived, the heat was treacherous. We unloaded our cars and carried endless bags and so forth inside. The difference was that this year the boys had their own cars—Max a VW Jetta and Luke a Ford Eddie Bauer Explorer. They were used cars because Adam had wisely decided that new cars were an unnecessary luxury. He helped the boys buy them by splitting the cost and the insurance, which meant the boys had to work. And over their summers they had worked alongside Adam's construction crews. Luke had taken a shine to the family business, but Max, no doubt as a result of Carl's influence, was interested in medical school.

"If you graduate from college with honors, I'll buy you both any car you want, within reason," Adam said.

"Lamborghini!" Luke said.

"Maserati!" Max said.

"When pigs fly," Adam said and slapped them on the shoulder. "Keep dreaming!"

Eve wandered in around five and invited us all over for dinner.

"It's just so good to see y'all again! I missed all of you!" Eve said. "Come eat with us."

"Oh, sweetie!" I said after giving her a big hug. "Me too! I've already got lasagna in the oven!" I had another casserole in the freezer but I could throw that in the oven as well.

"Then I'll bring my hot dogs and chili over here?"

"Of course!" I hoped the hot dogs had no nitrates in them and wondered if that kind of dinner pleased Carl and her mother.

"By the way, Daphne brought a friend with her." Eve rolled her eyes. "It was the only way I could get her to come."

"Teenagers," I said.

"We're going swimming, Mom," Max said, passing through the kitchen with Luke. "Hey, Miss Eve. Daphne here?"

"Don't go in the ocean!" I said. "They had a shark attack last week. Some poor man nearly lost his leg."

"Really? Yikes," Eve said. "Yeah. She's next door with her new best friend, Kelly. Kelly Engelbert. Kelly Engelbert who is reputed to have a tattoo of her astrological sign on her backside."

Luke and Max looked at each other and grinned.

"Boys, stop it!" I said. "I can read your minds!"

"And it's not Virgo," Eve said.

"Sweet," Max said and looked to Luke, who was struggling not to laugh.

"Yep, shark attack," I said, trying to change the subject. "There was a big article in the *Post and Courier.*"

"How terrible!" Eve said.

"Don't worry, Mom. We ain't afraid of no shark," Max said, grabbing a bottle of water from the fridge. He tossed a second one to Luke.

"Don't say 'ain't,'" I said.

The door slammed and the boys were gone.

"You know, my boys aren't going to be happy until they know Kelly's sign."

"Honey? I predict she ain't gonna be happy until she shows it to them."

The evening was spent getting caught up with one another. Daphne and Kelly (both of whom seemed as innocent as the driven snow) and the boys had eaten quickly, washed all the dishes, and gone for a walk on the beach. Two casserole dishes of lasagna and four loaves of garlic bread had been summarily consumed. The hot dogs and chili brought less enthusiasm from the crowd and, for the most part, languished in an aluminum container on the back of the stove.

"Did you count the beers?" Eve asked Carl.

"Kelly doesn't seem like the tattoo type," I said.

"I know," Eve said. "They're both Lilly Pulitzer and pearls on the outside. Teenage girls are very deceiving."

"No, I didn't count the beers, but I know I bought a case of Amstel Light and a case of Beck's," Carl said, looking across the table to Adam and me. "It's a whole new world this year. Let me tell you, a whole new world."

"What do you mean?" Adam asked.

"I mean raising a teenage girl is like having a terrorist in your house," Carl said. "I used to keep all kinds of medicine at home and now I have to lock it up in a vault."

"Why? Is Daphne fooling around with prescription medications?" I said. "That sweet child? I wouldn't believe it for a minute!"

"You don't know girls," Carl said.

Eve said, "We had a whole bottle of Vicodin go missing last month. She claimed to know nothing about it. I said, 'Oh, so it was here yesterday and today it just grew legs and walked?'"

"It's got some serious street value," Carl said. "When I realized it was gone I told her that if she got busted for selling drugs I'd take away her car."

"And send her to a Christian military school in Georgia where she would have to dig up onions and recite Bible verses before she would get to eat," Eve said.

"Good grief! Does such a place even exist?" Clarabeth said. "That sounds like the Spanish Inquisition, like child cruelty! I mean it's too much, it's medieval, it's inhumane, it's—"

Cookie interrupted Clarabeth. "A good idea. It sure scared the bejesus out of her."

"Heaven help us," I muttered to no one in particular.

"Unfortunately, this school only goes to twelfth grade," Eve said. "She's going to Elon this fall."

"She'll be having more fun than our boys," Adam said. "Luke's going to Georgia Tech for civil engineering and Max is premed at Duke."

Adam and I were very proud of our sons' academic achievements.

"I was so glad he got in," Carl said. "You know we'll keep an eye on him."

Carl had generously written a strong letter of support for Max's application and he had the head of admissions, an old friend, shepherd his application through the process.

"And I hope you know how much we appreciate that," I said. "Who even keeps Vicodin in their house?"

We never had anything stronger than Tylenol in our medicine cabinet.

"I get muscle spasms in my back," Eve said. "You must be so proud of Luke and Max."

"I am thrilled for them, but it's going to be pretty lonely for me!" I said.

"I'll bet so," Eve said. "Well, I'll come visit!"

"I'd love that!" I said.

"I told Eve to lock all the drugs away, but it's not like she listens to me," Carl said.

"Ow!" Adam said. "Muscle spasms are the worst."

I thought, Whoa, baby! Vicodin? Muscle spasms? Swallow two with a glass of chardonnay and call me in the morning? Eve definitely has a problem. Carl has to realize this. Doesn't he?

"Do your boys smoke weed?" Eve asked. "It seems like every single boy in Daphne's class smokes weed."

Cookie gasped and said, "Where are the parents these days?"

I turned bright red, thinking that the question was too personal to be addressed in front of Adam's father.

"Listen, in our world? Our boys never had the time to get involved with all that stuff. I kept them busy," Adam said.

"You sure did do that!" I said. "If they weren't chasing a ball or something else, they were catching fish or birds or helping Adam."

"Idle hands are the Devil's workshop," Clarabeth said. "That's what my mother always said, and she was right. She also said, tell me who your company is and I'll tell you who you are because birds of a feather flock together. Oh! She had so many sayings like that and they were all true! Kids today should have more supervision, if you ask me . . ."

"I agree!" Cookie said.

Ted reached over and gently patted the back of Clarabeth's hand to make her stop talking. She does enjoy the soapbox, I thought.

"Come on, old girl," he said, smiling at her. "Let's let the young people have their night."

"Who's an old girl?" Clarabeth said indignantly. "Not I!"

"I may as well call it a night too," Cookie said and got up. "Thank you for dinner, Eliza. Your lasagna is almost as good as Stouffer's."

For a moment, I thought she was kidding.

"Thank you," I said, because what could I say?

"Don't pay her no never mind," Clarabeth said. "Your lasagna is incredible! Paula Deen would kill for your recipe!"

I hugged Ted and Clarabeth and blew an air kiss to Cookie. Adam walked them all to the door.

"See y'all tomorrow," I said.

In due time, Carl and Eve reached maximum capacity in the department of stamina and announced they were ready to sleep.

"I'm sorry, but I can hardly hold my eyes open," Eve said and yawned.

"Long day," Carl said.

"Don't worry. We have two whole weeks to solve the problems of the world," I said.

We went through the motions of shutting the house down for the night. The boys drifted in and said good night, disappearing into their rooms. I set up the coffeepot for the morning and Adam turned off all the lights. It was eleven o'clock. That's when the screaming started.

"Help! Call 911!"

It was a man's voice. There was a man outside our condo, close by, huffing and puffing.

"Help! 911!"

"It sounds like Ted!" I said, panicked.

"I'll go see what's going on," Adam said, opening the sliding glass doors.

I watched as Adam raced across the terrace through the pool area and I saw Ted coming off the beach with Cookie in his arms. Ted's clothes were soaking wet. Cookie was naked and her leg was bleeding like mad.

"Get Carl! Shark bite!"

"Give her to me," Adam said.

Ted was nearly out of breath and passed Cookie's tiny body over to Adam's outstretched arms. Adam, decades younger and more fit, ran with Cookie straight to Carl and Eve's. I followed Adam, grateful that Cookie was unconscious. It didn't seem like her injuries were life threatening and I knew it was better that she was not entirely aware that her clothes were nowhere to be found.

And Adam would tell me later that he had the fleeting thought that this was the woman who'd ruined years of his life and he should've thrown her back to the sharks. But, on the other hand, he would rather that she owed him one. When I asked why he said, "I'll tell you the story someday."

At that point, I was on Carl and Eve's terrace. I ran to call 911. In minutes, Cookie was stretched out on Carl and Eve's couch, a makeshift tourniquet of clean dish towels around her wound and a comforter covering her up.

"What the hell happened?" Carl asked.

Carl and Eve were in their pajamas and had been half asleep.

"What's going on?" Daphne said.

"Go back to bed," Eve said.

"Oh, my God! Cookie! Is she okay?"

"She's going to be fine," Eve said. "It looks like a shark took a little nip of her thigh."

"Oh, Mom! Oh, no!"

"Calm down, sweetie," Carl said. "She's fine."

"I just went out to the beach to get some air. Clarabeth

had the thermostat up to eighty degrees and she was snoring like a bear. Don't say I said that."

Carl said, "Ted? Would you like a glass of water?"

Ted said, "Yes, I would. Thanks. I guess she decided to go skinny-dipping."

The doorbell rang. Eve opened it and there stood two EMS workers with a stretcher.

"Hurry! My mother was bitten by a shark!"

"I never even heard her leave the house," Carl said, filling a glass from the spigot and handing it to Ted.

"Thanks. I could see it was Cookie. She wasn't that far out in the ocean. Anyway, I saw her get pulled underwater and I knew she was in trouble."

"Wait two minutes. Let me get my clothes on," Carl said, then turned to the EMS workers. "Take her vitals. I'm coming with y'all. I'm a doctor and this is my mother-in-law."

Cookie was moaning as she was being loaded into the ambulance. Carl hopped in the back with her.

"I'm coming too!" Eve said. "I'll be right behind you in the car."

"Holy crap," I said.

"Wait until I tell Clarabeth this one," Ted said.

"We're going to be chewing on this one for years, no pun intended," Adam said.

"Worst joke ever," I said.

CHAPTER 9

eliza's catching up

wild dunes, 2009

It was a mere ninety-four degrees in the shade, but there was not a breath of air to be found. Eve and I were stretched out under the fronds of towering palmettos on recliners by the pool at Wild Dunes drinking iced water and rehashing the year. Our husbands were engaged in an afternoon battle to the death on the tennis courts.

"I still cannot believe it was Cookie who took the Vicodin," I said.

"And I can't believe it's taken me two years to tell you. I was so horrified. She had enough in her system to kill a person three times her size. Evidently she had built up quite a tolerance," Eve said. "We had a terrible fight over it."

"Who? You and Cookie?" I sat up, took a Ziploc of apple slices from the cooler, and offered it to Eve. "Here. Have a slice."

"Thanks!" Eve helped herself to two. "Of course, I had it out with her."

"It doesn't really do any good to argue with your parents."

"Well, it made me feel better. I've never been so angry. Don't you remember she let me accuse Daphne? She stood right there while I read Daphne the riot act. But I also had the battle royale with Carl."

"Tell me about Cookie first. What did she say?"

I wanted every detail. I was starved for gossip. It had been a slow year on the Stono. With the boys away at college, my pipeline to the latest dirt was shut down.

"I just said to her, I can't believe you let me threaten my daughter with that horrible boarding school when you knew you were to blame all along. She got all weepy and dramatic and tried to say she couldn't help herself and blah blah blah. It was really unbelievable."

"Well, drug addiction is terrible. To say the least," I offered. "It makes nice people do awful things."

"Agreed. But Carl heard me going at it with her and jumped in telling me not to be so hard on her. He called me a bitch. I didn't speak to him for a week."

"What? If Adam called me that he'd be sleeping in the barn for a year."

"I know! And I wouldn't blame you one little bit! Anyway, it took three trips to Betty Ford to get her sober. To be honest? I liked her better drunk and high."

Well, *that's* a helluva thing to say about your mother, I thought.

"Oh no! Was she drinking too? I never noticed her drinking that much. Gosh!"

"Listen, Eliza, I like my white wine, probably too much, and I *know* that, but *I* don't have bottles of vodka stashed in my closet and in the garage and under the sink and in more nooks and crannies than you'd find in an English muffin. *She* did."

"No kidding. My God. I never would've suspected that. Never!"

"Oh, she was clever. She had it all worked out so that she never had to drive or do anything that might arouse the suspicions of the authorities and land her in the county jail wearing orange or whatever color they wear here. She had Ted picking up her groceries and her neighbor picked up her dry cleaning and so forth. She sat home watching *The Golden Girls* on television and drinking martinis and popping pills all day and night!"

"Do Ted and Clarabeth know she went through rehab?"

"Nope. She never told a soul. I knew and Carl knew, but that's all. You know, in my blue-blooded family we don't like to talk about such things. Only trashy people get drunk and do drugs. Not the highfalutin likes of Cookie."

"Right. How in the world did you find out?"

"Well, it started with the shark bite. They discovered all the Vicodin in her blood. At the same time, they discovered elevated blood alcohol levels. The combination set off all the alarms in Carl's mind. He didn't say anything much at the time because Cookie was honestly traumatized. But it didn't take long for her to fall apart after the shark. She went home, believe it or not, with a big fat bottle of pain medication."

"Good grief! Didn't they know she was abusing pain meds?"

"Honey, these days? In a huge hospital, it's a miracle when the right hand knows what the left one is doing. The doctor who released her wasn't the doctor who admitted her and didn't make the connection in the records. And I think it's probably fair to say she did have legitimate pain. After all, that shark took a hunk out of her thigh. Anyway, a few weeks later, her UPS delivery guy saw her dancing in her garden. It was ten in the morning. She was . . . well, she was as naked as a jaybird, dancing in and around the azaleas. They weren't even in bloom!"

I was unsure of what to make of that last remark. Perhaps there was a special southern ritual of dancing with blooming azaleas that had escaped my attention. I thought, I am, after all and through no fault of my own, from the north. And at one time, Charleston did have a reputation for celebrating her eccentrics. Stories like this were not all that unusual.

"And he had a sense that something wasn't right. Drugs and alcohol go hand in hand."

"Uh, yeah, they do. He called 911. It was off to the Betty for Cookie!"

"Gee, that's too bad. But she's okay now?"

"If complaining and criticizing about every single thing under the sun is okay, then she's okay. I'm telling you, you're not going to like her like this."

"Well, I guess we're going to see what we see," I said. "I'm just so glad we could get together again. This vacation is my favorite time of year."

Eve leaned over to me and patted the back of my hand.

"Carl and I were so sorry to hear about your father," she said.

I sighed, thinking about my father's funeral, which was painful and sparsely attended.

"Thank you. He had a good long life, you know? And he died so suddenly, it was such a terrible shock."

"Yes, but that's better than some long-drawn-out illness where it seems like you're dying one cell at a time."

"No, that's absolutely the truth. He had a heart attack in his sleep. Went to bed on earth and woke up in heaven!"

"That's the way to go for sure." Eve smiled at me.

"My boys hardly knew him. He didn't like to travel and he wasn't particularly interested in us, for reasons I will never be able to reconcile."

We were both quiet then, Eve giving me a moment to reflect. I was dwelling on the fact that his death was so final and that I'd never have the chance to make him see me as a whole woman who was anything but another version of my mother. It was game over. To say my parental relationships had been less than satisfying would greatly understate the intense heartache and disappointment I felt. Eve finally spoke.

"Your mom passed away when you were young, right?"

"Yes, I was just eleven and it was terrible for all of us. I think my father never got over it. And I think one reason he ignored me is that I look exactly like her. My brother looks like him."

"Well, we both know people love people for the craziest reasons. But I'm sure your father loved you, don't you think so?"

"Oh, I'm sure he did. He was just very reserved, like my brother, who is a sweetie once you get to know him. But not a lot of juice, you know what I mean?"

"Yes. I know."

"By the way, your flowers were gorgeous. Thank you again."

"Oh golly, Eliza, you're so welcome, but I wanted to be there with you. I felt so badly that we couldn't come."

"You know what? Let's make a pact to come to our children's weddings! Let's celebrate the happy things!"

"I'll drink to that!" Eve said. "And Eliza, how much weight have you lost? You look fabulous! What are you doing?"

"Just drinking a lot of water," I said. I had dropped a few pounds.

We touched our plastic water bottles and smiled.

"And you know what else?" I said. "Cookie might have become a fussbudget, but at least you still have her. Let's see what we can do to cheer the old girl up!"

"Good luck with that!" Eve looked over to the pool, which was unoccupied by any of the other guests. "Gosh, this is some summer without Daphne! Where are the boys this afternoon?"

"They're down at Breach Inlet, kitesurfing or some sport designed to break their little necks," I said. "How was Daphne's year at college?"

"She did all right this year, but she didn't exactly burn the town down."

That was code for *barely passed*.

"So what's she up to this summer?"

"Well, as usual, we're rewarding her poor academic performance and assuaging our own guilt over Cookie's drug debacle by allowing her to go with Kelly for a six-week cultural immersion in France. How about your boys?"

If Daphne was mine, I thought, Adam would have her chopping wood all summer or something else equally torturous. In our family, poor performance brought consequences.

"Well, they're working for Adam, like they have since they could pick up a hammer. But he pays them the same as the other guys."

"Dean's List?"

"Yes," I said with an involuntary grin.

"Figures."

"They're competitive with each other. It really isn't about us pushing them. In fact, it might be the one advantage of having twins."

"I don't believe I could manage two Daphnes! Oh, did I mention she got suspended for plagiarism?"

"Well, girls are different," I said, thinking, I don't know if I could've managed the one she's got. "She was probably just not thinking. They give you a run for your money."

"She does. And she got three speeding tickets!"

"No!"

"Yes," she said.

I was quiet for a moment and then I said, "Listen, I don't think it matters if you have girls or boys. You worry."

"It's true. Hey, here come the guys. I wonder who won?"

Adam and Carl, red faced and sweaty, waved, peeled off their shirts, kicked off their sneakers and socks, and fell into the pool. In their tennis shorts.

"I'd swear I just saw steam rise from the water," I said.

"I hope he left his cell phone in the condo," Eve said. "But it's probably in the pool."

The boys came up for air, flipped over on their backs, and floated like dead men.

"Oh, thank you, God," Adam groaned. "I finally whupped the son of a bitch."

"Good, darlin'," I said, laughing to myself.

"I nearly died out there," Carl said. "It was so close."

"It was never close," Adam said. "You lost by a country mile."

"He got me on a dink shot," Carl said. "Very sneaky."

"It's called playing the net," Adam said.

"I want a rematch," Carl said.

"Stop! You're whining like an old woman," Adam said.

"Oh, really? Is that what you think?"

Their banter went on for a while, entertaining Eve and me to no end. Finally, when their body temperatures had returned to normal, Adam and Carl climbed out of the pool and sloshed over to us, dripping on us as much as possible, creating puddles all around their feet. We jumped away and complained, but we were laughing all the while. Carl pulled his cell phone from his sopping wet shorts and tried to make a call—sadly, to no avail.

"Fried another one," he said.

"What about putting it in the dryer?" Adam said. "You know, like in a sock or something?"

"Yeah, right," Carl said.

"What did I tell you?" Eve said, rolling her eyes to me.

"Oh, dear. There's water in the cooler if you fellas want a drink," I said.

Carl busied himself drying and blowing on his phone, thoroughly annoyed that he had ruined yet another one. He was embarrassed.

"Third one this summer," Eve said, happy to announce that perfect Carl wasn't so perfect after all. "Try covering it up in a bowl of rice. I read that somewhere."

"Can't hurt," I said.

I was delighted that Adam had bested Carl on the tennis court. Carl had been beating Adam at golf and tennis and even poker for years, so it was time Adam had his pride restored. And it was also good because Adam could justify the amount of money he had spent on tennis lessons. After all the years we had been vacationing together, it had taken the challenge of Carl to make Adam competitive.

Eve seemed happy to see Carl and Adam getting along so well. We both were. It meant that this vacation was going well and that there would likely be another. Like me, she had come to cherish this time we all shared. She didn't like Raleigh anymore. Daphne was gone, Carl worked all the time, and she was lonely. I knew what loneliness felt like. At least her mother's illness brought her to Charleston and that helped her loneliness—to be needed. On occasion, we would meet downtown for lunch. Maybe the fact that no one *really* needed her was at the bottom of her malaise. At least I could offer her genuine friendship, and spending time with me gave her a chance to catch a glimpse of Adam again, even if their relationship was as chaste as Abelard and Heloise. I could see Eve aching for Adam's company. And she worked mighty hard so that no one could detect the fact that she still had feelings for Adam. But it's pretty hard to hide love.

Somewhere along the line, as Carl continued trying to salvage his phone, Eve caught Adam's eye. I watched as Eve appeared to be eighteen again and so did he. Then I blinked and the moment evaporated as though it had never been. I needed to tell him that time had no patience for his longing. Guilt would eventually take a bite out of his soul and he should remember to be grateful for all he had—me, the boys, all that . . . still. I knew that something in him remained unfulfilled. But did anyone ever find all they dreamed of and all they needed in one person?

It's his age, I thought. He thinks he's going down the fucking tubes.

My husband had unquestionably arrived in middle age. We both had. There was nothing to be done about our advancing years except to embrace them and to pray that they continued to advance for decades to come. We were in perfect health and we looked pretty darn good for our age, and what else could we ask for?

If I could've crawled inside his head, *I knew exactly* what he would be asking for. Adam would ask for an epic blizzard to occur, and that he would be caught in a wonderful cabin in Vermont and Eve would arrive and they would lose power and sleep together for warmth. Nature would take its course more than once. But Eve would wake up with a total case of amnesia in the morning and it would appear to her that Adam had slept on the sofa under a pile of quilts. He would be making pancakes (that he didn't know how to make) in a cast-iron skillet over an open fire and brewing the most wonderful-smelling coffee in the world. Why not? Then he wouldn't have any guilt.

As I continued to watch him fantasize, I telepathically sent him a message that the odds of this happening were sharply not in his favor.

Shrugging his shoulders, Adam said, "Let's eat. I mean, what's up with dinner? Did we make a plan?" he asked as nonchalantly as he could, given his self-indulgent bullshit daydream. I knew this man.

"We have a table at Ronnie's at six thirty," I said.

Ronnie's was a popular seafood restaurant on Shem Creek in Mount Pleasant, just two tiny bridges and a stretch of causeway away. People from all over the country loved to gather there with locals to see the shrimp boats come in with their catch of the day and to watch the dolphins play in the water while the seagulls and pelicans performed their swooping dances and struts for free. It was a different show every night and one that never bored even the most jaded visitor.

"Great!" Carl said.

Adam said, "Are Cookie, Ted, and Clarabeth joining us? And what about the boys?"

"The boys, no. They're going to see a movie. But the elders, yes," I said. "We'd better get moving if we're going to be on time."

"Time to shake a leg," Carl said.

Soon all seven of us waited outside the restaurant as the throng of diners ahead of us slowly moved inside. I noticed that Clarabeth was having a little trouble with the steps, but I didn't say anything.

"This place is packed!" Carl said.

"How long am I expected to wait? Don't we have a reservation?" Cookie said.

"We're actually a few minutes early," Eve said and shot me a glance as if to say, *Here we go. Get ready to listen to some serious carping and complaining.*

I smiled and gave Adam a nudge. "Honey? Why don't you tell the hostess that we have some special seniors with us who need to be seated quickly?"

Clarabeth mouthed *thank you* to me.

"You bet," Adam said.

I watched as Adam worked his way through the people to the podium where two harried young hostesses worked in tandem, seating patrons as quickly and efficiently as possible. Adam explained the situation to one of them, who nodded and quickly counted out seven menus.

"Just follow me," she said.

Adam turned back to me and the others and gave us the sign to come along. Soon we were all gathered around a nice table with a view of the water, ordering drinks and enjoying the complimentary crab dip and crackers.

"This dip used to have more crab in it than it does now," Cookie said, piling a generous dollop onto a saltine cracker.

"Crabmeat is expensive," I said, thinking that Eve was right. Cookie had become a malcontent.

"Well, the dip is free, for heaven's sake," Eve said.

"I'll have a Heineken and a cold glass, if you have it," Carl said to the waitress.

"Yes, sir," she said and looked to Cookie. "For you, ma'am?"

"Well, I've been cut off at the knees, so I guess I'll have a glass of iced tea. Unsweetened," Cookie said with a smile that only barely concealed her dissatisfaction with her new alcohol-free life.

"Yes," Ted said, winking at her. "Our Cookie is sweet enough."

"Oh, you!" Cookie said and smiled.

"I'll have iced tea as well," Clarabeth said, smiling at Cookie.

"Misery loves company," Cookie said.

"There's strength in numbers," Clarabeth said. "My mother always said that."

Ted blew a kiss to Clarabeth for good measure. He always seemed to know how to bring Cookie around. In fact, Ted had become quite adept at improving and sustaining the dispositions of Clarabeth and Cookie, always seeming to strike the right balance so that one did not feel the other to be a threat to her status quo. They, in turn, fussed over him like two old hens.

I assumed their sex lives were something of a distant memory. So, if that hot button was out of the equation, things had to be way less complicated among them. Still, I thought it was marvelous that Ted could manage to keep both women so happy.

Over platters of fried seafood, crunchy and lemony, served with tartar and cocktail sauces, the conversation turned to age.

"So, y'all turned fifty this year? You're babies!" Cookie said.

"I remember fifty," Clarabeth said, adding, "vaguely."

"Cookie, that was a couple of years ago! But boy, I can tell you, fifty gets your attention," Carl said. "AARP is stalking me."

"Time seems to be moving faster," I said, "and there are still so many things I want to do."

"Like what?" Eve said.

"Go to Greece."

"She gets this in her head about twice a year," Adam said, adding very dramatically, "she thinks Greece is *calling her home*. Come home, Eliza!"

Adam laughed. I could tell that he thought that was a ridiculous concept. He looked around the table for support, but there was none. There was a brief awkward silence.

"Maybe it is," I said. "Maybe there's something there I need to know or see, or I don't know, I just feel like I really want to go back. Even just to see the house where my mother grew up again. Maybe there are still some relatives around."

"Most likely they won't speak a word of English," Adam said. "You really need to let this fantasy go."

"There's a lot of crime in Athens," Eve said. "I read that somewhere."

"They don't live in Athens," I said. "And don't talk to *me* about fantasy, mister."

The table got quiet. I was almost out of estrogen and Eve was still lacking in situational awareness.

Carl looked at Eve. It obviously frustrated him that she seemed unable to speak with authority on anything. I could see it in his face. Eve was embarrassed and didn't know why. Adam had dropped a bomb on the dinner and couldn't recover quickly enough. But then Clarabeth cleared her throat.

"All right, you youngsters, listen to your old Auntie Clarabeth." Her faded blue eyes twinkled with wisdom and kindness inside the reddened rims of her lower eyelids.

"Lay it on us," Adam said jovially, hoping she could restore the mood to something that felt more celebratory.

"Here's the thing. If there's something you see on television, like a cute little sports car or a beautiful vista in Switzerland or Hawaii, and you say to yourself, Oh! I'd like that! Or, I'd like to go there! But you turn off the television and go about your day. Chances are you're not going to Switzerland or Hawaii and you're not buying that little red sports car. But if you keep saying you want to go to Greece and you went there as a child and your mother was born there and the feeling stays with you for years? Good grief, girl! Take yourself to Greece!"

I gasped. Then I got up from my chair, went around the table to Clarabeth's side, leaned down, and kissed her on the cheek.

"You're right!" I exclaimed. "Not tomorrow, but soon. I'm going to visit Corfu and my family there."

On my way back to my seat, I gave Adam a little stink eye. He shrugged and threw his hands up in defeat, smiling sheepishly.

"Well, if you need an old lady to help you carry your bags, let me know," Clarabeth said. "I've got a little time on my hands and I'd love to see Greece!"

"I went out with a Greek man once," Cookie said and sighed wistfully. "We used to drink ouzo and make out like jungle animals in heat. He was a gorgeous thing."

"Mother!" Eve said.

"What? It's the truth."

Adam was smiling then. Cookie was a trip. She always carried herself like she was related to the Queen of England. She dressed like she was Anna Wintour's mother and tried to come across as royalty. When she opened her mouth, we all knew the devil had arrived.

And of course, Clarabeth was right. If you had a longing in your heart, it had to be dealt with. I saw Adam look at Eve. Eve was staring in his direction and then she quickly looked away. What were they going to do about their longing for each other?

CHAPTER 10

adam

wild dunes, winter 2010

A typical Lowcountry winter goes like this: In the early morning, it's cold and damp, the temperature ranging anywhere from low thirties to low fifties. If you're near any kind of a body of water, and the chances of that are high, there might be an otherworldly rolling mist. You need a sweater, a windbreaker, and a neck scarf. By noon, the mist has burned away, evaporating back into the genie's lamp. You've shed your jacket and scarf, and the sweater you're wearing is probably starting to itch, making you question your own judgment for ever buying anything made of wool. By three in the afternoon, you very well might be playing tennis in shorts, feeling like the weather is absolutely California perfect. But when you venture out to that backyard oyster roast later that night, it's cold and damp again. Bundle up, Bubba.

So much of how I plan my day depends on the weather. In

our house, we talked about it a lot. In the months following the holidays, it could rain frequently, causing my business to slow down somewhat. But not this year. Boeing had come to Charleston, and the need for housing was off the charts. I was insanely busy. We were in Summerville most days and for long hours. So long that I rented a trailer to use as an office and hired a receptionist to field all the phone calls.

It was the dead of February. Eliza was visiting Max at Duke and not due back until tomorrow. I decided it was a good time to work some handyman voodoo on our Wild Dunes condo. There was a dripping faucet in one of the bathrooms, a sliding glass door that was always getting stuck in its track, and some drawer pulls missing in the kitchen. I was sure that I would find a dozen other handyman jobs because DIY had become my specialty. So I packed up my toolbox, a cordless drill, a six-pack of beer, and an overnight bag. As soon as I rolled into Mount Pleasant I stopped at Lowe's to buy some drawer pulls that I hoped would resemble the original ones that were still in place. It would be nothing short of a miraculous event to find the same ones. I found some that bore a resemblance and they would have to suffice for now, which of course would drive me crazy and eventually I would replace them all. Call it builder's pride.

When I crossed the connector bridge to the Isle of Palms, I was struck for the millionth time by the natural beauty of the marshes and the changing colors of the marsh grass. The water seemed to be a deeper blue than it was in the summer, and maybe it was the current or the cooler temperature or the time of day, but the water beneath me shimmered and sparkled. To my right, long skinny docks with dry-docked boats dotted the Intracoastal Waterway. I thought then that I should try to make friends with the guy who owned that dock right down there because I could bring my boat over and enjoy my summer vacation even more. The Wild Dunes yacht harbor was always jammed. It would be so much nicer to just pull up to a private dock like I did at home on the Stono, which always made me feel like a man who had arrived.

I stopped at the Red & White grocery store to pick up a few things like coffee and milk and an Entenmann's coffee cake that I could eat unseen. Eliza was always telling me to watch out for my cholesterol like it was the family menace, some live thing lurking in the kitchen shadows, waiting to sink its claws into my good health. My cholesterol was perfect, thank you. Well, as long as I took my statin. Just gimme the coffee cake and nobody gets hurt. And I bought burgers and buns I could throw in a pan for dinner.

By the time I pulled into my driveway at Wild Dunes, the sun had slipped away for the night, leaving the horizon ablaze in deep crimson and majestic purple, like the color of a king's robe. I know that sounds a little sappy coming from me, but I don't know how else to describe the scene. It's *that* dumbfounding, like it deserves a soundtrack from an opera. I should go to work for Hallmark, I thought, I'm such a poet. A regular dang Walt Whitman.

I went inside, dropped my things on an armchair, popped open a beer, and went outside to watch the sky. Winter sunsets always gave me pause. How could they not? It was like being in church. I was calm like the great Buddha, reminded once again how small and insignificant I was in the scheme of things—the cosmos, the universe, all that was out there. Venus appeared in the western sky, the first star of night in the cold months. It was going to be a beautiful night. I was intensely grateful to be a witness.

Eventually, my hands grew cold, and finally every trace of day disappeared. I was freezing in the forty-degree weather. The skies above me began to twinkle as the stars came out of hiding.

I turned to go back inside and noticed that a few lights were on in Carl and Eve's place. Who was there this time of year? Surely not renters. I walked across our shared terrace to see if I could see anyone through the sliding glass door. I wasn't like a Peeping Tom or something. Just curious. A friend with a proprietary sense of duty, that's all. I mean maybe kids had broken in or something. Maybe kids were in there drinking or doing drugs or filming a porn movie. Who knew? Maybe it was Carl with that hot little nurse who was making Eve so paranoid. Whoever it was would give me a legitimate excuse to call Eve and report it. Eve had called me again. She was convinced Carl was having an affair. To be honest, we were sort of always looking for an excuse to talk to each other. The idea of talking to Eve fueled my determination to see just who was in their condo and exactly what the hell was going on.

This is what friends are for, I told myself as I crept up to the building and positioned myself ever so carefully on the edge of the sliding glass door against the siding made in China that probably caused a rash on contact. I could make out the bluish light of a television screen. Peering in more closely I saw that an old movie was playing. Oh, for the love of Pete. Someone was watching *Love Story*, with those two morons who said love means never having to say you're sorry. Good grief! What bullshit is that? The first thing I say in the morning is I'm sorry!

"Good morning, sweetheart. I'm sorry."

"Good morning, sweetheart. You should be."

Then I say it about another hundred times more a day. Okay, maybe not. Maybe I should, because Eliza always nails me for every little infraction, but I'm not going to say I'm sorry every time I do something she doesn't like. That would make me wrong all the time, and I couldn't live with that. And it would be further confirmation that she's right all the time and I couldn't live with that either. Currently Eliza had too much time on her hands. She had nothing better to do than think up shit she wasn't happy about. Or adding things to her bucket list. Now she wanted to rent a sailboat and sail from island to island around Greece! And who had the time? Me? I was so busy I could hardly think straight. I just signed a contract to build another hundred homes! And her latest deal was that she wanted a YouTube channel so she could offer cooking videos. She wanted to teach the world how to make chicken fricassee! Was she kidding? I didn't even know what that was! Make videos? For who and why? And how much would that cost? Listen, between us? I thought she had arrived at that time in life when women feel old, but I was keeping my mouth shut on that one.

So, who was in Eve and Carl's condo? I thought, bringing myself back to the situation at hand. I peeked in through the glass door again. Whoa! Whoever was on the sofa was getting up! I jumped back, plastering myself against the building once more, inches away from being discovered. Wait a minute, I told myself. You're not the criminal here! The person with the lousy taste in film is the one in trouble! Not *me*. So I took a step forward and looked squarely through the door just as the person inside turned to face me wearing some terrible-looking flimsy bathrobe and a lopsided shower cap. She screamed bloody murder loud enough to wake the scores of dead pirates buried on every island in the Atlantic Ocean.

"Aieeeeeeeeee!"

It was Eve!

"Eve! It's me! Adam! It's okay!"

She screamed again anyway, I guess just to be sure I wasn't lying. Finally, she stepped back and took a deep breath. Then she came forward and opened the sliding glass door.

"Sweet baby Jesus! You scared the life out of me, Adam Stanley."

"Sorry."

"Just what the hell are you doing on my terrace in the dark staring through the door like a pervert?"

"I saw lights on and I wanted to be sure everything was okay with your property." I looked hard at her. She'd been crying. And she smelled like alcohol. "Um, are you okay?"

"Sure. I'm just fine. Fine and dandy. Would you like a glass of wine?" she said.

"Sure. Why not?"

She pulled off her shower cap, her blond hair tumbled down her shoulders like filaments of gold, and she stood aside to allow me to cross the threshold. God, she was sexy.

"I've already had three," she said. "I was just going to take a shower and go to bed."

"It's only seven o'clock," I said.

She looked at me as if to decide whether I thought three glasses of wine before seven o'clock was too many or did I think seven was too early to go to bed?

"Adam? Are you judging me?"

"Who, me? Hell no! Where's Carl?"

"That son of a bitch?"

"Yeah, that son of a bitch."

"He's, he's, he's . . ."

And then she burst into tears and started to weep. She literally fell into my arms crying like a baby.

"Oh, God. What's happened? Eve? Talk to me."

But now she was sobbing, great big convulsive sobs. Blubbering sobs. Ugly crying. I wasn't good with this kind of thing. I pulled her into me, into a solid embrace, rubbing her back to console her. Maybe Carl was dead. Or dying.

Finally, she said in a whisper, "I came here to end it, Adam. I can't take it anymore."

"End what? What are you talking about?" She didn't mean to end her *life*, did she?

"My marriage is over."

"What the hell are you saying?"

"Adam, I'm a terrible failure as a mother."

"Don't say that! Daphne is a lovely girl!"

"No, she's not. She's a lying slut! She got kicked out of school for sending lewd pictures of herself to one of her professors to get an A."

"Oh, come on now! That's not so terrible. All the kids do that these days." Did they? Who knew? It *was* terrible. Good grief.

"Yes, it is! It's really terrible. And I have never done anything except disappoint Cookie."

"Eve? Let's be honest. Who could please Cookie? She'd find fault with the pope himself! He'd come to dinner and bring baked ziti and she'd hate it! She'd hate the pope's baked ziti! She'd tell him it tasted like dog shit. Believe me! I've given this a lot of thought! Years, in fact."

No trace of a smile. I thought she'd see humor in the truth of that, but she didn't.

"But she's my mother! Shouldn't your own mother at least fake it that she's proud of you for *something*?"

"Not necessarily. Not if she's always unhappy. Cookie's not too happy with herself, now is she?"

"No. She's a total misery. She always has been. And Carl is definitely not in love with me anymore. He's sleeping with one of his nurses. I have proof. I finally have proof."

"Oh, who cares, Eve? I mean, really, who cares if he's screwing all of them?"

"What do you mean? He's my husband!"

"He cheats at golf, Eve. That's the lowest of the low."

"Really?"

"Yeah, but who cares? He has other redeeming qualities. Listen, can we go back to Cookie for a minute?"

"Sure, but why?"

"Because I'm gonna explain this whole thing to you. It's her jealousy that's at the bottom of everyone's unhappiness. Don't you know that?"

"I don't know what I know anymore."

I led her over to the couch and made her sit down. Then I took an empty goblet from the bar cart, poured myself a glass of wine, and took a long look at her. Even in this pitiful state, she was still the most beautiful woman I had ever known. I took several long sips. She took another drink from her glass.

"This started a long time ago, Eve, before you and I ever met. But when we did finally meet Cookie saw something in our relationship that she'd never have and she couldn't stand it."

"What?"

"Real love. Genuine, honest-to-God love."

"She wouldn't know what love looked like if it was standing right in front of her and bit her on the nose. She was unhappy during my entire childhood. She cried every single night. My father finally dumped her for someone else, and I never saw him again."

"No. Your father dumped her because living with her made him miserable. Guaranteed. No man goes through the hassle of a divorce if he's happy at home. I'm going to guess that alcohol probably brought on her depression. The fact that another woman was there in the wings is almost immaterial."

"So, you think that she destroyed us because of her wounded pride?" she said.

"Absolutely."

"But did she succeed?" Eve asked.

"I'd say not completely, right?"

"We are in each other's lives anyway," Eve said. "And I still love you."

"And I love you, Eve. I always have and I always will."

It was the most natural thing in the world to say. There. At last it was out in the open. I sat down on the sofa and pulled her over next to me. I put my left arm around her and she leaned into me the exact same way she used to so many decades ago. It would've been so easy to let that robe slip. I knew I was crossing a line of propriety, because I would never have done this if Eliza was in the room. Not in a million gazillion years. And this had nothing to do with Eliza. Eve was a whole other situation. Eliza was my wife. I loved them both. Just differently. But at last there was honesty between us, and that seemed to excuse me for stealing a moment. I mean, it's not like I had her legs in the air.

"Oh, Adam. I'm so exhausted. I'm so tired of Carl's lies."

I was still having a hard time getting my brain wrapped around the idea that Carl would cheat on Eve. It just didn't ring true. He might have given himself a few strokes on the golf course, but I'd always thought that was because he couldn't stand to lose. Not because he was a womanizing lowlife.

"Cookie probably pushed you up the aisle to marry Carl. Am I right?"

"He's a doctor. She thought he could give me a certain status. And I was pregnant."

"Please. That's a topic for discussion another time. I'm going to guess she didn't even care if you loved Carl. She only wanted you to not love me." I leaned forward, refilled my wineglass, and took another sip. Somehow, I was making the occasion about Eve and me instead of Eve and Carl. But the question of Cookie's motivations had bothered me for years. This was as good a time to ask as any. Eve then took the glass from me and drained it. I was impressed. "If you got married and had a baby, in her mind, you'd be taken care of forever. That's how women of her generation used to think. Your happiness was never part of the equation to her."

"Carl only married me because I was pregnant." Eve yawned and put her head in my lap.

"Well, I don't agree with that. He loves you, Eve. He does."

"Carl loves medicine. He loves being a doctor. He loves the adoration of his patients."

"Show me one that doesn't," I said. "But that still doesn't mean Carl doesn't love you. And I don't think he's screwing his nurse."

That's what I said, but what I was thinking was something entirely different. All things being equal? If I wasn't screwing Eve—and I'd had a lot of opportunities over the years to do it—then there was no way Carl was screwing his nurse. Thinking about having sex and actually doing it are two completely different categories.

We were quiet then for a while and I realized Eve was fast asleep. I should've jostled her and sent her to bed. I should've disengaged, substituted a pillow for my lap, and gone home. I did none of those things. I looked at her. She was absolutely angelic. I loved having her close to me so much that I put my head back on the sofa and went to sleep as well.

The next thing I knew it was morning and I was being yanked off the sofa and held by the front of my shirt, looking into the angry face of my good friend Carl. Yes, *that* son of a bitch had his fist drawn back and aimed at my jaw.

"Stop!" Eve screamed.

"Hey! Wait!" I managed.

"I can't believe that my good friend Adam is screwing my wife! You fucking asshole! I ought to rip you to pieces!"

"Stop!" Eve screamed. "Stop it right now!"

"Shut up, Eve." Carl looked at me with the face of a madman. "If I had a gun, I'd blow your fucking brains out!"

"Carl! Nothing happened! Adam didn't even touch me!"

"She's telling you the truth, Carl," I said. "Listen to her."

"I came here because I found all the sexy text messages from your trashy little nurse. I'm leaving you, Carl. You can have her!"

"What? You mean Shonda?"

The screaming and the accusations went on for a while. Meanwhile, Carl stood over me, my shirt twisted into his fist, which was approximately the size of a ham.

"I wouldn't touch that filthy little whore! I'll fire her this afternoon! She's nothing but a crazy gold-digging bitch desperate for another husband."

"*Swear* to me you're telling me the truth!" Eve shouted.

"I swear it on a stack of Bibles!" Carl shouted back. Then he looked at me and eased his grip on my shirt slightly. "You swear to God you're not screwing my wife?"

"I swear it on my mother's grave! I'm screwing *my* wife! Whenever she will let me, that is. Truth." But I could've had

Eve's clothes off in about two minutes, I thought. Boy, talk about a missed opportunity.

"Then just what the hell are you doing here on my sofa?" Carl asked.

"That's a legitimate question," I said, racking my brain for a plausible excuse.

Eve stepped up quickly on my behalf. "He was here telling me that you loved me and that there was no way you were being unfaithful to me. That's the truth, Carl."

"You were?" Carl said to me. "You swear?"

"I already told you nothing happened between us," I said, deciding a dollop of self-righteous indignation was appropriate. "You want to let go of my shirt now?"

He released me, and in the back of my mind I knew I had escaped some serious hurt that I probably—no, definitely—deserved.

"Adam, I came here looking for my wife. Suffice to say, I am not happy about what I found when I got here. Let's leave it at that for now," Carl said.

"We've been friends for a long time," I said. And if I were in his shoes, I'd be pissed too.

There was a knock on the sliding glass door and we all turned as if on cue to see who it was. There stood Eliza. She was not going to like this story.

The door slid open.

"I brought a picnic for us, Adam," she said with a furrowed brow. "I drove back late last night from Duke because I wanted to surprise you. But it looks like you all started the party without me. What exactly am I interrupting?"

CHAPTER 11

eliza's fury

There was no answer from any of them. I turned around with all the dignity I could muster and walked out, leaving them all standing there startled and embarrassed. My mind was spinning. I didn't know what to do and I didn't know what to say and I didn't know what to believe. What had I walked in on? How was Adam going to explain this? What *did* happen? I'd never forget the look on Eve's face, that was for sure. She looked terrified to see me. But her fright seemed extreme if nothing had really happened between her and Adam. Maybe nothing happened. Maybe something did. But she looked as guilty as hell, and so did Adam. And she wasn't wearing any underwear under her robe. There was no panty line or bra strap. I was going to get to the bottom of this, and it wasn't going to be comfortable for anyone.

Adam followed me back to our condo almost immediately. I was standing in the middle of the living room, facing him, when he came in.

"Eliza," he said, "we have to talk."

"Really?" I was fuming with anger and devastated simultaneously.

"I know it looked bad back there, but it was nothing."

"Really? Because, you know, Carl didn't look too happy either."

"Just listen to me. I can explain everything."

"Go right ahead. Explain."

"Okay, so I got here last night after I went to Lowe's and picked up some drawer pulls. I remember I popped open a beer and went outside to look at the sunset. And you know this week has been extremely busy for me. I was either in my office at home or on a job site fourteen hours every single day."

"Maybe you were. Maybe you weren't." So, what if he was? It wasn't like he punched a clock. He worked for himself!

"Come on! Bear with me here for a few minutes. So, while I was outside I noticed that lights were on in Eve and Carl's place. I wondered who could be there this time of year, so I went over to see. You know, maybe kids broke in and were drinking all the booze or something."

"Sure." I knew I sounded sarcastic and I didn't care.

"Well, it wasn't kids. Eve was in there watching *Love Story*, of all the horrible movies ever made in the history of Hollywood."

"So?" I thought, Now you're a movie critic?

I noticed tiny beads of perspiration on Adam's forehead and top lip. Good. Sweat, you son of a bitch.

"Well, I almost gave her a heart attack. She started

screaming like I was a burglar or something. And that is the funny part."

"Uh-huh. So far this is a riot. Am I to believe she was surprised to see you?"

"Yes. She was surprised to see me. That's why she was screaming."

"Okay, so?" I knew better. Adam knew Eve was coming because she had probably called him to tell him so. We'd been through this before.

"Well, it turns out she was hysterically crying because she really believed Carl was carrying on with his nurse. She found a bunch of text messages on his phone that must've been pretty incriminating. She had left him and didn't know where to go, so she came here. To think. I mean, it's not like she was going to go to Cookie and ask for her old bedroom back, right?"

"Why should I care where she goes?" Although that sort of made sense to me. "What else?"

"So, she let me in and we drank a bottle of wine while she cried her eyes out. I just did what any friend would do. I just listened to her. And I told her I didn't believe Carl was fooling around with his nurse. Which, as it turns out, he wasn't. You missed that part."

"That's all?"

"That about wraps it up," he said.

"You wouldn't lie to me, would you, Adam?"

"God, no."

"You're not leaving anything out?"

"I don't think so," he said.

"Then you want to explain to me why our bed hasn't been slept in?"

I watched the color drain from his face. Faint, you bastard, I thought. See if I care.

"Shit," he said. "I was getting to that part."

"Like hell you were. I don't believe you for a minute, Adam Stanley."

"I fell asleep on their sofa." He said in a mousy little voice that kids use on their teacher when they don't have their homework.

"You did *what*?"

"I know. The next thing I knew it was morning and Carl was threatening to kill me, looming over me like a linebacker from the NFL with the front of my shirt all twisted into a knot. Not a nice way to start your day, lemme tell you."

He was trying to be funny in an effort to lower my thermostat. I was having none of it.

"So, let me understand this. You came here, intending to do some work on the house, which I seem to remember you told me you were going to do. You went outside and saw lights on at their place. You went over to see what was up and after you scared Eve to death, you drank a bottle of wine with her and slept on her couch with her naked under a silk bathrobe. Slept there all night long and nothing happened. And you were surprised she was there in the first place. Oh, and she was crying over Carl. As usual."

"That's the whole story. I'm sorry. I know it looks very bad."

He tried to take me in his arms and I jerked free of him and put my hands on my hips.

"You must really think I'm a total and complete idiot, Adam."

"I think no such thing," he said. "But I am telling you the truth."

"And you fell asleep because you had such a long hard week you couldn't hold yourself together to get off the couch and walk home, which is twenty-five feet away? It never entered your mind?"

"I actually don't remember falling asleep, Eliza. True story."

"I don't believe that for one minute. How long have we been married?"

"Forever," he said.

"Sadly, I've seen you drunk as a dog, but you always make it to bed. Always."

"That's true. I'm not quite sure how it happened. But I'm sorry, Eliza. I really am."

"I send you here to fix the dripping faucets and this is what you do?"

"I did go to Lowe's! Look! There are the bags of stuff!"

I looked over at the table and indeed there were bags from Lowe's. They proved nothing to me except that he had gone shopping as promised, maybe just to have an alibi.

"How could you, Adam? For all these years, the first thing I did every morning until I went to bed at night, was to put you and our boys first. I trusted you with my life! I gave you children. I took care of all of you, cooking and cleaning and listening to you go on and on about anything you wanted to talk about and birthdays and holidays and this is what you do? This is what you do to me?"

"It's really just an unbelievable coincidence that she was here at all and that it played out this way."

"Adam. Do you think I have lost my memory?"

"I know, I know. I remember that summer too, when I knew Eve and Carl were coming and you didn't. I knew you'd bring that up."

"This changes things, Adam. I feel betrayed and hurt. I don't like all this. I'm not this kind of person, the one who just looks away or gets over it."

"So, what do you want me to say? I told you the complete truth and I said I was sorry and I am. Look, Eliza, I love *you*. You know I do. What else can I say?"

"I don't think it matters what you say. You can explain it all away until the cows come home, but the fact is you spent the night with Eve and it isn't right."

"It was an accident."

"Accident my big fat behind. You sound like your sons."

"It was. It was an accident. I swear."

"You forget something, Adam. I know you. And I know you had the strength to get off that sofa and leave. You didn't because you didn't want to."

He started to speak and I cut him off.

"Save it, Adam. I know you down to your DNA. Don't forget that."

I went into the kitchen, took the Italian submarine sandwiches I'd brought for a surprise picnic out of the refrigerator, and put them back in the shopping bag with the homemade oatmeal raisin cookies. I made those cookies for him because I knew he especially loved them. But at this point I wasn't about to reward him with food. Then I took the cookies back out and left them on the kitchen counter, on top of the box of Entenmann's. Next I changed my mind and dropped the sandwiches on the counter too. I didn't want to eat them then and I wouldn't want them later. I had no appetite. I felt sick inside.

I went back to the living room, where he stood just as I had left him, and put on my coat.

"Where are you going?"

"I'm going home. I suppose you don't know how that coffee cake got in there either?"

"Eliza. Please."

"Nope. I've been watching you play games with Eve for too many years, Adam, and I'm all done. I love you too. But right now, I have a lot to consider."

I knew that Adam was shaken, but I had to get away from him. I picked up my overnight bag and my purse, left the condo, and threw them in the back of my car. I needed to get some clarity, put things in perspective. What had really happened?

I started the engine, turned around to back out of my parking space, and saw Carl walking toward me, waving. I rolled down my window.

"So what do you think, Eliza? What pile of crap excuse did Adam give you?"

I turned the car off and got out. I wanted to know what Carl thought too.

"Let's take a walk," I said. I felt light-headed. It was probably from the shock. It was probably also a really good idea to calm down before I drove a car anywhere.

"Sure," he said. "Are you okay? You look pale."

"I'm okay. But this was all quite a surprise."

"I hate surprises," Carl said.

"Me too."

We walked around the complex to the ocean side and took a seat at one of the tables.

The chairs were made of some heavy composite metal, and in the winter's morning air they were freezing cold to the touch. I sat and warmed my hands under my arms. I had left my gloves in the car. Carl had no jacket, only a lightweight sweater. I had never seen Carl so upset, and I was sure it was the same for Eve. We began to talk, and Eve's story matched up with Adam's. Apparently, Carl had a nurse who was in hot pursuit of his mind, body, and spirit. I had no idea whether that was actually so. I just knew what Adam had told me, which was that Eve was suspicious that there was someone else. Maybe he had said it was a nurse. I couldn't remember.

"So basically, Adam told me the same story."

"What do you think?" Carl said.

"I think he should have had the presence of mind to get his behind off your sofa and go home to his own bed. It's bad enough that they're here together without us. Given the situation, it's hard to believe nothing happened."

"I agree. You're giving me a lot to think about."

"Carl? Have you ever been so wasted you couldn't get up and walk home?"

"Never."

"Adam either. He stayed because he wanted to. Whether or not they had sex almost doesn't matter."

"And why didn't she go put some clothes on before they started drinking a bottle of wine?"

"Good question. I'm going to go with because she didn't want to."

"Jesus. I mean, I wonder if this was the only time this has ever happened. Eve's been coming to Charleston more and more often to check on Cookie. At least that's why she says she's coming. What do I know?"

"How is Cookie?"

"As crazy as every bat in hell."

"So, she's the same?"

"Yeah. Bat shit crazy."

"What are you going to do?" I asked.

"About what specifically?"

"Your nurse, for starters."

"Fire her immediately. You wouldn't believe how aggressive this woman is. There's a growing trend among women whose ovaries are a time bomb. They think it's easier to pick off an old dude who's perhaps weary of his marriage than it is to find someone nearer to their own age."

"You're not an old dude. But she must be out of her mind to think she could have you just because she wants you. What kind of person makes advances to a married man?"

"Amoral ones. I don't expect you to understand this and I don't quite get it myself, but out there in the great big world there is a perception that 'MD' stands for 'mucho dinero.'"

"It doesn't?"

"No. Well, I'm not rolling in it, anyway. I mean, I do fine, but I'm not rich. And there are some young nurses—as there are young women in any profession—who think they want to be a nurse or a nurse practitioner so they can snag a rich doctor."

I looked at Carl and I could see the pain in his beautiful eyes. He was so handsome. It was one thing that some little twit was pursuing him but quite another to find his wife on the couch curled up with his friend, snoozing like babies. He was going to fire the twit, but what was he going to do about his marriage?

"So. What do you think, Carl? How are you feeling about all this—you and Eve, I mean."

"I don't know, Eliza. I don't know."

"Me either."

"This definitely changes things."

"It sure does. It definitely puts a strain on things. You know? I just feel like I've been giving more than I've been taking for a long time. I gave up almost every dream I ever had for myself to try and become the best wife and mother I could be."

"Aw, come on. You make one helluva pot of gumbo," he said and smiled at me. "Best in the world."

"Thanks," I said and looked out over the water. "You're sweet."

"And you've got great boys."

"Thanks."

I began to cry. Quietly. I couldn't help it. I was so hurt and disappointed in Adam and in Eve. And I was angry. Really angry. How could Adam be so stupid?

Carl put his arm around my shoulder and gave me a squeeze. I sniffed and wiped my eyes with my sleeve, which was gross, but there were no other options.

"What dreams did you give up?" Carl said.

"Oh, golly. Dreams. Me and my dreams are pretty hopeless at this point."

"We are never without hope. Talk to me, Eliza. Tell me what else is on your heart."

I was quiet then. I wanted to tell him about my cookbook and about Greece and why I was so passionate about it. But those passions had been completely squelched every time they were mentioned. Maybe there had been other things at other times. I couldn't remember in that moment when I'd just seen my whole world blown to bits.

"My mother died when I was very young."

"I think I knew that."

"Yes. She was from Greece. Corfu, actually."

"It's in the Ionian Sea, isn't it?"

"Yes. Anyway, when I was really little we used to take a family vacation there almost every year. It was idyllic. I mean, there was an innocence about the village where my grandmother lived that's unlike anything I've ever encountered here. Or maybe wholesomeness is a better way to describe it. Dogs and chickens wandering around. When we arrived, it seemed like every single person in Dassia came to my grandmother's house to see the Americans. And they all brought my brother and me a little gift to welcome us."

"That's awfully nice."

"Yes. It was. And my grandmother! She couldn't get enough of us! She absolutely beamed with happiness to have us there. We had these elaborate meals that she spent all day preparing and then we'd set up tables in her courtyard with lanterns strung between the branches. These dinners went on forever. All the neighbors came and went. It seemed like meals started with lunch and lasted until midnight."

"Too bad life's not really like that anymore. Who has the time?"

"Well, family was everything to my grandmother."

"Like it is for you."

"Yes."

"And let me guess, she's why you love to cook so much."

"Probably. And it's also the place where I felt the most loved in my entire life."

"You know Adam loves you."

"I know. But not enough to get off the couch." I looked at Carl and he stared at me. I could almost hear him thinking, Yeah, and Eve loves me, but not enough to put her clothes on. "I've always dreamed of going back to Greece to see if there are still relatives and what happened to my grandmother's old house. Maybe see some skinny dogs walking around."

"I've never been to Greece. Always wanted to, but somehow it just never worked out."

"Well, this might be a good time for me to go. I think my brother said that one of our cousins has a B and B. We'll see. Mr. Stanley can have some time to stew and so can I."

"Maybe Eve needs a little time out herself," he said.

"That's your call. Hey, isn't it weird that we both came here this morning? What a coincidence." There are no coincidences, I reminded myself.

"Yes. I drove almost all night. I couldn't sleep. Something told me I'd find her here."

"Well, the four of us have been coming here for how many years?"

"Too many to count."

"It's where I always found peace. I feel like my church has been desecrated."

Carl looked at me then as he processed what I'd said. And then his face changed to one of worry and wonder.

"Do you think they're still in love with each other?" he said.

I didn't know how to answer him. I'd questioned it myself. But I thought then about the four of us and what we meant to each other. We had shared every single milestone of our lives with each other for decades. And it wasn't like we didn't have other friends, because we did. But no other foursome was as satisfying or as interesting to each of us.

Over the years, I'd often thought that God forbid something happened to Adam or one of the boys, Carl would be the first person I'd call. It didn't matter that he lived hours away. Heaven knows, he had saved the life of my son. Our relationships with each other went beyond the usual expectations of normal friendship, and they always had. The trust and reliance was built on years of care. There could never be another foursome that would supersede what we shared. No,

Eve, Carl, Adam, and I were solidly and forever entrenched deeply in each other's hearts.

"Carl? I think that to some extent we're all in love with each other."

"It's true."

"And I think it's been like that from the get-go. If Adam's affection for Eve has crossed a line, or vice versa, I couldn't say. But the whole business doesn't seem right."

"It sure doesn't."

"This morning I woke up a happy housewife thinking I'd surprise my husband with a lovely lunch and a nice bottle of Chianti. Now I'm wondering what to do about the rest of my life."

I sat there searching Carl's face for answers he couldn't possibly have for me. Or for himself.

"Eliza. Nothing is really changed, and yet I feel like I got blindsided too. I need to think about this. Meanwhile, I think it's time for me to start driving back to Raleigh. I've got some mighty sick children depending on me. Stay in touch with me, okay?"

"Okay. Let's go." We began walking back to our cars and I glanced at our windows. There was no sign of Adam. And when I looked over at Carl and Eve's place, it looked dark. Metaphorically? The life force had left the buildings.

Carl and I exchanged a familial hug, one of the somber, reassuring ilk. Then we got into our cars, me into my new white Benz SUV and Carl into his Lexus sedan, and left Wild Dunes and our spouses behind.

I drove home in something of a stupor, reliving the entire episode mile by mile. Had Carl and I overreacted? No. Did Adam still love me? I knew that he did. But how could I forgive this?

I got home and pulled my car into the garage. I went inside through the door to the kitchen, and suddenly my house that I loved so much seemed like a hall of gloom. It had a personality, to be sure, but gloom had never been a part of it. But crazy as it may sound, it was as though the house knew what had happened.

I don't know why, but I began to walk from room to room looking at all the objects and photographs Adam and I had amassed over the years. There were wonderful things, sentimental things, gifts from and to one of us from the other that reminded me of a special birthday or anniversary or Christmas. Lovely ceramics, engraved picture frames, bookends made of polished brass. There were lamps that looked Asian, embroidered hand towels with our monogram in the powder room in the hall near the front door. A brass umbrella stand that had belonged to Adam's grandfather. Suddenly it was just a bunch of stuff. If the house didn't have our love, it didn't have its soul. It had been snatched away by longing and deceit.

Some time passed with me basically standing in my kitchen looking out into the yard through the window over my sink, wondering if Adam was coming home right away or if he was staying with Eve or just why the hell hadn't he called me? I checked my phone. No calls. No texts. Shouldn't Eve have called to say something like "Oh God, I'm so sorry?" Um, I think so. How long had we all been friends? It seemed like forever.

I loved Carl with more affection than I had ever shown my own brother. My brother and I didn't see each other much because of the distance between us, and we both knew Adam didn't really care much for him and Tasha. Carl had almost filled his shoes. The more I thought about that I wondered, since my brother practiced family law, if I should run this story by him for a second opinion. JJ could offer a different perspective, because I suspected he had seen it all. And it was a good excuse to connect. I dialed his cell and he answered right away.

"Hey! You okay?" he said.

"I've been better," I said.

There was a pause then, and the fact that I didn't just spill my guts told him it wasn't a call about our boys. Intuitively, he knew it was about Adam. My brother had a squirrelly personality, but he wasn't stupid.

"Adam's a challenge for me and you know it. Tell me what happened," he said.

"It's complicated," I said.

"It's always complicated," he said. "But you've never come to me for advice before, so I'm all ears."

So I told him the story and he listened. When it seemed that I had recounted enough of the worst episode that ever occurred between Adam and me and I thought he could see everything from my perspective, I got quiet and he cleared his throat.

"People are so fucking stupid, men in particular," he said. "But I gotta say, Eve sounds like a real piece of work."

"She is. This whole thing is a little bit pathetic," I said. "How could I not have known how deeply he felt about her?"

"The wife is always the last to know," he said. "But before you tear up your whole life over this, let's think it through."

"That's why I called. I mean, in your experience, once something like this happens, how impossible is it to restore the marriage?"

"Well, I've seen couples patch things up and go on with their lives. But Eliza? You're not going to like this, but it all depends on your ability to forgive."

"Wait a minute. He commits the sin but I have to forgive?"

"Yes. That's how it works. Do you think they actually had sex, or maybe they were having an affair the whole time behind your back?"

"To be honest? I don't know. I still can't believe what my eyes saw. And I just don't think of Adam as that calculating and dishonest. Sneaking around has never been his style. I mean, he can't keep a secret for ten minutes."

"Well, it sounds like he did this because he thought he wouldn't get caught. And if he swears they didn't have sex, it leaves him a tiny little bit of moral ground."

"Like the smallest ant hill on this earth."

"I'll tell you what I don't like, besides the obvious."

"Tell me, JJ."

"I don't like that you're not getting all the things you

want out of life. None of us are getting any younger. You and Adam have plenty of money and your kids are in college. There's no reason why you shouldn't go to Greece if that's what you want to do."

"Well, Adam says it would be super expensive and that he's too busy. He is awfully busy these days."

"Hold on, sister. What if it's not expensive, and since when do you need him to go with you? Seems to me that right now might be an opportune time. You know? Let him worry a little bit? It won't kill him."

"Didn't you tell me we had a cousin with a B and B on Corfu?"

"Yeah, Kiki, Aunt Anna's daughter. Kiki's been sending Dad a Christmas card for years and I wrote her back telling her that Dad had passed. In fact, I think she owns one and manages four or five others. You want her contact information?"

"Yes, please. Does she speak English?"

"Jesus, Eliza. Practically the entire continent of Europe speaks English. She went to UCLA, don't you remember? She's as fluent as you and I are."

Adam had assured me for years that no one in Greece spoke English except for a few wealthy people and that from the way I described my mother's family, it didn't sound to him like they were particularly educated or rich people. Therefore, they couldn't possibly speak English. Suddenly I realized that there was a control problem here. Adam calling the shots was more important to him than me fulfilling a dream, and right then and there I knew that if Adam and I ever got over this, things would be very different between us.

"I am so happy to hear that, you couldn't possibly know."

"You have a pencil?"

"I'm ready," I said and took all the contact information for my cousin Kiki. "Thanks, JJ."

"Happy to help. I think you and Adam can work past this if you want to. Like I said, it's all up to you."

"Right. Thanks. I mean it."

"Let me know how things pan out."

I promised him that I would, and we hung up. The first thing I did was check my passport to be sure it wasn't expired. It was not. The only time I'd used it was for a short trip to Jamaica. I sat down on the edge of my desk chair and looked around the kitchen again. I still felt nauseated and light-headed. I ignored that and decided to go online and look for a cheap ticket. But first I sent Kiki an e-mail. What was the time difference? I thought it might be seven or eight hours. It was two in the afternoon and probably nine there. She might be having her evening meal.

> Kiki, I know you won't remember me but I'm your cousin . . .

To my surprise, she responded in minutes.

> Come, come! Come for a visit and stay as long as you like! I can give you your own house! Please . . .

Wow, I thought. Just wow.

I wrote back,

> I'm on my way!

An hour and a half later I had booked a flight, I had packed a bag, and I was in my car on the way to the airport. I called both boys. I said it was an impromptu decision. I told them about Kiki and that I'd be staying with family. They both knew this was something I had wanted to do for a long time, and they sounded genuinely happy that I was going. I wasn't sure which day I'd be back, but we'd be in touch through e-mail.

I'd left Adam a note on the kitchen table.

> *I'm going to visit my family in Corfu. For once, I'm putting myself first.*
>
> *I'll let you know when I'm coming back.*

Not *Oh God I love you but I'm taking my broken heart to Greece* or *Adam! How could you? I'm devastated!*

Oddly, I wasn't brokenhearted or devastated. I just felt very disappointed. I had depended on Adam's faithfulness for the better part of my life and now I didn't know if I ever could again. I remembered reading a line by Emily Dickinson about the heart wanting what it wanted. Was that how Adam felt? Had this friendship with Eve and Carl been a sham so that Adam and Eve could see each other every so often?

I checked my phone again. Nothing from Adam. Maybe he's dead in a ditch, I thought. The thought of it made me smile. This fucking till-death-do-us-part thing could have already happened for all I knew. Nah, the police would've tried to contact me. He was probably in the kitchen of the condo changing the drawer pulls and trying to figure out a way to blame me for snooping on him.

As I began to drive I had the thought that it would be a good idea to leave my car with Ted and Clarabeth. Why should I pay for parking for more than a week if I decided to stay longer?

I dialed Ted's cell and he answered.

"Ted? I need a small favor . . ."

I gave him part of the truth and left out the majority of the details.

"I'll drive you to the airport," Ted said. "It's no problem."

I went directly to Clarabeth's home on the Ashley River and parked under a sprawling live oak tree in front of the house. I got out and saw Ted, Clarabeth, and Cookie standing on the front porch. It was getting chilly, as it did in the afternoons in winter. I rubbed my arms and looked up to see that their faces were covered in concern.

"No reason to be alarmed," I said. "It's kind of spur of the moment, I know. It must seem funny but believe me, everything's okay."

I gave everyone a little hug and a pat on the back, which was how we all greeted each other.

"You got time for a cup of coffee?" Clarabeth said.

I looked at my wristwatch. I still had three hours before my flight to New York.

"Sure," I said, trying to sound as nonchalant as possible.

We all went inside the house together and I noticed that Cookie had her hand on Ted's lower back, a gesture that seemed too possessive.

I had the thought then that Clarabeth had sure seen better days. She looked decrepit. Cookie, however, was dressed for tea with the First Lady of the United States, should she drop by, and already circling the carcass before it gave up its ghost. And as usual, Ted was oblivious to Cookie's attention, or perhaps he just decided to take the stance that Cookie couldn't possibly be serious. In any case, Cookie and I sat down at Clarabeth's kitchen table while she opened a tin of shortbread and Ted took out cups and saucers. He made each of us a cup of coffee from a rather fantastic looking cappuccino machine. The thing was huge and a vision of chrome and knobs and gauges. I'd never seen one like it in someone's home. Starbucks? Maybe. Clarabeth's kitchen? It was a very high-end and luxurious accessory.

"Wow!" I said. "When did you get that?"

"I surprised him with it just this week!" Clarabeth said. "You know how he loves a good cup of coffee, and we've been using my old Mr. Coffee machine for a thousand years, so I saw this in a catalog and . . ."

"I'm a barista now," Ted said. "Would you like your milk frothed?"

"Why not?" I said. "Thanks."

"So where are you going?" Cookie asked.

"Greece," I said.

"That's wonderful! Is Adam going too?" Clarabeth asked.

"No. He has to work," I said.

"I didn't know you were planning a trip," Ted said.

"It came up sort of suddenly," I said.

"You and Adam had a fight?" Cookie said.

It was hard to get anything past Sober Cookie. She had feline instincts.

"I don't know if I'd call it that," I said. I felt my neck get hot.

"Must've been pretty gargantuan to prompt a trip all the way to Greece," Cookie said.

I felt tears welling up and knew that within a matter of seconds they'd be sliding down my face. She saw it too and pounced.

"Listen, Eliza, between Clarabeth, Ted, and me, we've got the better part of two hundred years of experience, and I've had more men in my bed than I can count or remember. You can tell us anything."

The story and the tears came tumbling out.

"Oh, honey," Clarabeth said.

"I can't believe my son would do something so terrible," Ted said. "I mean, I believe you, but I seriously doubt he would actually be unfaithful. I'd stake my last dollar on that."

Cookie looked at Ted and Clarabeth and then she looked at me.

"Look, I don't want to burst your bubble, Eliza, but here's the truth. When Adam and Eve were just out of high school, I caught them screwing their brains out in my house downtown. I threw him out of the house and told him to get lost or I'd call the authorities. When y'all met up with Eve and Carl at Wild Dunes I doubt that there'd been a word between them since then. But if you want my opinion? I wouldn't trust my daughter as far as I could throw her. Adam grew up to be a nice man. But my daughter? She's never happy."

I was stunned. I looked at Ted and said, "We'd better get going or I'll miss my flight."

CHAPTER 12

adam

Our condos had the same floor plans but hers was absent any crown molding or shiplap. And our fireplace was bigger. Still, they rented for the same money. As soon as Carl and Eliza's cars were gone I walked back over to Eve's. I rang the doorbell and stood there waiting for what seemed to be a long time. She finally opened the door. Her hair was in a towel and she was wearing that same silk robe.

"Sorry! I was in the shower. Oh, Adam, I feel so terrible," she said. "Come in. It's cold."

She had been crying and was holding a fistful of tissues.

"Well, you shouldn't. You didn't do anything wrong."

"Carl said I should've had clothes on. He's furious with me."

"He'll get over it. Eliza's not too thrilled with me either. But she'll come around, she always does." Truth? I didn't know how fast Eliza would calm down. I couldn't remember her ever being so upset.

"You want coffee? Did you eat anything for breakfast?"

"Actually, no. Coffee might be good, not that I need the caffeine today. Carl gave me a jolt that should last for a few days, at the least."

"Oh God, Adam, I've never seen Carl like that. I thought he was going to kill you!" She took the towel off her hair, which was wet. "Give me a few minutes. I'll be right back."

"Where are you going?"

"To comb out my hair and throw on some clothes in case Carl comes bursting in here again."

I hated that she was getting dressed. I loved seeing her this way.

She ran up the steps to her bedroom and I called after her.

"He's not coming back. Guaranteed he's on his way home to Raleigh."

"Maybe! Who knows?"

A few minutes later, I turned to see her coming down the steps barefooted in tight jeans and a tight long-sleeved turtleneck. Eve could put on rags and still look gorgeous. She went to the kitchen and I followed her. She poured me a mug of coffee.

"Splash of half and half, right?" she asked.

"I love that you remember that," I said.

"I love you," she said.

"I love you too, but let's face the facts. We're in trouble because of it."

"Want to split an omelet?"

"Sure."

I'd never seen Eve prepare anything more complicated than sandwiches and I wondered how her food was. She cracked three eggs into a bowl and added water. I'd never seen Eliza add water to eggs. Eliza *always* used milk.

"Want me to set the table?" I asked. "Make myself useful?"

"Sure. Leave me the plates."

"So, what do you propose we do about our spouses?" I said.

"Pray that they get over it and never mention it again?"

I took some flatware from the drawer and two paper napkins from the holder and put them on the table that was just outside the kitchen. I saw her spray the frying pan with cooking spray and thought, Oh boy, this is going to taste awful. Eliza always used a pat of butter to cook eggs, not some rank oil—and I knew it was rank because I could smell it as soon as it hit the heat of the pan. But Eve didn't seem bothered in the least by it, so I didn't say anything. She put the eggs in the pan and it sizzled again. The pan was too hot. Even I knew that.

"That would be nice, but I can tell you that Eliza is probably going to spank me for this the whole way into eternity."

"Carl thinks we had sex."

"I'm sure Eliza does too. But if we didn't last night, we never will."

"I'll say."

She attempted to flip the omelet and it broke. The bottom of it was brown with crust. How I was going to eat this abomination was anybody's guess.

"I think so too," I said.

"But if we're going to get blamed for it we might as well do it," she said, scooping the poor eggs onto plates. "Let's eat." She smiled and wiggled her eyebrows.

"You're kidding, aren't you?" I said, sitting down.

"Am I?"

"Eve Church Landers! Are you suggesting that we have a trashy affair or just a onetime trashy screw?"

She giggled and took a bite of the eggs.

"Who knows? Maybe both. Oh, God! This is delicious, isn't it?"

I took a bite and I swear to everything that's holy, I thought I was going to vomit. I tried to swallow without tasting them but the metallic oil was so overwhelming that my gag reflex kicked in and threw them out of my mouth. Thankfully I caught the whole unholy mess in my napkin.

"So, you don't like my eggs, huh?"

"It's just that I'm feeling a little hungover. Maybe I'll take some toast?"

"Sure! There's bread in the freezer."

"Oh? Do you want me to make it?" I said. I never made toast, except when the kids were little. Eliza did that for me.

"No, no! I'll do it! I've been wanting to make toast for you since the seventies!"

She practically hopped up from her chair and disappeared into the kitchen. I sipped my coffee, listened to Eve banging things around, and thought about Eliza. If she or Carl could see us sitting here having breakfast together they'd call lawyers. I really shouldn't be here, I thought. This is bad. Adding insult to injury. I'll just eat the toast and go, I told myself. Yes, that's what I would do. I would excuse myself as gracefully as I could.

She returned to the table with a plate of toast. It looked reasonable. I took a bite. The bread was still frozen in the center.

"So?"

I swallowed it anyway and said, "What?"

"About us?"

"Eve, I'm going to love you until the day I die. But you know me. I'm a coward."

We stared at each other and then we started to laugh.

"So am I!" she said. "Thank God! Otherwise I'd be dragging guilt around like Marley's chains!"

"But if, God forbid, something happened to Eliza and Carl I'd call you right away."

"Not funny, Adam."

"Sorry. I'm just saying that now is probably not the ideal time for us, unless of course they left here and have already decided to throw us out and divorce us."

"I really should probably call Eliza, but I feel like it would be admitting that something happened between us. Don't you agree?"

"Eliza has that Mediterranean temper that's so hot you could grill a rack of lamb with it. I'd give her a couple of days if I were you."

"I just hate being punished for something I didn't do," she said.

I looked at her again. God, what I would give to lie down next to her. But it wasn't to be. Not that day and maybe never.

"Eve, there's not a day that's gone by that I don't think of you."

"Me too."

"I knew the moment you came over that first night with Carl that I was still in love with you. I dream about you. I fantasize about you and a part of me longs for you like an addict."

"You know I feel the same way about you."

"I know. But like you, I've got a family and a spouse who has given me everything she has to give. Like Carl."

"It's true. Sometimes Carl is so sweet to me that I feel ashamed of the things I think about you."

"Well, I think for the foreseeable future we're going to have to put the elephant back in the attic," I said, not knowing how else to describe it.

"Elephant in the attic? Is that what we've got going on here?" She laughed and I laughed with her. "That's about the dumbest thing I've ever heard."

"I guess it is," I said.

At least there was solidarity between us. At least we were finally completely honest with each other.

"I should have fought for us back when we were kids. I've always regretted that," I said.

"I should have told Cookie she couldn't tell me what to do. I was too afraid of her," Eve said. "I always hoped I'd see you again. Somehow."

"Who knew we'd both be married when we did?" I said.

I thought about what we'd just said to each other. There was no point in reliving the past. It was over. I stood up from the table and said, "Okay, so I came here to do some repairs. I'm going to do them and then I'm going home. If she asks me what happened again, I'm going to reassure her. I'm going to take her out to any restaurant she wants to go to and for the next six months I'm going to watch chick flicks without complaining."

"Eliza's a good woman," she said. And she smiled that million-dollar smile that melted my heart every single time.

"And Carl is a great guy. Listen, Eve. Go home. Go home and tell him you love him."

"What if he won't listen to me?"

I walked to the front door and opened it.

"Keep telling him until he does."

We blew each other a kiss and I closed the door behind me.

By the time I finished everything I had to do and got in my Expedition, Eve's car was gone. She had a long drive ahead of her. As I moved along on Highway 17 I wondered if Eliza had a premonition that Eve might have been at Wild Dunes. Had she come there to catch me in the sack with Eve? Didn't she trust me? There was no reason that she shouldn't. None at all. And had Carl come for the same reason? Were they spying on us? It kind of pissed me off to think about it. I didn't deserve that. I could've had all the sex I wanted to with Eve and I hadn't. God knows she was certainly willing. And I was no saint. I knew that. But I'd always thought that stepping out on the wife was asking for trouble. First of all, I'd get caught. I just had that kind of luck. I mean, look what happened when I fell asleep on the wrong sofa. I got my ass handed to me, that's what. And second, I didn't want to hurt Eliza. Maybe she wasn't the beauty she used to be, but neither was I. Although Eve was probably better looking now than she was when she was a teenager. And Carl was distinguished looking, still very *GQ* handsome. There was no justice in the world. I looked in the rearview mirror. I was getting very jowly.

Well, I fucking hate the hell out of that, I thought.

Traffic on the Ravenel Bridge was murder. Well, it was five o'clock on a Saturday night. People were probably going downtown to have supper. I realized then that I hadn't heard from Eliza all day. And I hadn't called her either. Why should I? To apologize for what? Falling asleep?

Maybe I would give her a piece of my mind when I got home. I'd been a faithful husband for over twenty years and I didn't deserve this kind of suspicion. I really didn't. Maybe I'd entertained the idea of sex with Eve a couple of hundred thousand times, but I'd never acted on it, even when it was right there in front of my face. I mean, there was a big difference between thinking about sex and actually having sex. No, I was a good husband and I deserved better treatment than I was getting.

And, excuse me, but it was Carl who was banging his nurse. He could say what he wanted to Eve, but I saw the look on his face. He had definitely cheated on Eve. I'd bet my life on it. Okay, not my actual real life, but something big, like maybe some money, like a couple of hundred dollars. Or maybe he wasn't. But he was as red-blooded as I was, and real men enjoy flirtation from young pretty girls. I'd been in those shoes before with a secretary my dad hired one summer when I was in high school. Blow jobs weren't really sex anyway. Ask Bill Clinton. Yeah, that was a hot summer. What the hell was her name? Karen. She was a cute little thing with hair dyed jet black, big old floppy boobs, and fat marshmallows for lips. She thought she was playing hard to get, but I can attest to the fact that she spent a lot of time on her knees—and not in prayer. Then one afternoon Dad caught her going down like a German submarine on one of our roofers and fired her. Hell, he should've fired the roofer! I laughed remembering the whole situation. It was just an inch shy of a scandal, but nothing came of it. That was a good thing. No, I'd maybe say my dalliance with Karen was an indiscretion, but it wasn't sex and it sure as hell wasn't an affair.

The truth was that I could've taken Eve away from Carl any time I wanted to through all the years we'd been vacationing with them. I didn't want to. But what would it have been like if I had? It would've killed Eliza. But then Carl sort of had an eye for my girl and always had. Maybe we would've divorced and remarried each other. Boy, that would be a story no one would believe in their wildest dreams. But stranger things had happened in this world.

Life with Eve. What would that look like? Well, the food would be terrible. Let's start there. The woman couldn't even make toast! Pitiful. At least Eliza could cook. Jesus. Gorgeous, great in the sack as I recall. So was Eliza. But Eve shouldn't be allowed in a kitchen. I could've died from that omelet.

Traffic was moving along and I was almost home. I had

the thought that maybe I should stop at the grocery store and pick up a bunch of flowers for Eliza. She loved flowers of all kinds. Her azaleas and camellia bushes were simply astounding. And her gardenias were too. Years ago, she'd planted hydrangeas in front of the house, and now they were as big as my SUV. No, there was no doubt about it. Eliza was a woman of many gifts. Extraordinary, really. Well, I drove right past the grocery store because coming home with flowers would look like I had something to apologize for, and I did not.

Okay, I did have something to apologize for, but I wasn't going to do it. I swear to God, Eliza can read me like she's psychic or something. She was right about me not wanting to get up and go home, but I'd never admit it to her in a million years. Hell, no. And you know what? After all the years when I had denied myself the opportunity to be with Eve behind everyone's back, which would have been the easiest thing in the world, I couldn't see the harm in sleeping on her couch. I wasn't even lying down. I was asleep sitting up. Was that really so terrible? Was that a deal breaker? No way. Eliza would be pissed for a while, but she'd forget about it eventually. It wasn't worth tearing a family apart. Or destroying our friendship with Eve and Carl. They meant too much to us, as we did to them.

I pulled into the garage. Eliza's bay was empty. Now, where was she off to? I thought. Probably at Williams Sonoma, running up our charge card. Vengeance shopping. Oh, she could read me, but I knew her too. So it would cost me a thousand dollars to get things back to normal. So what? It was worth every penny. Sorry, but it was. I'd had my one turn at bat and

I'd proven myself to be a good and faithful husband. And if I had to, I'd argue with Saint Peter at the Pearly Gates that falling asleep on Eve's sofa was accidental. Man to man? He'd let me into heaven. Men understand these things, where the line is and all that.

I went inside and saw a piece of paper on the counter. It appeared to be a note from Eliza.

> *I'm going to visit my family in Corfu. For once, I'm putting myself first . . .*

What? Was she kidding? What family? This was craziness! She must've been playing a game with me. There was no way! No way in hell! She didn't have any family over there, did she? Wait! Yes, she did. I remembered her saying she did. And I remembered telling her they were a bunch of poor slobs who couldn't speak English. Maybe I shouldn't have said that. I'd never met them. Yeah. That was probably not a good thing to say.

Then I had another thought. What if she was actually just playing a game? It was possible. What if she was just checked into a hotel, like the Sanctuary on Kiawah? She'd get massages and do her nails and then she'd come home. Right? I mean, where was her car?

Before I had a chance to check her bathroom cabinet to see if her toothbrush was there, the phone rang and I picked it up. It was my dad.

"Hey," he said. "What are you doing for supper?"

"Eating whatever I can find in the fridge. Why?"

"I thought you might join us tonight. I've got some pork chops and Clarabeth is baking some kind of potato thing. God, she loves potatoes."

"Is Eliza there?"

"No."

"Well, I just got home from fixing some things in the condo at Wild Dunes and her car is gone. I just thought she might be there. That's all."

"Son, I was gonna tell you when you got here, but I may as well tell you now. She's gone to Greece. I drove her to the airport myself. And I've got her car."

I was stunned. Completely stunned. Her note was true.

"I'll be there as soon as I can."

I hung up the phone and looked around. Suddenly, my heart sank and the house felt dead. What the hell, Eliza? What the hell?

I drove to my dad and Clarabeth's like a madman, parking my car in the side yard, right next to Eliza's. I ran up the steps and into the house. Dad was in the kitchen seasoning the chops and Clarabeth had just pulled a potato casserole from the oven.

"Hello, son," Dad said. "Feel like a martini?"

"I could probably use four, but I'd hate myself tomorrow. Hey, Clarabeth."

I gave her a peck on the cheek.

"Hey, Adam," she said, in a voice I imagined doctors used on the criminally insane. "It's so nice that you could join us tonight. I was just saying to Ted that it was way beyond time that you came for dinner. It's so nice for him to share a meal

with his son now and then. It means so much to him, and I
know it does to you too."

When she stopped talking to take a breath, I jumped in.
"Do y'all have any wine open?"

"There's a pinot grigio in the fridge. It hasn't been open
too long," Dad said. "And I opened a Cab for dinner. It's on
the dining room table. Help yourself."

"White sounds good," I said. I went to the cabinet and
took out a wineglass.

My dad reached into the refrigerator and handed me the
bottle. I poured myself a half glass and sat down at the table.

"I'm going out back to the grill. You want to come with
me? Maybe I can help you get this situation all sorted out.
Here, carry this for me."

He handed me a tray loaded with a platter, tongs, a plastic tub of seasoning salt, a pepper grinder, and a roll of aluminum foil. I followed him outside to the patio. Clarabeth
stayed inside.

"I'll make a salad," she said. "Y'all go talk! You know, do
your thing. I'll just be here washing and drying lettuce. I
don't care if they say it's triple washed. Who knows if that's
really true? I've heard some of these California farms use
waste water to irrigate. Have you ever in your whole life . . ."

Jeez, does she talk on and on or what? I thought. Poor Dad.
He has to live with that wall of noise all the time.

He put the pan of meat down on the counter next to the
grill and said, "I'm used to it. Just goes to show that you can
get used to anything."

"I didn't say a word," I said.

"You flinched. I know your flinches. Now tell me what went on."

"How much did Eliza tell you?"

"She told us a story about how some long-lost relative contacted her and invited her to come to Corfu, so she was on her way. Then Cookie, who was here, and you know how she is, started digging. Eliza got upset and began to cry and told us what happened last night and this morning."

"I hate Cookie," I said.

"She can be difficult," he said. "You like your meat medium rare, isn't that right?"

"Yeah, that's fine. So what else did Cookie say?"

"Well, this may sound crazy, but I think she was trying to say you were innocent if you said so but that she didn't trust her daughter at all. And speaking as a parent, I could've lived out my days not knowing you had sex with Eve years ago."

"What? Cookie told Eliza about that? Is that woman out of her mind?"

"She might be. It didn't help your case, that's for sure."

"Dad, here's the thing. When I was eighteen years old I was in love with Eve. She was my first serious girlfriend. And she was amazing. I wanted to marry her. Cookie, ever the social-climbing bitch from hell, had other plans for Eve's future. Eve went off to school in North Carolina, met Carl the doctor, got pregnant, and married him. I never saw her again until that summer we met them at Wild Dunes. That's the truth."

"I believe you. Why wouldn't I?"

"And we've all become really great friends. All these years we've been vacationing with them? I could've had sex with

Eve any time I wanted. Last night, same story. I didn't. I happen to love my wife, although right now I'm plenty mad with her."

"I believe you. But all of this looks bad, you know. Put yourself in Carl's shoes. Or Eliza's shoes."

"Yes, but Eve and I swore to them that nothing happened. They ought to believe us."

"Even if they do? It still looks very, very bad."

"I'll give you that much."

"Listen, Adam, everyone knows you and Eve have some powerful feelings for each other. It's as plain as the nose on your face."

"But I have maintained a proper distance from her all these years."

"Okay. That's the funny thing about love. It never dies. And the fact that you didn't get off the sofa and go home speaks volumes to Carl and Eliza. Eliza feels betrayed. If the shoe was on the other foot, I think you'd feel the same way."

"So, what do you think I ought to do?" I looked at the grill. "I think those chops are done, Dad."

He stuck the long fork into the meat, grunted, and dropped the meat on the platter.

"I think you ought to call her and tell her you love her and you're sorry and that nothing like that will ever happen again."

"I've told her that. But you know what? Part of me is very pissed off. I don't like being punished for something I didn't do. She wants to go to Greece so badly? I say, have a nice trip."

"Slow down, Adam. She's the one who's hurt, and your self-righteous indignation won't rebuild her trust. You've got fences to mend. Don't get on a soapbox."

I just looked at him.

"Only love and forgiveness will fix this. Now let's go have supper."

I started piling up the foil and utensils on the tray to take back inside. I hoped that he sensed that I was in no hurry to sit around a table and discuss my shortcomings with Clarabeth over a potato casserole.

"It's too many years, Adam. Don't be a fool."

After dinner, which was very good, I made up an excuse to go home early. I had a lot of thinking to do and I was exhausted. They said they'd bring Eliza's car back in the morning. I thanked Clarabeth, and Dad walked me outside. You could hear the crickets and the steady hum of bugs. And you could smell the decaying life around the banks of the Ashley River. It was cool, so cool that I wondered if we were headed into a cold snap.

"Think about what I said, Adam. Eliza is a wonderful woman. She deserves nothing but the best. I don't think you really want to lose her."

"Of course I don't. I'm too tired to think about it anymore tonight. But thanks."

"For what?"

"Dinner and the pep talk," I said.

I looked back at him and in the dim yellow light of the porch I thought he looked older. Someday I wouldn't have him in my life. I knew that what had happened between Eve and me made things awkward for Carl and Eliza, but there was nothing to be done about it. I drove home wondering if I should call Eliza, but I figured she was somewhere over the Atlantic Ocean right about then.

I pulled into our garage and my cell phone rang. It was Eve.

"Hey. You okay?" I said.

"Yeah, I guess I'm okay. I just got home and Carl isn't here. It looks like he's moved out."

"Are you kidding me?"

"Nope."

"Holy shit! Look, Eve, I'll admit that when Carl walked in the situation wasn't optimal, but it shouldn't be grounds for divorce!"

"I agree!"

"That said, when I got home I discovered that Eliza has taken a trip to Greece."

"What? Are you serious?"

"As serious as I can be. And listen to me, you're not going to like this. Eliza went to Dad's to leave her car with him and Cookie was there and told her about you and me back in the day."

"You don't mean it. Please tell me you're lying."

"I wish I was. And she was explicit."

"Eliza must've told Carl."

"I'd bet the ranch on that one."

"Dear God. Adam, what are we going to do?"

CHAPTER 13

corfu

It's so strange what I remember. When I was a child and visited Greece with my mother, we always flew to Athens and took a ferry to Corfu. I had never experienced an aerial view of the island. But now I had booked myself straight through to the airport right outside of Corfu Town. As we circled to land I looked through my window and marveled at the mountainside filled with little white stucco homes with red clay roofs. I recognized the white convent on the tiny islet of Vlacherna. And I recognized the sparkling blue water of the Ionian Sea. I remembered that someone had told me that Corfu had over three million olive trees. That's a whole lot of olives. But I did not remember that Corfu was so green, even in winter.

The Aegean Airbus touched down gently and my own odyssey in the land of Homer was about to begin. It was around seven o'clock in the evening and the end of a thirteen-hour journey. I was bone tired and feeling pretty alone in the world. I felt like I didn't belong in Charleston, at least not until things were right between Adam and me.

Kiki's last e-mail said she would meet me in the baggage claim and bring me to her home in Dassia. I hoped I would recognize her. I had not been here since I was maybe seven or eight years old, and that was a very long time ago, never mind how many years.

I had cleared customs in Athens, so when we landed on Corfu it was very uncomplicated. The first thing that struck me was the delicious smell of strong coffee coming from a kiosk that sold cold water and a mountain of loukoumades, the Greek version of Krispy Kremes. I stopped to look at them. Then I realized that I resembled the woman selling them and also the majority of the people around me in the airport. It made me laugh and think to myself, Well, here I am in the land of my people. Like Moses in the Promised Land. Of course I looked like them. I was one of them. This was a good omen.

I made my way to the baggage claim area and to my astonishment, I recognized Kiki right away.

"Kiki!" I think I probably shouted her name a little too loudly, because people turned to have a look at me.

"Eliza! Welcome!"

She threw her arms wide open and hugged me hard. I was so excited to be there and to have found her. It was a marvel to me that in less time than it took the earth to take a spin on its axis, I was almost on the other side of the world, in a completely different culture.

"Oh, my! I can't believe I'm really here!"

"Look at you! You're beautiful! You look so young!"

"Thank you! You too! And I saw your face and knew it was you! I can't believe I recognized you after all these years."

"My God! How old are you?"

"Fifty-three, but don't tell anybody," I whispered.

"My God! I'm fifty-four, but I look like I could be your mother!"

"No! No, you don't!"

"You'll have to tell me everything you do to your skin! Are you hungry? No, of course you are! These airlines starve you to death these days, and who can eat the food anyhow? It's disgusting."

"I'm okay. Don't worry about me."

"Listen, we eat late here. Let's get your bags and we'll go to a little taverna that's owned by my friend. It's delicious! And my husband is his partner."

After a few minutes my bag came riding around on the carousel. I grabbed it and set it on the floor next to my feet to pull the handle out.

"That's it? One little bag? Are you going home tomorrow?" Kiki asked, and I laughed.

"It's deceiving," I said. "I have clothes in here for a week."

"Well then, let's go!"

We left the terminal, found her car, threw my bag in the back, and hopped in. I took a deep breath, exhaled, and fastened my seat belt. I thought about Adam. I really should send him an e-mail, but had he sent me one? I checked my phone. No. I was too tired to dwell on thoughts of him. At that moment, I was thinking he should go get Eve out of his system once and for all and then we would see where we stood with each other.

Kiki reached over and patted the back of my hand.

"I'm so glad you're here," she said. "There's nothing like seeing family. Nothing."

"Me too. I agree."

"I was so sorry to hear about your father's passing. He was a good man and we kept in touch, at least with Christmas cards."

"I know, JJ told me. Thank you, Kiki. I wish I had stayed in touch too," I said.

"The past doesn't matter, we're here together now, right?" Kiki smiled.

"Yes, Kiki, we are." I smiled right back.

This had been my dream—to come to Corfu. My heart was pounding with excitement.

She backed out of her parking space and off we went.

Soon we were sitting on small rush-bottomed chairs in an open-air dining room called Taverna Alexandros in Dassia. Alexandros, the owner, was not only Kiki's husband's partner but a very good friend of Kiki too.

"I tell everyone Kiki is my cousin, so you're my cousin too! Give Alexandros a hug!"

He was a big fellow wearing a somewhat stained apron, like a Greek teddy bear with crazy hair and a bushy mustache. Despite my reservations, I hugged him because it would've been rude not to. Then the food started coming. Over grilled octopus, Kiki wanted to hear all about my boys.

"They're twenty-one years old," I said. "Both of them graduate from college in May." I showed her their pictures on my phone and she was very complimentary. "Max is going to medical school in North Carolina and Luke is getting an advanced degree in mechanical engineering. He goes to Georgia Tech."

"My God, where does the time go? My one boy, Stephen, works in technology, doing something I can't understand. He's twenty-five and married to a sweet girl who still has to give me a grandchild."

"I don't understand technology either. And if my boys have girlfriends, I haven't heard one word about them!" I smiled at her. "And Aunt Anna?"

"She's dying to see you!"

"I can't wait to see her too. And your husband?"

"He runs the pharmacy in town. It keeps him out of trouble. He says he wants to retire soon and get a little sailboat to sail around the island. I will go crazy if he does that. What about your husband?"

"He's in the doghouse at the present time."

We looked at each other with that knowing look that only women with long marriages can share that tells the story without using words.

"Uh-huh. I understand. If you want to talk about it, you can. I'm a very good listener."

"He's a jerk, and for the moment that's about all there is to say."

Kiki smiled at me. "I've been married to Nicholas for more than half my life and I love him with all my heart. But he's a jerk too. They all are. You know why? Because their mothers tell them they are the Second Coming." She made the sign of the cross in the Greek Orthodox way and smiled.

I smiled too and nodded my head in agreement.

Next came a salad for us to share, with the reddest tomatoes and crunchiest cucumbers I'd ever eaten and a small cake of feta cheese on top.

"This looks like a picture!"

"We eat feta with everything!" she said and shook her head.

The salad was followed by sofrito, which is a meat dish cooked with vinegar and parsley. The wine continued to flow. By the time we got to the baklava, quince liqueur, and coffee I was stuffed within an inch of my life.

"He's a good cook, yes?" Kiki said.

"Inspired," I said, adding, "I'd love to get in the kitchen with him and see what's up with traditional Greek cuisine. But if I eat one more bite I'm going to die, and what will you do with my body?"

"You like to cook?"

"It's my passion," I said.

"How do you like that?" Kiki laughed and said, "Let's get you home and to bed."

We thanked Alexandros profusely. He wouldn't let us pay the bill, but we left a generous tip for our waiter.

It was just a short drive to the bed-and-breakfast where I would stay. I got out of the car and thought to myself that it seemed familiar. But if this had been my grandmother's house, I didn't recognize it. The house I remembered from my childhood was more Spartan. This little house was completely charming. Even in the darkness I could see that it was painted a coral color and trimmed in white. We stepped into the courtyard, which had a table, eight chairs, a long bar for serving buffet meals, and an olive tree in the corner, old and gnarled. Bougainvillea vines crawled all over, and I knew that when it bloomed in the summer it would be gorgeous. Planters filled with herbs were everywhere.

"It's empty this time of year, so you can have the whole house to yourself. I'll come by in the morning. Give me your cell phone number."

"It's not on an international plan, but you can e-mail me."

"Okay. Come in and let me show you around."

I followed her inside. We entered a plainly decorated living room with a sofa and four unmatched chairs. There were exposed beams and two terrible paintings of little sailboats on the water that looked like they'd been done by children. In the corner was a rough-hewn fireplace with an oil lamp on the mantel. It was rustic, to be sure, but it had a charm all its own. I felt very comfortable there.

"The lamp is there in case you lose power. That happens here a lot," Kiki said. "Come see the kitchen."

"It's the heart of the home," I said.

"You say that too? My mother says that and I think she is right. Listen, I should warn you about something."

"What? The kitchen is great!"

"Thanks. Every last person on this island who has the slightest relation to you wants to meet their American cousin. So don't be surprised when they start showing up."

"Wonderful! I would love to meet them all!"

"And there's going to be a dinner for you tomorrow night, so you have to stay. Anyway, three bedrooms are upstairs but the big one is down here. After Yiayia died we renovated. It could use another renovation now."

"So, this *is* Yiayia's house! I thought it felt familiar!"

"Her picture is hanging on the bedroom wall. She's the guardian of the house."

"Oh! I can't wait to see it. God, she was a wonderful woman."

"Yes, she was. When your mother died, it put her in an early grave."

"I'm still devastated over losing them and I probably always will be."

"I'm surprised you didn't say anything about our artwork in the living room," she said.

"Those terrible little sailboat paintings?"

"Yes! You and I painted them when we were about five! You didn't recognize our artistic genius?"

"Oh, my goodness. No!"

We hurried back to have a look, and sure enough, my tiny initials were there in the corner and Kiki's were on hers.

"It's a good thing I went to business school. I would've starved as an artist."

"Me too," she said.

Minutes later we said good night and I closed the front door behind her. I rolled my suitcase through the living room and the kitchen to the bedroom, where, sure enough, Yiayia's picture was on one wall and a picture of Helen of Troy was on the other. Strong women. Greece wasn't afraid of them and never had been. I stared closely at Yiayia's picture. I hoped she would somehow send me the courage and fortitude I felt I needed to figure out what to do with Adam.

I was too tired and there was too much Greek wine coursing through my veins to unpack and find my pajamas. I just kicked off my shoes, laid myself down, and pulled up a quilt that was folded at the foot of the bed. The next thing I knew, light was flooding through the windows, and for a moment I didn't know where I was. I got up. I was so stiff in all my joints that I decided a hot shower was in order. I unpacked my toiletries and pulled back the shower curtain to turn on the faucet. There was no shower, but there was a rubber showerhead attached to a rubber tube that I could affix to the spigot of the lovely old tub in case I didn't want to enjoy a good soak.

I started filling the tub with hot water and saw that there was a jar of bath salts right there, just waiting for me to toss a scoop in the hot water.

"This is just what I need," I said to the empty room.

I brushed my hair up into a bun and brushed my teeth while the tub filled. I checked the water now and then and adjusted the temperature as it grew warmer. Finally, I took off my clothes and slipped in, and oh my goodness, that bath felt like heaven. It was the bath to end all baths.

While I marinated, I thought about Adam and Eve. First of all, I needed to back up. I still couldn't believe I had actually packed my clothes, gotten on a plane, and left the country. I've always had nerve, but this was a huge leap over the boundaries of my comfort zone. I was just so shocked by what

Adam and Eve had done that I had to get away. I couldn't face him. Or her. What was I supposed to say to them? I'd said what I needed to say to Adam for the moment.

I still could not get over what Cookie had told me. It made every single aspect of Adam and Eve's betrayal that much worse. All the years we'd been friends suddenly seemed like an orchestrated fake-out—a sham, a big lie. They had used Carl and me so that they could see each other every summer. Plain and simple.

Was that really true? Had they really done that? No. I knew I was blowing everything out of proportion. Adam loved Eve. That much was clear to anyone who cared to have a glance at them. He had probably always loved her, since they were teenagers. But he loved me too. I could not honestly say that there had ever been a moment when Adam made me feel like he had settled for less by marrying me. I scrubbed my feet with a vengeance.

And Eve? She was absolutely 100 percent in love with Adam. But she loved Carl too. She was proud of him, and he truly did love her. She really was the beauty queen in our foursome, but he sure did have a roving eye. And to be honest, Eve didn't bring a lot to the table except her looks. God knows, that mother of hers was a liability. Between Cookie's mouth and Carl's eye, it's no wonder she was so insecure. She didn't have a career that could solidify her confidence. She was a really terrible cook. She overindulged her daughter and always had. Cookie didn't do anything except find fault with her. And Carl was probably chasing the skirt he accused of chasing him. What a screwed-up world this is,

I thought. I pulled the plug on the drain and began rinsing off with the hand shower.

But still, at the end of the day, Eve had been Adam's young love, maybe his first, and as far as I knew he had been hers. First loves. Young loves? They were fragile and precious.

I'd known a guy I'd thought I loved all through high school. Vince was Italian, and we looked like we were brother and sister. We were inseparable. I spent so many Saturdays in the kitchen with his mother, chopping onions, peppers, carrots, and celery. She taught me how to make ravioli. I still use her recipe for marinara to this day. His father taught me how to parallel park and how to make a good cup of espresso. I was crazy about his whole family. Everyone thought we would eventually get married. But we went off to college in different cities and it just fizzled out. I thought about him now for the first time in years.

While I was drying off, it didn't take me long to decide that if Vince had shown up at Wild Dunes with his wife and family I would've high-tailed it in the opposite direction. I wouldn't have invited him for drinks that night and I never would've agreed to go to Wild Dunes again for the rest of my life. Who needs the aggravation? Who needs to test their heart? So why did Adam do it? Because he was stupid. And Eve? There was no such thing as too much adoration in her world. I've known that since the night I met her and she complained about still being too skinny. I'm not saying that with snark. I'm saying she got the minimum from Carl, less than that from her mother and her daughter. Well, she was so self-involved I was sure she gave her mother little to no regard. Adam took up the slack for all of them. Once a year she got a two-week dose of Adam's adoration. And maybe more often, for all I knew.

I tightened my bathrobe around me and went to the kitchen to make coffee. There were some groceries—butter, milk, and juice—in the small refrigerator. Just basics, but they would be fine until I went to a store. It was evidence of Kiki's thoughtfulness. There was ground coffee in a canister in the cupboard along with a loaf of sliced bread. Finally, there were a few bananas and a couple of apples in a basket on the table. The coffeepot was the old-fashioned kind that percolated when you plugged it in. I hadn't seen one of those in years. I set it up and decided to unpack while the coffeepot gurgled and perked.

I made the bed, got organized, dressed, and had a little breakfast, thinking to myself that I actually felt pretty good, considering the difference in the time zones. I checked my e-mail. There was nothing from Adam. And there was a note from each of my boys checking in. I wonder if they were suspicious. Nope. They were busy with their lives. I sent an e-mail to Kiki.

> Good morning! I am up and dressed and wondering if you have any free time today? I think I'm going to take the bus to Corfu Town and be a tourist. Would you like to join me?

Minutes later she replied.

> Good morning! I hope you were able to sleep. Jet lag is such a pain. And yes, I am going into Corfu Town to do some errands. Why don't

I pick you up and drop you off at somewhere like the Palace of Saint
Michael and Saint George and then we can meet for lunch at the
Liston?

I wrote right back.

That sounds great! I'm ready anytime you are. Thanks!

Soon we were on our way to the palace.

"I think you'll really enjoy the Museum of Asiatic Art," she said. "Have you been there?"

"Who knows? Maybe? If I was there I was too young to appreciate it."

"Well, the collection has over ten thousand pieces of Asian art and artifacts. It was put together by a Greek ambassador one hundred and fifty years ago. It's fascinating."

When she dropped me off I said, "Only I would come to Greece to see Asian art! Ha!"

"That's too funny! So, let's say we meet at Café Liston at one o'clock? It's not too heavy, and you know dinner tonight is going to be a big meal. My mother is cooking lamb and fish and everything in the world."

"That sounds great! I'll be there."

I paid the small entrance fee with my Visa card and went inside to see the Asian art. There were endless statues, pieces of armor, ceramics, and silks. In the Chinese galleries, there were somber, beautiful funerary pieces that fascinated me. One in particular caught my eye, a lone female equestrian, oddly sitting western style, astride a noble horse, bound for the afterlife. The rider was dressed for a grand occasion, her hair atop her head in a great swirl and her clothing ornate and detailed. Her face was expressionless, as though the trip was not unexpected. It was not serene but resigned. The statue struck me as kind of a notation of life in general, that we arrive alone and we will leave alone. It was attributed to the Tang Dynasty, sometime in the late sixth or seventh century.

"Wow," I whispered to the empty gallery.

I moved on to the Japanese galleries. After passing dozens of kimonos and painted fans, ceramics and domestic objects, I came upon a gallery of woodblock prints. When I was a young woman and taking an art history class, thinking erroneously that I'd get an easy A, we studied the art of making woodblock prints. I stood now in front of an eight-color woodblock showing two women in traditional Japanese dress, long kimonos tied at the waist with wide obis. Their hair was in an updo secured by hair sticks. They were wearing geta sandals and one woman held a fan, an indication of warm weather. They were tending a small garden, and one of the women held a morning glory blossom between her fingers. It reminded me of the great pleasure gardening gave to me. It wasn't just about the harvest of flowers or vegetables. It was about the time spent there. I always came away with a feeling of peace. What would happen to my garden now?

I went on and on, from one gallery to another, and I looked at everything until it became a blur. Maybe visiting a museum on my first day here wasn't such a great idea. My heart was so heavy every time I thought of Adam that I definitely wasn't giving the collection the focus it deserved. It was still early enough to go see something else before lunch. I decided a church was in order.

I asked the ladies at the entrance which one to see and they were emphatic.

"You must see Agios Spyrídon!" said one.

"He is the patron saint of Corfu. He works many miracles!" said the other.

The first one added in a whisper, "He still protects us, and every now and then they have to replace his shoes."

"Why?" I said.

"Because," she said, again in a whisper, "he roams the streets at night, checking on us!"

"He wears out the soles of his shoes," the other one said.

"No kidding," I said. "Can I walk there from here?"

"It's no problem at all."

They gave me directions, and I thanked them and left.

I looked into the sky for the church with the red dome on its steeple, which was easy to find. The tower clock in the church's belfry began to chime and I looked at my watch. It was ten to twelve. Saint Spyrídon was early, I said, smiling to myself.

In the entrance of the church were stacks of brochures about the life of the saint and the miracles he performed. Well, I'm a sucker for a miracle story, and I thought I sure could use one right about now. I took a brochure, sat down in a pew, and read. Then I looked around me. He stopped armies. He stayed the enemies of Corfu. He healed the sick.

Incredible, I thought. The church itself was a gorgeous sixteenth-century building with a ceiling covered with murals of Saint Spyrídon dressed in deep red robes performing miracles. All around the altar were beautiful icons. I couldn't think of a single church in Charleston that was so ornate.

The brochure said that as a bonus, his incorrupt mummified remains were there, including his right hand, which no one seems to know how he lost but which is also in an alleged incorrupt state. That hand had traveled a bit—to Rome, Russia, and other spots. Saint Spyrídon? Well, let's just see what the remains of a seventeen-hundred-year-old incorrupt saint looks like, I said to myself. I got up and went up to the altar, where others stood in a line. I assumed they were there to ask the saint for a favor.

There was an Orthodox priest with a bushy salt-and-pepper beard positioned there behind the altar, chanting in Greek. As he sang, it became clear that he was chanting to the saint on behalf of each petitioner. I only had a few minutes to think of what I wanted to ask. When it was my turn, I awkwardly introduced myself to the priest. The saint was lying there in an open silver coffin, so elaborate I could not even imagine anything more grand. It was completely unprotected by a glass panel or anything. I was astonished by the lack of security. Just me, Saint Spyrídon, and a crusty old Orthodox priest.

"Hi, I'm Eliza Stanley from Charleston, South Carolina," I said, instantly realizing that I could've said I was Marilyn Monroe and it wouldn't have made a lick of difference.

He just smiled and said, "Ask Agios Spyrídon . . ."

Then he touched his own heart several times and I knew

he meant for me to ask for my favor from my heart to the heart of the Saint. I thought of Adam. Please help me put us back together again, I asked silently.

I took a good look at the saint. He looked terrible. But I had to admit, he still had skin. You'd think someone who died in A.D. 325 would be nothing but a pile of bones. And I took a look at his shoes. They were velvet slippers. I looked back at the priest. He motioned his approval to touch the foot of the saint. So I did. I know this will sound insane, but for one tiny moment it felt like time stopped and I was in midair, and then without so much as a watch your step, I was on my feet and back in the world.

"Thank you," I said and moved on.

So, that's probably what LSD feels like, I thought. I couldn't wait to tell Kiki.

I left the church and hurried down the bustling streets to the Café Liston where I was to meet her. I passed dozens of shops selling souvenirs, whiskey, olive oil, and the quince liquor that was so popular. I reminded myself to buy some to take home. If I went home.

The restaurant was swarmed with midday diners, everyone talking at once. Kiki was there waiting at a table, doing e-mail on her phone. We could have been having lunch under the colonnade on the Rue de Rivoli in Paris, the architecture was so similar. She looked up at me smiling.

"Hey there!" she said.

"You won't believe who I just saw!" I said, and we swapped air kisses.

"Sit! Sit! Tell me everything," she said.

I told her what I had learned about the saint and she said, "Oh please! When I was a schoolgirl, the teacher would call roll. She'd say, is Spiros here, and twenty boys would raise their hands!"

"Well, do you believe the stories about his shoes?" I said.

"Why not? This is Corfu! The home of mythology and truth. Now, do you feel like a sandwich or a salad?"

I looked at the menu and saw it was heavily influenced by Italian cuisine.

"I came to Corfu to see Asian art and eat Italian food!"

"That's the way it goes these days. But believe me, you'll eat plenty of Greek food before you leave here!"

We ordered lunch, which came quickly, and I ate like I had not eaten in weeks. Kiki was telling me more about Saint Spyrídon between bites. Prayers to the saint resulted in the failure of an invasion by Turkey. The Turks had fifty thousand troops on the ground and a good number of ships surrounding the island. It was 1716, and Saint Spyrídon appeared in front of the troops holding a raised sword in his right hand. Never mind that he had been dead for almost fourteen hundred years. The Turks were so terrified, they ran for their lives. The governor of Corfu once wanted to do something to honor the Orthodox saint. A visiting Roman Catholic cardinal suggested that it would please the Almighty if the governor would build a marble altar in Saint Spyrídon's Greek Orthodox church where he could say a Latin Mass. Naturally, the governor agreed. The materials were gathered and they were ready to begin the conversion of the church from Greek Orthodox to Roman Catholic. The islanders got into an uproar because they considered this to be an unthinkable blasphemy. The governor was outraged that the people should question his judgment and authority. So the people prayed to their saint for deliverance, and deliverance they got. Saint Spyrídon began appearing in the governor's dreams telling him to back off. Saint Spyrídon brought about a storm so powerful that the lightning bolts exploded the powder keg at the Old Fort and killed nine hundred Roman soldiers and zero Orthodox. The remains of the governor were found crushed between heavy beams, and the cardinal's body was found in a sewage ditch, holding on to his—well, there's no nice way to put this—family jewels.

"Boom!" I said. "So much for those guys!"

"Exactly! The stories about him are spectacular, but I tell you, everyone who lives on Corfu believes them. They believe every single word. He is a very powerful saint."

"Well, it certainly gives you hope about the hereafter being a reality. What else did he do?"

"Oh, all sorts of things. During his lifetime when he was saying Mass, people nearby reported hearing a huge heavenly choir in the church. But when they went inside to see who was singing, there was only Saint Spyrídon and a couple of members of the congregation. Do you want dessert?"

"Baklava?"

"Of course! But we're going to get fat."

"I've been craving it. You can't get this in South Carolina. Saint Spyrídon. Wow. No wonder my mother loved this place so much."

Kiki smiled at me. I could read her mind. Well, almost.

Maybe if I could understand all the reasons my mother loved Corfu so deeply, I would somehow have her back with me. Instead of pushing Greece away as I had for years, I would begin to embrace it again, the way I had as a child. There's not a whole lot that's lonelier than being a motherless child. Discovering Corfu might give me some new roots.

"My mother is about to explode with excitement to see you. You might want to catch a nap before tonight, because I can tell you they're going to have you up until all hours."

"That's not a bad idea," I said.

The mere mention of the word *nap* was making me sleepy.

Kiki dropped me off at the house and said she would pick me up at seven that evening. I thanked her and waved as she pulled away from the curb.

To my surprise, there were packages piled up at the front door of Yiayia's house. I picked them up and went inside.

What in the world? I thought and dropped them on the dining table.

They were gifts! Exactly as my grandmother's friends and neighbors had done when I was so very young, some very sweet people had come around to the house to welcome me with a few little surprises.

I began to open them. There was a purple hand-sewn silk cover that held a pack of tissues with a signed greeting card. Very thoughtful! I couldn't have told you what that card said for a million dollars. But I wrote a description of the gift on it. I'd get Kiki to help me decipher and to thank the right people. Then there was a set of beautifully embroidered dish towels that someone had spent hours working on. Someone else had brought a tiny, pretty, blue and white ceramic pot with rosemary planted in it. I ran my hand across the needles and smelled it. I loved rosemary. Next I unwrapped a homemade loaf cake filled with fruit and nuts. It would be a wonderful treat for breakfast. Someone had brought a box of butter cookies topped with pistachios that smelled amazing. Finally, I opened a flat box that contained a pretty scarf, blue swirls on white, like the water that surrounded the island. I made notes and looked at all these thoughtful things and realized that one of the many things I was missing in my life was a sense of community. The quietude of living in the country had become almost complete isolation. The boys were gone. Our pets were gone. Well, if I went back to Adam—and it was awfully strange to even think of my situation in those terms—I was getting a dog. And maybe I'd spend more time at Wild Dunes. Like, a lot more time.

I stretched out on the bed and looked at the ceiling. What did I want? Well, that one was easy. What I wanted was for this never to have happened. I was pretty sure I couldn't turn back the clock. Did I really want Adam to be free to see Eve? Well, he was going to anyway if he wanted to. It wasn't like I had him on a leash. Should I tell him to do whatever he wanted to? Hell, no. It would be much more interesting to watch and see what he would do than to give him permission or a mandate. My great disappointment was based on the fact that I'd been living with a man for all these years who really loved somebody else. That broke my heart. My lesser disappointment lay in the fact that he placed his wants and needs too far over mine. I would never be so submissive again.

I turned over on my side, punched the pillow into submission, and somehow drifted off to a dreamless sleep.

Nearby church bells roused me at six in the evening. I rolled over and looked at my watch. It was six fifteen. I smiled, thinking about the tower clock in Corfu Town that had been wrong earlier in the day. Evidently, punctuality wasn't all that important. I took a deep breath and thought, I'm in the Mediterranean! People come here from all over the world to relax. I should just take a page out of their book and not worry so much. I had been trying to act normal with Kiki, but she knew something was terribly wrong. Who flies to Greece on a moment's notice?

I washed my face and brushed my teeth, thinking that after all the strong coffee I'd enjoyed my breath probably smelled dreadful. What should I wear to Aunt Anna's? What would she say about me never being in touch with them? Would she want to know why I was here? I hoped she'd never learned to speak English.

I decided on black slacks and a red sweater with flat black ballet slippers. I dressed, applied a little makeup, and looked in the mirror. I looked sad. Well, hopefully it could be explained away as jet lag.

CHAPTER 14

adam

Eliza had been gone for barely twenty-four hours and I was completely discombobulated. I had a first-class seat on a high-speed, death-defying emotional roller coaster. Angry one minute, penitent the next. Furious again and then weepy like an old woman. The first phone call came from Max at about ten thirty the same night Eliza left.

"Hey, Dad? You okay?"

Hell, no, I wasn't okay. But I wasn't going to get him all riled up.

"Of course, I am. How are you?"

"Good. Dad? Mom called. Why is she going to Greece? Did y'all have a fight?"

Now, what was I supposed to tell him? The least amount possible, I decided.

"No, no. Nothing like that. You know she's always wanted to go back there to see if she could dig up some more family. I said, fine, go! That's all there is to it. She'll be back soon."

"That's a heck of a long way to travel alone."

"Nah, your mother knows her way around."

"Okay, then. I was just checking on you."

He was still suspicious.

"Well, thank you, son. I'm still above ground and taking sustenance. How's life for my brilliant future doctor?"

"Oh, you know. About the same. Killing myself over the MCAT."

"When do you take it?"

"End of May."

"You'll do fine. Talk to your brother lately?"

"Not lately. He's okay?"

"As far as I know. If I hear differently, I'll call you."

"Okay, then. Just checking in."

"Sure thing. Love you, Max."

"Love you too, Dad."

I poured a generous measure of Scotch over a glass of ice. Sometimes I had a beer or a glass of wine and then hit the sack, but I wanted to be sure I didn't toss and turn. Scotch would put me out like a light. Yes, I was sedating myself with alcohol because I didn't have anything like Ambien in the house. And I assured myself I would only be a self-indulgent boozehound for this one night.

It was eleven o'clock. The phone rang again. Eve.

"I can't sleep," she said.

Oh, God, I thought. Here we go. Somehow, for the first time in all these years, she called me when the mood struck, and I didn't want to talk to her. It would complicate things that were already complicated enough.

"Warm milk," I said. "It has melatonin in it."

"You're not going to have a problem sleeping tonight?"

"No, because Scotch has melatonin in it too."

She laughed and I began to warm to her, as I always did.

"Oh, God, Adam. What have we done?"

"Well, I can only speak for myself, but what it appears *I've* done is throw my marriage on the fucking shoals. Before this is over, I'm sure I'll be the family asshole for the rest of time."

I never cursed in front of Eve. Dr. Dewar's was taking effect.

"Potty mouth," she said.

"Sorry."

"Have you heard from Eliza?"

"Nope. You heard from Carl?"

"Nope. Silence like the tomb. How angry do you think Eliza is?"

"I think she's more hurt than angry. What I did really rattled the foundation of everything we had together. She probably thinks I've been in love with you all along."

"Well, she wouldn't be wrong."

"No, but loving you is wrong." I wasn't going to tell her that now that I could have her, she was less appealing, less of a beautiful dream. But for some reason I never saw coming, it was true. The cost of having Eve was way too high, especially if it meant that I'd have to give up Eliza. I loved Eliza in a different way, a deeper love. Hell, I'd spent my entire adult life with her.

"So, what should we do?"

Who's this *we*, I thought.

"I don't know. It's too fresh. Let's think about it. We can talk tomorrow."

"Okay."

"Okay, then. Good night."

"Adam? We didn't do anything so horribly and terribly wrong, really. Did we?"

"Eve? What we did was probably legitimate grounds for a lot of things—murder and divorce, for starters. Let's talk tomorrow."

We hung up and I knew that my conversation with her had left her sort of hanging. I had not given her any reassurances. It wasn't like Friday night at Wild Dunes when I told her I loved her. That had been more like acting out a fantasy. But then reality had hit me, because Eliza was gone. And to make things worse, I couldn't get it out of my mind that Eve was looking for more than a friend in me. And she wanted it now. This was no time to begin an affair, even if it would be with Eve. I felt pretty rotten over the idea that I'd run Eliza out of the country. I hadn't meant to hurt anyone. I'd only meant to steal a few hours with Eve. But mainly, I never thought we'd get caught. Jesus, this monogamy thing was hard. It sure didn't have much leeway.

I don't know why in the world I said yes to her, but when Eve called me yesterday I agreed to meet her for dinner. She was coming back to Charleston to take Cookie to the doctor. Cookie couldn't take a taxi? Somehow, I got through the day, checking my e-mail every ten minutes to see if there was anything from Eliza. Not one word. Now I was annoyed again. I mean, it might have been nice if she'd dropped me a line just to say she was there and safe or that she was finding what she went searching for in the first place. I drove home from the job site where I was currently working the biggest crews I'd ever hired, building another two hundred starter houses in Summerville for Carolina One Realty to sell to Boeing employees. Boeing was bringing a renaissance to our local economy. With all the new residents came housing needs, obviously, and a demand for other things like new restaurants, dry cleaners, bank branches, grocery stores, health clubs . . . the list was endless. Every builder in Charleston had all the business they could handle.

I was going to shower and change and meet Eve at Charleston Grill, at the Charleston Place Hotel. She'd made the reservation. Charleston Grill was a little fancy for my taste. I think I took Eliza there once for her birthday, and I remember that I nearly had a heart attack when the bill came. But I gave Eve no objection because it was sort of a momentous occasion, if you could call your wife of twenty-two years dumping you because of one tiny transgression a momentous occasion, and I guess you could.

I realized I wasn't in the best humor as I went through my closet looking for a clean dress shirt. There were none to be found. Eliza usually picked up the dry cleaning on Saturdays. Well, that was the day she ran out on me, wasn't it? Big deal. I'd pick them up myself. Wait, I thought, what dry cleaner did we use? Easy to find out. I'd have a look at the checkbook or maybe the Visa bill. I'd do that tomorrow morning. Meanwhile, it was pretty chilly for a February evening, so I pulled out one of the infamous sweaters from that Christmas of abundant knitwear and thought, okay, this doesn't look too bad. It was just a pale blue lightweight cashmere pullover with a collar and a zipper. It looked pretty good with khaki pants and my navy blazer. I splashed on a little smell-swell and regretted it right away. Eve would take a sniff and think I got myself dolled up for her. I locked the house and left to meet her. But the devil in me would be sure to let her get a good whiff.

Why in the hell was I doing this? I was still playing with fire. What kind of expectations did Eve have of me? Men and women were wired so differently, and that had never been more clear to me than it was at that moment. I had given my marriage a lot of thought and I knew I could outlast Eliza. She would have her Greek adventure and eventually come crawling home. We would resume our respective roles in our life together and never speak of the incident again. But Eve? I didn't have a clue, really.

I pulled into the circular driveway at Charleston Place and gave my keys to the valet.

"Checking in, sir?"

"No, just having dinner," I said.

"Enjoy your evening," he said.

I might have to remortgage the house, but thanks, I thought.

I walked through the lobby of the hotel toward the restaurant and spotted Eve at the bar. She looked more beautiful than ever. My resolve to keep the evening free of titillation started to waver. She was sipping on a glass of white wine.

And her long legs were amazing as she perched on the barstool, rare and exquisite, wearing super high heels, making her legs look even sexier. And let me tell you, she was wearing something one would not wear to church.

"Hey, Eve. I don't know if this was such a good idea," I said, suddenly nervous.

"Oh, for heaven's sake," she said and kissed me lightly on my cheek. "You smell delicious. You worry too much!"

"Jesus, Eve. I only have so much willpower."

The bartender said, "Can I get you something, sir?"

"Um, let's see . . ."

A lawyer? I thought.

Just then the maître d' approached.

"Your table is ready," he said.

"Oh, good," I said.

"We can take the lady's drink to the table if you'd like," the bartender said.

"That's fine," I said and watched Eve slide down from her barstool.

It occurred to me then that this might not have been her first glass of wine that day. And Friday night she nearly put away a bottle by herself. What was going on with that? I thought Cookie was the one with the alcohol problem.

I followed her to the table and the maître d' pulled out her chair for her. They were very heavy chairs. He handed me a wine list and a menu.

"Have you dined with us before?"

"Yes," I said, "but it's been a while."

"I've always wanted to come here," Eve said to him.

The maître d' said, "Welcome!" to Eve and then, "Welcome back!" to me. He was one chipper fellow, I'd give him that.

"Well," he continued, "when y'all are ready I can explain how the menu works."

Our waiter came up to us and placed Eve's glass of wine in front of her. She flashed him that million-dollar smile and he all but fainted. That smile had some megawatts.

"I think we're ready," I said.

"All right then. As you can see, we have four distinctive menus. This one is called the Cosmopolitan, because all of the dishes have exotic flavors from around the world. The next one is the Regional, because it includes updated versions of classic southern favorites. Third is the Pure offering, so named because the dishes are lighter, and the last one is Lush, because all the choices are more lavish. Feel free to mix and match. And, take your time. Sir, may I offer you a cocktail?"

"Sure. I'll have a glass of red wine. Do you have a nice zinfandel by the glass?"

"Yes, of course. May I suggest the Turley?"

"That sounds fine," I said, thinking, Who knows what that is?

I didn't remember this place as being so formal, and then I realized it wasn't any more formal than Cypress or Peninsula Grill. It was simply very polite and very professional. I began to relax a little.

"What looks good to you, Eve?" I was busy scanning the menu.

"You look good to me, Adam."

"If you think you're going to flirt with me like this and nothing will happen, you're dead wrong."

She narrowed her eyes and stared at me.

"Oh, Adam! Since when can't you take a joke?"

"I can take a joke just fine."

She wasn't fooling with me. But dang, she was beautiful.

The waiter returned with my glass of zinfandel.

"Cheers!" I said to Eve.

"Cheers!" she said.

I thought about Eliza. If she were here she'd order the seared foie gras and the Thai fish. I'd have the sturgeon salad and the Norwegian ocean trout. We always ordered dishes she didn't make at home and we'd share them. She would actually feed me with her fork. Let me make you the perfect bite, she'd say, and put a bit of glistening meat and a tiny bite of potato or vegetable together and lean across the table to me. Then she'd sit back smiling while I savored it. Eliza had such a healthy curiosity about food. She liked to try everything. Whenever we went to a new restaurant she always came away inspired, determined to re-create whatever crazy thing we had just eaten. There was a Thai restaurant near the Citadel Mall she loved. And a sushi bar downtown. Even the Mexican food in Charleston was an adventure. Eliza would have worshipped this menu.

"What are you thinking about?" Eve said. "Your eyebrows are all knitted together."

"Hmm, Eliza used to say it was my furry brow."

"Instead of furrowed?"

"Yeah. I think Luke started that when he was just a little boy."

"You do know you just referred to her in past tense?"

I just looked at Eve and thought, Oh my god, she's right. I just referred to Eliza in the past tense. What does that mean?

"Well, just because it's something she did in the past," I said. "She's not dead."

"No. Thank heaven. But is she in your past?"

Boy, Eve really had a helluva campaign laid out, didn't she? I couldn't remember her being this aggressive. Maybe she couldn't separate from Carl unless she had someone else in her life. Like me. A lot of people were like that. But I wasn't going to be her exit ramp.

"No, Eve, she's not."

Eve shifted in her seat, uncomfortable with my response.

The waiter returned.

"Have we decided? Ma'am?"

"I'll have the beet salad and the flounder," she said, handing him the menu. "Thanks."

Jeesch. That had to be the most unimaginative thing on the menu.

I said, "And I'll have the steak tartare and the rack of lamb."

"Medium rare?"

"Yes," I said.

"Very good. And would you like to order a bottle of wine?"

"Well, since my friend is having fish and I'm having red

meat, maybe we should just order by the glass. How's that, Eve?"

Her glass was empty.

"Would you care for another glass?" the waiter said.

"Please," she said. "It's a sauvignon blanc."

He disappeared into the throng. The restaurant was filling up. There was jazz music being played on the other side of the dining room. All in all, I knew Eliza would shoot me dead if she could've seen me then.

Then the next worst thing that could have happened, happened. In came Cookie, Clarabeth, and Dad, all dressed up for a night on the town. Dad was even wearing a suit. When Cookie saw me she started screaming. She all but ran to our table and began to rant and rave like a crazy person. The other guests in the restaurant became very quiet.

"Are you kidding me? Are you kidding me? Eliza is gone for forty-eight hours and you're already fooling around with my daughter again? Have you no shame?"

"Mom! Stop! I called Adam and invited him to dinner!"

"You call yourself innocent in that dress?" Then she whispered, "You're a tramp."

"That's not nice. We're just having dinner, Cookie," I said.

That shut Cookie up for about five seconds, then she leaned into me and said, "You listen to me. You should've said no." Then she stood back and looked from Eve to me. "Shame on both of you."

My father came and took Cookie by the arm to lead her away. He looked disgusted.

"Enjoy your dinner, son."

Gone was the look of approval I was accustomed to seeing in his eyes.

He turned and walked away. I saw them leave the restaurant, abandoning their reservation. I was mortified. Eve, on the other hand, was perfectly sanguine.

"You still hungry?" I said, thinking it was time for the check.

"I'm starving," she said. "My mother is a lunatic." Then she turned to the other patrons and said, "Mom's off her meds. Sorry for the excitement."

They nodded, and the ladies gave me looks of pity, as they thought I was a recent widower, but on the faces of the men were silent thumbs-ups for having such a gorgeous dinner companion and, may we add, she has the most delightful sense of humor?

"Eve, Eve, Eve. What am I to do with you?"

"Just love me, Adam. That's all I want. I just want to feel like someone in this world loves me."

"Carl loves you, Eve."

"Then why did he walk out on me?"

"Because you and I did something selfish that broke a boundary." Then I thought, Um, did I really say that?

Our first courses were delivered.

"I'm not happily married and you know it."

"And we're doing it again tonight." I paused for a moment, watching her push her salad from one side of the plate to the other. I took a bite of my steak tartare. It was melt-in-your-mouth good. "Would you like a bite of this?"

"Raw meat? No, thanks."

I'd never realized she was such a picky eater.

"So, Eve? Do you really think that you want to divorce Carl?"

"Adam, I didn't tell you this at the beach, but he has pictures of a woman's breasts on his phone and they're not mine."

"Are you serious?"

"He might be a doctor, but he's no Einstein. He uses the same password on everything. His mother's birthday. Not mine, not our daughter's—his mother's."

"A good shrink would know what to do with that. I don't. So, he knows that you know this? About the pictures, I mean."

"He has to know. I think that maybe he moved out to avoid getting kicked out."

"Where did he go?"

"I think he's at a hotel next to the hospital," Eve said.

"Jesus, Eve, I'm so sorry." I leaned back in my chair. "What a mess."

The waiter took away our appetizers and another waiter delivered our entrées.

"Yep. I've got a nice fat big mess on my hands."

"I've gotta tell you. I'm surprised, and I'll be really surprised if there's not a reasonable explanation for this. Make that a believable explanation."

If I were Carl, I'd have an ironclad alibi for everything on my phone. How could he be so sloppy?

She began to pick at her fish, taking the tiniest of bites. Maybe she'd simply lost her appetite. I could've picked up my lamb chops with my hands and gnawed them to the bone like Henry VIII, they were so tender and tasty.

"Something wrong with the fish?" I said.

"No, I was just thinking that I planned to stay with my mother tonight, but now I *really* don't feel like going there. And it's too far to drive out to the beach. Maybe I'll see if they have a room here."

"Well, at least you'd be able to sleep in peace," I said.

CHAPTER 15

eliza

It was dusk when Kiki rolled up to the house, and off we went to her mother's house, my *theia* Anna. I wondered if I would recognize anyone there. Or if they would remember me at all. And maybe there would be stories about my mother I'd never heard. I knew that would be asking for a lot. After all, my mother died forty years ago or more.

"Oh, my God, wait till you see! Mother has gone off the deep end! She's been cooking all day and night and so have her friends. There's moussaka and lamb and lamb sausages and octopus and breads and oh, you won't believe. And desserts? There's enough baklava to feed the entire Greek navy! I don't think there's a grape leaf, a block of feta, a pistachio nut, or a teaspoon of honey left on this island!"

"I can't wait!" I said. "I loved our dinner at your friend's taverna. I've always loved Greek food anyway. There's only one Greek restaurant in Charleston and they make the juiciest roasted chicken. I can't wait to see everyone." I was a nervous wreck.

"We're going to have a wonderful night."

"I wish I spoke Greek," I said. "I apologize in advance for all the translating you'll probably have to do."

"Don't be silly," Kiki said and turned to smile at me. "Nicholas speaks English and the others are somewhat fluent."

She turned her eyes back to the road and we drove very slowly as we wound our way through the village. The streets were busy. And I suddenly realized I had no gift for my aunt, which would be unforgivable considering all the trouble she went to to prepare this dinner.

"Kiki, I need a small favor. Is there a place I can buy flowers? I can't see my aunt after all these years and show up empty-handed."

"Of course! Just ahead is a little bakery that sells flowers too."

She pulled over and I got out, then realized I didn't have any euros.

I turned around and Kiki already had her wallet out.

"You can pay me back," she said, and handed me a twenty-euro note.

"Thanks," I said and thought, Well, now she knows I left home in a hurry.

Indeed, this tiny shop sold pastries and bread and flowers. I picked out two small bouquets of wildflowers and paid for them. I got back in the car.

"Those are lovely," she said. "Mother will love them."

I buried my nose in them and took a deep breath. They reminded me of something, some smell from long ago.

"Why do these flowers smell so familiar?" I asked.

"Maybe because they smell like the hills around us? It's a fragrance as old as the hills themselves."

"Like the dirt," I said, remembering playing with my brother and Kiki in my aunt's yard, digging holes to China.

People were everywhere, old ladies arm in arm, mothers with youngsters in tow going to the stores for last-minute items for their supper, children kicking a soccer ball in the square by the church, their pet dogs of dubious pedigree scampering all around them. The air was thick with contentment, something you might run through your fingers if you held your hand outside the window. I wished I could grab some, put it in a jar, and keep it with me. Soon we had passed through the tiny business district and with a few more turns, we arrived.

"Yassou! Yassou!"

The tiny old woman who came rushing from the ancient fading pink stucco house with her hands in the air had to be my aunt Anna. It was. Across all the years that had divided us, I could tell her by her eyes. I got out of the car without my purse or the flowers, we threw our arms around each other, and we burst into tears, even Kiki.

"*Yassou*, Theia Anna," I said, remembering that Yassou was how to say hello in Greek.

She threw her arms around me again and I hugged her for all I was worth. I was hugging the next best thing to my mom. Her only sister. Now nearly eighty years old. Something in me began to crumble. Maybe it was the place in my heart that had closed the door to Greece when we buried my mother and then Yiayia. I felt a flush of warmth from my head to my toes. She was a wall of love. Love emanated from her entire being. I could not say that I had ever felt so wanted and welcomed.

We stood there in her courtyard in the breeze of the evening and she began to chatter away in Greek so fast that I strained to understand her. Somehow, I could pick up the meaning of a few things. She touched my face tenderly and hugged me again. She asked so many things. How was I? Did I bring pictures of my children? She was sorry to hear of my father's death. I answered her in English as she nodded and responded in Greek. Kiki stood by watching all of this in amazement.

"How do you know what she just said to you?" Kiki said.

"Because I remember some words, I guess. She just said, 'Oh, look at you! You look just like your mother!' and I hope she's right."

"That is exactly what she said," Kiki said, still shaking her head.

I grabbed my purse, wiped my eyes with the back of my hand, handed Aunt Anna the flowers that Kiki was holding, and we all went inside.

Her home was very similar to my grandmother's. And it was brimming with people, some of whom were related to me. There was a huge smile on every last face.

"*Kalinita*," a handsome man said. "I'm Nick. Kiki's husband!"

Kalinita meant *good evening*.

"*Kalinita!* Oh! I'm so happy to meet you!"

"And we are so happy to see you here! Let me introduce you around."

The next few hours were filled with broken English, broken Greek, and an absolute feast of food. I took pictures on my phone of everyone and all the food so I could show my boys. When dinner was finally done and almost everyone had gone home, my aunt took me by the hand and led me to her bedroom. Kiki followed us. We sat on the edge of her bed while Anna went into the bottom drawer of an old armoire.

"What did she just say?" I said.

"She wants to show you something, something she'd been saving for you and your brother all these years."

Anna dug around and produced something wrapped in linen. As she unwrapped it I could see that it was a book, and when she opened it I saw that it was an album.

"Come by the light," Kiki said. "This old house has never had enough light. You could go blind trying to read a book at night." Then Kiki said something in Greek to her mother and my aunt hurried from the room.

"What did you say?" I asked.

"I said, we need a magnifying glass to really see the details. I can't see anymore. Can you?"

"Are you serious? I must have ten pairs of reading glasses."

"Me too, but I can never find a pair when I need them."

We were having the same thoughts simultaneously— where had the years gone? Now we are older women who need reading glasses. How much richer would our lives have been if we had only made the time to see each other? And now that we were together again, it was so wonderful and we got along so well. It felt so natural, not forced.

This time I was the one who reached over to pat the back of her hand.

"I'm so happy to be here, Kiki. Thank you for all the many things you've done to make me feel so at home."

"But you are at home," she said. I could feel her sincerity.

It was true. I had found my place in the world.

My aunt returned with a magnifying glass and together we went from page to page. This album had belonged to my grandmother and it was filled with childhood photographs of my mother and my aunt Anna. There was my mother at six or seven years old, all dressed up for Easter. Then there were pictures of my mother and aunt in their pajamas. There were pictures of graduations, birthdays, and Christmases. Then there were more of my mother and father, and of course pictures of me and my brother with Yiayia and with Kiki. I had never seen any of them before. I just marveled at them all, moved that my Yiayia had chronicled my mother's life so completely and grateful that my aunt had saved them.

My aunt said something I didn't understand. I was tired and my intuition was shot for the night.

"She wants you to have this," Kiki said.

"Oh! Are you sure?" I said.

"*Nai, nai!*" my aunt said, nodding her head. "*Parakalo!*"

"She saved it all these years, hoping you or your brother would come to visit."

"*Sagapo. Efharisto,*" I said to my aunt, and I welled up

again. I had just told her that I loved her. And, of course, I thanked her.

My aunt said *parakalo* again and handed the linen wrapper to me as well, saying something to Kiki I didn't catch.

"What was that?" I said.

"She wants you to have this too. Yiayia kept this on top of the chest of drawers in her bedroom to protect it from scratches. She embroidered it herself when she was a girl."

It was just beautiful, bordered with flowers and butterflies.

"It's a treasure," I said.

After so many hugs and thank-yous and promises to come by the next day and the day after and every day that I was still in Greece, Kiki and Nicholas drove me home.

"We have a little surprise for you for tomorrow," Kiki said. "I hope we have a sunny day."

"Really? What?"

"Do you remember when you used to come here when you and JJ were really little? We used to go out into the country and have picnics and gather *horta*?"

"I remember the picnics. They were such fun. We used to fly kites. I remember that. What's *horta*?"

Nicholas said, "Kiki, my sweet, you don't pick *horta* in the summer. It's out of season."

"Ah! My love, you are right!" Kiki said.

"What's *horta*?" I asked again.

"Wild greens! Dandelion, honey wort, chicory . . . so many things. They grow all over the place. You pick it, bring it home, clean it up, and boil it until it's tender. Then you pour olive oil over it with salt and pepper and serve it as a side dish with potatoes and fish and bread and, of course, feta."

"We cook greens like that," I said, "but with a smoked ham hock, and we serve them with sherry pepper vinegar."

Kiki laughed and said, "That sounds terrible!"

"I'll admit, it's an acquired taste."

Kiki said, "I see. Well anyway, tomorrow my mother and I are going to take you to where we used to go and see if we can find some *horta*. It's a traditional thing to do. Whatever she has left over from tonight will become tomorrow's lunch and we will eat in the countryside!"

"That sounds wonderful," I said.

"Yes, you have to be able to say you've done this if you want to truly be Greek!" Nicholas said.

"*Horta*," I said. "Okay."

We said good night and I went inside my grandmother's house.

As I washed my face and got ready for bed, I thought again about how remarkable it was that I felt so comfortable here. It would be so easy to slip into a life in this place. The weather was mild, like Charleston was in the winter months, but the light was different, crisper. It seemed like there was more blue and the edges of everything were more clearly defined.

Maybe there were other places I could call home.

I loved the little village, my aunt's friends, and the long-lost cousins that I'd met. Life here seemed so easy and un-encumbered from the daily stresses of my life with Adam. At least no one here had to drive an hour to buy groceries. I needed to do something nice for my aunt. Maybe I'd make her a southern pound cake. In the morning, I told myself, I'd dig around in the kitchen to see what kind of pans there were. The oven looked ancient, but sometimes old stoves worked better than new ones. I wondered if my grandmother had ever used it.

I put my phone on its charger and checked my e-mail. There were notes from the boys and one from Carl. I opened his first.

> Hey! I hope you had a safe and uneventful trip over the pond. After our conversation when you were changing planes in New York, I decided to move out. Boy, they sure had us fooled, didn't they? Stay in touch. Take care. Carl

I felt sick knowing that something I told Carl led him to leave Eve. Eve had to be ripping mad. I wondered if she was going to stay in Raleigh. I wondered if she was with Adam, sleeping in my bed. And I didn't make Carl leave Eve. I reminded myself that it was what Adam and Eve had done that was the catalyst, not a side note from me. I should respond to this, I thought. But I wanted to think about it.

I opened Max's e-mail next.

> Hey, Mom! I can't believe you're really in Greece! Wow! When are you coming home? Have a ball! Love, Max xx

I'll be back, Max, but I don't know when, I thought.
I wrote him back.

> Max, baby, yes, I'm on Corfu visiting my family and having a wonderful time. I wish you and your brother were here with me to see all that I'm seeing. This is a gorgeous place. We'll have to come here together some day. Love, Mom xxoo

And from Luke . . .

Mom! Are you okay? I still can't believe you just got up and flew to
Greece! What's really going on? Are you sure you're okay? Love
you, Luke xx

That's my tenderhearted Luke, always worrying about
everyone's happiness. At some point when I knew what the
future looked like, I'd have to say something to my boys. The
future, which I'd been imagining as eight to ten years from
now, was supposed to include my boys coming home with
their lovely wives and babies and Adam and me spoiling
them all to death. And Adam and I would get old together,
snuggled up on big sofas watching old movies and laughing
at our house on the Stono in the winter. And we were supposed to be walking the beaches on the Isle of Palms holding
hands, watching the sun set, and just being happy to be alive
and with each other.

My smartphone pinged and I knew I had e-mail. It was
Kiki.

Pick you up at eleven?

Perfect!

I replied.

The rest of my e-mails were all junk. Nothing from Adam
or Eve. You'd think that by now I would've heard something
from Adam. Was I alive? Dead in a Greek ditch? Did he
care? Eve's behavior still baffled me. I went over last weekend again in my head, as I probably would a hundred times.
How in the world could she possibly have thought it was okay
to entertain my husband half naked in some slinky negligee
and then sleep on the sofa with him all night? Was she losing

her mind? Or did she have some latent gargantuan need for attention that I had never noticed? I mean, yes, Eve loved being the prettiest girl in our gang, but I had never had an inkling of anything like this coming. It was a little bit as though a freight train had come right through my house and made matchsticks of everything and I was standing in my own front yard looking at the wreck.

If I'd been in her position—which I cannot even imagine how I ever would be—I'd have run away to change clothes in the first instant. And even if I put on sweatpants and a sweatshirt, I wouldn't have gone to sleep with my head in my husband's friend's lap. Even if I had a fever so high that I was delirious! No, what they did was outrageous and there was no excuse for it in the world.

I missed Adam, of course, although the pain and disappointment I was feeling overshadowed it. He would've loved dinner tonight. I wondered again if he was spending time with Eve. Then, suddenly, I felt sorry for him. How terrible to carry a torch for someone else for decades. If he thought Eve would make him happier than I had, he should go be with her. He really should. One thing was for sure, I didn't want to live out my days with a man who really wanted to be someplace else with someone else. I was still in shock over the whole incident. And for all those years I'd thought I had a perfect marriage.

I crawled into bed and turned out the light. The night was quiet and the sheets were cool and comfortable. Was I sleeping in my grandmother's bed? Or my mother's? I'd have to ask Kiki.

What would become of me? I thought. Should I have been thinking about hiring a lawyer? No, it's too soon for that, I told myself. I didn't feel like I wanted a divorce anyway. But would I wind up divorced? How stupid! Maybe it was time to call Adam. Or maybe I'd just send him an e-mail. I wondered how long I should stay in Greece. Should I make some day trips to other islands and be a tourist? I was so tired. My skin felt itchy. I'd go to Nicholas's drugstore in the morning and buy some body lotion. Supposedly long flights dehydrated your skin. I'd heard that somewhere.

When the village lights went dark for the night, I could see a slice of the millions of stars in the sky from my bed if I turned on my side and looked through the window. I wondered what constellations were visible in a Greek winter sky. I would ask someone. Didn't Calypso tell Odysseus to keep the Bear on his left? Ursa Major. I couldn't find it if my life depended on it. But I had to say that celestial navigation was a piece of brilliance. Maybe someone had a telescope or maybe there was an observatory on one of the islands. I couldn't remember how to find Polaris, but I sure did love to look up at the heavens at night. Eventually I drifted off to sleep.

In the morning, I washed my hair and bathed. There was no hair dryer in the house, or at least I couldn't find one. I decided to just go native, so I braided my hair and tied it off with a rubber band. No one was looking at me anyway. I thought it might be a nice idea to bring something to the picnic, and I hadn't forgotten about the cake I intended to bake. While the coffeepot was percolating, I looked through all the cabinets. I found no cake pans, but I did find an old cast-iron skillet. I could make an upside-down cake. This would require a trip to the market, and the cake I'd make would depend on what I found there.

I drank two cups of coffee while I dressed and put the house in order. I thought about Carl's e-mail again. I still felt very upset that I'd had a part in Eve and Carl's separating. Having had even the slightest role in it was deeply troubling. I composed an e-mail to him.

> Carl, I have to tell you that I feel a little sick inside for telling you what Cookie said to me. If that is what caused you to leave, then there is blood on my hands too. I'm so sorry. Eliza

There. I'd spelled it out. I'd apologized. There was nothing more I could do. As my father used to say, that cat is already out of the bag. I hit the send button.

On my way to the shopping district I laughed, thinking, How am I going to buy anything with my pathetic command of the language? This ought to be good, I said to myself. My first stop was a bank that had an ATM on its outside wall. If I had cash it would make a transaction that much easier. I took five hundred euros from my account and thought about how wonderful technology was. And while five hundred euros was a lot, if I didn't spend them, it didn't matter. I knew I was coming back to Corfu. That was the moment when I knew I would never deprive myself of my family again. How had I allowed this much time to pass without ever visiting my Greek relatives? I thought about it and I had no real viable answer, except that Adam had no interest in my origins and I let everything he wanted come first. But I did know this much—for starters, I was going to bring JJ and his family back into my orbit. And I'd never be so weak again.

The village grocery store was small and had limited inventory. But I made my way around the aisles and picked up eggs, flour, butter, brown and white sugar, vanilla, and the other things I needed for a basic cake recipe. Then I noticed the clementines. They were bright orange and heavy with juice. I took a dozen. Then I bought some large green olives in oil, some stuffed grape leaves, a few tomatoes and cucumbers, and a block of feta. They had fresh bread, so I took a loaf and added it to my basket. It was a good idea to have a little food in the house. To my surprise, the market sold Pellegrino, and I wondered how a rather expensive Italian water came to be on these shelves next to the Greek varieties. I took a large bottle of the Greek water. And lastly, I picked up a bottle of local Greek white wine.

I paid for everything and the cashier was a little surprised that I didn't have my own shopping bags. She pointed to the stack of straw ones with leather shoulder straps. They were great looking—bright red with yellow stripes, navy with red stripes—and each one was different. Only five euros each. I took two and added them to my pile of groceries, and she began to fill them.

"American?" she said.

"Yes," I said, adding, "and Greek."

I loved saying that.

I had not considered that I would have to carry what I bought back to the house, as I walked along the cobblestone road, giving the strength of my shoulders a challenge. The next time I went food shopping I'd take the weight of everything into consideration. Like, if I wanted a case of water, I'd call a taxi or hitch a ride with Kiki. I was definitely no longer in Kansas.

On the other hand, for that short while I felt like a local—just an ordinary woman going out in the morning to do some errands. I passed schoolchildren in uniforms on their way to class and men whitewashing the street. The shops were opening, and people filled the little cafés, having coffee, frappés, and pastries, reading the newspaper, working on their laptops, beginning their day.

I was falling in love with the place.

Nicholas's pharmacy was open. I went inside and did not see him there, but there was a clerk behind the pharmacy counter. I sauntered over with a bottle of shampoo and a tube of some kind of body lotion and hoped a wide smile could substitute for my lack of proficiency in the language.

"Is Nicholas here?" I thought, I can't ask in Greek, so let's see how far my English takes me.

"No, no. Noon."

"Okay," I said.

I continued to smile and paid him for whatever it was I had chosen, hoping it wasn't hemorrhoid medication or something to relieve some godawful thing like herpes. I didn't need that bit to get back to Nicholas and by suppertime to Kiki. The thought of it put me in a lighthearted mood. Wouldn't that be nice?

I got home, unpacked everything, and turned the oven on to preheat, doing the conversion from Celsius to Fahrenheit with the help of Google. What did we do before Google? I said to the room, and adjusted the dial to 176 degrees. Then I opened up the Epicurious Web site and entered *upside down cake* in the search bar. And right away I found a recipe for clementine upside down cake.

I got to work. There was only a hand mixer to help me cream the butter and sugar, but it worked just fine. Pretty soon I was pouring the batter over the sliced clementines and a bed of caramelized brown sugar and butter. In half an hour, my grandmother's darling little house smelled like the citrus department in heaven.

I checked my e-mail. There was something from Carl.

Eliza, you had nothing to do with me moving out of the house. It's Eve. She is so unbelievably self-centered and desperate for attention she did what she did and still doesn't think she did anything wrong. Pathetic. Sad. Any word from Adam? Carl

I answered him right away, although it was something like four in the morning in Raleigh.

Carl, not one single word. Do you think they are together? Eliza

He would not be able to answer me for several hours. And I knew it was a sign of weakness to ask the question, but I wanted to know the truth. Carl would not lie to me. Unlike my husband, who massaged the truth, but only when he needed to. That he ever uttered those words in the first place was without question the stupidest thing ever said by a man to his wife in all of recorded history. I should've given him a trophy.

I checked the cake by touching the top. It felt firm. There were no toothpicks, so I broke a straw from the broom and dipped it into the center of the cake. It came out clean. I took it from the oven and put it on the cutting board to cool. After I put the cream all over my body, I dressed for the picnic, put the rest of the groceries away, and washed up the dishes. I hung the straw shopping bags on a hook by the door and thought that hook was probably there just for that reason. I'd bring one of the bags with me to gather herbs. Then I ran a knife around the edge of the cast-iron skillet and flipped the cake onto a large plate. It was beautiful, if I said so myself. In fact, I'd probably made fifty of that exact cake and they never turned out this well. It had to be the oven.

Kiki and Aunt Anna arrived promptly at eleven. I'd always thought Europeans were perpetually late. I sure was wrong about that. I took the cake wrapped in foil with a knife and a handful of paper napkins and dropped it in one of my new bags, thinking how versatile it was.

We all said hello and kissed cheeks, then Kiki took my bag and put it in the back of her car with the rest of the picnic, and off we went into the countryside to gather *horta*.

We drove in the direction of Arillas, a seaside town an hour and a half northwest of Dassia. We passed under many canopies of pines and countless olive groves, through a half dozen tranquil and charming villages, before we descended down to our destination. I wanted to stop every ten minutes and just have a look to try and sear the landscape into my memory. But Kiki and Aunt Anna said, "Wait, wait. Wait until you see." And of course, they were right. Arillas was breathtaking.

"Gorgeous!" I said, thinking there must be a thousand shades of green and blue out there and the sandy beach was so white. Soon my phone was filled with photos.

"Isn't it something?" Kiki said.

"Yes, it really is unbelievably beautiful."

We drove along the top of a cliff and parked there, where we could enjoy the panoramic views of the whole coastline. And there were picnic tables there in a grassy area for people just like us. We got out and Aunt Anna swept her arm across the whole sight before us, urging me to take it all in. I took a lot more pictures with my phone.

We began to unpack lunch. There was a warm breeze, despite the time of year, and we were quite comfortable to eat outside.

"So, Kiki? Is any of the furniture in Yiayia's house hers?"

"Eliza, you are sleeping in the bed where your mother was born, but of course it has a new mattress!" Kiki said and interpreted my question and her answer for Aunt Anna, who had a good laugh.

I unwrapped my clementine cake and my aunt gasped and said something in Greek that seemed to be complimentary.

"Thank you!" I said.

"It's gorgeous!" Kiki said. "Where did you buy it?"

"Honey, I didn't buy it. I made it!"

"In *that* kitchen? With Yiayia's old oven? You've got to be joking!"

Aunt Anna had already cut a wedge and was eating it with her fingers. And even though she was moaning with delight and she had a mouthful, she muttered something in Greek.

"Don't pick on that oven. I think it's got a little magic in it. What did she just say?"

"She said, life's short, eat dessert first!" Kiki said. "Maybe she's right." Kiki leaned over, cut herself a big wedge, and took a bite. "Omagawd!"

"Good, right?"

Eat dessert first. It was on T-shirts, cocktail napkins, greeting cards, painted on driftwood in every gift store in America for the last twenty years. And the saying had finally made its way to Greece. Maybe it started in Greece. Who knew? It didn't matter if it was old or cliché, there was a lot of truth in it. I cut myself a piece of cake and joined them.

"Yes, ma'am! You could be a professional pastry chef!" Kiki said.

"I really love to cook and bake. Hey, do you think your friend Alexandros might let me in his kitchen before I go home, you know, to cook alongside him? I'm still dreaming about that meal."

"Are you kidding? I think that if you made him a cake like this he'd give you the keys to the place. I'm not joking, Eliza. This cake is that good."

We ate cake and leftover chicken cooked with lemons and creamy moussaka and picked on some marinated olives. There wasn't a salad in sight, I thought. I'm going to gain a hundred pounds.

After lunch, we repacked the car with our leftovers and locked it up. It was time to pick *horta*.

"You're going to have to show me what's edible. I'll probably pick out bad mushrooms and poison ivy!" I said.

"No worries," Kiki said. "I'll show you."

We walked deep into the woods. The air smelled sweet, and it was a lot cooler under all the trees. For the next hour, we picked Neapolitan garlic, wild asparagus, wild mustard, and chicory. Soon, our bags were stuffed with greens. But with all the bending down and getting up I was feeling awfully tired. Exhausted, in fact.

"I could lie down right here and sleep for ten hours," I said to Kiki.

"Jet lag," she said. "It takes about a week, I think, to feel like you're in your own skin."

"You know, I can't just stay here forever. I wish I could, but I can't."

"We wish you could stay too! I feel like I've found the sister I never had."

"Oh, Kiki! Me too!"

And I don't know what got into me at that moment, but I burst into tears. The next thing I knew, Aunt Anna had her arms around me, making *sssh, sssh* sounds to console me, and Kiki was giving me tissues to blow my nose.

"It's about your husband, isn't it?" Kiki said.

I nodded my head and the whole story came tumbling out. Kiki interpreted as I blurted out the facts, and by the end of it, we were all quiet.

"It's okay," Kiki said after a minute. "He's worried about getting old and dying. But I don't think he loves her. He loves the *memory* of being young and the *memory* of her."

"Maybe." I hadn't thought of it that way.

"Your life with him is reality. Not this silliness of pretending. Your Adam wouldn't trade one of you for a thousand of her. Wait. You'll see."

Aunt Anna said something in rapid-fire Greek to Kiki.

"What'd I miss?" I said.

"Old Greek saying," Kiki said and giggled, covering her mouth with her hand.

"What is it?" I said.

"My mother says, when it comes to love all men are idiots."

I had stopped crying long enough to laugh.

"They don't just say that in Greece. It's a universal truth."

CHAPTER 16

adam's snake in
the garden

It was only seven thirty in the morning when Dad knocked
on my door. The bed was unmade, but I had showered
and shaved and dressed for work.

"You got coffee?" he said.

"Of course I do. I'll pour you a cup."

"Thanks," he said.

I went to the kitchen and saw him walk down the hall
toward the bedrooms. Why was he doing that? Maybe he
needed to use the bathroom. I filled a mug for him, gave it
a splash of creamer, and put it on the counter. Then I threw
some bread in the toaster and took the butter out of the refrigerator. He reappeared and took a long drink.

"You want some toast?" I said.

"Okay, sure. Listen, son, I have to talk to you."

He climbed up on a barstool and I leaned back against the sink, steadying myself for some unsolicited advice.

"Okay. Talk to me."

The toast popped up and I removed it, quickly dropping it on the cutting board. It was hot. I began to scrape butter across it and put a slice on a paper napkin for him. Now that I was maybe a bachelor, my goal was to never need to run the dishwasher more than once a week. I was going to conserve energy and save a little money.

"It's about last night," he said.

"What about it?"

"Well, look, you're a grown man and what you do is your own business."

"Thank you for that," I said.

"Eve didn't stay here last night, did she?"

"That's a helluva question to ask. Didn't you always tell me that discretion was the better part of valor? But no, she didn't. Do you think I'm completely crazy?"

He sighed heavily and said, "Women." He folded his toast in half and took a big bite.

"Agreed, but which women?"

"Well, Eve was supposed to be staying with Cookie and she never came home last night. And when Cookie called her she didn't pick up."

"She probably didn't feel like getting read the riot act again. Maybe she drove herself over to Wild Dunes. Oh wait, she said she was going to check to see if Charleston Place had a room."

"So, you left her at the hotel then?"

"I left her *in the bar of the restaurant.* Dad, please. What do you think?"

"I think you have the wrong attitude, son . . ."

"Oh, come on! I have not done anything wrong here. What the hell is the matter with everyone?"

"Since when are you such a knucklehead? I am still your father and I want you to listen to me."

"Okay, I'm listening."

"Perception is everything. Finding you two together at Charleston Place and knowing the story about last Friday night, it looked like monkey business. No matter what you say you were or weren't doing, it still looked like some monkey business was going on. I can tell you Clarabeth wouldn't like it if I took Cookie out to some fancy restaurant without her."

"And from my vantage point, I wouldn't be surprised if Cookie would pick up the check just to have you to herself for a few hours. Want a refill?"

"Sure," he said and granted me a sort of half smirk. "Thanks."

I filled his mug again and pushed the carton of half-and-half toward him.

"I just don't want to see you do something stupid and mess up your whole life, that's all. Eve is a pretty girl and all that, but between us? Not much between the ears. She can't even begin to measure up to a woman like Eliza. I think you know that."

I didn't disagree with him.

"Eliza thinks I lied to her."

"Well, if you did, then you need to do something to make it up to her. Lying is very bad for business."

I remembered then that Eliza had let me tell her the story of Friday night and I had left out the part about sleeping on the sofa. She had set me up knowing I would reveal the story only on a need-to-know basis. Omission of unnecessary facts was not the same thing as flat-out lying, in my book. When she nailed me on that detail I fessed up, didn't I? And I apologized, didn't I?

"Dad? My conscience is clear."

I put my cup in the sink and looked at my watch. It was past time for me to go to work. Then I realized I'd need someone to do payroll for the week, because Eliza wasn't here. Great. Thanks, Eliza.

"Well, that's good, Adam. One other thing. I hope you and your clear conscience will be happy together. If I were you, I'd be on a plane to Corfu. But that's just me. If you want to have dinner this week, let me know."

He put his mug in the sink next to mine, turned around, and walked out.

I could not remember a time in my entire adult life that my father had spoken to me that way. He had always had my back. His disapproval made my confidence wither a little. I hated it that he couldn't or wouldn't even try to bring himself to see things my way. In fact, I had a very strong suspicion that he believed there really was something sexual going on between Eve and me. He should have heard how I turned Eve down. I could have had her panties off in no time.

I just really wasn't interested in doing it. The timing was all wrong. Now, if Eliza wanted to play the wronged woman to the hilt, we'd see. If Eliza wants to do something crazy like file for divorce, I might give Eve a whirl. But it wasn't likely that Eliza would be so rash. She had always been reasonable, except on a few topics I don't like to think about.

Go to Corfu? For what? I didn't have the time for drama. No, I knew Eliza. It was better to let her live her dream. She'd be home in a few days, and if we still had issues to settle we would settle them like civilized adults, the same way we always did. I'd show her where she went wrong and she'd agree and we'd be okay again. That's how a marriage is supposed to work. I'd forgive her for taking off and then we'd have a nice dinner. And then we'd have an epic night in the sack. Yeah, I was especially looking forward to that part.

Well, I'm sorry to report that that's not exactly how it worked out. Two weeks went by and I still hadn't heard a word from her. I know, I know. I could have e-mailed her, but I was plenty pissed. I could stonewall too. What was she thinking? This was lunacy! Did she think she could just walk out on me and our family and resume living in another country? And then something terrible happened. Clarabeth tripped over the hem of her nightgown or bathrobe—it was unclear—and she fell down the long flight of steps in her entrance hall and broke her neck. She was carrying a tray of breakfast dishes because she liked to have her breakfast in bed. Dad called me right away.

"There's been a terrible accident!" he said. "Clarabeth fell down the stairs!"

"Call 911, Dad! I'll be there as fast as I can! Stay calm! Is she conscious?"

"No. I think she might be . . . God, I can't bring myself to say it."

"Don't touch her, Dad. If it's a neck injury, you might do her more harm. I'm in my car. Just hang on for a few minutes."

I raced there from Summerville, and for once traffic was with me. I got there in time to see a fire truck, an ambulance, and two patrol cars, with the lights spinning and doors left open. I moved through the crowd just as Clarabeth was being taken away with a sheet over her head. My poor father was sitting on the stairs with his head in his hands, weeping. I sat down next to him, put my arm around his shoulder, and gave him a good squeeze.

"It's gonna be okay, Dad."

"I know, I know, but I blame myself. I told her I'd bring the dishes down and she insisted on doing it herself. I was in the bathroom shaving and I heard this horrible crashing sound and a thud and then silence. The most awful silence I have ever heard. Oh, God, I feel so terrible about this. I wouldn't have hurt a hair on her head, much less be the cause of her death! Oh, my God! What have I done?"

"Nothing, Dad."

"She had to wear those crazy slippers with all that marabou! I told her they were dangerous."

I could not and did not want to envision Clarabeth in chiffon and marabou. It hurt my brain. And where the hell was

Eliza when I needed her? What would she have done if she was here?

"She loved being glamorous. You know that. And Dad, her accident was not your fault; it was her time. That's all. Come on now. Let's call Cookie and tell her what's happened. She'll want to know right away."

So, he made the call to Cookie, who called Eve, who called Daphne, who called Carl. I called my boys, and then there was the matter of notifying Eliza. I wrote her an e-mail.

Eliza, Clarabeth has passed away. Dad is bereft. Funeral is Friday.
Please come home.

Twenty-four hours later she was walking through the door. When she didn't find me at the house, she'd called Dad. Not me. Dad. Dad, Cookie, and I were at Dad's house for dinner.

"Your car is parked in your garage," Dad said to her, and he said something more I didn't hear and then hung up. "She's coming over."

"Fine," I said. "It will be good to see her, I hope."

"Listen to your old man. Put a smile on your face and be nice to her. I don't care how much you try to convince yourself that she's in the wrong, she's not. You are. And if you don't want to lose her forever, stop acting like this."

"Let's see how she acts too."

"Yeah, boy. Is that clear conscience keeping you warm at night?"

I didn't answer him.

"Your clear conscience is going to bite you in the ass," he said.

I didn't answer that either.

We were in his den. I was watching the Golf Channel. Dad was reading the paper and considering a nap in the recliner. He was miserable, trying not to cry. What good would tears do?

"So, Dad? What exactly are the plans for a funeral?" I said.

"Not going to be one," he said. "I'll tell you all during supper."

"Okay," I said.

Dad was clearly very unhappy and there was no reason to press him for details then.

Cookie was in the kitchen, also miserable. She was putting supper together and weeping for her lost friend. And I was avoiding her as much as possible. I had enough trouble on my hands thanks to her.

I decided to take a middle road with Eliza and pretend that everything between us was, as my boys used to say when they were little, hunky-dory. Max and Luke were coming in late that night, both of them driving. I didn't know if they had clean sheets on their beds and I didn't think they would care if they had them anyway. Eliza had always seen to that kind of thing.

Eve and Carl were bringing Daphne down Thursday. Whatever the plans were to lay Clarabeth to rest, we would all go along with them. Anyway, we had more than enough food to get us all through the weekend, and on top of everything else, Cookie made a trip to Harris Teeter for soft drinks and other groceries. Nobody was going hungry. Clarabeth was barely cold, and as expected, Cookie was at the helm. The thought of Cookie making serious moves on my father sent a chill up my spine. I could possibly have that horror show of a woman in my life at every turn instead of once a year at Wild Dunes, which I imagined was canceled anyway until further notice.

Dad was struggling to hide his emotions but doing okay, all things considered. He was still weepy now and then. When something would get to him, some memory of something or when he noticed an object she treasured, he would break down. That's why I was there—to offer sympathy and to give him a shoulder. I think the abrupt circumstances of her death made everything harder to handle. It had to have been traumatic for him to hear her falling and then to see her lying there motionless at the bottom of the stairs. I couldn't imagine the pumping adrenaline rush and the surge of panic he must have felt. He was lucky he hadn't given himself a massive stroke.

Dad and Clarabeth had been married for only four years, but I'd say all their years together had been very happy ones. I knew he was going to miss her something awful. She did everything for him. While Clarabeth was much older than Dad, it had never really seemed so until just recently. I could see signs of her slowing down, and she'd had slight mobility issues for the past ten years or so. We just chalked it up to osteoarthritis. If you lived long enough, something would most likely hurt.

I heard a car door close. Eliza. I got up, went to the front door, and opened it. There she was, walking toward me. She seemed different. Maybe there was more purpose in her stride or maybe she had on a new coat. I couldn't remember ever seeing the one she was wearing.

"Hey, there!" I said, with a friendly smile on my face.

"Hi, Adam," she said, flatly.

She took off her sunglasses and looked at me straight in the eyes in such a way that I knew I was still in very deep shit.

"Are you okay?" I said.

"I'm perfectly fine, Adam. How's Dad?"

"He's broken up but he's coping pretty well."

"Where is he?"

"He's in the den," I said and stepped aside for her to cross the threshold.

She moved past me without touching me and I thought, Wait a minute! Not even a hug? Apparently not. I followed her inside.

"Hey, Dad!" she said. "I'm so sorry about Clarabeth."

Dad got out of his recliner and held out his arms to her. They embraced each other and he kissed her cheek.

He said, "She was a great lady and I loved her. Thank you. I'm glad you came, Eliza."

"I wouldn't let you go through this without me at your side," she said.

I smartly said, "Because you're a great lady too." She turned around and looked at me as though I had on one of those gag arrow headband things that appears to be going in one ear and out the other. "Can I get you something to drink? That's a long flight, I guess, huh? Dad? You want something?"

"No, son, but thank you."

"Eliza?"

"I'll get something for myself in a few minutes," she said, obviously not wanting to accept any hospitality from me.

I left the room and headed for the kitchen, thinking, So, is this how it's going to be? Well, I can spread the frost too. I could hear Clarabeth in my mind saying, what's good for the goose is good for the gander. God, she was a funny woman. A motormouth, yes, but a nice one. I'd miss her too. I was half wishing her spirit would haunt the house and scare Cookie away.

Cookie was there in the butler's pantry taking plates from a cabinet and flatware from a drawer.

"Eliza's here," I said. "Straight from the airport."

"Oh! Wonderful! How was her trip?"

"Long, I imagine."

"Is everything between you two all right?"

Emboldened by the somber occasion that brought us together, I said, "Thanks to you? No."

She gasped and said, "What possible thing could I have done to add to your unhappiness? I merely told Eliza the truth. What I can't believe is that the four of you have been gallivanting together for all these years and you kept your history with Eve a secret! You and Eve never told your spouses! Lying is disgraceful." She then busied herself opening and closing cabinets, looking for something that wasn't where she thought it should be. "This kitchen was organized by a crazy person."

I reached in the refrigerator, took out a beer, and popped

the top. I took a long drink and stared at her, giving her the most murderous expression I could muster.

"Some things are better left unsaid, Cookie. And you know what? It might be nice if we buried Clarabeth before you redecorate her house."

"Don't be ridiculous, Mr. Stanley. Your father is a dear friend to me and nothing more."

"Right," I said.

"I'll have you know I have a date this weekend with a very nice man I met on social media."

"Is that so? Watch out. He might be an ax murderer."

"He happens to be a retired investment banker from New York City, for your information."

"Well, if he wants a referral, tell him not to call me. I'm going back to talk to my wife."

"You want my advice?"

"Not especially."

"Well, here it is anyway. Make up with her. She's the best thing that ever happened to you."

It was the first useful thing I'd heard come from Cookie's mouth since this whole debacle started. I liked her better when she was a drunk. So, she had a date, did she? God help him.

I found Eliza right where I'd left her, in the den with Dad.

"Eliza? Can I peel you away from Dad for a moment? I want to talk to you."

I saw her inhale and accept the inevitable. She stood up and started walking in my direction. She had to talk to me.

"Let's go in the living room," she said.

"Okay," I said. "The boys are coming in tonight."

I sat on the huge floral-print sofa and she sat on the opposite end.

"I know. They sent me an e-mail," she said and looked around at the room. "This room is very aqua."

"And pink. Well, you know Clarabeth."

"And long on fringe. Yeah, well, she was a glamour-puss."

The walls were pale green, like Granny Smith apples, and the raised panels were painted gold. It was too Marie Antoinette for my taste.

"Yeah. She was that. So, Eliza? Where are we?"

"What do you mean?"

"Are things okay between us?" May as well get right to the point, I thought.

"I think you know that they aren't."

"So what are you telling me? That you live in Greece now? That you want a divorce?" I was trying to get the truth without letting her know how upset I was.

"I'm telling you nothing of the kind, Adam. But here's what I am telling you. I have family there that I haven't seen since I was a child. Lovely, educated, successful family with children and lives that I've known nothing about all these years. I feel like the last twenty-something years flew by so fast and I was so busy working for you and raising our boys that I never, ever saw a window of time that I could use to see what the rest of my family was like. And that's crazy."

"But you haven't been miserable with me and Luke and Max, have you?"

"Let's not put my relationship with the boys on the same

table as my relationship with you. I would've given my heart and my time to my sons with or without you. But we raised them together, and I think we did a pretty good job."

"Thanks for giving me some credit."

"No, you deserve a lot of credit for how well they turned out. And *then* there's my relationship with you."

"Which is . . . ?"

"In trouble."

"I love you, Eliza. I only love you. I don't love Eve. I swear I don't."

"I used to believe *anything* you told me and I have overlooked so much, wanting to keep things on an even keel. But since Carl and I found you and Eve together, why would I think you're telling me the truth? How am I supposed to trust you? I don't know what to believe. I don't know, Adam. You need to know that when this is over, I'm going back to Corfu."

"What? Why? You can't just go off when the mood strikes, Eliza!"

"Oh, yes, I can."

"You're my wife, you belong at my side, and you have responsibilities to me and to our business! Do you have any idea how much I've had to deal with since you've been gone?"

"I'm sorry for any inconvenience, and I'm going back to Corfu because I have unfinished business there."

"What kind of unfinished business?"

"My first cousin, Kiki, and her husband own a little restaurant with a friend, and I've been running the kitchen with him while his sous chef is on vacation."

"Let them hire someone else!"

"I don't want to. For once in my life I'm doing what *I* want to do!"

"Okay, Eliza. You go back. Meanwhile, why don't we try to put on a good face for the sake of the boys and the others?"

"I'm here, aren't I? But then, you're the better actor, Adam. You've been putting on a good face for years."

I thought about what she meant. She still thought I'd been in love with Eve all along. She wasn't going to get away with making me eat shit forever.

"Eliza. I love you. I have always loved you. I thought I loved Eve, but I don't. Not one bit."

"How do you know?"

Now I had her attention.

"I just don't feel it."

"Let's see how the next few days unfold, Adam."

Cookie appeared in the hallway outside the living room. She stood there under a crystal chandelier that had to be as big as a small car with this big fake smile on her face. God, I hated her guts. She was such a meddling troublemaker.

"Hello, Eliza. Y'all ready for some supper?"

eliza

We sat down to dinner in the kitchen. Cookie had bought two rotisserie chickens from Harris Teeter and hacked them into chunks with no regard for aesthetics. There was dry salad from a bag in a bowl and a cut-up baguette in a basket. I got the butter from the refrigerator, cut some pats, and put them on a small plate. Then I took the olive oil and balsamic vinegar from the pantry and mixed up a quick dressing.

"You use salad dressing? It makes you fat," Cookie said.

"No, it doesn't. Processed carbohydrates and refined sugar make you fat," I said. "Salad dressing in moderate amounts just makes your food taste better. And olive oil is good for you, especially your skin." I was fed up with her too.

Cookie snapped back, "I'm sure you know better."

"Maybe she does," Adam said.

I refused to meet his eyes or to give any indication that I appreciated his support.

The atmosphere was awkward. Adam was feeling no love.

"So, Eliza, how was your trip to Greece?" Cookie asked.

"Incredible," I said. "I'll show you pictures of my long-lost family after dinner."

"Did you have nice weather?" Ted asked.

"Beautiful," I said. "It's a lot like a Charleston winter except for the humidity."

"Did I tell y'all about the letter I found?" Ted said.

When Ted went looking for Clarabeth's will, he found an envelope stapled to the folder with his name on it.

"What did it say?" Cookie asked.

"Yes, what did it say?" I asked.

"Here, y'all can read it yourselves," he said and pulled it from his back pocket.

Clarabeth had probably left very specific instructions in her will about how her funeral was to be conducted. Cookie and Adam got up and stood behind me to read it over my shoulder.

My darling Ted,

If you are reading this it means I'm already singing in that great big choir in heaven, at least I hope that's where I go! (Please pray for that to happen to my soul!)

Although we found each other later in life, you are my most favorite husband of all and your family became like my children and grandchildren. I want you to know that you brought me the greatest joy I have ever known and that I loved you with all my heart. Everything I'm leaving behind is yours to enjoy. I do not want you to fret.

When you think of me I want you to smile and remember all the happiness we shared.

As to my funeral, I don't want one. What I'd prefer is to have my body delivered to McAlister's, have it cremated, and tell them to put my ashes in the urn that's on the fireplace mantel in the living room. Then I want you, Adam, Eliza, the boys, Cookie, Carl, Eve, and Daphne to take my ashes out to dinner in the private room upstairs at Cypress, my favorite restaurant. Hire a string quartet or a piano player, put my ashes in the middle of the table, order a fabulous dinner, expensive wine, arrange for gorgeous flowers, and say nice things about me. After dinner please take my ashes home in the urn and put them back on the mantel. The cash to pay for all of this is in the pocket of my baby blue cashmere robe in the guest bedroom closet. Now, go have fun!

All my love,
Clarabeth

"Wasn't that just like her?" I said.

"She was a practical woman. Thoughtful too," Ted said. "So, that's the plan."

Clarabeth was also very dignified but not particularly into any kind of organized religion. I knew she believed in God because we talked about it once or twice. And I was very glad indeed that she didn't want to do something crazy like hire the Burke High School Marching Band to lead her casket down Broad Street in a Cinderella coach. Some people make a spectacle of themselves even after they die. I mean, what's the point? One last hurrah on the way out? Give your money to a worthy cause instead.

Ted, Clarabeth's worthy cause, was now a very rich widower, but he didn't care about money so much. He never had been exposed to all the trappings of wealth until he met Clarabeth. But he would rather have had Clarabeth alive than all the money in the world. That much was clear to everyone.

"So, did you look in the pocket of her baby blue bathrobe?" Adam asked.

"Yep. And I found the biggest wad of hundred-dollar bills I've ever seen in my life. So, it looks like Clarabeth is taking us all out to dinner. Should I call Cypress for Saturday night? I'm picking up the urn on Saturday morning."

"Why not?" Cookie said. "I know a pianist I can call if you'd like. And I can call Charleston Flowers."

"I thought you had a date," Adam said.

"That's Friday night, Mr. Stanley," Cookie said.

"Who do you have a date with?" Ted asked.

He looked surprised and, to be honest, a little shaken.

"Why? Are you jealous?" Cookie asked.

"Ever the provocateur!" I said.

"Certainly not!" Ted said. "I just like to know what's going on."

"Boy, is that the question of the day or what?" Adam said, laughing with an annoying little *heh, heh, heh*.

I bit my tongue so I wouldn't tell him how not funny he was.

"No, I met a very nice man on one of those dating sites for seniors and we're meeting at Rue de Jean for an early supper."

"Well, that's wonderful, Cookie. If he seems creepy at all, I want you to get up and leave," Ted said. "Tell him you're going to the ladies' room, but walk out the back door."

Ted wasn't fooling me. I could see that he was a little jealous that Cookie's attentions were diversified.

"I have another escape," I said. "Why don't I call your cell at around seven thirty and pretend to be a sick friend who needs you right away? If he's awesome, tell me to call someone else. If he's not, just ask me where I am and tell him you have to go."

"Those are both great ideas," she said. "To tell you the truth, I am a little nervous. After all, this man is a stranger. I'm sure he's very nice, but who knows? Anyway, Rue de Jean is close enough to my house. I can walk home if I need to."

The meal ended pretty quickly, as there was no compulsion to stay at the table and eat any more of the long-dead chicken than we had to. I helped Cookie clean up the kitchen while Adam wiped down the counters and Ted took out the trash.

"Well, I'm about to fall on my face," I said. "It's been an extremely long day for me. Thanks for dinner, Cookie. Good night, Ted." I gave him a kiss on the cheek.

"I'll follow you," Adam said.

I gave him the smallest smile humanly possible. I mean, I didn't hate the man.

I drove home with Adam right behind me, so we pulled into the garage at the exact same time. We closed the doors with synchronized *thunks*. I sat there for a moment, just to think about how I was going to handle the sleeping situation. Well, the boys were going to be arriving soon. Did I really want to let them know something was wrong between their father and me? No, I did not. I thought a minute more until I hatched a plan.

We got out of our cars and went inside.

"I'm glad you're back," Adam said.

"Only until Monday, then I'm going back to Greece."

"I know, but how long will you be away?"

"A week, maybe two. I'm not sure."

"Eliza! You can't just leave me like this and expect everything to be the same when you get home, you know."

"Adam? That's the point, isn't it? I don't want everything to be the same when I return. Got it? You've got a whole lot of soul-searching to do before there's a chance to make things right between us again."

"I've already done that. I want things right between us."

"How do you know?"

"Because I saw Eve. And I know now that I'm just not interested in her like that."

"Really? Where'd you see her?"

"Well, Cookie probably already put it on the front page of the *Post and Courier,* so I may as well tell you first. Eve called me after Carl left her. She was almost hysterical and she said she needed to see me. I felt bad for her, you know? I told her to make a reservation and I'd meet her somewhere for dinner. So she booked a table at Charleston Grill, and I—"

"Charleston Grill? You're kidding me, right? You couldn't meet her at Home Team Barbecue?" He took her to Charleston Grill? Was he insane?

"Anyway, I walked into the bar and there she was. It was very obvious to me that she thought you and I were finished and now was her time. It was like the biggest turnoff ever. Suddenly, I knew she was the last person I'd ever be interested in. Besides, she can't hold a candle to you, Eliza, and I think we both know that."

"Telling me the truth is not scoring you any points with me. You know, sometimes you are so incredibly egotistical and stupid at the same time that it simply takes my breath away."

"What does that mean?"

"First of all, this isn't a contest between me and Eve. Second, the last time you felt so badly for her you slept with her on her sofa and I went to Greece. I'm glad you've come to a decision about Eve and I'm sorry for her, I really am. She sounds like a rudderless boat. But what really galls me is that you say she turns you off."

"What's galling about that? I came to realize that I don't want her."

"Because it was too messy? Too complicated? Or was it just because the fantasy of her being unattainable died?"

"What's that supposed to mean?"

"People want what they can't have. When they can have it they don't want it anymore."

"Oh."

"Adam, until Carl and I caught you two red-handed, I was blissfully unaware that you had a serious history with Eve. And just because you don't want *her* anymore doesn't mean that everything between *us* is okay. You slept with her, Adam.

I don't care if you say something happened or it didn't. You slept with her. So I'm going back to Greece on Monday. I'm giving you time to think."

He looked at me as though he didn't know what else there was to consider.

I poured myself a glass of water and drank it all at once. He was exasperating. I refilled the glass and turned to him. "I'm going to bed, Adam. Please wait up for the boys and lock up the house."

"Okay," he said.

I brushed my teeth and washed my face and fell into bed. If he tried to so much as touch me I'd kick him right into next week.

It must have been around three in the morning when I felt him slip under the covers. Very quietly, he turned out the light, and soon he was snoring lightly. He didn't even attempt to spoon. I guess he was getting the message. I couldn't believe he didn't understand that what he had done had an impact on how I felt about him. The more I learned about his secret longing for Eve, the less I liked him as my husband. He had reframed himself in my mind as a thickheaded man who couldn't conceive that his words and actions hurt me deeply, benign as he may have thought they were. The consequences were that what he had done changed the way I felt about him. And a halfhearted apology wouldn't restore my love for him.

The time difference between Greece and Charleston of seven hours was working against me. I felt like it was time to get up. I rolled over and looked at our digital alarm. Four forty-five. Too early to rise. I'd had about six hours of sleep, which was enough to keep me awake. I tried to drift off again, but my mind was racing as though the day had already begun. I'd come home because Adam said the funeral was Friday, but there was to be no funeral. Another lie. Another manipulation. Or Adam was just being sloppy.

Eve, Carl, and Daphne would be arriving tonight. This should be the most magnificently awkward meeting in the entire canon of life gone awry, I thought. They had to come. They had known Clarabeth nearly as long as we had. And they loved Ted. And it wasn't like Ted would be swarmed by the families of Clarabeth's ex-husbands and old friends showing up for the first time in decades. We were a small tribe, and their absence would be conspicuous and hurtful to Ted. But it would be awkward. There was no doubt about it. I assumed they would all stay at Cookie's, but maybe I was wrong. It didn't matter to me where they slept, but boy, who slept where was becoming a popular topic for discussion.

I got out of bed as quietly as I could. I headed for the shower, where I would stand under the water for as long as I could take it and rinse away all the germs from the long flight from Corfu to Athens to New York to Charleston. I was probably carrying a hundred different viruses. Then I would blow out my hair, dress, and make breakfast for my boys. After I had looked at them from head to toe and decided they were all right, I'd go get some groceries, because I knew without looking that Adam had not been to the store. He probably didn't even know where a grocery store was.

By seven thirty, I was in the kitchen frying sausage patties from the freezer and scrambling eggs when Luke appeared.

"Hi, sweetheart!" I said. "How are you?"

He threw his arms around me and hugged me hard.

"God, I love my mom! We got any coffee?"

"In the pot," I said. "Help yourself. What time did you get in? There's some milk in the fridge."

He took a mug from the cabinet and filled it with milk and coffee.

"Right at midnight. Dad was snoring his guts out in his recliner. Max rolled in around one."

"So, how are you? You doing okay?"

"Oh, yeah. I'm doing great. Too bad about Miss Clarabeth, huh?"

"Terrible. But at least it was quick. And she was eighty-seven. Although I suspect the closer you get to eighty-seven, the younger eighty-seven seems."

"That sounds right. So, what's the drill? When's the funeral?"

I gave him the plans and he said, "I skipped two days of classes and I could've just come down on Saturday?"

"That's true, but your grandfather is pretty torn up. Having you around will be a great source of comfort for him."

I scrambled two eggs in a bowl for him and melted a pat of butter in my skillet. Just as I was about to empty the bowl into the pan, Max came strolling into the kitchen and hugged me.

"Hey, baby!" I said. "You hungry?"

"Starving!"

I cracked two more eggs into the bowl, added a little more milk, and whipped them around. Just as I was about to pour them into the sizzling butter, Adam showed his face.

"Family breakfast? Just like the old days! Good morning, gentlemen. Eliza." He came around the stove and gave me a kiss on the cheek. I let him, as the boys were right there watching.

I got a bigger bowl and deposited the contents of the small bowl and two more eggs into it. Then I reached into the freezer and pulled out the emergency English muffins I kept there, as there was not a crust of bread to be found in the pantry. I opened the whole package, broke them apart, and put them into the microwave to defrost. I added more sausage to the other pan and opened a new jar of my strawberry jam, placing it on the counter. I should've known I'd be hosting a kitchen party this morning. Men are just like houseplants. They flourish when tended to and become dull and lackluster when you ignore them.

"So, how's Pop handling this?" Max asked.

"He's devastated," Adam said. "Worse yet, he blames himself."

"Let's go over there after breakfast," Luke said.

"Absolutely," Max said.

"And I think part of the reason for the Saturday night dinner is he couldn't get the ashes until then," I said.

"Cremation is weird," Luke said.

"I don't know," Max said. "Considering the world popula-
tion? Pretty soon there won't be any room left for cemetery
plots. Cremation reduces carbon footprint."

"What?" Luke started laughing. "Reduces carbon footprint? That's some bull, brother."

"Okay," Max said, "maybe it's a bit of a stretch."

Adam said, "Clarabeth might have left us unexpectedly,
but she sure did it with style."

He told the boys the details of her plans for her own small
memorial service and they were impressed.

"Cool. She was always a very classy lady," Max said.

"Yeah, she was," Luke said. "But, man, she sure liked to
work her jaw."

"Yep, she could go on and on about nothing forever," I
said. "I loved her. And I'm going to miss her."

"Me too," all three men said.

And men they were. It was hard to reconcile the near
adults my boys had become with the way I felt about them
in my heart. To me they were still little boys with skinned
knees, full of the devil, my ever-reliable source of endless
happiness and laughter. It seemed like I turned my back on
my sweet little fellows one day and on the next they were
strapping young men, boys no more. I looked at them and
marveled at how they resembled the best of Adam and me.

Adam and the boys moved everything from the counter
to the table and actually set it without being asked, another
sign of their approaching maturity. I put a platter of scrambled eggs and sausage in front of them with a basket of hot

English muffins, butter and homemade jam to go with it. My boys descended on it like locusts, but Adam didn't seem to have much of an appetite.

"Remember how Rufus used to sit under the table, hoping we'd feed him something?" Max said.

"What's life without hope?" Adam said and looked my way.

"Cue the violins," I said.

Ignoring us, Luke said with a sigh, "He was a great dog."

After breakfast was cleared away, the balance of the day was spent with Ted. Televisions were on wherever there was one, because we needed white noise. We took walks around the property. Mountains of sandwiches were consumed. Later in the afternoon, Cookie's caterer dropped off a rib roast and a potato casserole with a container of roasted root vegetables. The fragrance of all the onions, garlic, and red meat made our mouths water. I took the task of setting the dining room table with Clarabeth's best. That's what she would've wanted.

Her formal china was white with cobalt blue bands edged in gold. I liked that kind of china because a simple design worked with the food. Busy plates loaded with food seemed to detract from the overall look of the table. And I found a chest of dinner-sized sterling silver flatware. To my surprise and relief, it was untarnished. In the buffet drawer was a beautiful white linen tablecloth with matching napkins. By the time I was finished playing house with Clarabeth's gorgeous things, I had set a table worthy of royalty.

At around six, when the cocktail hour was nigh, Carl, Eve,

Cookie, and Daphne arrived. I watched them get out of the car from the dining room window. Their faces were serious, as was appropriate for the occasion. Cookie was wearing Chanel from head to toe with a triple strand of pearls. They didn't know, and neither did I, that Adam intended to get everyone through the evening together in an alcoholic haze. He was already pulling corks and shaking martinis.

The doorbell rang, and I saw Ted go toward it to open the door. I could hear them offering Ted their condolences. Of course, Cookie sailed past them and into the dining room to assess the progress.

"Well!" she said, smiling like a cat that had swallowed the proverbial canary. "The table looks lovely, Eliza! Very nicely done!"

Cookie had just paid me a compliment, which was highly suspect. When Cookie was nice in one situation, it always meant she had just dropped a giant stink bomb in another. In an instant I knew that she'd told Carl about seeing Eve with Adam at Charleston Grill. This woman could not control her tongue. There was no filter.

"Thanks, Cookie. It reminds me of a table at Charleston Grill. They have the most beautiful dining room, don't you think?"

Put that in your bong and smoke it, I thought.

That stopped Cookie in her tracks for a moment. Then I watched as all the good humor in her expression drained, just like I'd pulled the stopper.

"I'm not the troublemaker, Eliza."

We stared at each other for a moment. I wasn't going to answer her. Cookie turned and left the room without another word.

How we were going to get through the weekend was anybody's guess. I was determined to be polite to Eve and Adam because this was not the time or place to duke it out. I went to the kitchen to warm the container of jus that came with the roast and to reheat the vegetables. I was looking inside the refrigerator for ingredients to make another sauce.

"Hey, Eliza. How was Greece?"

I looked around the door and there stood Carl, handsome as ever, with the kindest eyes.

"Well, you know . . ."

I put a container of sour cream and a bottle of horseradish on the counter. We hugged and then he held me back to examine my face.

I said, "Greeks hate change as much as Charlestonians do! So it's about the same as it was in the days of Plato except it's wireless. How are you?"

"About the same. Adam and Eve can't seem to help themselves," he said.

"Adam says he's over Eve, but why should I believe him?"

"True. I wouldn't. Well, Daphne is clueless about all this. Do your boys know anything?"

"No. Unless Adam has told them, but I doubt that he has. And why would he? He still doesn't think that he did anything wrong."

"Incredible. Well, I think the best plan is to keep our differences quiet for now. This weekend is about Clarabeth and for Ted. Of course, Cookie is just waiting to stir up trouble."

"She's truly one dreadful woman."

"Yes, she sure is. Would you like me to carve the roast?" he said.

"I'd love it. Thanks."

I dropped two heaping tablespoons of horseradish into a small bowl that held the contents of the container of sour cream and finished it with a little lemon zest and a good pinch of salt.

"Instant sauce," I said and began opening cabinets looking for a bowl nice enough for the dining room.

There was a small crystal bowl in the butler's pantry and a serving spoon in the silver chest. I put it down on the dining table and brought the empty gravy boat from the china closet back to the kitchen. Carl was doing an expert job on the roast.

"You should've been a surgeon!" I said and we laughed.

"Right. So, are you going back to Corfu?"

"Yes, I am. Monday."

"What exactly are you doing over there? Did you dump Adam?"

"Good grief! No!"

"Too bad," he said and smiled at me.

"Your flirting has the worst possible timing," I said, teasing him back.

"Just tell me there's a chance," Carl said.

"Okay, Romeo, that's enough." I was laughing then.

I told him about my cousin Kiki and my aunt and the

restaurant and all about how beautiful the island was and that I was so fascinated by the history that was literally at your fingertips.

"It's a simpler life, but it's so gorgeous. I mean, Carl, everywhere you look it's like a movie set. I love it there, and not just a little bit."

"So what are you going to do?"

"Well, I'm not sure how, but I'm definitely going to spend time there every year."

"With Adam?"

"Maybe. Maybe not. We'll see."

"You're really furious, aren't you?"

"Furious? No. It's more like this. I thought I knew what was in his heart, and I didn't. And for some asinine reason he doesn't understand why what he's done changes the way I feel about him. And now he says he's not interested in Eve because he'd rather have me. Well, excuse me, is that really supposed to make me feel good about our marriage?"

"I hear you. Eve's very busy swearing her love to me too. I don't know. It all seems like too much work. And Cookie is on the sidelines, stoking the fires. Where's that damn shark when I could use him again?"

"You said it."

I pulled the container of vegetables from the oven. If we didn't eat very soon it would all be cold. We lined all the food up on the counter to serve it buffet style.

"I'll call everyone to come fix their plates," I said.

Remarkably, everyone moved quickly to the kitchen to

serve themselves and then to the table. And Eve, of course, swanned into the room.

"Hi, Eve," I said. "How are you?"

"Fine," she said, fighting back tears I wasn't the least bit interested in seeing. "Isn't it just terrible about Clarabeth?"

And did she expect me to believe the tears were caused by Clarabeth's untimely death?

"Yes. But as you know, life goes on, right?" I said.

"That's kind of cold, Eliza," Adam said, having overheard.

I didn't answer him. I didn't take my directions from him anymore. I could decide what to say all on my own.

I kept myself very busy on Friday when Adam was at work and on Saturday I did errands, got my hair done and my nails too. Cookie's date had gone fine the night before. So fine, in fact, that she wanted to bring him Saturday night. There was no objection, so she brought Reginald Finley IV to Cypress for all of us to ogle and interview. He looked harmless with his white hair and wire-rimmed glasses. Reggie, as he liked to be called, sat on Cookie's left and Ted sat on her right. He simply smiled and nodded all through dinner until Cookie started picking at Eve and it looked like a fight might break out.

"Stop! Stop!" he said.

The group stopped talking and he cleared his throat.

"Give me a minute. I have to put my hearing aids in. I don't want to miss this. God, I love a good catfight."

That was the nugget of the evening, as everyone had something to say about it.

Adam said later, "That's the only way you could have a relationship with Cookie. Take your hearing aids out."

"That was actually very funny," I said in agreement.

The dinner at Cypress was so delicious. Again, I noticed Adam was pushing his food around the plate.

"What's wrong? Is your food okay?" I asked him.

"Yeah, it's fine. I'm just not very hungry."

We told stories about the old days and Wild Dunes when our children were little. We reminisced about Max's fall and how Clarabeth felt responsible. And, once again, described how Carl all but saved his life. Clarabeth had always had a kind word and a little surprise in her pocket for the kids. She was the most thoughtful woman I'd ever known. We got through the weekend, but only with God's grace and quite possibly Clarabeth's loving eye looking down on us. I was so happy to see my boys and to see with my own eyes that they were satisfied with their lives and their futures.

Sunday night, the last night Adam and I were together, was awfully sad. The boys had left, Luke to Atlanta and Max to Durham. I wouldn't see them again until Easter, and even that wasn't certain. It had begun to dawn on Adam that he had done some serious damage to our marriage and that it might have been irreparable.

We were sitting in the kitchen, eating the hamburgers and French fries that I'd made for supper.

"I don't want you to go, Eliza. I know I've probably been an idiot."

"Not probably," I said.

"Come on, Eliza, cut me some slack. You know I love you

and you know that whatever I did that you think was so wrong, well, I'm sorry. From now on, I'll be the perfect husband. I swear."

"That's not enough, Adam."

"Jesus! What do you want from me?"

"I want you to understand that you hid your desire for Eve from me for over twenty years. How would you like it if I was miserable inside because I couldn't be with someone but I put on a brave face for you for all these years? How would you feel if you found out it was a friend of yours?"

"Probably not so great. But this wasn't like that."

"Yes, it was, Adam. From where I'm standing, it was exactly like that. You think about it and I'll see you in a couple of weeks. I'll let you know."

"God, Eliza. I feel so terrible inside. You make me feel so terrible."

"Classic man. Blame transference. All this heartbreak is a result of your ego. Not mine. Yours."

"So what are you telling me? That I can never make things right?"

"To be honest, Adam? I don't know."

CHAPTER 18

back in corfu

I was in the kitchen at the restaurant with Alexandros rolling dolmades, known in America as stuffed grape leaves. He showed me how to roll them tightly so they didn't fall apart, something I'd never been able to accomplish at home on the two occasions I attempted to make them. And he was tickled pink to show me how to make all the traditional dishes of Corfu. His hospitality was irresistible. I had arrived with a lemon cheesecake with meringue topping that won his heart. He sliced himself a piece immediately.

"This is delicious!" he said and licked his fingers. "Will you make this for me to sell?"

"Of course!"

"It's so good to have you back! Tell me about your family. Is everyone fine?"

"Well, it was very sad to lose our dear friend, especially in such a sudden way. She was like an adopted grandmother to my boys almost all their lives."

"Yes, I understand. Terrible. And the boys handled it okay?"

"Yes, yes. My boys are doing very well, thanks."

"And your husband?"

"He lives in the doghouse now. In the backyard of my house."

Alexandros laughed so hard his little belly shook. I wondered if Kiki or Nicholas had said something to him about my situation. Probably.

"What did he do to get moved into the dog's house?"

"He got caught," I said.

"Ah!" he said.

No further explanation required.

I said, "Hey, do you want me to make the tzatziki?"

Alexandros made tzatziki fresh every day. It was a simple dip made of garlic, cucumber, and plain yogurt. His patrons used it on everything and with everything.

"Yes, please." He looked at me long and hard. "I don't know this husband of yours, but I am one hundred percent positive that he is very foolish."

Alexandros was so serious and dramatic it made me laugh.

"Why do you say that?" I was peeling cucumbers then, happy just to be there.

"Humph. Because he let you out of his sight. If you were mine, I'd never take one eye from you."

I knew what he meant. He had no intention to remove one of my eyeballs.

"Oh, Alexandros! You are too sweet." I blew him a kiss. "You don't let your wife travel to see her family?"

"Oh, yes. Of course I do. I wish she would travel more!"

"Alexandros! Are you flirting with me?"

He was smiling from ear to ear. "Oh, no! I'm simply explaining the situation. She is a bitter woman and no longer a pleasure to live with."

He was flirting not because I was an object of his affection but because he was so gregarious it was impossible for him not to flirt.

"Is this because you got caught?"

"No, it is because she gained one hundred kilos."

"Seriously?"

"Yes. She is a whale. I want her to be happy, but please, go be happy on Mykonos with her relatives. Please. Would you please get us a liter of olive oil from the storage room?"

"You bet!" Was his wife really that fat? I'd have to ask Kiki. "Alexandros? How much olive oil do you think you use every week?" It seemed to me that he was always opening another can.

"Six, seven liters? What does this 'you bet' mean?"

I put the huge can of olive oil on the counter near him and took the empty one away to discard.

"Well, it means 'you can bet money that I will do it.' Slang versions vary from 'ya bet your booties, baby!' to 'you can bet your life on it!' or 'you betcha.'"

"Wouldn't it be more efficient to simply say, 'of course I will,' or 'with pleasure'?"

"Yes! But isn't it more charming and colorful to paint the picture with an image than to be precise and succinct?"

"Yes, I agree. Greek is like that too. Well, you improve my

English and I'll teach you how to make taramosalata! And kleftiko!"

Taramosalata was a rich dip made from cod roe and bread crumbs, a kind of Greek caviar. Kleftiko was a lamb stew, cooked slowly in a special oven. Both were incredibly delicious.

"That's a deal," I said. "Hey, I saw the prawns that came in this morning. They're beautiful!"

"My friend goes out in his boat every day and brings them back. The octopus are his too. I'm gonna make bourtheto with octopus and swordfish. It's the best fish stew in the history of fish stew! When I make my fish stew it's all gone just like that!" He snapped his fingers in the air.

"The best in the whole world?"

"In the whole world!"

"I can't wait to taste it!"

"I'll put some aside for us for later."

"So. Alexandros? May I ask a personal question?"

"Of course! You are almost my cousin!"

"In your mind, is there a circumstance that excuses infidelity?"

He sighed deeply and became very serious.

"Men and women ask that question for centuries," he said. "And love is very powerful. People fall in and out of love all the time."

"Even with the same person?"

"Of course!"

"So if my husband comes to his senses and your wife loses all that weight, we might love them again?"

"Who knows? Anything is possible."

I had a sense that he wasn't quite comfortable talking about the subject.

"It's probably better if we keep the conversation focused on Greek cuisine. If I was your wife I'd be on a diet."

"And if I was your husband I'd be on a plane!"

We laughed again, but this time it was a knowing laugh, one shared by friends who knew a dark truth about each other.

I'd been back on Corfu for only a few days, and in that short time Alexandros had taught me so much about traditional Greek cuisine. But I couldn't seem to shake the fog of my jet lag. Maybe I hadn't spent enough time in Charleston and I bounced back to Corfu so quickly that my brain was somewhere in between and I needed to reel it back into my head. And my clothes seemed to be looser. Maybe I just needed a full night of sleep.

Kiki and Nicholas came to the restaurant late that night, and after all the patrons were gone, Alexandros and I sat with them eating the fish stew, which was absolutely divine, and drinking local wine until the wee hours.

"Would it be so terrible just this once to lick the bowl?" I said.

"Best in the world!" Alexandros said, then threw back his head and laughed.

By the time they dropped me off at Yiayia's house the sun was coming up.

"I think tomorrow we will start the day sometime in the afternoon," Kiki said.

"That's another thing that's so wonderful about living here," I said. "You can do that if you want to."

I told them good night, we blew each other kisses, and it occurred to me that if I was going to stay much longer it really would be a good idea to rent a car. Or at least a scooter of some kind.

I got ready for bed and climbed into it with my cell phone, checking my e-mails. There was something from Carl.

> Hey, hope you got back there in one piece. I don't know if you knew this but Eve and I were supposed to go to Italy next week. Well, forget that. But the tickets are nonrefundable, I already have the time blocked out and doctors to cover for me, so I'm thinking of coming alone. Where exactly are you? And would it be a huge inconvenience if I came to Corfu for a few days? I can fly there from Naples, I think. Or maybe a ferry? Do you know where I might stay? Thanks.

Poor Carl, I thought. He's floundering around. He needs a friend. I'm that friend.

> Carl, No one understands how you're feeling better than I do. Of course! Come! I'm at Dassia Beach, just north of Corfu Town . . .

I gave him my address. I told him I'd love to see him. It was true. I was excited to see him. I'd take him out to the countryside to gather *horta*. And I'd take him to see Saint Spyrídon and his hand. Maybe we'd visit the churches on the islet of Agios Nikolaos. And there was the architectural museum. He could stay a hundred years and never see all there was to see.

The days until his arrival flew by. During that time, I rented a precious red Vespa and got used to handling it after nearly killing myself a dozen or so times. The first morning I took it out for a spin I ran into a hedge. Scratched my face a bit. Once I stopped it too abruptly and fell off. Banged my knee. Another time I was going too slow and it fell over, taking me down with it. Black and blue hip. But I finally got the hang of it and actually loved zipping around on it. It was a strangely liberating experience.

Kiki and I arranged for Carl to stay in another charming little cottage that she managed. This one was within walking distance of the village too. It was a lot smaller than mine, but it had a clear view of the sea. It seemed that spring was coming early, as there were buds on the trees and determined purple and white crocuses pushing their way up through the earth everywhere you looked.

The day before his arrival, Kiki and Nicholas came to the taverna for dinner. By then they knew every detail of my friendship with Carl and Eve and the whole wretched business of what transpired with Adam and Eve, including the dinner at Charleston Place.

"We must be very nice to Carl," Kiki said to Nicholas and me. "This is a difficult time for him and for all of you."

"Except for Adam, who thinks that he's done nothing wrong," I said.

"I don't know what to tell you about that," Kiki said.

Nicholas said, "I am looking forward to meeting Carl. We need a decent pediatrician on this island. Maybe we can persuade him to stay!"

"He practically saved my son's life," I reminded them.

Nicholas had unknowingly planted a seed for a wild and woolly fantasy my brain could entertain. Here's how it would go. I'd stay here and become a popular chef and then a partner in my own little restaurant with Alexandros. Carl would fall in love with Corfu and move here. The island would embrace him and all the children would love him. He'd save lives every day. My moussaka would enchant him. My baklava would drive him over the edge. We would actually fall in love and find passion we had never known before. We would live out our days together in a little stucco house with a courtyard, an olive grove and vineyard, cooking and laughing our way into our nineties together. Maybe we'd even live to be a hundred. No! Wait! Because we couldn't live without each other, at 101 we'd hold hands and jump to our deaths from the cliffs of Lefkáda, like Sappho.

Good grief, I thought and laughed to myself. That is one huge load of feta, Eliza, I told myself. Too cheesy for it ever to happen except in a romance novel.

Kiki and I drove her car to the airport to meet Carl. I had the night off from the restaurant. Alexandros's chef was back and the plan was for me to bake for them. I could make whatever I wanted, Alexandros said. Or I could come in and cook. It was up to me. I loved the idea of baking for the restaurant, but I'd need better equipment than what I had. There had to be a cooking supply store in Athens. I'd ask Alexandros. Maybe he had a catalog.

That's what was rattling around in my head while we waited for Carl. We stood in the baggage claim area and after a few minutes I saw him coming. He towered over the people and walked with ease, as though the carry-on bag slung over his shoulder was filled with cotton balls.

"That's him," I said to Kiki.

"Sweet Mary, Mother of God," she said with a dumbfounded expression.

"He has that effect on most people," I said, smiling.

"Eliza!" He called my name and I giggled.

He pulled me into a bear hug and kissed me on the cheek.

"Carl! Welcome! This is Kiki, my cousin!"

"Eliza told me she had a cousin, but she didn't tell me you were so beautiful!"

It was the same line he had used on me so many years ago. Kiki took the bait and almost swooned.

"Well!" Kiki said, flustered. "Thank you! And welcome to Corfu!"

"Do you have any checked baggage?" I asked.

"Yeah. I overpacked, of course."

"That's okay," Kiki said.

Kiki was still a little bit verklempt by Carl's appearance. Even in middle age, Carl looked like a movie star, in the same way that Paul Newman aged so well. Carl and Paul couldn't get ugly if they wanted to.

"Well, I'm sure your bag will be out in a moment. Are you hungry?"

"Of course!" he said. "I'm always hungry when I get around you!"

"What?" Kiki said.

"He didn't mean that the way it sounded. Did you, Carl?"

"What? Oh! Oh, sorry! Gosh, that did sound a little carnal! No, Kiki, Eliza is such an amazing cook, it's impossible to be around her and not think of food! That's all."

"If you say so," Kiki said and smiled at me.

Oh, fine, I thought. Now Kiki suspects there's something going on between me and Carl. Or maybe she was just teasing me. I decided to just ignore it and focus on getting Carl some dinner, the way Kiki had for me when I first arrived on the island, and then on getting him settled.

His bag arrived on the carousel, he grabbed it, and off we went. Carl sat in the front with Kiki and I crawled into the backseat feeling a lot like a human pretzel, twisted in too many directions at once.

"You all right?" Kiki asked.

"Oh yes, fine, fine. I'm just back here auditioning for Cirque du Soleil. So how was your trip?" I asked. "How was Naples?"

"I wasn't really in Naples. Big cities are too crazy for me. I was in Ravello, a quiet little hill town above Amalfi. It's absolutely beautiful."

"Ah, Ravello!" Kiki said. "I went there with Nicholas on our honeymoon a million years ago! It's so gorgeous! Where did you stay?"

"The Hotel Palumbo. Eve and I stayed there years ago and we always wanted to go back. I had lunch yesterday on the terrace of their restaurant that hangs over the water a thousand feet below, and I'm telling you what, I can't imagine a more beautiful place anywhere."

"It's truly breathtaking," Kiki said. "I remember it well."

"Wait until you see this island in the sunlight!" I said, bragging like a native.

Carl laughed and said, "So I'm going to fall in love with Greece?"

"I think we would like to see you try not to!" Kiki said. "It's not possible to resist her many charms."

We pulled into the parking lot of the restaurant. It was about nine thirty and the dining room was full. We decided to sit outside on the terrace. Despite the budding trees and flowers, the nights were still cool enough for a sweater, more comfortable still if you sat by a heater, and Alexandros had them placed strategically. I went inside to tell Alexandros we had arrived, and of course he came out to greet Carl and begin the feast. A huge platter of grilled octopus was being delivered to our table just as Nicholas arrived minutes later. He shook hands with Carl. They liked each other immediately and started talking about medicine and the rising costs of pharmaceuticals.

"It's out of control," Nicholas said. "Even here."

"I agree completely," Carl said. "Corporate greed is the devil."

Everything was served family style, so he had the opportunity to try many things. Of course, Alexandros wouldn't let anyone order from the menu or pay for the meal. It was sometime after one in the morning when we finally left the restaurant and Kiki and I delivered Carl to his cottage by the sea.

The little house where he would stay was half the size of mine but a lot more contemporary. It was white with navy blue shutters, and flower boxes under the windows were filled with herbs and hardy ferns. There was the requisite courtyard with a round table and four chairs. Lights were strung in the trees and an old olive tree, gnarled with age, stood like a sentry in the far corner where it had probably been for a hundred years or more.

"This is very nice," Carl said.

"It stays rented in the summer months, but this time of year . . . well, it's not exactly the busiest time for tourists," Kiki said. "It's not the Hotel Palumbo, but I think you'll like it."

We went inside.

This one-bedroom house was a candidate for a magazine shoot next to the rustic simplicity of my grandmother's house. The stone fireplace was the focal point of the living room. All the furniture was low slung and slipcovered in white canvas piped in navy. The coffee table was large, rectangular, and entirely constructed of glass. In its center was a cobalt hand-blown glass vase filled with calla lilies that Kiki and I had bought earlier at the market. Of course, we had stocked the refrigerator for him with the basic things he would need. Instead of a percolator this house had a Nespresso machine. And the appliances here were all stainless steel and almost new. It was very modern. Off the open kitchen/living room/dining area was a small powder room, and a large master bedroom was behind a sliding barn door. The master bath had a view of the ocean. And a shower. He opened the window and the sounds of the waves coming ashore filled the room with just the perfect perfume of salted breeze.

Carl smiled at me and then looked to Kiki.

"Who owns this house?" he asked.

"A French woman who bought it for an investment. She works in the fashion business in Paris and she's hardly ever here."

"She certainly has great style," I said.

"She does," Carl said. "This house is really great, Kiki. Thank you so much for arranging this for me."

"You're very welcome, Carl. So, we will see you in the morning? Why don't you e-mail Eliza when you get up?"

"I'll do that."

We said good night and Kiki drove me back to Yiayia's house, a few blocks away.

"He's very nice," Kiki said.

"Oh, Carl's a great guy, for sure. I've known him forever."

"What's the matter with his wife?"

"And my husband too. I think they just have a couple of loose screws in their heads."

"Well, I think you could spend a million years studying human behavior and it would always be a little irrational. People seem to like to make trouble for themselves. Maybe they just get bored. Who knows?"

"It sure looks like self-destructive behavior to me. But I think, as you said, that it's more about their fear of getting old and dying."

"It's true!"

I said, "I just want to get old, and then I'll worry about dying!"

We laughed and hugged. I got out of the car.

"See you tomorrow?" I said.

"You know it! The neighborhood is gathering and my mother is at the stove!"

"God, she is so great," I said and blew her a kiss.

I could not wait to get into my bed. And I was really looking forward to dinner with everyone at my aunt Anna's house.

The next morning I woke up to sun streaming through all the windows. It was going to be another beautiful day. For some reason, I thought of Clarabeth while I brushed my teeth and dressed. I wondered then for just a few moments what she would do in my situation. Given the many husbands she had had, she would probably say to give Carl a serious once-over. Even considering Clarabeth's age, she was a very pragmatic woman. She believed that men and women needed partners for life and that it wasn't healthy for most of humanity to be alone. She would've told Adam to take a hike, because although she never came right out and said it, she had not liked what Adam and Eve did one little bit. I was sure of that much. But then, she didn't have to voice her opinion, because she had Cookie. Cookie was more than happy to mortify Adam and Eve in public and to cast buckets of disparaging words in their direction whenever possible. It had never been in Clarabeth's nature to dress down sinners. She was definitely a member of the love the sinner, hate the sin camp. And she knew when a thing was too broken to mend. Would she say Adam and I were too broken? No, she would say she couldn't answer that question.

Then I thought of my mother and Yiayia as I set up the

coffeepot and plugged it in. They were from such a different time and place, they'd be horrified. To them, family was everything. They would tell me to do whatever I had to do to work things out with Adam, to go home and be his good wife, to forgive him and to never speak of this unfortunate business again. They didn't buy into that idea about pursuit of happiness being an individual's inalienable right. Hell, no. You take the oath? You honor the oath. It was just that simple. They would tell me that I was a smart girl and that I should find a way to work Corfu and whatever else I wanted to do into the equation. But it was my job to hold the family together. Men strayed from time to time. They would probably tell me that it should be expected or that it was just a flaw in the nature of the male of the species. If a man does something stupid, it shouldn't ruin the whole family. Besides, it ruined holidays and weddings, and, well, it would just put a nasty cramp in everything for the rest of my life if I divorced Adam.

That was all true. And if I was being completely honest with myself, I'd admit that both arguments had merit. The real question was what did I want to happen now? I didn't know. I really didn't know.

I straightened up the house and had a little breakfast. I wondered if Carl was awake, so I sent him an e-mail. He responded right away.

> I'm drinking coffee, eating cake, and wondering why you don't spend some of Adam's money and get yourself an international plan for your phone so I can just call you? Ha ha! Do you want to meet somewhere this morning?

He was right. It was time to upgrade my phone service. I could meet him at one of the cafés on the main drag in Dassia. We could have another cup of coffee and then take a taxi or a bus to the city. I could wait until later to impress him with my Vespa skills. First stop in Corfu Town? The Church of Saint Spyrídon. As a doctor, he would be stunned by the uncorrupted remains of the saint and his traveling shoes. We'd have lunch at the Liston and we would map out a few trips to some other islands. But mostly, I wanted to hear what he was thinking about his marriage. And at some point, I'd find a phone store.

I e-mailed him back with the plan and he responded by saying he would meet me in the village in half an hour.

I found myself smiling for no reason as I brushed my hair. Was it because Carl was here? Yes. Was it because I was attracted to Carl? Absolutely not. Okay, yes, but only in a platonic way. I mean in reality, I wasn't about to do something really stupid like have an affair with Carl to punish Adam and Eve. That was ludicrous. But his being here would strengthen my resolve and help me make some decisions. For better or worse, we were in this soup together.

I took one of my shopping baskets with me, dropping my phone and wallet inside with a hairbrush and a scarf to cover it all up in case I might be followed by a pickpocket. There was almost no crime in Dassia, but that didn't mean I shouldn't be cautious. I'd buy a bottle of water and maybe a newspaper if I could find one in English. I locked the door of the house from the outside and began the short walk.

There were two cafés in the business district. One sold

pastries and shots of ouzo with briki, a strong Greek coffee brewed in copper pots and frappé, a cold coffee drink. The other café sold those things as well, but it had a larger menu and was open late into the night. Both had tables outside. I spotted Carl seated inside the second one. It was called Athena, as many business establishments were.

"Good morning!" I said.

He stood and gave me a kiss on my cheek.

"Good morning, gorgeous! Sit, please." He held my chair for me.

Carl had lovely manners. I had to give him that.

Café Athena was a modest affair. The dozen or so tabletops had brightly colored mosaic designs in their cement tops, which rested on metal bases. The chairs were ladder-backs with thick rush seats. The entire eating area was under a thatched roof over a floor of large square rust-colored tiles. It was casual but very simple and easy to maintain. Most of the tables were filled with young women with little dogs on leashes and men reading the newspapers and discussing the events of the day. And just as in coffee shops all over the world, there was a contingent of an old dudes' club, a table of eight older men, leaning in to hear each other, nodding and drinking coffee.

"Did you eat enough?" I said. "Want to split an omelet?"

"Sure. What kind?"

"Well, you have to have feta cheese. This is Greece and you get feta with everything. After that? I don't know. How about spinach?"

"Sounds fine to me," he said.

We ordered the omelet and two cups of coffee. He pulled out a guidebook and we made a plan for the day's sightseeing. Our food arrived and we began to eat, finally bringing up the obvious.

"So," he said, "Cookie sure spilled the beans. Why do you think she did that?"

"Because she's really as mean as a snake?" I said. "I mean, she had to know that telling the story of their teenage romance would do more harm than good. Not to mention the story of their dinner together. What were we supposed to believe?"

"Exactly. This omelet is pretty good."

"The food here is pretty good right across the board."

"And you know what? For years, I thought Cookie was a sweetheart! Of course, once her addictions came to light I knew she was more complicated than I'd originally thought. That's one problem with being a physician. Too many hours are spent away from home, so you never really know what's going on."

"Listen, Carl. I always knew Eve was very fond of Adam. And I knew Adam felt the same way about her. But I didn't think they'd step out on us. I really didn't."

"Cookie said Eve was dressed like a hooker when she saw her at Charleston Place."

"Now why would she tell you that? She knows she's just causing more heartache and trouble for all of us."

"Yeah, it seems pretty mean-spirited. Since then, Eve gave up alcohol."

"No kidding?"

"Yes. She said she needs clarity, and wine clouds her judgment."

"Wow," I said.

After breakfast, we took a taxi for the short ride to Corfu Town. Carl was staring out the window, enjoying the coastal views.

"The water's beautiful. It might be nice to take a long walk along the shore. How's the beach in Dassia?" he said.

"Rocky. It's not the best for walking, but there are plenty of other smooth spots not too far away." I was quiet then, thinking of how much Adam and I loved to walk the beach hand in hand on the Isle of Palms. "It is beautiful here."

"I fired that nurse, by the way."

"Well, that's good," I said, wondering if anything had gone on between them.

"I never touched her. She wanted to know why she was being fired and I told her sexual harassment in the workplace. How's that?"

"She probably denied it," I said.

"She did. How'd you know that?"

"It's all about ego, isn't it?"

"It sure seems like it."

We got out by the Church of Saint Spyrídon, which was crowded with people walking in every direction. I had told him the whole story of the wandering saint and he was fascinated.

He said, "I'll be the judge of whether his corpse is corrupted or not."

He was ahead of me, walking into the church, and I stopped him.

"Let me take your picture, Carl! Stand right there on the steps!"

Then someone stepped up to me and said, "Go get in the picture with him!"

"Oh! Okay! Thanks!"

I quickly trotted myself to where Carl stood, he threw his arm around my shoulder, I put a big smile on my face and the nice stranger clicked away.

"Thanks!" I said as the man handed my phone back to me. Then I turned to Carl and said, "Now let's go see Saint Spyrídon and ask him to bring Eve and Adam to their senses."

We stepped inside the apse of the church and Carl looked up.

"Wow," he said. "How old is this place?"

"Sixteenth century."

"That's old," he said. "It's a little spooky in here, don't you think?"

"A little. Okay, want to go see the saint?"

"Let's do it."

We stood in line waiting our turn as others went before us. The same Orthodox priest was there chanting for each pilgrim. When it was our turn, I let Carl go first. He took a long look into the lavish silver coffin and seemed transfixed. He said something to the priest and the priest nodded his head. As I had done when I was here, Carl touched his foot. I saw the same look of astonishment come over Carl's face and I knew he'd had a similar experience to mine. He moved on and I took his place. I repeated my petition to the saint and to the priest and just to be sure I hadn't imagined it, I touched the saint's foot again. Once more I felt a rush of something, and then it was over. Carl was waiting for me in the front pew.

He got up and followed me outside.

"How'd you like them apples?" I said. "Cool, right?"

"If I hadn't seen that guy with my own eyes and experienced it myself, I wouldn't have believed it."

"It's a little like touching the doorknob after you skate across carpet in nylon socks."

"Yes, it is."

I stood there and shook my head, thinking, Well, who knows? Maybe the saint had heard our prayers and was going to intervene on our behalf.

"Where should we go next?" Carl said.

"Let's go to the Antivouniotissa Museum. They have a mind-boggling collection of Byzantine icons and all kinds of other religious treasures."

"Let's go! I'll get us a cab."

He managed to flag one down and I took his picture again before I got in.

"We have to document your vacation," I said.

We played the role of tourists all morning, and then one o'clock found us seated in the Liston. We had just ordered lunch when his cell phone rang.

"Ted? What's going on? Is everything okay?"

"What? Oh, my God. Okay, okay. Don't worry." Pause. "No, I'm away. But I'll be on the next plane." Pause. "I'll text you. Thanks."

His face was drained of all color.

"What's happened?"

"It's Adam. He's in the ICU at the Medical University. It looks like he may be in liver failure."

"What?" I thought I was going to faint dead on the floor. *Liver failure?* I started to panic.

"It sounds like hep C. Let's get a check and get out of here."

CHAPTER 19

eliza

I made my apologies to Kiki and Aunt Anna and threw my clothes in my suitcase. Carl booked airline reservations, and we were off to the airport one more time.

"I'll return your Vespa for you," Kiki said.

"The paperwork's on the kitchen table," I said. "Kiki, good grief, how can I thank you for everything you've done?"

"I know. I should open an airport limo service." She looked at me in the rearview mirror. She was smiling. I knew she was teasing me then. "Maybe I'll come to Charleston and stay with you for a vacation. I've heard it's beautiful."

"Yes! Come and stay! I'd love to have you. I have a big old house and lots of empty bedrooms and a place at the beach on the ocean. Bring Aunt Anna too!"

"Well, let's let you get through this crisis first and then we'll talk about it. I have a feeling that Adam will be fine. Here, take these." I took a string of beads from her.

They were amber *komboloï*, or worry beads—a secular Greek version of the Roman Catholic rosary.

"I sure hope you're right. Oh, Kiki! They're beautiful! Thank you!"

"You're welcome. When I'm worried, I say my prayers and run my fingers over the beads. Somehow it helps."

"Let's see," Carl said, and I handed them to him. He had a look at them and then gave them back to me. "Very nice."

Carl was very quiet. Too quiet. That meant he was worried and not telling me what I needed to know. I would ask him what he was thinking as soon as we were alone.

At the airport Kiki and I hugged and hugged, and I promised to give her the update on Adam as soon as there was one. Just when I thought I had Greece to myself I got yanked away again. I hated leaving, but there was no alternative. I couldn't stop thinking about Adam. I was going to be at his side as fast as humanly possible. I e-mailed the boys too. I couldn't stand it that Adam was suffering, much less entertain the thought of anything worse.

Three hours later we were over the Atlantic Ocean, on a direct flight from Athens to Kennedy Airport in New York. From there we would take a United Airlines flight to Charleston. Ted was going to pick us up at the airport.

"Please tell me everything Ted said again."

"He said that Adam had been complaining of extreme fatigue and that two nights ago he began vomiting and couldn't stop. He called Ted, who came and rushed him to the ER. He was admitted right away and given fluids and they ran tests. They check for hep C now all the time."

"Carl? How much danger do you think Adam is really in?"

"Big time. If it's hepatitis C, and he's already in danger of his liver failing, he's going to need a liver transplant right away. If it's not hep C, I don't know what it could be."

"Dear God. How in the world would Adam get hepatitis to begin with?"

"I don't know. Did he ever get blood, like a transfusion?"

"Not that I know of. He's never even been in a hospital since we met each other."

"Does he have any tattoos?"

"Adam? No. He thinks they're déclassé."

"Well, they can be a health risk because tattoo parlors don't always have the most antiseptic environments. Think about it. Hospitals are supposed to be germ free, but they're not. People get MRSA or *C. diff* in hospitals!"

"I've read about that. It happens all the time," I said.

"Well, he must have gotten blood somewhere along the line, because I can't believe he'd share a needle with someone—not in a million years. He's not a drug user."

"In fact, he's the furthest thing from one."

"And hepatitis isn't contagious. It has to be an exchange of blood."

"How did he get so sick this quickly?"

"He's probably had it for years. It hides. By the time you become symptomatic, you could be in the late stages of the disease. Bad odds."

"How's he going to get a liver transplant?"

"Well, there are only two ways—cadaver donor or living donor."

"Oh, God. Poor Adam. What are the chances of a cadaver donor?"

"Probably not good. I don't know the exact stat, but it's something like only seven thousand people get them and seventeen thousand people need them every year."

"Otherwise he dies?"

"No, he can have a live donor. I'm sure the doctors are already looking for a match for him."

"How serious is this, Carl? I'm really worried."

"Eliza, it's dead serious. You can't live without a liver. But you know what? You should try to get a little shut-eye. There'll be plenty of time to fret later on."

I thought to myself, He has to be kidding. He tells me my husband is in a life-threatening situation and I should take a nap? Then I understood: what he meant was that he wanted to focus on Adam's illness and think it all through.

After tossing and turning in the seat for several hours, I crawled over sleeping Carl to just take a walk in the aisles. I didn't need deep vein thrombosis any more than Adam needed hepatitis C. I used the powder room and took a bottle of water from a bar the flight attendants had set up near the galley. I looked at the faces of all the people on the plane as I passed them and thought, So many lives, so much love, and so much sorrow. I had never expected happiness every day of my life. But I had never expected anything like this. And certainly, not for tragedy to happen to Adam, who was as healthy as you would hope to be. If we lost Adam it would kill Ted, and my sons would be utterly and completely devastated. It would break my heart into a million pieces as well. I loved Adam, more than I had ever loved anyone. He made me as mad as every fury in hell, but if I lost him I couldn't imagine how I would go on without him in the world. The thought of losing him made me feel my love for him deeply, as though I were feeling it for the first time. I knew then that our love had been rattled hard, but it wasn't broken beyond repair.

Our flights were an endurance contest. I thought I would honestly lose my mind if I had to withstand one more minute of travel time, but after we landed at Kennedy, cleared customs, and changed terminals, we still had another hour and a half to go.

"I'm scared," I said to Carl as we waited in line to board the flight to Charleston.

"I know but don't be. I'm here." He put his arm around my shoulder and gave me a squeeze.

I leaned into his side and thought about how safe Carl made me feel. It was like the day he lifted my little boy from the ground and rushed him to the hospital. Carl was imperfect, as we all are, but he was a dear, sweet friend. I knew he had to go back to Raleigh, but I also knew that since he had the time off, he would likely stay by my side until Adam was out of harm's way. I couldn't even consider any other possible outcome. Adam had to get well. And I needed Carl's steadfast spirit. I really hoped he would stay.

He held my hand the entire flight home to Charleston, and I dozed off for a while. I was so tired I could've slept standing up. But I woke up and looked out the window as we passed over the Waccamaw River. I knew we were close to home. Minutes later we were on the ground and taxiing to the gate.

Passengers began to disembark.

"What do you think is waiting for us?" I said. I put the straps of my duffel bag over my shoulder and picked up my purse.

"Whatever it is, it's going to be all right, Eliza. I'm right here."

"Our very own Rock of Gibraltar," I said. "Thank God."

We worked our way through the terminal to the baggage claim area and spotted Ted. Cookie was with him. First, she saw me, then she saw Carl. I watched her face contort as she made a snap judgment. Inside of about two seconds she started huffing and puffing like a blowfish, and then she blew her stack. She rushed to Carl first and started poking his chest with her finger.

"You! You! You son of a bitch! Don't even try to tell me that it's a coincidence that you're on the same plane!"

"Whoa! Cookie, calm down!" Carl said.

Then she turned to me.

"Shame on you, Eliza Stanley. Your poor husband is lying in a hospital bed, fighting for his life, and you're up to no good! Well, I have never . . ."

"Excuse me, Cookie, this is not what you think . . ." I said, realizing she thought I'd been in Greece or Italy or somewhere carrying on with Carl.

"Then explain yourselves!" she demanded.

"No, sorry, Cookie. I don't answer to you," I said. "How dare you!" I was getting pretty mad and I felt like Mount Etna, ready to spew. I was a grown woman with grown children, and no one spoke to me that way.

Ted finally saw what was happening, grabbed Cookie by the arm, and pulled her away.

"Cookie, get ahold of yourself," he said. "You've got to stop jumping to conclusions. There's no reason to make a scene."

"Are you blind, Ted? Don't you see what's going on here?" she said.

"Lower your voice, Cookie. Whatever is going on is none of your business," Ted said firmly. "You're embarrassing yourself."

She turned on her heel and blustered away to the ladies' room. I looked at Ted.

"There's a perfectly reasonable explanation," I said.

"Let me explain it to him, Eliza," Carl said.

While we waited for the bags Carl talked and Ted listened. As Carl finished talking, Ted crossed his arms and let it all sink in. Then he spoke.

"That's a good story, but it looks like monkey business to me. Sorry, but it does."

"Ted! I'm surprised at you," I said. "I've been your faithful daughter-in-law for almost twenty-five years and you know it. I'm not interested in Carl! He's my friend! And that's all there is to it!"

"Right. Okay. Now, why don't you two just get your bags and let's get to the hospital. My son is a very sick man."

Cookie returned with her jaw locked up as tight as a clam

and refused to make eye contact with either of us. The bags came up and we took them from the carousel. We rolled them to Ted's car in silence and rode to the hospital in silence. Finally, Carl broke the tension.

"This is absurd," he said. "Never once have I touched Eliza or any other woman, with the exception of my wife, in all the years I've been married. I wouldn't be here if Adam wasn't one of my dearest friends. By the way, where is Eve?"

"Why, she's by Adam's bedside! Where else would she be?" Cookie said.

"Sweet Jesus," I said.

"That figures," Carl said.

"Look," I said, "Carl and I don't need anyone to accuse us of something we didn't do. So why don't we all just cool it and focus on Adam."

Carl and I looked at each other. They were accusing us the same way we had accused Adam and Eve, because on the surface it probably did look like there was some monkey business going on between Carl and me. But this was different. Wasn't it? Although a tiny little bubble in my conscience gave me a nudge to remind me that if Carl and I had been in Corfu for an extended period of time and Adam and Eve were out of the picture, something might have happened. No, something *would've* happened eventually.

We pulled into the MUSC driveway and gave the keys to the valet parking attendant. We got out and hurried to Adam's room in the intensive care unit. Ted pushed the door open and there was Adam in the bed with an IV and all sorts of machines monitoring his status. Eve was in the chair by his side. Her face was all blotchy from crying. Adam was asleep. The whole scene was surreal.

"I'm not a match," she said quietly and began to cry again.

"You were going to give him part of your liver?" I said. At first blush, the idea seemed as extraordinary as it did inappropriate. She thought it would be a good idea to put her liver in my husband's body? Was she crazy?

"Wouldn't you?" she said.

In that moment, everything changed between us. Of course she would offer to be a donor! So would I and so would Carl. Any one of us would do anything to save the other.

"Of course I would," I said.

"As would I," Carl said. "I'm going to go find the doctor in charge and see what I can find out." Carl looked at the machines and all their readings and shook his head. "I'll be back in a few minutes."

Cookie said to Eve, "Why don't we go get some coffee and let Eliza have a few minutes with *her* husband, hmm?"

If there had been a news ticker crawling across Cookie's forehead, it would've said, *My daughter's such a slut, she doesn't see anything wrong with weeping on someone else's husband who she's still in love with, and she's such an airhead she thinks no one knows.*

Ted said, "I'll come with y'all. Eliza? Would you like coffee or something?"

"No, I'm fine. Thank you."

Not until you apologize, I thought. He shrugged his shoulders and left.

Ted, of all people I'd ever known, should've been the

last person to suspect me of having an extramarital affair with anyone, much less with his son's friend. He and Cookie thought they had caught us red-handed at the airport, as if Carl and I on the same flight proved a single thing. If it hadn't been so absurd I might have laughed it off. And it struck me then that at that very moment, Cookie was telling Eve about Carl and me flying to Charleston on the same plane, that we had been in Greece together, most likely having sex every five minutes on a beach somewhere, even though it was winter, and chugging ouzo the way she'd done with some Greek stud years ago. Oh, Cookie, I thought, I'm buying you a muzzle for Christmas.

I leaned over Adam and kissed his cheek. He was warm to the touch, but his color was off. Yellow. Jaundiced.

"I'm here, sweetheart. It's me. Eliza. I love you, Adam. We're going to get you back on your feet."

There was no response. I sat in the chair beside him, reached into my purse for Kiki's worry beads, and began to pray.

Soon, Carl returned and motioned for me to come out into the hall with him.

"The hepatologist's report says that Adam was admitted with severe abdominal distress and heavy bloating. And he was agitated. That's why he's so heavily sedated. If we can find a donor quickly we can save him quickly. I just got tested to see if I can donate. Do you want to get tested too?"

"Yes! Right this minute! And I'm sure the boys will want to be tested too."

"Have you spoken to them?"

"I left a message for Max and I sent Luke a text. Luke is already in his car. I'm sure Max will show up by the end of the day."

"Okay, so if you're a match, there are several tests to be performed. Mainly, you have to swear you have a close personal relationship with Adam, if you are not a family member."

"We can check that box."

"And you have to be made to understand all the risks involved. But basically, your liver would be completely regenerated in just a few weeks."

"Too bad my neck can't regenerate."

Carl looked at me like I was crazy.

"Gallows humor?" I said.

"Of course. And you'd have to get an MRI so the surgeon has a road map of your internal organs. We don't want any unnecessary poking around in your gizzards."

"Please!" I must have looked horrified at the thought that the surgeon might not know where to find my liver. "MRI! No big deal. I'll take two!"

"Well, first we have to find out if you're a match. Since Adam is critical, the labs will be on it."

I went back down the hall with Carl to a lab where a technician took blood from my arm. While I sat there with a very tight tourniquet just above my left elbow, Adam's predicament and the horrific possibility of his dying weighed heavily on my mind. I'd do anything I could to save him. He would move the world for me and I knew it.

"Carl?"

"Yes?"

"I'm so afraid for him."

"So am I."

When we went back to Adam's room Cookie and Eve were gone. Ted was standing outside in the hall looking in through the plate-glass window. There was a nurse inside, reading the machines.

Carl slapped Ted on the back, a gesture between men that said, *I'm here for you, buddy.* Then he said, "Let me ask you something, Ted. Did Adam ever have to get blood for any reason?"

"Yeah, when he was a kid. Burst appendix or something. I don't remember, but he did get some blood. Why?"

"Because that's a possible cause of Adam's hep C. Not that it matters now. How he got to here is practically moot."

Ted nodded.

"And Ted?" I said.

"Yes?"

"There is no monkey business going on."

"That's what Adam told you too, and you didn't believe him. So why should I believe any of you?"

"Because I'm giving you my word," I said, incredulous that I should be accused this way.

"Listen, Eliza. Right now, there's what I care about, right there." He pointed toward Adam. "I just want my boy well. That's it and that's all."

I didn't blame him, really. Besides, Ted was not a busybody.

The nurse came out.

"How's he doing?" I asked.

"He's holding on," she said with a hopeful tone and left.

I sat by Adam's bed until my sons arrived, first Luke and then Max. I was so sleep deprived and jet-lagged, it was incredible I could even think straight. I must've been running on pure adrenaline. We went outside with Carl and he explained to them what was going on and how they might help.

"Who wouldn't want to save their father's life, Doc?" Max said.

"Absolutely! Where do we have to go to get the test?" Luke said.

"Come on," Carl said. "I'll take you to the lab."

Time dragged so slowly that it was torturous. At around eight o'clock, after a hospital cafeteria supper that was actually not completely terrible, Ted declared he was exhausted and wanted to go get some sleep.

"Ted, go home," I said. "If anything changes, I'll call you right away."

"Thanks," Ted said. "Carl? Where are you sleeping tonight? As you and Eve are in sort of a state of flux I thought I might offer you a room."

State of flux. Well put, I thought.

"Uh, thanks, Ted. I actually thought I might stay with Cookie, raving lunatic that she is. One, to set her straight, and two, because Eve seemed pretty down. I think this is the time for us to all pull together, not to bicker and point fingers."

"I see. You're right, of course. Well, let's get your luggage out of my car and put it in one of the boys' cars."

"I'll take you downtown, Doc," Max said to Carl.

"I'll take Mom home," Luke said.

"To be honest, Adam is stable right now," Carl said. "Nothing's going to change until we find a donor. We may as well all try and get a good night's sleep. It's been a very long day."

I went back into Adam's room and looked at him, lying there. In the morning, I'd bring his nice pajamas for him and his slippers. And I'd put a picture of all of us next to his bed. He needed a shave. I'd arrange for that. I smoothed his hair away from his face and leaned over him, kissing his forehead as gently as I could.

"Good night, sweetheart," I said softly. "Just hold on. I love you."

We all said good night to each other and Luke drove me back to our house on the Stono.

"So, can we talk about this donor thing? If I'm a match for Dad and they decide I'm a good candidate, what happens to me? I mean, not that it matters, because I'd do anything to help him. But I'm just wondering."

"I think it's a few days in the hospital and you can't do strenuous exercise for about a month. I don't know all the details."

"Still. That's not such a big deal," Luke said.

"You know what, son? I find that whenever I've been cavalier about something it winds up being about fifty times bigger. We should probably wait and see."

"Yeah, I'm sure you're right. I'm glad you're here, Mom."

"Are you serious? I would've crawled home from Tibet if I'd had to. I wouldn't let your father go through something like this without me. No matter what."

"So, you and Dad have been sailing in choppy waters for a while?"

"Yes, but there's nothing going on that won't be all right eventually. We just have different opinions sometimes."

Different opinions as in, I prefer the truth and he likes to invent truth that suits him. But I didn't tell Luke that because my children did not have to have their lives destabilized from worrying about how their parents got along. Especially at a time like this.

"I'm thinking you couldn't be more vague, Mom. But, hey, that's okay. And you know, Max and I aren't stupid."

"I know that. Let's just get Dad well. Then I can kill him."

"That sounds reasonable."

In the morning, I was surprised to see that I had slept until almost eight thirty, which was very unusual for me. But I'd crossed so many time zones in the last weeks that my body had no clue when it was time to wake up. I scrambled out of bed to find that Luke and Max were still sound asleep. I stood there in the hallway outside of their bedrooms just looking from one of them to the other, remembering them when they were little boys and shared a room. Now they were so tall and filled out that they looked like men from where I stood. How old would they have to be before my rational mind would recognize them as adults? And, I asked myself for the millionth time, where did all the years go? I felt like so many years had blitzed right by me. I made a pot of coffee and went back to my bedroom to dress and to put together some things for Adam. I put his pajamas, his Dopp kit, and a picture of all of us in a tote bag by the door, and then I started cooking breakfast.

The smell of bacon frying brought Luke and Max back to

the conscious world. Bacon, by-product of the almighty pig, worked its irresistible magic on everyone. Luke kissed my cheek, then Max. I loved being with them and it made me deeply happy to have them under my roof, even if they were here for another absolutely terrible reason.

"Scrambled okay?" I said, referring to the eggs I was about to crack into a bowl.

"Anything's okay," Luke said, and filled an iced-tea glass to the top with orange juice.

"I'll make toast," Max said.

"I'll set the table," Luke said. "Anybody else want juice?"

We ate breakfast as quickly as we could and almost threw the dishes into the dishwasher in an effort to return to the hospital as early as we could. Despite our best efforts, it was still ten o'clock by the time we all got into my car.

As we were walking down the hall toward Adam's room we could see Ted, Cookie, Eve, and Carl there with someone else. It was Daphne, Eve's daughter. She looked like an adult. When did that happen?

"Well, wasn't that nice of Daphne to come," I said.

"I'm pretty good friends with her. She lives in Raleigh now," Max said.

"Oh. Did she ever finish her undergraduate degree?" I said.

"Not yet. She's taking courses to be a dental hygienist and working at Quail Ridge Books on the weekends," Max said.

"Yeah, remember her friend Kelly?" Luke said.

"Yes, I do," I said, remembering the summer of Kelly's tattoo—and oh, by the way, she's a Leo.

"She lives in Atlanta," Luke said.

"What a coincidence," I said, and then I knew exactly what my boys were up to. "You should never try to pull a fast one on your mother."

And to think I'd ever given their love lives a moment of concern. What was I thinking? Of course they had girlfriends. They'd probably had a hundred, for all I knew.

"Good morning!" I said to them all. "How's Adam doing? Any change?"

"None," Carl said. "But here's what I've learned. Luke? Max? You're off the hook. So are you, Eliza. I, however, am type O. So is Adam. I am a match."

Oh, dear God! I started to panic. Would Carl be willing to be Adam's donor or not? Eve looked like she might start crying. Ted was pale. He had to be thinking that what he had accused Carl and me of doing wasn't going to help his case now. In fact, he had given Carl a reason to walk away from all of us. Cookie, for once in her life, was silent.

"Why don't the three of us go get a cup of coffee," I said.

"Good idea," Carl said.

Eve, Carl, and I left the others there and went down to the cafeteria where we could speak in relative privacy. We all got coffee and sat a few tables away from the people who were there reading and eating. We took a seat and Carl cleared his throat.

"Here's the thing," he said. "I don't feel so great about giving part of my liver to a guy who's been mooning over my wife for years."

I was speechless. Absolutely without words. And then Eve spoke.

"You listen to me, Carl Landers. I'd had it up to *here* with all the accusations flying around us. How long do you think it took Cookie to tell me about the two of you being in Greece together? Two seconds, *that's* how long! And do you think I believed that you were sleeping together? Hell, no, I didn't. I know the two of you! So you were both in Greece. So what? You're not sleeping with Eliza any more than I was sleeping with Adam. If I'd wanted to sleep with Adam I would've said, I'm sorry, Carl, I want a divorce. I had a million opportunities to do that over all these years and I never did. You want to know why? Because I love you. And I love you, Eliza. And I know Adam loves both of you too. Carl, he's the closest thing to a brother you've ever had. This is ridiculous. Adam's up there hanging on to life with a wing and a prayer. And he needs you now. And Eliza needs you too. And no matter what Cookie thinks with her stupid mind games and insinuations, she's wrong, just like she's been wrong all my life. And Ted?"

I said, "He's not thinking straight right now. Clarabeth's hardly cold and Adam's as sick as he can be. He's scared to death."

"Carl? You know Adam loves you and has looked up to you all these years," Eve said.

I said, "It's true, Eve. Everything you said is true. Please, God, don't let Adam die. Not like this. Not because of Cookie's lies."

"They're not all lies," Eve said. "There was a time when

we were practically babies, that Adam and I knew each other in an intimate way. Now, and every time he sees me coming, he remembers being so young and carefree. But listen to me, he's not in love with me. He was just infatuated with a ghost of the past. He's not that young man anymore, and I'm not that young girl! We're not even who we were when *we* first met each other, that first summer when our children were so young and you were whipping Adam's self-esteem on the golf course! We are who we are *now*, and we're still together because of the nearly twenty years of love between all of us. Real, deep, and abiding love. If you want that all to end, Carl, it can end right now. It's your call."

I'd never heard Eve speak so eloquently and with so much passion. She was right. That ditzy blonde I met at Wild Dunes decades ago was long gone.

Eve and I stared at Carl, waiting for him to say something.

After what seemed like an eternity, he finally spoke.

"I never said I wouldn't give him part of my liver. I just said I didn't feel so great about it. I'm a little nervous, you know?"

"I can't blame you for that," I said.

"He's a doctor," Eve said. "He knows too much for his own good."

"No more blame," Carl said. "Let's get these wheels in motion."

I was so overcome with emotion and gratitude that I threw my arms around Carl and cried.

CHAPTER 20

eliza

The worst part of major surgery for the family is always the waiting. According to the transplant surgeon Carl's surgery would take about five hours. They were going to take only part of his right lobe, but still—five hours under anesthesia was no small thing. Most of his liver would regenerate in two weeks, and his hospital stay would be five to seven days. That didn't sound so awful, but we all knew Carl would have significant discomfort. But he was willing to withstand it for Adam's sake. Saving your friend's life was the most heroic thing I could imagine a friend could do, and I loved Carl for it.

"Greece would've been more fun than this," he said.

"Adam and I owe you a vacation there," I said. "We'll foot the bill."

"Eve, I want to show you the cottage where I stayed, right on the ocean," Carl said.

"And I want to see it with you. Greece. Something for us to look forward to!" Eve said.

We were more worried for Adam. He was fifty-three years old and until now, he had been in excellent health. Or so we thought. Hepatitis C had been working on his liver for a long time. But even though otherwise he was pretty strong, a million things could still go wrong. Immune system rejection. Bile duct complications. Internal bleeding. Infection. I knew the risks involved, but it wasn't like we had a choice. My hand shook as I signed the consent form allowing them to perform the surgery, since I was Adam's medical proxy. Still under heavy sedation, Adam was wheeled to the operating room to wait for Carl's liver. I kissed Adam's forehead before they took him in. I even kissed Carl's cheek and squeezed his hand, thanking him a thousand times. Eve and I stood together as they rolled our husbands away. We tried to look brave and we smiled, but our insides were gelatin. Well, mine were anyway.

We were all there, gathered in the waiting room, the elders all second-guessing ourselves to death. The kids were fixated by their iPhones, doing Facebook and tweeting or whatever it was that they did these days. I'd finally upgraded from a flip phone last year because Max and Luke told me it was an embarrassment. Now the wrong phone is an embarrassment? I was beyond redemption in all areas of cool, but it didn't bother me, which was probably another confirmation that I was seriously over the hill. So, to let them know I wasn't completely out of it, every now and then I'd send them a text. Sometimes with an emoji. Or I'd upload one of their baby pictures on their birthdays and leave a comment with it on their Facebook page, expecting to be unfriended. I thought it was hilarious, and oddly, they didn't really complain. To me, so-called social media and all that stuff was just a colossal waste of time. I had better things to do. Like worry.

Now Adam was in one operating room and Carl was in another. I was so frightened, I wouldn't have been surprised if I'd looked in a mirror and saw that my hair had turned white.

Ted said to Eve, "I cannot begin to tell you how grateful—"

"I know that, Ted. We are *all* so grateful to Carl."

"Oh, my God, are we ever!" I said.

I looked up to see a hospital volunteer approach. There was an official badge featuring her smiling face hanging from a lanyard around her neck. She was a lovely woman. I would've put her age somewhere in the sixty-five area, a little younger than Cookie for sure. She was dressed very stylishly. For whatever reason, she zeroed in on Ted.

"Mr. Stanley?"

"Yes?"

Ted all but jumped to his feet.

"I'm Judy Linder, the head of our patient-family support group here at MUSC."

"It's nice to meet you," he said.

"I just wanted to know if I can bring y'all some coffee or a cold drink? Or today's paper? Waiting is so hard. We try to make things a little easier for the family."

It was obvious to me from the way that Mr. Stanley

preened that he found Ms. Linder to be quite attractive. Seventy-eight and still preening.

"What can we bring you, Eliza?" Ted said.

"A bottle of cold water would be great. Thanks." But a bottle of wine and five milligrams of valium would be better, I thought and did not say.

The kids—I call them kids even though they're all twenty-one—wanted water too.

Eve said, "So would I. Thanks!"

"Cookie?" Ted said and looked at her. She was suddenly visibly annoyed.

"I'd like a bottle of Evian."

"Everyone is so health conscious today," Ted said to Judy. "In my day, I drank Cokes by the dozen!"

"Oh! So did I!"

"Why don't I come with you and help you carry everything back?"

"Why, thank you. That would be so nice! You know, ever since my husband passed away—"

Cookie interrupted. "Everyone's husband is dead these days."

"Mother!" Eve said.

Claws in, Cookie, I thought.

Ted and Judy walked away, and as soon as they were out of earshot, Cookie said in a high-pitched whine, "Oh! So did I!"

"Mother! What is wrong with you?" Eve said in nearly a whisper.

"Nothing," Cookie said.

I remembered the distinguished older gentleman she'd

brought to Clarabeth's memorial dinner. What was his name? Reggie? Reginald?

"Cookie? What happened to that nice man you brought to our dinner at Cypress?" I said.

"Well, nothing, I imagine."

I said, "Oh, I was just wondering if you saw him again."

"No, ma'am. It turns out that he wasn't as available as I was made to believe. Unlike *some* people, I don't fool around with married men."

"That's enough, Mother!" Eve said.

"Why don't you kids take a little stroll down the hall?" I said to Max, Luke, and Daphne.

Despite the fact that they were so mesmerized by their phones, they'd all been around Cookie long enough to smell trouble. They got up and walked away.

"Mother? All this talk and innuendo about me and Eliza and Adam and Carl has to stop this minute. We are friends, Mother. Nothing more than friends. But we are friends on a level that you've never enjoyed because you're always saying terrible things about everyone and looking for the worst in people. Think about it."

"Friends without boundaries! That's what you all are!"

I had to jump into the fray. She was now gone over the top of incredible rudeness.

"No, Cookie, that is *not* who we are," I said. "We are very respectable middle-aged men and women who have known each other for decades. Eve's husband is in there trying to save my husband's life. If Carl didn't hold Adam in very high esteem, do you think he'd undergo this surgery?"

"How should I know how a man thinks?" Cookie said.

I don't know. Because you've had enough of them in your bed to write an encyclopedia on the male species? I thought.

"Well, Cookie, here's the bottom line. We are responsible adults, not philandering fools. You need to stop this ugly talk right now," I said, and realized that I was surprised at myself. It was the first time I had ever called down an elder, but what was she going to do? Spank me?

"You're just projecting your mean-spirited behavior onto us, Mother. The four of us are practically family. You've turned into an old crone."

"Don't you dare speak to me this way," Cookie said. "I'm your mother!"

"Yes. You brought me into the world. But I sure don't like who you've become. No matter how badly you've behaved— whether it was drugs, alcohol, or just starting trouble—we always showed you respect. It's time for you to give us the respect we deserve."

It was like trying to drill some sense into a spoiled, stubborn child. There was no use in it. I got up to rescue the kids. They were just down the hall at the next waiting area. Daphne stood and looked at me.

"My grandmother is not very nice," Daphne said. "She's always making up awful things about other people. It's totally embarrassing. Why does she do that?"

"Well, honey, if I had the answer to that I'd bottle it and sell it and probably be a very rich woman. I think some people are just the glass-is-half-empty kind."

"I guess. She used to be so sweet when I was little."

"Well, those were difficult days for her as well."

"Yeah, like when she tried to nail her drug abuse on me! Who does that to their only granddaughter?"

"Hurt birds," I said. "But Adam and I and your parents? We all love you to pieces! And you're awfully nice to be here with all of us today."

"I'm glad I could come. I figured, God forbid, if something happened to my dad I'd better be here for my mom. Cookie would probably say it was Mom's fault."

"You're right. She might."

"And I didn't want Luke and Max to be here without me either. I mean, this is happening to both of our families."

Luke looked up.

"Any word?"

"No, sweetie, I think it's going to be a while," I said. "Let's go back and join Eve and Cookie." And pull Cookie's claws out of Eve's throat, I thought, but kept it to myself.

Eve and Cookie weren't speaking. Cookie was flipping through a six-month-old *People* magazine and Eve was pacing the floor.

"I'm so worried," she said. I could see it in her eyes.

Something had changed in Eve's demeanor since the three of us had that cup of coffee a few days ago. The lines between us were no longer blurred and never would be again. Eve, who surprisingly assumed the lead, was reclaiming Carl. And Carl was stepping up to validate the worth of our relationships with each other with conviction, nobility, and great personal sacrifice. Adam was unaware still that it was Carl who was going to save him. Somehow, I knew though that when Adam woke up and learned what had transpired he would be a changed man for the rest of his life.

"You know, Eve, you told me something years ago. Do you remember when Max had that awful fall and Carl stepped in? You said to me, you don't know Carl. If something terrible is happening, Carl can make it right. I believed it then and I still believe it now. Carl is going to be fine. I just hope Adam will be fine too."

"Yeah, except this time, Carl's taking a bullet."

"You're right. But Carl knows how to judge the risk, don't you think?"

"I think so. I mean, Carl knows Adam is in real trouble and that the odds of Adam living without a transplant are nil. And waiting for one would take too long, at least that's what Carl told me. Of course, if we'd known this just a few weeks ago, we could've taken Clarabeth's. But who knew? Anyway, she was probably too old to be a donor. I don't think your organs are transplanted after sixty."

"Clarabeth was close to ninety!"

"Well, then, Carl had to be the man," Eve said. "And that's that!"

"Too late to change his mind now," I said.

Eve scowled and I thought to myself that I'd painted a gruesome picture for no reason. I should learn to keep my mouth shut.

"I guess it is," Eve said. "And Eliza?"

"Yes?"

"All of Cookie's clothes are from a consignment shop. Even her shoes."

"Wow," I said

We went back to where Cookie was sitting. Ted returned with Judy. Her arms were filled with magazines and newspapers. Ted passed out the water bottles.

"Sorry, Cookie, no Evian. Just Dasani."

Cookie took the bottle from him and mumbled, "Thanks."

"You know, there's a VIP lounge with a television and Internet access," Judy said.

"We might be more comfortable there because there are sofas and club chairs," Ted said.

"And it's stocked with snacks. The minute I realized that your donor is a doctor, I pulled a few strings, and y'all are very welcome to wait there," Judy said.

"Why not?" Cookie said. "These chairs are terrible for the old bony derriere."

"She said it was old, not me!" Ted said. "Come on, Cookie."

Ted outstretched his hand to Cookie and she got up, taking his arm. I wouldn't say she actually sneered at Judy Linder, but she held Ted's arm in a proprietary way, sending a message that Ted was hers. But Cookie was too late. Ms. Linder had moved in for the kill. We were all walking down the hall, following her to the new lounge.

"Eliza? Ms. Linder is going to have dinner with me next week. Isn't that wonderful?"

I thought Cookie would faint. But it only took a few seconds for her to recover.

"What? But Clarabeth hasn't been—"

"Dead long enough?" Ted said. "Cookie, at my age, I don't want to spend what might be the last year of my life in mourning. Clarabeth wouldn't want that for me either."

"Well," she said, "I'm going to wait until Carl is out of the woods, of course. But here's my news. I'm going to spend eleven months out of the year on cruise ships. I'm going to see the world!"

"What?" Ted said and stopped dead in his tracks. "Why?"

"Because it's cheaper than moving to Bishop Gadsden."

Bishop Gadsden was a very nice retirement community in Charleston.

Cookie went on. "And life here has become intolerably dull. Cruise ships can be so glamorous! Broadway entertainers! Black-tie dinners! My accountant did the math for me."

"That's insane," Ted said.

"It most certainly is not! A lot of people are doing it now. It's all the rage," Cookie said. "I just listed my house with Carolina One. When it sells, I'm going to buy a little one-bedroom condo on the harbor in Mount Pleasant and it's sayonara, baby! I'm spreading my wings!"

Eve and I exchanged looks of surprise.

Sayonara, baby?

"This is the first I'm hearing about it," Eve said.

"I don't know. Maybe. Well, what the heck? I think it's a great idea," Ted said.

"So do I," I said.

"Sometimes a change of scenery is the best thing for you," Ted said.

"Well, if I had a reason to stay, I would," Cookie said.

Eve and I looked at each other and rolled our eyes.

The sign on the door of the VIP lounge said *Hollings Society Room.* Senator Fritz Hollings was something of an icon in contemporary South Carolina politics, having served in the United States Senate all my life until his recent retirement. There were wings of buildings, schools, dormitories, parks, and all kinds of spaces named for him. I imagined that there was a substantial price tag that came with the privilege of membership in the Hollings Society.

We went inside. It was as beautifully decorated as it was serene. Big leather sofas and club chairs provided several sitting areas. There was a conference table with twelve chairs and two large-screen televisions. The lounge had a Pullman-type kitchen and a bathroom. I thought, if this just had a bedroom and a better kitchen, I could live here.

Ms. Linder assured us that as soon as Carl was in recovery someone would let us know. My boys and Daphne made a beeline for the refrigerator.

"It's only water," Luke said.

"But there are apples and bananas over here," Daphne said.

"This drawer has a ton of pretzels and potato chips," Max said. "But if you eat this stuff you clog up your arteries and wind up here getting bypass."

Judy Linder laughed and said, "Well, we have to stay in business, you know." Everyone looked at her with surprise. "I'm kidding! I'm just kidding! Golly! This is how conspiracy theories get started, isn't it?"

"Yeah," Max said. "Actually, that was pretty funny."

"Thank you," Eve said. "This is so nice of you to let us be here."

"It's our pleasure!" Judy Linder said and went toward the door. "Ted?"

"Yes?"

"I'll be expecting your call."

"Of course!" he said.

If I'd only had a superhero's extrasensory vision, I would've been able to detect the steam billowing from Cookie's ears.

We made ourselves comfortable and time passed. I looked at my watch. Carl had been in the operating room for almost three hours. I said a prayer for him and one for Adam, holding my beads from Greece and drank another bottle of water.

Ted, Max, and Luke, who had been deep in a powwow on the other side of the room, approached me and sat down.

"What's going on, gentlemen?" I asked.

"You should be very proud of your sons," Ted said.

Max and Luke grinned and I said, "I am! I'm very proud of my boys. Why are you telling me this?"

"We're coming home to take over Dad's business until he's well," Luke said.

"And I'm coming out of retirement until Adam is back on his feet and ready to resume his duties," Ted said.

Cookie butted in and said, "Well then, you're not coming to the Galápagos with me."

Ted looked at her like she was off her rocker.

"Ted, thank you. Boys! You can't do that!" I said. "You're both supposed to graduate in May!"

"I got a special leave," Luke said. "All of my professors

said I could make it up in summer school and still graduate, but I'll walk with the next graduating class in January. If I want to walk."

"I don't know," I said and thought it didn't seem right to yank Luke out of Atlanta like that.

"I got a family emergency dispensation, but I wasn't as lucky with my professors about course work," Max said. "Premed is a special kind of hell. But if I go back in June, I can graduate in December."

"Are you boys sure you want to do this?" I said.

"One hundred percent," they both said.

I wanted to weep with joy. These were good boys. I had raised really good boys.

The door of the lounge opened again and in walked JJ and Tasha.

"Oh, my God!" I said. "I can't believe you're here! I was going to call you, but everything happened so fast!"

We all hugged and kissed.

"I wasn't going to let you go through this without Tasha and me!" JJ said. "What are families for?"

"How did you even find out about Adam?" I asked.

"Kiki called me and told me the whole story. How else? She was very worried, and so is Aunt Anna. I decided that we should just get on a plane and come give you some support."

"Oh, JJ! Thank you! Thank you so much. And Tasha, thank you too. I'm so happy you're here. I want you to meet Cookie and Eve."

"So! You're Cookie?" Tasha said. "You look just like I thought you would."

"Oh? And how's that?" Cookie said.

"Gorgeous! And you're Eve! You look just like your beautiful mother!"

Cookie and Eve liked nothing better than a compliment. Who didn't?

JJ said, "So what's the story? Is Adam still in the operating room?"

"Yes, and he still has a few hours to go, I think," I said.

"But the doctors expect a good outcome?" JJ said.

"Yes, but Adam's going to have a long recovery in front of him," I said.

My boys had been standing by politely waiting for their chance to say hello to their aunt and uncle.

"Uncle JJ?" Luke said.

"My God, you've become a man! Look at you! All grown up!" They hugged and then JJ turned to Max. "And look at you! You're an adult!" Then they hugged.

"Thanks, Uncle JJ, it's so good to see you."

"Well, when our cousin Kiki called me from Greece and told me what was going on I looked at Tasha and said, 'We have not been doing a good enough job for Eliza and her family. We get so wrapped up in our own stuff that it's ridiculous. We're going. Start packing.'"

"That's exactly what happened. And I decided something, Eliza. I've been a lousy sister-in-law and aunt to these beautiful boys. Ever since I went on the board at the Isabella Stewart Gardner Museum, all I do is go to meetings. I'm in my car driving back and forth to Boston four times a week! It's ridiculous. We're going to see each other more often. And I want Luke and Max to visit us too. I'd love to take them to the big city and show them all around. Have you boys ever been to Boston?"

"Not since we were little," Luke said.

"He's right. We must've been what? Five?" Max said. "Can we go to a Sox game?"

"Absolutely!" JJ said.

JJ and Tasha settled into a sofa with bottled water and a magazine and we all resumed the wait. We talked about Greece and Kiki and how amazing and historical Corfu was. I showed them all my pictures. And then came the news about Carl.

"He's in the recovery ICU," the doctor said. "He did just fine and we don't expect any complications."

"Can I see him?" Eve said.

"She should let the man rest," Cookie said.

"Hush," Ted said. "That's her husband."

Cookie pressed her lips to one side of her mouth, looked at JJ and Tasha, rolled her eyes, and shook her head as if to say, *he thinks he knows everything.*

The doctor said, "As soon as he's awake, we'll come get you."

"And my husband? Adam Stanley?"

"I think they'll be winding the surgery up shortly. I'll come let you know, or someone will."

There was nothing left to do except continue to wait.

Someone came to get Eve. Carl was awake and asking for her. She left Daphne there with Cookie and went to see him. Two more hours went by. We had sandwiches from downstairs and the kids got pizzas. We watched CNN and then *I*

Love Lucy reruns. We talked, played cards, and paced the floor.

Then Ted came to me and sat down.

"I'm sorry for what I said, Eliza. I was so worried I couldn't think straight."

"It's okay, Ted. It really is."

Finally, word came that Adam was in the recovery ICU as well. I broke down in tears—tears of gratitude, tears from stress, and tears of exhaustion. Ted gave me a giant hug and so did the boys and JJ. We were all so relieved. And so grateful.

About forty-five minutes later a nurse came to lead me to his room. He was in an ICU room right next to Carl. Our whole group went there together. Everyone stood outside the plate-glass window while I went inside.

There he was, stretched out in his bed, attached to more monitors then I thought could possibly be needed by just one person. But his eyes were open, and although he was still groggy, he was awake. The joy I felt was indescribable. I leaned over him.

"Hi!" I said in a whisper.

"Hi," he whispered back.

"Sweetheart," I said, "you're going to be all right."

"I love you," he said.

"I love you too," I said. In my heart, I had forgiven him for everything.

"It was Carl?"

"Yes. He was your donor."

"Gotta let the son of a bitch take me on the tennis court, I guess," he said and smiled again. In fact, it seemed like neither one of us could stop smiling. Adam's color was improving by the minute and I was happy, no, overjoyed, to see it.

"Nah," I said. "Just buy him dinner."

"I'm gonna live, Eliza."

"Yes, Adam Stanley, and *we're* going to live happily ever after."

He drifted off to sleep, still smiling. Where he went when he dreamed I did not know. But I could tell by the look on his face that it had to be somewhere beautiful. We were a family again. Given a second chance to be happy and productive and in love because of Carl and Eve's generous hearts. I had so much to tell Adam. But the updates could wait for another time. It was the time to heal.

CHAPTER 21

eliza

2010

Adam's illness had terrified us. Carl's gift had purified us. It was as though he had taken us by the hand down to the River Jordan and baptized us. A group baptism *and* an exorcism. All our devils were gone. We resumed our rightful places with each other with renewed vigor and deepened commitment. There was nothing like staring death right in the eye to wake us up. Everyone around us could see the changes in us, especially Ted, which Adam and I appreciated.

"I'm so glad to see y'all worked things out," he said one night when we had him over for dinner with Judy.

Ted and Judy had become quite the pair, and Cookie just hated the hell out of it.

Carl recovered quickly and went back to the business of saving children's lives. As we knew it would, it took Adam longer to regain his energy and strength. I was his home nurse. I saw that he got up and walked in the first days he was home. I took him to all of his doctor's appointments and had all of his medications ready for him to take when the time came for another dose. And I kept his spirits high by reading to him, watching feel-good movies, and discussing the events of the day. And I began and ended each day with a positive attitude. How well a person heals has as much to do with attitude as anything else.

During that spring, Ted and the boys did a wonderful job of getting all those houses finished on time for the Boeing employees, with Adam consulting from the sidelines and me paying all the bills. Slowly, slowly Adam became himself again. He was so grateful to all of us for the parts we played in saving him and putting him back together again. Carl, naturally, received the largest share of the gratitude pie.

I was in touch with Kiki all the time. She was overwhelmed with joy to hear of the success of Adam's transplant, and the fact that Carl had been the donor was incredible to her.

"Now that's a true friend," she had said.

"Yes," I said. "It is."

Adam and I were planning a trip to Greece in August, with Carl and Eve as our guests. JJ and Tasha were coming too. And, in a moment of oh, what the heck, Ted and Judy decided to come along.

Kiki said, "We cannot wait to have all of you here with us! What wonderful news! Mother will start cooking the minute I tell her!"

"I can't believe I have to spend a week with JJ and Tasha," Adam said.

"Don't you dare complain," I said, and that was the end of that.

I was so happy to have my boys home with me. I wasn't lonely at all. And no one ever heard a peep from me over having mountainous laundry to do or more mouths to feed. They loved being home too.

"I never realized how much you did for me until I had to do it all myself!" Luke said.

Max said, "Duh."

Suddenly it was summer and we literally had to push Max and Luke out of the house and back to college. They didn't want to leave us. Maybe they were afraid Adam would take on too much too soon and that something might happen to him. For the first time in their lives they'd had to reckon with the fact that they wouldn't have us forever.

I was making waffles one morning in May, happily stirring a compote of blueberries in a pot to pour over them. They were at the table with Adam, drinking coffee and reading their favorite morning newspapers on their iPads. Another sign of their adulthood.

"You know, Dad," Luke said, "I could just stay here and we could run the business together."

"You need your degree," he said.

"Oh, come on," Luke said. "I've been training for this job all my life."

"You need your degree," Adam said again in his most serious parental voice.

Luke mimicked him in an even deeper voice, saying, "You need your degree."

Max laughed, then Luke laughed too.

"I think Luke's got the picture, Dad," Max said.

"Good," Adam said.

In May, Adam got the okay from his doctor to resume full-time work, and it was time for the boys to go. They went back to Atlanta and Raleigh and Cookie embarked on her first cruise.

Cookie was testing her plan to live on cruise ships for the rest of her life. It didn't work out exactly the way she hoped it would.

"She came home yesterday and said she'd never met such inhospitable people in her entire life," Eve said. "She told me she's suing the cruise company and she wants her money back."

"Good grief! What happened?" I said.

It was a couple of weeks later, and we were having a barbecue at Ted's house. Carl and Eve had come for the weekend and were staying with us. We were standing in Ted's backyard watching him baste four racks of baby back ribs. Judy was bringing potato salad and mac and cheese but had yet to arrive. And I had brought my grandmother's photo album and all my pictures to show them so they would have an idea of what to expect when we got to Dassia.

Eve said, "Well, you know Cookie. She had it in her head that she'd meet fascinating widowers from around the world who would find her allure irresistible."

"She forgot to pack her allure," Carl said to Adam. "You want another beer?"

"Nah, thanks. One's plenty. Gotta be good to my new liver," Adam said.

"Oh, Cookie, Cookie, Cookie. Tell me more," I said.

"Don't you know, I had to squeeze the truth out of her, but it seems those widowers from around the world *were* there. But they brought women with them who were half Cookie's age, which she didn't like one little bit."

"She doesn't like Judy either," Ted said. "And Judy's almost her age."

"Jealous," I said, and Ted nodded.

"She probably would've had a better time if she had not felt it was her moral duty to offer her staunch opinion against May-December romances," Carl said.

"Come on!" Adam said. "I mean, we know Cookie's bold, but that's social suicide."

Eve said, "Yes, it is! And it was. Here's how bad it got. By day three on her trip down the Seine, people left the room or moved to another sofa when they saw her coming. And she ate almost all of her meals alone."

"That's terrible," I said. I felt bad about it, but I had to laugh.

Even Ted snickered. Carl and Adam were snorting and laughing.

Eve said, "When she got home I told her, Mother? This is how the world is today. You have to learn to be happy on your own before you can be happy with somebody else."

"We all have to learn that lesson," I said.

"Some of us more than once," Ted said.

"Ever since Eve stopped drinking, she's a font of knowledge and advice," Carl said.

"Her mind is razor sharp," I said.

"I can't get away with jack," Carl said.

"You never could!" Eve said and laughed.

Eve swearing off wine had given her a mental clarity I didn't know she could access. These days she never missed a trick. Sober Eve was much more desirable company. If we had lived in the same town, we would've been inseparable.

Eve said Cookie thought that her advice was a lot of hooey, but she'd signed up for another river cruise in July, this time down the Rhine River.

"She promised she'd try harder to be more congenial and less judgmental on her next trip. She's determined to make this idea of retiring on cruises work."

Well, that's where Cookie found love, on a side trip offered by the cruise line, in the picturesque village of Kinderdijk, snuggled in the southern tip of the Netherlands. His name was Hans, and he was a cheesemaker, a big man, she said, who wore wooden clogs everywhere he went. Or maybe it was the windmills that stole her heart. She called Eve to say she was staying. She got off the river cruise with all her belongings and checked into a quaint bed-and-breakfast.

And of course, Eve told me all this as soon as we got to Wild Dunes and had a moment to ourselves.

"Oh! My goodness! You're kidding! Wait until I tell Adam!" I didn't know whether to be horrified or to start laughing hysterically. "Clogs?"

"Yes! She told me his house has a thatched roof and that you can see the windmills from his bedroom. She said, 'He gave me a night of Dutch magic.'" She imitated Cookie in a dreamy teenage girl's voice.

"Dear holy mother!"

"Then she said, I'll let you know if I'm ever coming back."

I thought, maybe all Cookie ever needed was a good roll in the hay herself.

Eve continued, "Ew. Dutch magic? I don't even want to know what that means. How's Adam feeling?"

I had to laugh. Cookie was happy? Puh-leaze!

"What a story! Adam? You'd never believe he was ever so sick, to see him running around these days. So how are you and Carl getting along?"

It was as hot as Hades, the dead of July, and Eve and I were sitting by the pool like we always did. The boys were out playing nine holes despite the heat. We weren't going to let a little thing like an organ transplant and Cookie running away from home ruin our annual vacation. And that year was sans children. And sans Ted, who had stayed home to oversee the construction of new porches and a new roof on the old plantation house.

And Clarabeth, of course, was absent too. Wild Dunes seemed a little strange and haunted without her.

"Carl is just the greatest guy in the world," Eve said. "What's that old Joni Mitchell song? 'Don't it always seem to go, you don't know what you've got till it's gone'? Something like that. I almost blew it! But you know, Adam's illness saved us, crazy as *that* sounds!"

"I almost blew it too! Yes, Adam's illness saved us all," I said in agreement. "He's always said, there are no coincidences."

"I think I might actually agree with that," she said.

"Me too."

That night we went over to the Shem Creek Bar and Grill for dinner. Ted and Judy met us there. We ordered tons of food—salads, deviled crabs, fried shrimp, hush puppies, and flounder.

"That ought to do it," Angie Avinger, the restaurant's owner, said.

"They got you waiting tables, Angie?" Ted said.

"For you, darlin'? Anything."

"She's my favorite," Ted said.

"Do I need to be jealous?" Judy said.

Ted reached over and squeezed her hand. "Not for one second. How's everything at Wild Dunes?" Ted said to Adam and Carl.

"Hot on the golf course," Adam said.

"Today was a scorcher," Carl said.

"That's because you boys don't have the sense to get in the shade! Ted, it's the same beach as last year," Eve said. "I love it there."

"Me too. I love the Isle of Palms. And it will be the same beach next year," I said. "I hope."

"Well, next year I'll put aside a week and join you," he said. "This year it just didn't seem right."

Adam said, "Dad, we understand completely. How's that new roof coming?"

"It's coming, but so is Christmas," Ted said.

"I'm so looking forward to our trip to Greece," Judy said. "I've been to some of the islands but never Corfu."

"It's pretty special," I said. "My mother was born there

and her sister still lives there. And I still have lots of cousins all around Corfu Town. They all say we can't get there fast enough."

"Well, your family looks so nice," Ted said. "This is going to be a real treat."

Later that night, Adam and I took a stroll on the beach. It was low tide and there were approximately a billion stars glittering above us. We found an old palmetto log and sat there for a while, just musing. Adam took my hand in his and kissed it.

"I love you so, so much," he said.

"Enough to live here a few months out of the year?" I'd been waiting to ask that question for a while.

"Which months?"

"Oh, I don't know. March, April, May? It's a slower rental time."

"What about your garden?"

"I can put it in with Mr. Proctor and he can watch it, don't you think?"

"Yes, he could. What about the commute?"

"Well, sweetheart, if you're still building in Summerville, it's only about ten minutes longer from here than from where we live."

"True. You really love this place, don't you?"

"Yes, I do. And to be perfectly honest, it's a lot closer to civilization."

He looked at me, and even in the dark I could see him thinking about the many inconveniences of living so far away from all the places we liked to go, inconveniences that had impacted my day-to-day living and my social life for twenty years.

"Maybe we should just build a house over here. What do you think? I can bring a dump truck of black dirt from our property and you can have a garden here. That is, when we find a piece of property to build on."

"Oh, Adam! Do you mean it? Oh, you're the most wonderful man in the world!"

"That might be overstating it, but only slightly," he said, smiling. "Hey! We had a great year and all I want to do is make you happy!"

"Oh, I love you, sweetheart!"

The next morning, Adam and I were lying in bed. Neither one of us felt like getting up. We were talking about buying property. He said we should take a ride around the island that afternoon and see what was for sale. I was so excited. He was too.

"Last night was fun, wasn't it?" Adam said, fluffing his pillow and turning over on his side to face me.

"Yes. I love deviled crabs," I said. "I never think to order them because of the breading. But theirs are really good. I love them."

"I love you," he said.

I turned over to face him. "And I love you."

For the next few minutes we just lay there, like two lovers do, and stared into each other's eyes. Then he took his hand and began to rub his knuckles lightly along the side of my arm. I had missed his touch for a long time. I had a fleeting thought about how much time we might actually have left together, then I let it go. I had been avoiding sex because I was afraid it might hurt him somehow. I was waiting for him to let me know when he was ready. He was ready.

"Are you sure?" I said.

"I played golf and I didn't drop dead," he said. He had that devilish smile on his face, the one I fell in love with so long ago. "Feel this."

He took my hand and pushed it down to his Lowcountry.

"Good Lord! Adam!" He was like a teenage boy seeing a *Playboy* magazine for the first time.

"This won't take long," he said, unabashedly and brazenly, and then he smiled like he used to when we were younger—wide smile, full of beans.

He's bragging about a quickie?

"Okay, but if you die, don't blame me."

"I won't."

He pulled my nightshirt over my head and threw it somewhere and slipped out of his pajamas at the same time. Before I could say anything, he was inside of me, and I thought, Oh, God. I have missed my husband!

"I love you, Adam. You feel so good."

"I love you, Eliza. Yes. You feel wonderful."

Well, I should've made note of the time. It was not a quickie. It was an Olympic trial if not a main event. Adam was in charge and going for the gold. I was holding onto the headboard for dear life while he enthusiastically plunged in me over and over for at least fifteen minutes, maybe longer. The headboard was banging the wall so loudly, I knew our neighbors knew what the rhythmic sounds meant. At that moment I didn't care. I could barely participate or add anything to what was happening. I could hardly think. All I could do was lie back and enjoy it. So I did. When he finally reached orgasm, he began touching me. An onlooker (not that there had ever been one, except for that one time the boys caught us when they were little and thought we were killing each other) would've said Adam had a future in gynecology. I would've said to that onlooker that Adam knew how to make my body sing arias like a diva. There was no way sex got any better than that.

We were lying there in a pool of our bodily fluids and sweat, trying to bring our heartbeats back to normal.

"I'm pregnant," I said. "I'm sure of it."

"No, you're not. You're menopausal."

"Screw you," I said and laughed.

"You just did," he said.

The doorbell rang.

"I'll get it," I said. "You just stay right here."

"I'm not going anywhere," he said.

I pulled my nightshirt over my head and yelled, "Coming!"

Adam said, "You just did!"

"Very funny, Mr. Stanley."

"Be right there," I said. I looked through the keyhole. It was Carl and Eve. I thought, Oh, okay, and I opened the door. "G'morning!" I said, chipper as a baby bird just out of the shell.

"Sweet Jesus, girl! What happened to your hair?" Eve said.

I ran my fingers through my hair and stopped at the rat's nest in the back of my head the size of a grapefruit.

"Um," I said, feeling its Rastafarian mass. "Yeah, wow."

"And your nightshirt is inside out," Eve said. They both snickered. "Busted!"

"Yeah," Carl said, innocently. "So what's going on in the Stanley house this morning?"

"Exactly what you think, Mr. and Mrs. Landers! We're giving each other a little thrill. So, why are you here at the crack of dawn?"

"It's actually nine o'clock and we're supposed to be going out for breakfast at the Sea Biscuit? Remember?" Eve said.

"Really?" And then I remembered. "Well, why don't y'all get us a table and we'll be there as fast as we can."

"Come back to bed, woman!" Adam yelled from upstairs. "I'm not done with you!"

"Adam! Stop! You're just going to milk this to death, aren't you?"

"We'll see you soon," Carl said and took Eve's elbow. "Let's go, sweetheart, and let these old people try and recoup their dignity."

They left, and by the time I got upstairs, Adam had the shower running. He was brushing his teeth and I began to work on the knot in my hair.

"I have three choices," I said, looking at it with a hand mirror. "I can grow dreadlocks starting now, I can cut it off at the roots, or I can carefully untangle it."

"I'm going with dreadlocks," he said. "I think they're interesting."

"I'm interesting looking enough," I said. "Get your shower. The Landerses are waiting."

When we got to the Sea Biscuit, Eve and Carl were still waiting for a table.

"This place is impossible," I said.

"You should open a breakfast place on this island," Eve said. "You'd make a fortune!"

There was a shortage of breakfast places on the Isle of Palms and nothing on Sullivan's Island, the next island over.

"What do I know about running a restaurant?" I said, and then I remembered I knew someone who did. Alexandros.

I'd talk to him when we returned to Corfu. Maybe he'd like to have a second restaurant here? Maybe I'd be his partner? It was certainly something to think about. A Greek diner on the Isle of Palms? Why not? I'd had crazier pipe dreams than that.

Later on, Carl and Eve went downtown to check on Cookie's house and Adam and I scouted the island, looking for a real estate opportunity. Sadly, there was nothing on the market that we liked.

"You should call that guy who's on all the Carolina One For Sale signs—Everett Presson. Looks like he's listed every darn house on the market! Tell him to let us know when something good comes up."

"Good idea," I said.

Three weeks later, the elders of our tribe were all on the way to Greece and I had a cell phone with an international plan. My bag was stuffed with gifts for everyone I could remember. JJ and Tasha were flying to Athens from Boston, and we were able to coordinate our flights to land within thirty minutes of each other. Then we would take the domestic airline to Corfu together. I called him the night before we left just to see if they were all ready.

"I'm psyched," he said. "Tasha's been shopping around the clock."

"I'm really excited too," I said.

The plan was that Eve and Carl would stay in the precious house on the beach where Carl had the most expensive one-day vacation in his life. Adam and I wanted them to have the best property to themselves. Ted and Judy were going to stay in Yiayia's house with us along with JJ and Tasha. There were two small bathrooms upstairs and three bedrooms. One for JJ and Tasha, one for Ted and Judy (we knew what was going on with them. They were seventy-eight, for heaven's sake. So probably not much) and the last one for whoever snored. A snoring room sounded crazy, but no, it wasn't.

On the trip over, after sleeping for three or four hours and a breakfast of rubber eggs and inedible fruit, Ted and Judy peppered us with questions about Kiki and Nicholas. I assured them over and over that it was not an imposition to stay in Kiki's house and how insulted she would be if we did not.

"But remember, it's rustic. Don't say I didn't warn you!"

"What does that mean?" Judy said.

I could see she had a little trepidation over the accommodations and spending a lot of time with people with whom she could not communicate in English.

"We're going to live like the natives. You'll see, Judy. I promise you it will all be fine."

I went to check on Eve and Carl in their seats.

"Y'all okay?" I asked.

"Oh yes, we're just great," Carl said. "Did you sleep?"

"Yes. But I think I'll be taking a nap this afternoon. Hey, Eve?" She looked up at me. "I kept forgetting to ask you about Cookie. Does she know we're going to be on Corfu?"

"Yes, she sure does. I asked her to come spend a night or two with us. God only knows what she's really gotten herself into."

I shook my head, thinking, Oh no.

"And?" I said.

"She never responded."

"We can hope," Carl said.

I laughed and returned to my seat. The plane was preparing to land. As before, we cleared customs in Athens, then we found JJ and Tasha at the gate for our next leg and boarded the plane for the short flight to Corfu.

Kiki and Nicholas met us at the airport with a large van.

"Hello! Hello! Welcome back! Welcome home!"

Kiki was effusive, overflowing with love and warmth. I hugged her hard and so did Carl.

"This is Adam!" I said proudly. "And do you remember JJ?"

"Oh, on the head of my saint! It's you! JJ! Do you remember me?"

"Yes, I sure do, and it's great to see you again! This is Tasha, my wife."

Carl said, "This is my wife, Eve, and that's Ted, Adam's father, and his friend Judy!"

"And here is my Nicholas," Kiki said.

Everyone shook hands and over the next twenty minutes

we gathered all our bags. We were a gregarious and bois-
terous crowd, and the people around us must've thought we
were all hard of hearing because we were loud. Loud Americans. I hoped we weren't offending anyone.

The plan was to get us settled and then Nicholas and Kiki
would pick us up at around nine that night and we'd go to
Alexandros for dinner. Aunt Anna would join us as well.

On the drive to Dassia, I realized that the island was in
bloom. There were abundant flowers everywhere, cascading
over garden walls, spilling out of window boxes, climbing
anywhere the blooms could attach themselves. Morning
glories, bougainvillea, and others I didn't know. Oleander
bushes, like the ones all over the Isle of Palms, blossomed in
every shade of pink and white too.

"Looks like home, doesn't it?" Adam said.

"It is home," I said.

"That's right," Kiki said. "It is! And now it's your home
too, Adam! And Tasha!"

The first stop was for Carl and Eve. Eve's eyes grew wide
and I could see that the little white house with the navy
shutters had already worked its spell on her. Bright pink blos-
soms of bougainvillea tumbled out of the window boxes and
covered the courtyard trellis. Nicholas and Carl pulled their
luggage from the back of the van and Carl, Eve, Adam, and I
went inside with Kiki and Nicholas. We walked through the
rooms, Kiki showing them how things worked. Eve gasped
when Carl pulled the bedroom windows open.

"Oh! My! Goodness! Would y'all look at this view?"

"I thought this place was unreal in the winter, but in August it's really unreal!" Carl said.

In Manglish, that meant it was really beautiful.

"I could live here," Eve said. "Oh, Kiki! Thank you!"

"You're welcome!" Kiki said. "Now, get some rest and we'll see you all later!"

We took the short drive to Yiayia's house, and as at the house where Carl and Eve were, our window boxes and courtyard had flowers and herbs galore. The lemon tree was loaded with fruit and the olive tree with olives. I was so happy to be there.

Judy said, "Well, this is the most adorable little house I've ever seen!"

"It sure is!" Ted said, with noticeable relief in his voice.

We went inside with all our bags.

"JJ? Do you remember this house?" I said.

"I do! I actually do! I can almost feel Yiayia here."

"I'll bet! Come see," I said, and took him to the main-floor bedroom.

We stood before her picture, which hung on the wall right where it had been last February.

"She was a great lady," he said.

There was a sentimental tone to his voice I didn't often hear. I knew it was something special to JJ to be there, and it meant something to me, something important, because we were all there together. Old memories, new beginnings.

"Yes, she was. Wait until you see Aunt Anna. Yiayia is in her eyes."

"Well, that's creepy," he said.

"No, it isn't. It's wonderful!"

Kiki took Ted and Judy upstairs with their bags. JJ and Tasha followed them. I looked in the refrigerator to see many small bottles of fruit juice, soda, and water. And there were eggs, cold cuts, fruit, butter, and the basic necessities. I was sure Carl and Eve's kitchen was stocked as well. Kiki's never-ending thoughtfulness was in evidence once more.

Adam was in the bedroom unpacking his bag.

"What do you think?" I said.

"I think this place is wonderful and I think you're wonderful."

"No, come on. Really. Tell me."

"Eliza, I've never seen you so happy as you were when your foot touched the tarmac in Athens. You seemed a lot younger and just, I don't know, really happy? I think Corfu's going to have a similar effect on everyone. I really do."

"I hope so. Adam, I really love it here."

"I know you do. So I will too."

I gave Kiki my cell phone number, and we said good-bye to her and to Nicholas and settled in for a little bit of quiet time and a much-needed snooze. We were all feeling like zombies.

When Kiki called at eight to rouse us, I was already up and dressed for dinner, too excited to sleep much. I went from bedroom to bedroom and gave everyone's shoulders a little shake.

"Time to go to dinner," I said, and they all groaned, even Judy.

"I was sleeping *so* hard," Adam said.

"That's what happens. We have to get on Greek time."

Soon we were all in the van and on our way with Kiki, Nicholas, and Aunt Anna, who was so overcome to see JJ that she cried like a little girl for a full five minutes, stammering her words and hiccupping. JJ put his arms around her and patted her back. He was so touched. He gave her his handkerchief. Yes, my brother used linen handkerchiefs. I know. Very old school. Everyone was moved by her emotional outburst.

"You see," Kiki said, "this visit means the whole world to her. She thought you wouldn't come back and she thought she'd never see JJ again. For a Greek woman, to find more family is the greatest gift she can receive."

Touché, Kiki, I thought. I couldn't have said it better myself. I hoped Adam took her words to heart.

Alexandros Taverna was in full swing when we got there, and of course Alexandros hurried out from the kitchen to greet us.

"*Kalinta! Kalinta!* My cousin is home!" he said, grabbing me into one of his bear hugs and then kissing both of my cheeks. "How are you, Eliza? Where is your husband? Did he stay at home, I hope?"

We all laughed at Alexandros's joke. Of course, he knew Adam was right there, waiting to shake his hand.

"I understand we have a very special reason to celebrate, yes?" he said to Adam.

"I'm alive," Adam said, "and very happy to be here."

"That's good!"

"Yassou! Yassou!" Alexandros said to everyone, and the feast began.

For the next six days, we ate, we drank, and we played tourist. Of course, Nicholas arranged for a boat to take us to see other islands and guides to various churches, ruins, and museums. Needless to say, every one of us touched the foot of Saint Spyrídon. I wondered if my plea to him had influenced the peaceful resolution of our marital strife. I thanked him and threw in a prayer for my sons to find happiness.

The last night found us back at Alexandros Taverna, discussing a visit to our neck of the woods.

"I know America," Alexandros said. "I went to New York and saw the Statue of Liberty and I went to many Greek restaurants in Astoria. And I have been to Disneyland in California and I have seen where Clark Gable lived. What else do I need to know?"

"Oh, come on, Alex," Kiki said. "He is teasing all of you."

"Actually, I wanted to talk to you about an idea I have for a restaurant. Should I e-mail you?" I said.

"Yes, please!" Alexandros said.

Suddenly, the restaurant got very quiet. I turned to see what was going on. There stood Cookie, in a diaphanous white linen caftan, laden with turquoise jewelry everywhere it could be hung, and with her was a large man, at least thirty years her junior, holding a wheel of cheese. He was wearing a navy double-breasted jacket and white pants with wooden clogs. Hans was in the house.

Adam, Ted, Carl, JJ, and Nicholas stood up.

"Oh my dear God," Ted said, and he shook his head, as though he'd seen something that didn't register.

"Hey, y'all," Cookie said. "Hey, Ted. Y'all say hello to Hans!"

I had to admit, Cookie looked radiant. But this man she was with was very age inappropriate. Very. And, hello? May, December?

"I sent her a text yesterday," Eve said. "I never thought she'd come."

Alexandros stepped forward to greet them as though it was a perfectly normal situation.

"*Yassou!* I'll get two more chairs."

"Thank you," Cookie said and sat down in Carl's chair.

Tasha reached for the bottle of wine and refilled her glass.

"Anyone else?" she said.

Ted said, "Sure. Thanks."

Hans just stood there grinning like a three-hundred-pound, six-foot-long merman out of water. He had long ringlets of blond hair and beautiful blue eyes.

"Mother! What are you thinking? Don't you know he's using you for your money?"

Cookie looked from my face to Judy's and back to Eve's and said, "Maybe I'm using him. Did you ever think about that?"

There was a look of horror on Judy's face, and Ted was just aghast. Tasha began to laugh like a hyena. JJ tried to calm her down with death ray looks, but she couldn't stop.

"She gets like this," JJ said, clearly exasperated.

"It's okay," I said. "We love her. She's family."

The cheese was a gift for Kiki.

"We brought this for your hostess," Cookie said to Eve. "Hans made it. And we knew you'd show up empty-handed."

Cookie had not changed all that much.

Don't ask me how we got through that awkward dinner, but we did. After all, the concept of *hospitality* was coined by the Greeks, and all my years in the South had taught me a thing or two about how to handle a sticky situation. In fact, everyone used their best southern manners and soon, when it appeared to be time for the bill, Cookie and Hans—who spoke not one word of English or Greek—went off into the night.

"Well, this was certainly a memorable evening," I said.

"Thank you, Cookie," Adam said and chuckled.

"It certainly was," Kiki said. "Anyway, Nicholas and I have talked. We think we should take turns visiting one another each year. Next summer we will come to you with Mother for one week if that is a good plan?"

"Oh! It's just perfect!" I said.

"Yes," Adam said. "We'll just get another condo at Wild Dunes!"

I was so sad to leave Corfu and most especially to leave Kiki, Nicholas, and my sweet aunt, Theia Anna. They had gone the distance to give us all the most memorable visit and vacation any of us had ever had.

"This vacation has been so great because we actually lived like locals," Judy said. "Eliza was right."

"Eliza is always right," Adam said.

"May I have that in writing?" I said with a laugh.

After cruising the incredible blue water of the Ionian Sea together, we would never be the same again. As we said good-bye in Athens to JJ and Tasha, Adam and I made them promise to stay in touch.

"We're going to do a better job, JJ," Adam said.

"That sounds good," JJ said. "We will as well."

We watched them walk away, heading to their gate.

"Tasha wasn't so terrible," I said.

"No. She really wasn't. She got a little tanked last night and went off the hyena scale but hey, she's family!"

"I love you, Adam Stanley."

"I love you, Eliza Stanley." Adam gave me a kiss on my forehead. "Let's go home."

epilogue

2016

It was right after Christmas and we were eating leftovers. I had finally given Eliza the gray pearl earrings she'd been dying for. They were pretty dressy for leftover roast beef sandwiches but she wouldn't take them off.

"They look really good on you," I said.

She touched them and said, "I can't believe you bought them! Adam! You're a madman!"

"What should I do? Leave our money to the kids?"

Luke piped in, "I don't know. That sounds okay to me."

"Right," I said. "You won't need it."

"I talked to Max," he said. "He's coming down for New Year's Eve. He thinks we should all spend it at the house on the Isle of Palms. He wants to have a black tie New Year's Eve Dinner."

"Why black tie?" I said. Black tie was a pain in the neck.

"You know him," Luke said. "He's always been the dramatic one."

"Oh, Lord. That's more shopping and more work," Eliza said. The holidays always wore her out.

"Nope," Luke said. "He's got it all handled."

I looked at Eliza. "Do you know anything about this?"

"I seem to remember he mentioned something about it last month, but maybe not," I said.

"All he told me was that he had a big surprise for all of us. The Landers are invited. I know that much," Luke said. "Do we have any more cranberry sauce?"

"Sure," Eliza said. "Well, what do you think, Adam? Want to go back to the beach for New Year's? We can always roast some oysters."

"I'll get a couple of bushels from Crosby's," Luke said. "They've got a ton from the May River."

"Up to you," I said. "I don't have any other plans. And I'm always happy to see Carl and Eve. Especially Carl."

She put the cranberry sauce in front of Luke and sat down again. I thought, a couple of bushels? One bushel was a lot for a dozen hungry people. Two would feed a lot of people. But I didn't say anything. I knew then that Eliza and I were being set up. I smiled because I thought it was great that Max wanted to surprise us and because he didn't want Eliza to do any work. He was going to make it easy on his poor old tired momma.

I had noticed lately that Max and Luke were treating us like old people, always asking if our doctors were happy with us. So Eliza and I were a hair shy of sixty. Was that so old? Or maybe they thought that if they took some weight off our shoulders we'd last longer. Or! Maybe he was planning a surprise birthday party for us? That was possible. I hadn't had a birthday party in ages! Neither had Eliza. Yes! That was it. So, I decided to be coy and just go along for the ride.

"Well, I think it might be nice to be on the island for New

Year's Eve. It will probably be damp and cold but we'll be able to see a lot of fireworks. That's always fun," I said.

"Good," Luke said. "I'll tell him to meet us there."

He shot Max a text message. "I told him the parentals were in."

The parentals, indeed.

"What time?"

He texted Max again.

"Max said to be there at eight o'clock sharp."

"Okay. He's got something up his sleeve," I said.

"Obviously," Eliza said.

On New Year's Eve we packed a bag for two nights, got dressed to the nines and drove out to the Isle of Palms. When we got to our house, as I suspected there would be, there were cars all over the place. The catering trucks from Cru were there blocking our garage, and a valet parking service was there, taking cars.

I said, "What the hell is this? Should I tell these guys to move their trucks so I can get into our parking space?"

"No," Eliza said. "Let's not be the difficult ones. Whatever is going on, Max went to a whole lot of trouble to make this happen."

I pulled up to the front of our house and got out. A courteous young man opened Eliza's door and helped her out. I opened the back of the car to remove our luggage and nodded to Eliza that we should go inside.

"This is some night. Here I am in a tuxedo and you're in a gown and we're going to a party in our house and we don't know why."

"I feel like the Magic 8 Ball—all will be revealed." She giggled and up the stairs we went, guests in our own house.

"Well, you look beautiful," I said. She really did.

"I told you I needed these earrings!" She smiled.

When we walked into the foyer, all our living room furniture had been removed and ballroom chairs were arranged in rows. Max hurried toward us.

"Mom! Dad!"

"Are you selling something, Max?" I said. I was thinking Amway products?

"No! I'm getting married!"

"*What?*" I looked further into the room and saw Luke, Kiki, Nicholas, Aunt Anna, Cookie, Carl, Eve, Ted, Judy, JJ, Tasha, and a dozen others.

"To whom?" I said very seriously.

"Daphne, of course. You probably know we've been together for almost eight years and she said it was time. I said, okay."

You could've knocked us over with a flick of a finger.

"We knew no such thing. Why didn't we know, if you don't mind me asking?" I said.

"Oh! You didn't then. Wow. Well, initially we thought you'd object because of the trouble you had with her mother and grandmother. Then she got pregnant . . ."

"*What?*" I said.

"Yeah, we're having a baby in May. So we thought it was a good idea to tie the knot."

"Holy shit," I said. "It wasn't enough that Carl gave me a piece of his liver. Now his daughter is going to give us a grandchild. I'll be damned."

"We love Daphne," Eliza said. "Oh! Max! This is the most wonderful surprise of my life! Now, let's not keep your bride waiting at the altar."

So we had a little wedding that night, performed by a universal minister, one that seemed impromptu to me. But Eliza said, and I'm sure she was right, that it wouldn't have gone more seamlessly if they'd taken a year to plan it. There was a photographer, beautiful music, and delicious food. And Daphne, beautiful Daphne was going to be our daughter-in-law. I was absolutely thrilled. So was Eliza. During the ceremony, I looked to see if Luke had brought someone and when the maid of honor appeared, I had my answer. Kelly Engelbert. She was making eyes at Luke. Suddenly the whole world made better sense.

After the ceremony, we all greeted each other with huge hugs and expressions of wonderment and surprise.

"I wanted to tell you so badly!" Kiki said to Eliza and me. "But they swore me to silence."

"It's fine! Oh, my goodness! I'm so happy you're here! I have to go kiss my daughter-in-law. I'll be right back!"

But before I got to Daphne, Cookie stopped me.

"Hi there, Cookie! How is the Netherlands?"

"I broke up with Hans."

"Oh, dear. What happened?"

"Somehow he got ahold of that language-learning program Rosetta Stone? He tricked me. Then he said I wasn't nice and he took his clogs and left."

"Younger woman?"

"No, older than me with more money," she said in disgust. "She speaks German. It will take him a while to learn another language and then he'll find out she's a bitch too. Where's your father?"

"I don't know," I said. The room was very crowded and there were a lot of young people there I didn't know.

"Is he still with that Judy woman?"

"I assume so," I said.

"Well, we'll see about that," Cookie said and smirked.

Give it a rest, Cookie, I thought, realizing I was now related to her by marriage. Oh, God.

I finally made it to Daphne's side and I took her hand in mine and kissed her on the cheek.

"I am happy, so happy," I said and one big traitorous tear slid down my cheek.

She looked at me and it was as though a young Eve stood before me instead of her daughter. It was poetic justice that my son married Eve's daughter.

Eve came to me and hugged me.

"Friends forever?" she said.

"Forever friends, but now we're family too," I said and hugged her back.

They say *man plans, God laughs*. It was never more true than it was that night.

Carl caught my elbow. "How do you like this little surprise of theirs?"

"I think I love it," I said. "They sure saved us a lot of anxiety. And money."

That's when we started to roar with laughter. Eve and Eliza joined us and when Carl pointed out to them that we were all finally related, they laughed at the beautiful irony of it all. Not one single thing about our friendship was coincidence. Each step brought us to the next one. Maybe it was true what the Good Book said—the good Lord had a plan for each and every one of us. All we had to do is pay attention.

Acknowledgments

Acknowledgments at the end of a book look like an opportunity to write a mini-memoir each year, so for just a few lines, please bear with me. A lot happened during the writing of *Same Beach, Next Year.* Our daughter and son-in-law are expecting their first child in June 2017 and our entire family is wild with happiness. Then our son got engaged to a wonderful young woman and is to be married this coming October. We are completely thrilled to welcome Maddie into our family. And Peter and I are still hard at work with our crazy careers and retirement is nowhere in our plan. Nonetheless, we are at a watershed moment in our lives, one where we are looking back in time and realizing how much our friends mean to us. We have seen them marry, bring children in to the world, send those children off to college and walk them down the aisle. Our friends are almost all grandparents now and we are about to take our place in that lineup as grandparents too. I am wondering about how we will be changed. I am already filled with so much love for this unborn child my heart could burst. How many grandchildren are in our future? Please share your stories with me and any advice on how to do this in the very best way would be welcomed.

Now to the business at hand. Using a real person's name for

a character has been a great way to raise money for worthy causes. And in *Same Beach, Next Year* three generous souls come to life in these pages as my characters. I have never met these folks so I can assure you that I would be astonished if the behavior, language, proclivities, and personalities of the characters bear any resemblance to the actual people. Special thanks go to the family of Eliza Stanley for their generous support of Christ our King Stella Maris Grammar School, my alma mater oh so many thousands of years ago. Although Eliza Stanley is a freshman in high school, and no doubt, a lovely young lady with impeccable manners, in these pages she is the female protagonist, a married woman and the mother of adorable twin boys. She gets into a lot of mischief and has a bit of a potty mouth, which I'm sure you don't. I hope you'll take all the character does in stride! Remember, this is just fiction!

And special thanks to Kelly Engelbert for her generous support of Abby's Friends, a non-profit that works to end type-1 diabetes. We combined her two daughter's names, Clare and Elizabeth to make one character, Clarabeth. Clarabeth is an elderly lady with a lot of style and something to say about everything. And just for good measure we made Kelly Engelbert a teenaged girl with a lot of attitude. On the house.

Everett Presson, Angie Avinger, and Judy Linder? I hope y'all will be pleasantly surprised to find yourselves in this drama. It was fun being reminded of you each time I wrote your names!

Special thanks to George Zur, who is my computer web

master, for keeping the Web site alive. To Ann Del Mastro and my cousin, Charles Comar Blanchard, all the Franks love you for too many reasons to enumerate!

I'd like to thank my wonderful editor at William Morrow, Carrie Feron for her marvelous friendship, her endless wisdom and her fabulous sense of humor. Your ideas and excellent editorial input always make my work better. I couldn't do this without you. I am blowing you bazillions of smooches from my office window in Montclair.

And to Suzanne Gluck, Alicia Gordon, Clio Seraphim, Michelle Feehan, Clarissa Lotson, Andrea Blatt, Matilda Forbes Watson, Tracy Fisher, and the whole amazing team of Jedis at WME, I am loving y'all to pieces and looking forward to many more years together!

To the entire William Morrow and Avon team: Brian Murray, Michael Morrison, Liate Stehlik, Lynn Grady, Tavia Kowalchuk, Kelly Rudolph, Kathryn Gordon, Carolyn Coons, Frank Albanese, Virginia Stanley, Andrea Rosen, Josh Marwell, Andy Le Count, Carla Parker, Donna Waikus, Michael Morris, Gabe Barillas, Mumtaz Mustafa, and last but most certainly not ever least, Brian Grogan: thank you one and all for the miracles you perform and for your amazing, generous support. You still make me want to dance.

To Debbie Zammit, okay, so how long have we known each other? No one needs to know! Our years together in this endeavor have now surpassed our years together on Seventh Avenue. What a spectacular friend you are! We finish each other's sentences, reading each other's minds—what's left of them anyway. As the years try to snatch our mental acuity and recall, we need to stick together. Thank you over and over for well, everything.

To booksellers across the land, and I mean every single one of you, I thank you from the bottom of my heart, especially Aaron Howard and Melinda Marquez of Barnes and Noble and Vicky Crafton of Litchfield Books.

To my family, Peter, William, and Victoria, I love y'all with all I've got. Victoria, you are the most beautiful, wonderful daughter and I am so proud of you and I'm just crazy about our Carmine, which he knows. I love everything about y'all. William? You are so smart and so funny, but then a good sense of humor might have been essential to your survival in this house. And proof of your intelligence is to be found in the simple fact that you're bringing Maddie into the fold. We are so very excited. I'm so proud of all of you. Every woman should have my good fortune with their husband and children. Peter Frank? You are still the man of my dreams, honey. Thirty-four years and they never had a fight. It's a little incredible to realize it's only thirty-four years, especially when it feels like I've loved you forever.

Finally, to my readers to whom I owe the greatest debt of all, I am sending you the most sincere and profound thanks for reading my stories, for sending along so many nice e-mails, for yakking it up with me on Facebook and for coming out to book signings. You are why I try to write a book each year. I hope *Same Beach, Next Year* will entertain you and give you something new to think about. There's a lot of magic down here in the Lowcountry. Please, come see us and get some for yourself! I love you all and thank you once again.